AUC

From Time to Time

G·K
Hall
&Cº

Also published in Large Print
from G.K. Hall by Jack Finney:

Time and Again

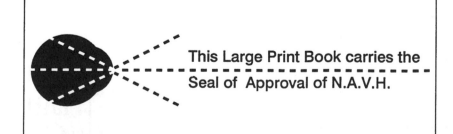

This Large Print Book carries the
Seal of Approval of N.A.V.H.

From Time to Time

Jack Finney

G.K. Hall & Co.
Thorndike, Maine

f/F
(Large Type)
(Fantasy)

Published in 1995 by arrangement with Simon & Schuster, Inc.

G.K. Hall Large Print Core Collection.

The text of this Large Print edition is unabridged.
Other aspects of the book may vary from the original edition.

Set in 16 pt. News Plantin.

Printed in the United States on permanent paper.

Library of Congress Cataloging in Publication Data

Finney, Jack.
   From time to time : a novel / Jack Finney.
     p.   cm.
   ISBN 0-7838-1387-2 (lg. print : hc)
   1. Titanic (Steamship) — Fiction. 2. Time travel —
Fiction. 3. Large type books. I. Title.
[PS3556.I52F56   1995b]
813'.54—dc20   95-9462

WELCOME, ANNELISE!

ACKNOWLEDGMENTS

TWO SUSANS helped me with this book. Susan La Rosa of New York found all the photos I needed, and also some fine ones I didn't know I needed until she produced them. Susan Ferguson did the same in California archives.

AUTHOR'S NOTE

THIS BOOK is a continuation of — a sequel to — a novel called *Time and Again*. In that book a young man, Simon Morley, is invited to join a secret government-sponsored Project housed in an old Manhattan warehouse. The purpose of this Project is to test the theory of a retired professor of physics, from Harvard. He is Dr. E. E. Danziger, who believes that the past still exists, and that under certain conditions it might be possible to reach it.

Si Morley is one of the very few candidates in the Project who succeeds. He reaches the 1880s . . . returns to the present to make his report to the Project . . . but then returns to the 1880s to marry a girl of the time, Julia, and stay there forever.

But he doesn't. And this book is the story of what happens when Si — out of simple curiosity — returns to the present just to see what's going on.

Historians say so: The years between 1910 and 1915 were the pleasantest this country has ever known . . .

— Allen Churchill,
Remember When

PROLOGUE

THE MAN at the end of the long table — he wore a trimmed black beard streaked white at the ends of his mouth — looked up at the wall clock: three minutes past seven. "Okay," he said to the dozen men and women around the table, "we better get started." But he turned once more to look at the open doorway behind him, and so did everyone else. No one appeared, though, no footsteps approached along the wood-floored hall outside, and he turned back to the group. He was the oldest of them, a trim youthful forty, wearing blue denims and a plaid cotton shirt — and the only full professor. "Audrey, you want to begin?"

"Sure." She bent up the clasp of a manila envelope on the table beside her purse, and partly pulled out a newspaper folded to quarter size. Only a portion of its masthead was visible, reading, *w-York Courier*, and one or two people smiled at what they took to be the deliberate drama of this. All were casually dressed, casually seated; aged from twenty-five to forty. This was the little Chemistry Department library, cheerful with shelved books and framed sepia photographs of the old laboratories. It was early evening, September and still light, and here in Durham still

9

warm. Someone had opened the three tall round-topped windows, and they could hear birds wrangling in the campus trees.

"So far my network is only four people," Audrey said. Her hand, wearing a plain wedding ring, lay on the tabletop, curved forefinger just touching the word *Courier*. "If you can call that a network. One is my brother-in-law, and I honestly never thought he'd turn up a thing. But he has. A friend of his owns a floor covering store of some kind in Brooklyn, New York. One of his men was working in an old house there, tearing up worn-out kitchen linoleum, and underneath —" She stopped: rapid footsteps sounded woodenly outside, and they all turned to watch the doorway. But the hurrying figure, glancing in at them, moved on by. "Under the linoleum the floor was covered about half an inch thick with newspapers. To cushion it, I suppose. And of course he looked at some of the papers, read the old comics — you know. I envied him. They were all really old, been there for decades. And he kept this one." She drew the folded newspaper from its envelope, and passed it to the man beside her.

He opened it, spreading it flat on the tabletop, and the others around the table hunched forward to look. *The New-York Courier*, read the complete masthead, and the man who'd opened it began reading the headline aloud. " 'President Urges Trade Recip—' "

"No, not the news, the date."

"Tuesday, February 22, 1916."

After a moment she said, slightly annoyed and disappointed, "Well, don't you see? There *was* no *New-York Courier* in 1916. It went out of business — I looked this up — on June 8, 1909."

"Hey," a woman across the table from her murmured, and someone else said, "Looks like a good one. Let's see that thing," and the paper was passed down to him.

"Is that it, Audrey — the date?" said the chairman.

"Yes."

"Okay, well, it's a good one. Write it up, will you? Use the new form; we got new ones, we're getting organized, sort of. Can we keep the paper?"

"Sure." Her face flushing with pleasure, she ducked to give close attention to bending down the clasp of her envelope.

A woman of thirty, small, with straight dark hair, said, "Dick, I have to leave early; I've got a babysitter who can't stay long. Can I be next?"

"Sure, go ahead."

She touched a cardboard folder on the table before her. "I got this from my aunt in Newton, Kansas. The local library there has a little history room. History of the town; people give them old photographs, clippings, and so on, and she had one of these photos copied for me." Opening the folder, she exposed a large, glossy black-and-white photograph. "This was taken in 1947" — she touched the date inscribed in white in a lower corner of the photograph. "It shows the main street. As it was then, of course. It includes the movie theater, and you can read the marquee. I'll pass this around in a minute, but let me just read it to you first." From the table she picked up her reading glasses and put them on, bending over the photo, pushing the glasses slightly higher on her nose. "It says, 'Clark Gable and Mary Astor in *Devil's Judgment*, Cartoons, and Pathé News.'"

She sat back, snatching her glasses off, sliding the photograph to the man beside her. "I've checked every old-movie book in the libraries here; listings of old pictures. And this summer in New York I checked a lot more in the main library there. No such movie is listed. I wrote to the studio, never got an answer, so I phoned, got through to someone eventually who said he'd check it out, and call me back. To my amazement, that's just what he did. Phoned a couple days later. Very pleasant; had a nice voice. They had no record of any such movie, he said. And — well, that's my offering." She glanced around at the others.

The chairman said, "Well, it's interesting, but we've got to be rigorous. The movie listings could be incomplete. Or the studio's mistaken. Or, nice as your man's voice was, maybe he didn't really look hard. Old pictures that weren't too popular get forgotten. Lost."

"But a Clark Gable?"

"I know, but" — he moved a shoulder re-

12

luctantly — "we've got to be impeccable. It could be only a title change. Released as *Devil's Judgment*, then changed to something else. I think they do that."

"Okay." She reached across the table as someone returned her picture. "I had some more checking in mind anyway, but I wanted to bring this to the meeting to show I haven't been loafing all summer."

"Well, it sounds good. Keep on it, see if you can really pin it down. Steve, you got something?"

"Yeah. Took me all summer." He was twenty-five, his extremely fine yellow hair thin on top. "Had to write a million letters." With his knuckle he tapped a little pile of stacked papers. "Want me to read them, or just tell you?"

"Just tell us for now. Can you xerox copies for next time?"

"Sure. Ben Bendix put me in touch with this. Remember Ben? He was in my class. Parapsych degree like me."

Someone said, "Sure, I remember him."

"Well, he's married now, lives in Stockton, California, and he put me in touch with this family. Their name is Weiss; father, mother, two grown daughters. One married, the other divorced and back in Stockton, living with the folks. Well, the divorced one remembers another sister. Sort of."

"Steve." The chairman sat shaking his head. "I don't know about the sort-ofs. Is this one of those little fragments of memory things?"

" 'Fraid so."

"Well . . . what's the rest?"

"She thinks the other sister was called Naomi. Or Natalie. Not sure. A year younger, maybe. Thinks she remembers them playing together, when she was around twelve."

"She says it reminds her of trying to remember a dream?"

"Yep; one of those. Little memories like walking to school together. Dinner with the family. Just stuff like that. And you know the rest: no one else in the family remembers this other sister, there never *was* another daughter. The divorced daughter actually checked out birth records, and they finally insisted this one cut it out, quit talking about it." He touched the papers before him. "What I got here is three letters, pretty long, from her; what she remembers, what she doesn't. And one each from the others. They didn't want to write at all, but I pestered them into it."

"I think we have to pass on this, Steve; sorry."

"That's okay."

"The vague ones, remember little bits and pieces — what can we do with them? Appreciate the effort, though."

Footsteps coming fast sounded outside, and two men walked in quickly, the younger one tall and stick-thin in a wrinkled white suit, saying, "Sorry, sorry, sorry! We're late, late, late! But you won't mind." He nodded proudly at the other man as they stopped beside the chairman, who was rising to greet them. "My fault," the other man said; he looked about forty-five, lean in the face, and

14

wore a blue nylon windbreaker over a very clean white T-shirt. "I had to work, so supper was late."

To the group, the younger man said, "This is Lawrence Braunstein," and Braunstein said, "Larry." The younger added, "Larry drove in from Drexel."

People near the chairman were standing or leaning across the table to shake hands with Braunstein, or smiling and flicking hands in greeting from the other end of the table. They were liking him because he responded so pleasantly, nodding, looking pleased to be here. He was incompletely bald, a thinning, straight stripe of brown hair from forehead to crown.

Someone moved to another chair so that he could sit at the middle of the table, and when he was seated, the chairman said, "Larry, a lot of us know your story from Carl here, though I understand you have an addition to it tonight. But some of us haven't heard; would you mind telling it over again? From the top?"

"Sure. Okay. And if you want to laugh, folks, go to it. I don't mind, I'm used to it."

"We won't laugh," the chairman said.

"Well." Braunstein slid down the zipper of his jacket and sat back, settling himself comfortably, one arm lying relaxed on the tabletop, hand loosely clenched. "There's not that much to tell; it's just that I remember Kennedy's second term." The group sat quiet and intent, some leaning forward to see him. "I don't really remember a lot

15

about it, tell you the truth. I vote. Sometimes. But I don't pay much attention to the politicians. Never did; what's the use. They're all — well, you know well's I do. But I do remember him running again. Watched a little of the convention. It was in Atlanta. Heard some of the campaign speeches. Not much. A little of that goes a long ways, you know?"

Someone said, "Who'd he run against?"

"Dirksen — isn't that a shout? I remember the commentators, remember Cronkite, saying the Republicans only ran Dirksen because they knew he didn't have a chance against Kennedy. And they were sure right. Kennedy won forty-nine states and was close in the other; Illinois, or something. And that's about it. I watched Dirksen concede less than an hour after the polls closed in California. And I remember Kennedy headquarters then, the Mayflower Hotel in Washington, him there at the microphones smiling, everybody yelling, then him lifting his arms, thanking his people, and — you know; all that stuff. Jackie was there, and I think his mother. Don't remember about Bobby or Edward."

They sat silent for a moment. Then one of the men said, "I know you've already answered this, but do you also remember —"

"That he never had a second term? Sure. Carl asked me that first thing, and sure I remember, just like everyone. He was shot. In Dallas. In . . . 1963? Then they shot Oswald." He shrugged, apologizing. "I know it don't make sense, but

16

— I got both memories; what can I tell you?"

"Do you remember where you were when he was shot?"

"No."

The chairman said, "Okay. And tonight you've got something more?"

"Yeah. A couple days after Carl came out and we talked, I remembered something, but I didn't get around to it for a while. I run the shipping department at Vector over in Drexel, and we been working a lot of overtime, sending out a lot of stuff. But last Sunday I got out my top dresser drawer and set it on the bed." He smiled around at them, inviting them in on this. "That drawer is a joke at my house, everybody laughs about my top drawer. It's my junk drawer. Packed full of nothing; you can hardly open it. You know: old ticket stubs from movies, receipts from stores, guarantees from stuff we wore out years ago. And snapshots, stuff I clip out of magazines, a couple of watches'll never run again, old lenses from glasses after the prescription was changed. My high school graduation picture. And a coonskin tail I had tied to my radiator in high school. Shoelaces, pencils, pens that don't write, matchbooks, soap from motels, worn-out flashlight batteries. You name it, it's all there.

"Well, I dumped that whole drawer right out on the bed, and started putting stuff back. One by one, till I found this." He opened the fingers of his loosely clenched hand, exposing the palm, and at sight of what lay there people shoved chairs

17

back, legs scraping the wood floor, as they stood up to see. Faceup on his palm lay a flat round object a little larger than a half-dollar. It was white, of plastic or enameled metal. Imprinted on it in blue were the head-and-shoulders photographs of two men, facing each other. The one on the left was a confidently smiling John Kennedy in three-quarters profile; the other, in sharp profile, a serious, almost scowling Estes Kefauver. Above these photos, white letters on a red band that followed the button's curve read: *One Good Term*. In a similar band of blue at the bottom of the button: *Deserves Another!* Directly under the photos in a ribbon shape: *Kennedy-Kefauver, '64.*

"A campaign button," someone said softly, and another voice said, "I'll be goddamned." Someone said, "May I?" Braunstein nodded, and the button began moving slowly from hand to hand around the table.

They had coffee, as they usually did, made in a cone-shaped Chemistry Department flask and glass funnel with filter paper. And as they stood around or near the long table or sat on its edge sipping at their Styrofoam cups, the button continued to move from one to another of them, inscription and printed photos held close to the eyes, the little blue union bug on its reverse touched.

"All right," the chairman said presently, "let's finish up. Bring your cups to the table if you want." As they took their seats again, he said,

18

"Mr. Braunstein's leaving now; he's got a little drive ahead of him. Any last questions?"

"Yes, please," said Audrey. "Mr. Braunstein, did you ever run into anyone else who'd had this . . . experience?"

Braunstein, standing with the chairman at the head of the table, nodded. "Yeah, I did once. At my brother's. He was on a softball team, and I was over to go with him to a game, watch him play. He had another player there, a guy from Chicago originally. My brother had me tell my story, and the guy said yeah, he'd heard that before. In Chicago."

Steve, the young man with the thinning yellow hair, said, "Well, did it check out the same? I mean about Kefauver and Dirksen. And the convention in Atlanta?"

Braunstein was shaking his head. "I asked him that but he said he didn't know or didn't remember or something. Maybe he was just kidding me, you know? 'What's so hot about your story? I heard it before!' But I don't think so. I think it's true."

Their guest left, well thanked, Carl walking out with him. The donated button remained lying on the table, occasionally picked up and examined again during the rest of the meeting. The chairman said, "Okay, we've got Teddy Lehmann to hear from, but" — he nodded, smiling, at a young woman in an army lieutenant's uniform seated near him — "you're a new member?"

"Yes. I hope so."

"You are if you want to be. Were you a student here?"

"No, but my husband was. We're divorced now, but — I got interested. Still am."

"Good. Well, I'm sure whoever recruited you briefed you. Was it Frank?"

Frank nodded. "How'd you know?"

The chairman said, "Lucky guess," and several people smiled. To the young woman, he said, "Let me just make sure everything's been covered. You understand what we're doing? Right now we're simply gathering and recording certain incidents. Documenting them as well as we can. We don't know what they mean yet. If anything. And may never know. We all have our guesses, of course, and it does seem obvious that occasionally two versions of the same stretch of time seem to exist. Or to have existed, one of them replacing the other. *Looks* that way, I should say. Maybe it's not what's happening at all. We're not even close to formulating a theory yet, we're just tracking down incidents any way we happen to hear about them. We're organized to do that, very loosely. And we keep a low profile. We're as secret as we can reasonably manage without being nutty about it. Each of us is building a little network of friends, relatives, acquaintances — anyone you might think would know, or hear of, or come upon the kind of incident we're collecting. So start your own network. If you haven't already. Use your own best judgment about who you should use and who not, that's about all I

20

can tell you. And explain as little as you think you can get by with. Make it seem as though you're alone; your own nutty little interest, nothing important. Because above all . . ." He paused for emphasis. "We are *not* an official part of the Parapsychology Department. Officially they know nothing about us; we're a private group of . . . hobbyists. We've never even met in any of the department's rooms. I don't have to tell you why if your husband was a student here. For forty years the department has taken a lot of guff" — his eyes began to narrow — "from academics in other fields, the *respectable* fields, who wouldn't know solid evidence or proof — or *refuse* to know, which is worse — if it came up and bit them in the ass." He smiled at her and at himself. "Sorry. I'll wipe the flecks of foam from my lips in a minute. But we're carefully unofficial. And as secret as we can manage. Okay? Ready for the sacred blood oath?"

The young lieutenant nodded, smiling.

"Then welcome aboard. Ted, I understand you took quite a trip on our behalf this summer. To Arizona?"

"Well, I was in California anyway. On vacation. In L.A., if you can believe it." Ted, a researcher here, was a handsome man who didn't seem to know it, his brown hair cut close, nothing made of its curl, his glasses of wire-thin metal, the lenses round as a coin. He looked thirty, and wore a hand calculator in his shirt pocket. "So I took a couple of days, flew over to Phoenix,

21

rented a car, and drove out to this guy's place."

"Okay. Tell us about it."

"My mother heard about this years ago from a friend, a woman her age; they both lived in New York then. I phoned this woman, and got the man's name — my mother couldn't remember it. He used to be a lawyer, a really big-time lawyer in New York, partner in a big firm, all that. He's well remembered, I've discovered. Retired now. I tracked him down, which wasn't hard. Talked to him by phone, and arranged to see him this summer." Ted reached down beside his chair, brought up a worn black leather briefcase bearing a scuffed Stanford sticker, opened it on the table, and slid out a small, chrome-rimmed, gray plastic recorder. He pushed in a control, and a beadlike bulb turned amber. "I taped what he told me, so you might as well hear it from the source. Just picture us sitting by his pool, a nice Arizona morning, getting hot but very dry. Pleasant. He had cactuses around, here and there, some natural, some in pots. We were in the shade from his house, adobe painted so white it hurt your eyes.

"He's an old man now, but smart; no trouble imagining him as a damned effective lawyer. Intelligent face. I don't think it was because I was in Arizona but he really did look — well, not truly like Barry Goldwater, but if someone told you they were maybe cousins you'd believe it. Had most of his hair, snow white, and the same kind of bushy white sideburns. Wore expensive-

22

looking tan linen pants, dark blue shirt. Name is Bertram O. Bush, and he was stretched out in a lounge chair, me in a straight chair where I could manage the recorder. I had it on a glass-top table between us, and we both had coffee, real big cups. It's a nice place, some twenty-odd miles out of Phoenix. He and his wife retired there, but now he's a widower. Lives alone, but he has grown children with families and two of them live near Phoenix. The other in California. He seems to see them fairly often. And did I say he has money? Well, he obviously has; it's a nice place.

"We got our preliminary chitchat out of the way, he said it was okay to record, and here's what I got. Nice and clear; I'm a master with these things." He pushed another control, and after a second or two his own voice came from the machine. "Okay, Mr. Bush, tell us about it if you will. Though you must be tired of telling it."

"Well, I used to be, but it's been quite a while since I've told it." This voice was deep, measured, assured; did not sound old. "When I was a kid in grade school and told this, I got hooted and jeered at, naturally, boys being the sensitive considerate creatures they are. Which I didn't mind; I hooted right back, my insults often superior to theirs. And it was somewhat the same in college. Mostly people assumed I'd made this up, but at least I got credit for being mildly imaginative and entertaining, a clever fellow. But

23

always some people listened thoughtfully. And a few were impressed. When one of these was a girl, I sometimes found that her interest and attention transferred to me, and I'm afraid I sometimes used my story for the wrong reasons, though I feel no shame. But after I began practicing law in New York, and particularly when I understood the solid possibility that I might someday become a partner of the firm in which eventually I did just that, I stopped telling this story. It was harmful now, made me seem odd and eccentric. So I shut up about it, except very occasionally to someone I knew would be interested and could be trusted. Doesn't matter now, of course. I'm retired. Old."

"Oh, I don't think —"

"None of that. And if you dare even pronounce the term 'senior citizen,' I'll demonstrate that I'm capable of throwing you into this pool. Headfirst. And hold you under. I am *old*. I was born near the turn of the century, so I've never had any trouble remembering my age.

"Anyway, when I was a boy we lived in New York. On Madison Avenue. We had a house — long gone — a four-story brownstone. My father, mother, two sisters, and me. And a dog actually named Fido. Plus several servants; my father was a successful marine-insurance broker, and we were well-off. Every morning our whole family breakfasted together, by paternal fiat, in the dining room. And one spring morning, a Wednesday, I remember, my father asked me whether I'd

24

like to skip school that day. Well, I was twelve years old, and I acknowledged that just possibly I might; but why? Well, there was a ship coming in, he said, a liner, and it had occurred to him that I might like to see her come in, from his office. He knew very well I would. I was wild about the big liners in the same way, I suppose, that my grand- and great-grandchildren are about planes today. Although come to think of it, I don't believe they really are. They seem to take everything in stride, pretty hard to impress. They know more than I did when I was twenty years old. And some things, I'm sure, that I don't know yet.

"But I loved the big liners. Thought about them, read about them, looked at their pictures and drew my own. And would have given anything I had or ever would have to sail on one. As we all did four or five years later. To Europe on the *Leviathan*. That was the old *Vaterland*, as you know. You do know, of course?"

"Sure, who doesn't?"

The old man laughed. "In the years since, I've sailed on the *Mauretania*. More than once. The old *Mauretania*, of course. And the *Normandie*, the *Laurentic*, the *Isle de France*, God bless her, and the *Queen Mary* many times. Wonderful ship, the *Mary*, one of the great ones. Compares with even the *Mauretania*, and I don't like it that she's tied up and engineless in southern California, where she doesn't belong and never did. I suppose we should be grateful, though, that she still exists. None of the others do. All scrapped the moment their profitable days were done. Suppose we'd saved them? Had them all lined up in Southampton from the *Kaiser Wilhelm* on, say, right on through to the *Mary*. Be wonderful, wouldn't it? Then someday finally we'd add the newest and last, the *Queen Elizabeth, Second*: the *QE Two*. Which I'm happy to say is fully in the grand tradition. Modern, yes. As she should be. But a most worthy successor to her ancestors. You must sail on her, my boy, if you never have."

"Can't afford it."

"Stow away then, but do it. Because when she's gone, when they scrap the *QE Two* as of course they will, picking her bones and selling the skeleton for the last dime of profit, there'll be no more Atlantic liners. Not ever. She's your last chance to know one of man's most pleasurable experiences, including sex, though a young man like you should be able to combine the two and avoid the comparison: I can assure you it makes for a wonderful crossing. Sail on the *QE Two* while you still can; I insist. Where was I?"

"Your father."

"Yes. My father. Of course he knew what my response to his invitation would be, but he was aware, he said, of my burning thirst for knowledge; maybe, after all, I'd prefer to go to school? He'd understand if I did. My father liked to tease us a little, and we enjoyed it, at least I did.

"We went downtown to his office after breakfast, at Battery Place and West Street. The White-hall Building, new then; it had a good view of New York harbor, and the old Battery. I wore corduroy knickerbockers, long black knit stockings, a kind of Norfolk jacket, and a cloth cap with a peak. All boys did; it was compulsory. We took the El downtown to his office, which had a huge rectangular window overlooking the entire harbor and bay as far as the eye could see. He had a big leather-bound brass telescope on a wooden tripod. I expect every office on that side of the building had one.

"The ship was already visible when we arrived, still far out, hardly more than a speck, but my father found it in the telescope, focused carefully, then turned it over to me, and I stood hardly breathing so as not to jar the telescope, watching that ship grow in the tight little circle of my vision. She was coming straight on, with a bit of white bow wave, and her stacks smoking; I could see that almost tangible blackness curling straight back. She was coal-fueled, and I expect she had a full head of steam. She grew, filling the circle, then expanding beyond it, and I stood erect and found her again with my own vision, shrunk back down in size. But once more she grew, very fast, and then I could see the colors of the pennants strung in her rigging for the occasion. Fireboats appeared, moving out to meet her; then they swung around to escort her in, their long brass hose tips pointing up, pumping great pluming jets of white water and spray. First time I'd ever seen that, though not the last.

"The tugs reached her next, as I recall, and now — she seemed very close — she turned to port, and I saw the full astounding length of her, the great stacks streaming smoke straight out over the port side. They all had four stacks, you know, and I still think it's the way a liner should be. It's the only thing wrong with the *QE Two*; she ought to have four stacks as God intended. Just as He meant automobiles to have running boards, and airplanes two wings. Right, my boy? You agree, of course."

"Of course," said Ted's voice. "It's what I keep saying all the time."

"I'm sure you do, but you must try not to be boring about it; you're not old enough. She turned, as I say, I saw the magnificent length of her, the sun lighting those millions of portholes, and of course in just that moment she sounded her horn. I saw the steam puff first, a sudden whiteness, and then oh, the glory of that deep sound. All the lost sounds: wagon wheels, ships' steam horns, the whistle of steam locomotives. Yes indeed. God also meant locomotives to run only by steam."

"I know. Diesels are the devil's work."

"You're right! You're right! You know, you don't look eighty at all."

The chairman laughed. "You two got along, didn't you?"

Ted poked a control, stopping the tape. "Yeah, we did. 'Course he's a lawyer, a pro; instinctively wants you on his side, and knows how to get you there."

Ted started the machine again, the reels turned for a moment, then the old man's recorded voice continued: "The sound, the cry of that ship, actually rattled the windows, and I do remember clearly that I could feel the vibration of it in my chest. So deep. Such a low, rough, growling, utterly thrilling sound.

"And then very quickly, the tugs assembling around her, little blobs of color fussing at her waterline, their stacks blowing black, she was gone, cut from our view by buildings, but then I learned that the best was yet to come. My father had passes, he announced now, which would admit us to her dock, on the Hudson; she was a White Star liner. And if I liked, we could go watch her dock, unless — and some more nonsense then about my deep love of school and learning.

"The only thing that might conceivably have made that day more wonderful for me would have been to find that down in the street at the cab rank one of the waiting cabs was an automobile. But this morning there were only two waiting cabs, both horsedrawn, and we climbed in, and moved up Broadway, through Washington Square, then over on Fourteenth, I think, and along the Hudson on West Street, to the docks.

"We walked down the stairs onto the pier, a partly roofed but otherwise open platform of thick splintery planking. It may be there yet for all

I know, a long shedlike structure without sides, and our ship was already in sight, out there on the river. She was already turning toward the pier, in fact. For a moment or so as she made the quarter-turn, the black smoke boiled out — I loved this — more thickly than ever, and I stood staring across the water at her, truly spellbound. Very suddenly the smoke abated, almost stopping, as the tugs took over the work of moving her. Then, their own stacks pouring black, they brought her in, quite slowly, slowing even more as they neared, heading straight for the pier as it seemed to me. I stood watching, staring rather, and could not believe that anything could grow so large. The tugs turned her very slightly, and now I saw her not quite head-on. Saw her stacks now, painted beige, as I recall, with a black band at the tops. Four stacks, almost merged, like the pickets in a fence viewed at an angle. She grew taller. And taller. More and more enormous as she came at us, almost frighteningly, until — alongside the dock now, impossibly only a few feet away — she had become so tall, her sides swelling outward so far, that I could no longer see her superstructure, and I stood there stunned at the enormity of this thing.

"The tug far out at her stern suddenly boiled water, immense churning pools of greasy gray bubbles. At her other side tugs shoved her sideways with a sudden rumbling sound, and the dirty water separating ship from dock shrank to a yard, a foot, to inches, and then — very slightly, gently as an elephant accepting a peanut — she touched, and through the soles of my shoes I felt the movement of the entire dock, and heard the vast creak and groan of its planks and nails, and understood the enormousness of the weight that had just barely nudged us.

"Now the ship was still, immense hawsers flying out from openings in her sides to drop, uncoiling, and be snubbed tight to the bollards by waiting men. A gangplank, slanting up toward the black hull, was being wheeled to her almost at a run, and before it could even be fully secured a swarm of uniformed porters in white jackets and black-visored caps were running up it.

"Almost immediately then, hardly a minute's delay, down came the first-class passengers, the porters carrying hand luggage spotted with colored stickers bearing the names of foreign hotels. Don't think of these people moving down that gangplank as dressed in 'casual' clothes, 'sport' clothes, like tourists from Hawaii with paper leis around their necks. There *were* no casual or sport clothes, unless you count the white flannels in which men played tennis. These people, many smiling, some haughty, coming down from that great ship, were dressed for arrival in New York, the City, the metropolis. And the women wore hats. Huge wheels some of those hats, the brims wide as small umbrellas; I mean it. Others had jeweled turbans of intricately folded cloth, feathered, and worn down to the eyebrows. And dresses to just above the ankles, and sort of . . .

31

curved in at the hem. Hobble skirts, yes. They wore or carried coats, some of fur or fur-trimmed. These women, believe me, were *dressed*. Dressed, I suppose, for the uplifted eyes of all of us down there on the dock, and for the reporters with press passes in their hatbands who had boarded from the pilot ship to interview some of them.

"The men wore suits, mostly. With vests and ties. A few wore black frock coats with gray, striped trousers, and stiff wing collars. A very few wore tall shiny silk hats — bankers and Wall Street people, I suppose, going straight to their offices. My father wore a felt hat, as most younger men did.

"As these godlike passengers stepped onto the dock, they were met, and hugged, and kissed. They were presented with bouquets, and with telegrams and cablegrams by uniformed boys. Nearby, waiting and smiling, stood clusters of servants, the women not quite in uniform but you could tell who was maid or nanny. The chauffeurs, some carrying folded lap robes like badges of office, wore livery and polished leather puttees. Out front, parked directly beside the dock entrance — we'd passed them coming in — stood a line of limousines. I knew every automobile made by sight, and these were Isotta-Fraschinis, Pierce-Arrows, a Stutz roadster, and so on.

"The heavier luggage of these people was coming down from the side of the ship on a kind of plank of rollers, sweating men in porters' smocks heaving them off at the end. Most these were huge steamer trunks lettered wi names or initials followed by the name of th city: *New York, Wien, Constantinople, London.*

"Not until the first-class passengers, except for stragglers, were gone from the pier to customs were other gangplanks wheeled up for the second-class, third-class, and steerage passengers. Down they came now, and I remember them as simply uninteresting. They walked down their sloping gangplanks dressed like ordinary people you'd see on the streets. And not talking, almost as though they didn't have the right. A few waved a little to waiting friends, smiling but not calling down to them. And for me it had all turned . . . drab. These people, I truly believe, knew their places in society. And without resentment. And little snob that I suppose I was then, though I did not remain one, I had no interest in them.

"Yet I didn't want to leave. Couldn't. And my father indulged me. I walked on toward the prow — wandered, really, sometimes stopping to lift my chin and look up at that immensity of curved black plating all riveted together to form a ship. Along this portion of the dock were fewer and fewer people, and as I approached the very nose of the ship, there were no others. But far up, several officers in their visored caps leaned on the rail looking down. I wanted to wave but didn't for fear they might simply stare and not return it.

"Then I stood directly opposite the prow just

looking at the very end of the great ship, the prow a perfectly vertical knife edge as ships were then. Far overhead, just short of the top of the hull and well back from the prow, hung the white block letters that spelled out the name of this great new ship. They were a long way off, those white letters, and I could feel the weight of my own head tipped far back to look up at them. But I could see them perfectly plainly. Read them with no difficulty. I can see them in my mind right now, seven big white letters standing absolutely plain and clear, and of course you know what they spelled: It's why you're here."

"Yes, but . . . say it."

"The white letters high on the painted black hull of that ship read *Titanic*, as I've told people for the rest of my life. And that's that. Feel free to ask whatever you like, though you'll surprise me if you have a question I haven't often been asked before."

"Could this have been a . . . particularly vivid dream? One of those dreams so real it comes to seem like an actual memory?"

"A dream, could it have been a dream? Of course you must ask. But this is my answer: Occasionally you yourself have had a dream — everyone has — that was astonishingly real. Nothing fantastic about it. And that stayed in your mind afterward, clean and clear. Perhaps never forgotten."

"Yes."

"But this is also true, always. You know that

34

nevertheless it was a dream. No one ever mistakes a dream for reality. The experience I've described to you — happened."

"Did you also know that the *Titanic* never reached port?"

"Yes, I remember hearing the news as a boy. The *Titanic* had struck an iceberg. On her maiden voyage. And sank, drowning two thirds of her passengers and crew. Oh yes, I remember that. I can't, of course, explain this rationally, but . . . I remember what I remember: that I also saw the *Titanic* dock."

A silence through several seconds, the tape hiss continuing. "One last question. Have you ever run into anyone else —"

"Twice. One yes; the other maybe."

"And — ?"

"Both heard my story. A woman, middle-aged at the time, who said yes, she'd always had the same two memories. I believed her. Another, a man of my age, said the same thing. I simply wasn't sure about him. Maybe so."

Ted pushed a control. "The tape ran out. There's a little more on the other side, but you've heard it all actually. He does go on a bit."

"Yeah, well, it's a good one. It's a good one. Do us a report, Ted, and — do we get the tape?"

"Oh, sure, that's what it's for."

"Okay. Well, it's a little late, folks. I had an interim report, but it'll hold till next time. It's a little more on the old book, is all: the Turnbull biography. For those who came in late last time

35

or fell asleep, that's Amos Turnbull, friend of Jefferson and Franklin, member of the Continental Congress. But mentioned nowhere else, and no other copy of my book known by anyone. All my interim really says, though, is that I spent a lot of hours this summer reading Colonial newspapers on microfilm. Which will either drive you blind or crazy; it's a photo finish. And found nothing, not a mention of Amos. Oh, Irv — you had some film?"

"Yeah, but no projector: this is thirty-five-millimeter. Thought I had a projector borrowed, but it fell through. I've got about a hundred feet of old black-and-white."

"Showing?"

"A couple of blocks of a street in Paris; 1920, '21, along in there. Very bright and sharp. Shops, people walking around, nothing much. But at the end of this particular street you should see the Eiffel Tower."

"And it's not there?"

"Right."

"Okay, like to see that. Next time?"

"Count on it."

"All right, then, it's a wrap. See you all in a month, those I don't see tomorrow; Audrey will send out notices. Anybody need a ride?"

No one did, and chattering — less of the meeting than of work, classes, children, clothes, recent vacations — they began gathering belongings from the tabletop, shoving back chairs. The bearded chairman stood by the door speaking good-nights as they left. When the last of them had passed through the door, the sound of footsteps in the wood-floored hallway diminishing, the nighttime silence beginning, he glanced at the campaign button in his hand, then flicked down the light switch and pulled the door closed, standing in the hall listening till he heard the lock click.

1

WE STOOD bunched in with the little crowd you can see on the balcony down there at the right — see it? — just over the pillared entrance to the Everett House: Julia and I, her hands in her muff, and our four-year-old son, chin on the balcony rail. When I leaned over him to see his face in the light of the marching torches below us, his expression was fixed in wonder. I was here on assignment, but this was also a part of nineteenth-century life, a great parade, that I liked a lot. We had no movies, radio, or television, but we did have parades, and often. Now every possible inch of standing room down there in Union Square was lost under the packed-together shoulders and the tops of derbies, tall hats, fur caps, shawled hair, and bonnets. Winding around the roadway through that thick crowd, hundreds of marching men, and floats, flags, bands, horses, all fitfully visible in the bobbing firelight from rank after rank of gimballed canisters of smoky flame.

The sound was a thrill: the splendid brass blare of marching bands and the yells of the crowd. What they yelled, I'd noticed again and again, was "Hurrah!" — actually pronounced *hurrah*. We stood hearing fireworks whistle up, watched them burst gorgeously against the black sky with that muffled fireworks *pop*. Skyrockets shot through these bursts and curved off, dying. Where did they land? And paper balloons, their swinging baskets of orange fire shining through the sides. Every now and then flame crawled up a paper panel, and the balloon would drop, blazing. Where? Were there men waiting on the dark rooftops around the square with buckets of water? Must have been, must have been.

It was glorious, all black dark and flowering color, marching leather shuffling on cobbles, drums banging, cymbals smashing. Only a political parade, the election weeks ahead, but fun. Another band moving past now, this one in tall flat-topped shakos with plumes and tiny peaks, the snares rattling, lots of powerful horn and trumpet and that bell-like thing that tops it all off. Splendid blaring sound, very close, and once again that night I felt the actual chill right up the spine, and the slightly embarrassing eye sting, of easy emotion about nothing.

Now a turnverein band in funny costumes, and we stayed for that — Willy insisted. Then we left to beat the crowd, coming down through the hotel. I liked the hotel because someone had told me that a couple of the old men sitting around the lobby were veterans of the War of 1812, but there were none there tonight. I didn't believe it anyway. Out the side entrance of the hotel, and across the street, around the square, the curbs were solid with waiting carriages, their lamps lighted, an occasional iron horseshoe stomping the stone. Just as we approached him a horse began urinating, fascinating Willy, who wanted to stop and watch, Julia's arm under mine tugging us past, me grinning. A few carriages further on we stopped to lift Willy to pat the soft nose of a more genteel horse, something he loved.

Then we walked home, the streets near to silent except for an occasional passerby or clip-clopping carriage. It was nice out, not too cold. There'd been a moon earlier, but I couldn't find it now. Plenty of stars though, the sky a great enclosing blackness over this low city; millions of stars, those near the horizon spiky and glittery.

Willy was asleep, head sweetly heavy on my

shoulder when we reached the little square of greenery which was Gramercy Park, turning to walk partly around it. We rented a house here, a three-story brownstone with basement and attic, across the park from Julia's aunt. Julia liked being near her aunt, and so did I. I liked Aunt Ada, and it gave us a convenient and willing babysitter. We passed a carriage, horse tethered to the hitching post, carriage lamps shining orangely, and I wondered about it. Then, as we passed I heard a door, turned and saw light from the Bostwick entrance hall shining out on the steps, a man leaving, putting on his derby as he came down, and I saw the little satchel in his hand: a doctor. I said, "Old Mr. Bostwick must be sick," and Julia said that in the park with Willy yesterday, she'd been told by another mother that he was. Old Mr. Bostwick interested me because I knew he'd been born in 1799, the year Washington died — were they contemporaries for a few months or weeks?

My name is Simon Morley, I'm "thirtyish," as we say, and although I was born well into the twentieth century, I live back here in the nineteenth, married to a young woman born long before I was or even my parents. Because — according to Dr. E. E. Danziger, retired professor of physics from Harvard — time is like a river. It carries us forward through its bends, into the future . . . but the past remains in the bends behind us. If so, said Dr. D, we ought to be

41

able to reach it. And got himself a government grant to try.

We are tied to the present, Dr. Danziger said, by countless threads — the countless things that *make* the present: automobiles, television, planes, the way Coca-Cola tastes. An endless list of tiny threads that tie us to *now*.

Well, study the past, he said, for the same kind of mundane details. Read its newspapers, magazines, and books. Dress and live in its style, think its thoughts — all the things that make it *then*. Now find a place that exists in both times unchanged; "Gateways," he called them. And live in that place which also exists in the time you want to reach — dressing, eating, and thinking the way they did — and presently the ties holding you to the present will relax. Then blank out even the knowledge of these ties through self-hypnosis. And let your knowledge of the time you want to reach come flooding up in your mind. And there — in a Gateway existing in both times — you may, you just may make the transition.

Most people failed, at the Project where we were trained. They'd try and — just couldn't. But I could, one of the very few. Made it back into the nineteenth century, returned to make my report, then went back to stay — to marry Julia, and live out my life in the nineteenth century.

Now at our house, in familiar routine, Julia stepped on ahead up the stairs to unlock and open the front door for me; and in the hall she turned up the light. Then I passed Willy over to her because our dog — a fairly big woolly black dog with dabs of white here and there — was doing his little dance around my feet, trying to trip me for laughs. I let him out, and sat waiting on the front stoop while he wandered around, sniffing, checking to see that nothing had been changed out here. He's a fine fellow, called Rover, a fairly common name that hadn't yet become funny. Big black dogs, I'm afraid, are often Nig.

Rover came back to sit down beside me, and I gave him his ear rub, which he accepted graciously, tongue lolling to show appreciation. I had various little routines with Rover, adding to and improving them from time to time, but it was best, I'd learned, to keep them out here. Julia is bright, quick-minded, and as subtle and perceptive as anyone. Yet one evening when old Rove came wandering in to join us in the sitting room, with a long thread of drool hanging from his black lips, I suggested to Julia that he might be an enchanted prince and that she ought to give him a big wet kiss to release him from his spell. But all I got for that was trouble, because her sense of humor, naturally, is pure nineteenth-century. One evening fairly early in our marriage we sat reading in bed, and she laughed aloud and pointed to what she'd just read in her newspaper. I leaned over and read it; it was a joke, a filler at the bottom of a column. The little omnibuses on Broadway and on Fifth Avenue are called stages by some, others call them buses, and the joke was: " 'Don't you think I have a good face for the stage?' asked a lady with histrionic aspirations. 'I don't know about the stage,' replied her gallant companion, 'but you have a lovely face for a buss.' " I imitated a chuckle, nodding my head very rapidly to suggest appreciation. As I once did at a Harrigan and Hart performance which was truly terrible, dreadful "faith and begorra" Irishman jokes. But Julia actually cried from laughter, along with everyone else but me. I faked it.

"I understand you're Man's Best Friend," I said to Rover now, there on the front stoop, and he agreed. ("Man's Best Friend" was serious business here, a subject for sentimental newspaper poetry, which Julia no longer read aloud to me.) "But it seems to me," I told Rover, who sat listening politely as though he'd never heard this before, "that it's kind of a one-sided friendship. We do all the work. We get your dinners" — his ears lifted at the magic word — "get your water, provide beds, fireplaces, baths" — the ears flattened — "all the necessities, nay, luxuries of the carefree dog's life." I began leaning close to him. "But what do you do in return, Best Friend?" I leaned still closer. "Where are my slippers?" He didn't know, but now he could, and did, as I'd expected, give me a wet tongue up the side of my face. "That's the *deal?*" I said. "Dog spit all over the face? Listen" — I grabbed him around the shoulders, hugging him close while he tried to pull his head loose, but I had him. "Where did you guys ever get this idea that a face lacquered with dog spit is some kind of favor? Thousands of years, but you never learn." I let him go, and he sat paying attention to whatever I might want to say. Dogs try to understand, they *want* to; cats never do. I gave Rove a friendly tail yank; then he followed me in, and out to his back-porch bed.

Up in our big bedroom Julia and I moved around, getting ready for bed, not saying much, still under the spell of a good evening. I liked this room, liked them all, but this especially: carpeted; gaslit; furnished with what I was aware were almost ridiculously massive, overornamented tables, chiffoniers, two big wardrobes, a leather chair, our big bed. But a place I loved: peaceful, a refuge.

Above my right shoulder — we were in bed now, sitting up to talk for a few moments the way we usually did — an open-flame light burned steady behind an etched and frosted shade. On the small marble-topped table beside me lay a copy of the new January 11, 1887, issue of *Leslie's Weekly*. I had two drawings in it this week, and I liked looking at them; so did Julia, who saved them all. My watch and chain, the watch tick-ticking pleasantly — I had just wound it — lay on the *Leslie's*. From below, outside at street level and approaching our slightly opened window, footsteps — made not by shoes but by boots, striking not concrete but cut stone, to make a

45

sound not twentieth-century but nineteenth —
footsteps approached, then moved on by, the
sound distancing. As so often, I felt the thrill
and mystery of simply *being* here, hearing those
unseen late-at-night footsteps deep in the nineteenth century. Whose? Going where? For what
never-to-be-known purpose? And to continue
how far on into the future?

We sat against the dark carved wood of the
great bedstead, snug under a thick quilt, in our
nightgowns; I'd long since and absolutely refused
to wear a nightcap, cold as it could get when
the coals in the fireplace across the room burned
out. Once in a while you're momentarily conscious
of being happy. But I'm superstitious, and I picture Fate — best be respectful, and use a capital
F — as a misty presence somewhere up in the
sky but not too far away. Always listening, alert
and ready to punish forbidden optimism. But I
couldn't help it, feeling as purely content as it
is possible to be, I would think, and in that moment as sometimes happens, Julia said, "Are you
happy, Si?"

"Not at all. Why should I be?"

"Because of me maybe?"

"Well, okay. Right now . . . here in this house
. . . Willy safely asleep across the hall, Rover
snug in his bed, two drawings in the paper this
week, and here in this cozy bed with you —"

"Stop that. It's much too late."

"I'm about as happy" — I glanced at the ceiling
to say, "Only fooling!" — "as any human being

46

could be without throwing up. That suit you?"

"Just barely better than nothing at all."

"Best I can do. Why'd you ask — something bothering you?"

"Oh, no. It's just that you've been singing again."

"What?"

"Those strange songs."

"Oh Lord, I didn't realize."

"Yes. After you gave Willy his bath on Sunday, I was getting him into bed, and he was trying to sing something about 'Raindrop fa' my head.'"

"Damn it, I've got to cut that out! I don't want to burden that boy with any twentieth-century knowledge, not a scrap! Not for a long time anyway. If ever. *This* is his time, the one he'll grow up and live in. And I want it to be for him just like any other —"

"Yes, yes, don't worry, he's forgotten, it won't hurt him. It's *you* I worry about" — she put a hand on my forearm — "when I hear you singing those songs. You don't even know you're doing it. Sometimes you just hum, but I know it's from your own time because the tune is so odd."

That made me smile. Julia's idea of a good song — everybody's idea — was one her aunt had just bought, the sheet music, called "Baby's Gone to Heaven." All about a dead baby, and the cover — a truly bad black-and-white drawing I'd have secretly buried late at night — showed a woman, tears streaming, arms lifted toward a floating baby drifting up into a heavenly glow.

Aunt Ada's boarders and friends, and some of our friends, too, would sing that kind of song standing around the organ. Some would smile, demonstrating sophisticated amusement, but most sniffled, eyes moist. And *my* songs were odd?

But I was smiling at more than songs. Here in the deep of the nineteenth century, I'd become a part of it, certainly. I knew how this time lived, thought, felt, and believed, and their ways were mine now. But like a man living permanently in another country, knowing its language and customs, becoming indistinguishably a part of it, I nevertheless carried hidden things that remained forever foreign. Things like my idea of humor and of what a song should be come from earliest childhood, and can't be changed.

"And when I hear you humming your songs," Julia said, "I know you're thinking of your time." The late twentieth century scared Julia; she hated everything she knew about it. She wanted me to be happy, but happy *here*.

"Well, of course I think about my own time occasionally."

"*Could* you go back, Si? Can you still do it?"

"Well . . . I'm not sure; it's been five years. At the Project we learned that if you can move into another time, you can usually do it again. But I really don't know. Don't want to anyway."

"Do you think others have done it?"

"Martin Lastvogel thought so; he was the teacher at the Project. He showed me an ad once, a personals ad in an 1891 *New York Times*. Said

48

something like, 'Alice, Alice, I'm here but I can't get back! Say hello for me to the city, MOMA, the library, and Eddie and Mom. Oh, pray for me!' And he said there's a tombstone in Trinity Church cemetery that reads, 'Everett Brownlee, Born 1910, Died 1895.' Martin said people assume it was a mistake, but that people don't make that kind of mistake on a tombstone. He thinks the dates are correct. Yeah, of course there've been others; always. The concept isn't hard; Dr. D couldn't have been the first to think of it. Not many can manage to do it though," I added, and detected a hint of smugness in my voice.

"Do you ever want to go back? Just as . . . a kind of visit to your own time?"

"No."

"Because of what you did."

We'd had this conversation half a dozen times in the past five years, but I knew she needed reassurance, and nodded. "On February 6, 1882, her eighteenth birthday: I can *see* her standing in the theater lobby in her new green dress. Just eighteen, and about to meet the man she'd eventually marry."

"You mustn't blame yourself, Si."

"Oh, I don't, really. But I think about it. Me standing there, knowing what was coming, knowing what I had to do. And watching him outside walking toward the lobby doors. Young Otto Danziger, about to step into the lobby where he'd be introduced to her: he even *looked* like Dr.

D! Then I see myself treacherously stepping out, unlighted cigar in hand, asking him for a light. Deliberately delaying him. Till I saw her leave the lobby to go inside. So they never met, it was that simple. Never met, never married, so Dr. D was never born. And without him, of course — so strange to think about it — there was never a Project." Julia lay beside me, listening like a child to a familiar story, and I smiled and said, "But what I do like to think about is Rube Prien. And Esterhazy. Living entirely different lives now, far ahead in the future. Never knowing about a — a what? — a different sequence of time in which there *had* been a Project. But I liked Dr. D, Julia. And he trusted me. What I did was like murder. So I don't want to visit my own time, because you know the first thing I'd do? I'd pick up a New York phone book and look up E. E. Danziger. Knowing it wouldn't be there. Couldn't be. Because I came back to the past . . . and changed the future."

One of the pleasures of nineteenth-century life had been giving up some of the relentless self-examination of the twentieth. And now — enough! I smiled at Julia lying wide-eyed beside me, and said, "So I'm staying right here. With the girl who led the intruder from the twentieth century up the back stairs of her Aunt Ada's boarding house. While I followed, watching her marvelous legs in those truly lovely, thick, blue-and-white-striped wool stockings."

"You should have looked elsewhere."

"I did. Here."

"Now, now."

"And here."

"Si, we are talking seriously. And it's very late. This is not the time for that." But it was.

2

THE YOUNG woman looked up from her computer keyboard, smiling pleasantly, and gestured the next patient into the doctor's office. He appeared to be in his late thirties, was bald, with red-blond hair at the back and sides, and — crossing the small room purposefully, very nearly belligerently — looked to be just under average height. Heavy shoulders, though, and thick through the chest.

Waiting at his desk, the doctor said pleasantly, "Sit down, please," nodding at a small couch that faced his desk. "Be with you in a sec. Just looking over your sheet." The doctor looked thirty-five, wore a faded green tennis shirt, and his hair was yellow brown and thick. But not air-blown, the patient decided, approving. No goddamn alligator on the shirt either.

He sat down to wait, his back barely touching the cushion behind him, sitting almost bolt upright, not accepting the offered softness and comfort. His hands lay unmoving on his thighs, and he kept his pink-skinned face placid as he looked around. More like a living room than an office, he thought: overlapping miniature rugs; the entire wall behind the desk bookshelves; a wide window ledge at the side scattered with publications; framed photographs of sailboats; wooden shutters darkening the room, secluding it from the world. He didn't like it. Then he made himself sit back, and forced his shoulders to release their tension. Hostility at the self-imposed necessity of being here was unproductive.

The man at the desk tilted head and paper simultaneously to read along a margin. "My secretary has noted that you prefer not to give your name."

"Well, we'll see. Tell me something first. Are you a regular doctor?"

"I'm not an M.D. I have a doctorate in psychology."

"I've always understood that what a man tells a doctor is confidential. That apply to you?"

"Absolutely."

He considered that, nodded thoughtfully, then unexpectedly smiled, so warmly and genuinely that the man at the desk felt an immediate response, a surge of wanting to help; but aware, too, that the patient was taking charge. "We can add my name later if need be," the patient said. "The thing is, I'm an officer in the Army."

"I thought so."

"Oh?" he said in a prove-it tone.

"Well, I don't want to come off as Sherlock Holmes, but there are no cuffs on your pants. A solid-color knit tie. White shirt. And you haven't unbuttoned your coat. There's a neatness about you that says Army to me. If your suit were khaki instead of blue, I'd salute."

"Well, you're pretty good. A brother officer claims my pajamas have epaulets. I like the Army. Only reason I'm out of uniform is the work I'm doing these days. And the only reason I'm here instead of an army shrink — sorry."

"That's okay. I say it too."

"I don't want it in my jacket, my army file, that I consulted a, uh —"

"Psychologist: I'm not a psychiatrist. And this won't be in any record but mine. So come on now. You have to tell me, you have to make a start."

"I know. All right. About ten days ago I was working. I'm a historian, an infantry major assigned just now to the Center of Military History. I'm a specialist in World War One. These days I work at the main branch of the New York Public Library at Forty-second and Fifth, and one day something happened.

"I had a stack of books in front of me. Taking notes. I was copying out names, German names and military titles. Going slow, printing carefully, getting the Kraut spelling absolutely right. And out of the blue I felt a sudden" — he hesitated — "well, rage. And I mean *rage;* absolutely unexplainable. It just took me over. Instantly. Like somebody had walked up and slapped me across the mouth. And I said — this was out loud, you understand; me sitting there at one of those long tables they have, heads all over the place turning to look at me. I said, 'Damn you. Oh, God *damn* you!' And I was kind of struggling, fighting to push the chair back and get to my feet.

"Then I more or less came to. Just standing there, everybody staring; I must have been *loud*. Well, I walked out of there pretty fast, and stood out on the Fifth Avenue steps for a while, cooling off. Thing is, I don't know why I said that. I just do not know. After a while I made myself go back, staring everyone down, and resume my work." He stopped, waiting.

"Go on."

"Well, not the next day. There was the week-end, and then it must have been Monday I was back at work. In the main reading room again. I'm there when they open, every weekday and Saturday. And I stay till they throw me out. But this time, thank God, I'd taken a break. I was out on the steps having coffee. There's guys out front with carts selling coffee and stuff."

"I know."

"Miserable coffee. But something to do. I give myself a ten-minute break, by the clock, in the middle of the morning, and another in midafternoon. And the quickest lunch I can manage. And I drink the lousy coffee because I don't smoke. I did, but I quit. It's been —"

"Come on now."

"Okay. It happened again. A terrible anger. Sudden. Out of nowhere. A rush of it. I could feel my face go red, my collar choking me. Raw emotion with nothing to explain it. And I said, 'You son of a bitch. Oh, you *bastard. You did it, you did it!*' There was a woman standing next to me — those steps get crowded — and I just trotted down the stairs, tossed my cup at a trash basket, coffee and all, and got the hell out of there. I couldn't help but look back, and you know" — he smiled — "she was still there, not even watching me. I was just another New York crazy far's she was concerned. But I was still wild. Walking along, going fast, headed north but going nowhere I knew of. And if I could have grabbed him by the throat, I'da never let go."

"Grabbed who! Quick!"

The patient shook his head. "I don't know. Just don't know. But the feeling did not go away; for a while it got worse. Finally it eased off, but I didn't go back. Not that day. Quit early and went home, first time in years. I keep a little apartment in the East Village; I'm up here a lot; the Army pays for it. My real place is in Washington. And that's about it. I don't know what the hell is going on. Do you?"

"Not yet."

"I see. I gather you think I'll be coming back."

"For a time maybe." The doctor picked up the patient-information sheet from his desk. "Maybe we should get this finished up. You married?"

"No."

"Ever been?"

"No."

"Okay." He made a check mark. "And you're how old: thirty-seven, thirty-eight?"

"Thirty-nine, and if you're really asking how come I'm nearly forty and never been married, it's simple: I haven't time. I like women; quite a lot. Sexually, and just for themselves. Women are nicer than men, they're better people; I have women who are friends, and women usually stay my friends. I've had a lot to do with them, and expect to continue, and I hope that takes care of that. But what I like most — better than women, men, cats or dogs — is work. Life is work, and work is life, that's my opinion. It's why we're alive; procreation is just to keep the thing going. I have fun, I have pleasure apart from work. I go to movies, have a drink, see friends, men and women; I do what everyone does. But that's only recreation. What I really do is work. Sixteen hours a day often, and for day after day when I know I should. Twenty hours if need be. There's no way I could be married."

"Well. You haven't asked me this, and it's not why you're here. But there are other years to come, you know, other kinds of years."

"I know it. And I'll be old and lonely, all that. But these are the years that matter. And this is how I'm going to spend them. Nothing is more important: I've got things to do, and they're going to be done. I'm a ruthless son of a bitch, Doc, and I'm not kidding. Ruthless with myself, too."

"Yes. Okay." He stood, so did his patient, and

— skilled at ending his sessions — the doctor led the way to his office door, the other man following, opened it, then waited for the almost inevitable last question or, occasionally, the final withheld-until-now revelation.

This time it was a question. "You have any clue at all on this?"

"No. And you don't want guesses."

"Okay, Doctor. I call you Doctor, by the way?"

"My name is Paul. Call me Paul."

"Okay, and my name is Prien, Ruben Prien. Call me Rube."

"Okay, Rube. Make an appointment with my secretary as you leave. I'll see you soon."

But he was wrong. Rube Prien never came back.

3

HE'D BEEN on his way to keep the appointment four days later, a Friday, walking north on lower Fifth Avenue toward the doctor's office on Sixty-second Street. As often as possible, moving about the city, Rube Prien walked, a chance for exercise. This morning he wore a sharply pressed olive-green gabardine suit, a white shirt, maroon knit tie, tan cap. The day was sunny and cool, and he noted, pleased, that after nineteen uptown blocks, usually overtaking other pedestrians, he was not perspiring. He believed that meant he was in condition.

Shoulders, elbows, and legs moving easily, the rhythm of it a pleasure, the air pressing his face, he felt his mind at rest, very nearly not thinking at all. But some twenty blocks later, crossing Fifty-ninth Street — glancing appreciatively over at the Plaza Hotel — to walk along now beside Central Park, he felt a little nudge of . . . apprehension? Unease? Something. It grew and then very suddenly it had him again. He felt it in his stomach, felt it building very fast, and he glanced around, afraid he was about to yell, curse, go out of control. On past Sixty-second Street, not even glancing east toward the building in which he had an appointment; turning to walk across the Park at Seventy-second; sweating now, hurrying, angry, scared, eyes bright with curiosity. Further west, then north again, block after block.

Then he was walking through a shabby, rundown little industrial area, cars solidly parked on both sides of the narrow streets, wheels up over the curbs. The sidewalks along which he walked were scattered with paper and plastic wrappings, newspaper fragments, plastic cups, crushed cans, pull tabs, food containers, bottles, broken glass. *Buzz Bannister, Neon Signs*, read an unlighted neon window sign in a dirty-white stucco building, windows crowded with stacked cardboard boxes. *Fiore Bros., Wholesale Novelties*; a heavy padlock on the door, a broken shoe lying in the doorway. No one in sight, not a soul. On he walked, fast, going somewhere, knowing which way to turn at corners, getting there.

Then it ran out. And he stood on the walk helpless as a dog who's lost the scent. He walked on uncertainly. Stopped to glance around for something, anything familiar, not finding it. Walked on looking for a street sign.

The feeling roared back, and he swung around to about-face and retrace a block, turned west at the corner, and stopped. There it was. "That's it," he told himself, "that's the . . ." The what?

It was a six-story red brick building, the sides blank and windowless except for an office at street level at the distant corner. But it looked right. Flat roof, he could see the conical top of the old-style wooden water tower up there. Yes. And along the building's sides just below the roofline in a band of weathered paint, BEEKEY BROTHERS, MOVING AND STORAGE, 555-8811. Yes. In a painted panel, LOCAL AND LONG DISTANCE HAULING. STORAGE OUR SPECIALTY. AGENTS FOR ASSOCIATED VAN LINES. A green, gilt-lettered Beekey truck stood before a metal-slat truck door in the side of the building. This was it, whatever it was, and Rube Prien turned to walk beside the block-long building toward a door he could see in his mind.

It was there. At the end of the building. An ordinary, unmarked weathered gray door, the paint peeling here and there in narrow strips. He knocked, heard steps on a wooden floor, the door opened, and he saw what he knew he'd see: a young man in white coveralls, his name embroidered in red over a pocket. "Hi there; come on in." The man turned away as Rube stepped in. Lettered in an arc on the back of his coveralls: *Beekey Brothers, Movers*.

Rube glanced around, pulling the door closed behind him. He knew this little room: the worn oak desk behind which — the name over his pocket was *Dave* — the young man sat down. Knew the wooden chair before it, at which Dave gestured, inviting Rube to take it. Knew the framed photographs on the walls: moving crews lined up beside their trucks; *The Gang*, some were labeled. Some of the trucks were old, with un-roofed cabs, no windshields, steering wheels huge and perfectly upright. Dates lettered in white under the lined-up crews: *1935, 1938, 1912, 1919* . . .

"What can I do for you?"

Rube turned, gripping the back of the empty chair, and said, "Do you know me? You recognize me?"

"No, can't say I do." Voice polite.

"I've been here before, I know I have." But Dave shook his head. "Well . . ." Rube's mind supplied an answer. "I'm . . . winding up a small business. Got some stuff to store. If I could look around?"

"Sure." Dave stood to walk to a gray-painted metal-sheathed door, pushed it open, and held it for Rube, who stepped through into a tiny, concrete-paved area lighted by a bare high-watt-age ceiling bulb. Dave pushed a button beside closed elevator doors, they heard a starting clunk up in the shaft, then the steadily descending whir, and Rube held himself still and expressionless, everything here utterly familiar, to the very scratches on the green-enameled elevator doors. And yet — what was he about to see?

Up to the top floor; the doors slid apart, Rube stepped out, and stopped so abruptly Dave had to dance a sidestep around him. They stood at the head of an aisle wide as a narrow street and so long its sides contracted far ahead with distance. Caged ceiling bulbs lighted the area poorly, shadowing the wooden floor rutted by years of iron wheels. Both sides were lined — like houses on the two sides of a street — with side-by-side cubicles of wood-framed wire netting, their simple plank doors stencil-numbered and padlocked. Rube stepped forward, his shoulders bulled in angry frustration, head jerking from side to side, glancing into the nearest cubicles; at household furniture, chairs inverted on tabletops; at a space paved with shadeless lamps, another stacked chest-high with framed pictures; more furniture. Angrily he said, "What is this! God damn it, what *is* this!"

Dave took his time answering, staring levelly at Rube. "It's a storage space, what do you think it is? This is a moving and storage company."

"And . . . what about the rest? The other floors."

"Three more just like this. And below that, temporary storage, stuff they're assembling into truckloads for long-distance hauls. You say you've been here before?" But Rube was swinging away, back toward the elevator.

Out in the street, walking away fast, he found a cab at curbside on Sixth Avenue, opened the door, ready to say, "Library on Fifth," but instead gave his home address. A moment or so later, sitting back, trying to think about what he had seen and what he had not seen, Rube murmured, "Oscar . . ." He did it again, deliberately,

63

"Oscar," waited for more, but there was no more, and he cursed silently, staring out at the street.

That evening, his gabardine suit hung in his bedroom closet to preserve its press, Rube sat facing the windows in the one upholstered chair of his furnished apartment. He was barefooted, wore a sleeveless underwear top and faded blue pajama pants. On his lap lay a clipboard, a pen clipped to the blank sheet. Not reading, not listening to or watching anything, eyes deliberately unfocused, and not consciously thinking, he sat in the faint wash of orange light reflected by the ceiling from the streetlamp below. He held a measured ounce of bourbon whiskey, with water, in a glass, occasionally sipping, staring out the window, waiting. His bare forearms and biceps looked powerful; first thing every morning he did push-ups, down on the floor only seconds after his alarm had rung.

Presently he said, "Dan . . ." and waited. "Dan . . . forth? Dan . . . bury?" He shook his head, said, "Don't force," and allowed eyes and mind to drift out of focus again.

He printed *Oscar* on his clipboard sheet. Then *Dan* — in elaborate doodle he strengthened the letters, added serifs and shading, then sat back again, staring at the rectangle of window. He sipped from his glass, set it back on the sill. "Dan . . . iel?" he said. "Dan . . . cer? Danboogleboogle? Danblahblahblah? Dandantheaccordionman? Okay, cut it out."

Across the street, he noted, the sky above the roofline of the apartment building really was a sky, not a whitish nothingness but a blue-blackness behind a thin scatter of stars. A light came on in a window of the building, then off. He stood up to walk absently through the three rooms, something he often did, often singing softly, usually an incompletely remembered fragment of the old popular music he understood. "A new room," he sang now, "a blue room for two room . . ." He knew he was a lonely man but didn't mind. *Oscar Rossoff.*

Swiftly he walked into the living room to a small wooden table against one wall that he used as a desk, and from a ten-foot length of books on an unpainted pine shelf he'd attached to the wall over the desk, took down the Manhattan phone book. *Rossoff, Michael S. . . . Nathan A. . . . Nicholas . . . O. V. . . . Olive M. . . . Omin . . . Oscar!* He dialed the desk phone, and on the third ring a man's voice said, "Hello?"

"Mr. Rossoff? Oscar Rossoff?"

"Yes."

"My name is Prien, Mr. Rossoff. P-R-I-E-N, Ruben Prien. I am a major in the United States Army, and I've phoned because I once knew an Oscar Rossoff. In . . . New York. And I wonder if it's you. Do you remember me? Rube Prien?"

"No-o," the man said slowly, politely reluctant to say it. Then, "Actually I'm not sure. Prien. Ruben Prien. It *does* sound . . . not quite unfamiliar." He laughed at his own cautious phrasing. "Maybe I do. Clue me in."

But all Rube Prien could do was refer to a nearly formless mental picture. "Well, the Oscar Rossoff I knew was . . . in his thirties, I'd say? Early thirties, but this was . . . a few years ago, I think." Suddenly he added, "Had dark hair and a trimmed mustache."

"Well, I don't have a mustache now, but I did. The trimming got to be a nuisance. And yes, I have dark hair, and I'm thirty-seven now. Rube Prien, Rube Prien. Sounds as though I ought to remember. Where was this?"

The words spoke themselves: "At the Project," but he didn't know what he meant.

"*What* project?" The voice on the phone had gone cold. "What is this? You're the second person who's phoned about 'the project.' "

"*Who was the other!?*"

"Look, I want to know what's going —"

"*Please.* Mr. Rossoff, *please;* I have *got* to know. *Who was the other?*"

Reluctantly: "McNaughton, he said his name was, John McNaughton. From Winfield, Vermont."

"Thank you, thank you very much," Rube said swiftly. "Won't keep you any longer, sorry to've troubled you," and he pressed the button to break the connection. Then released it, dialed information, got the area code for Vermont, and dialed long-distance information. "I am sorry, we have no listing for a John McNaughton." As though

66

he could be seen, and as though he'd expected this, Rube nodded, took down the Manhattan phone book, and began leafing through the H's for Hertz Rent a Car.

4

JUST PAST nine o'clock next morning, he turned off the throughway onto an asphalt-paved county road. Ten more miles, then off onto a narrower, winding, weed-bordered road, once paved but potholed now, chunks of asphalt missing. The final eleven miles took over half an hour. Out of a last slow curve, and the road turned into concrete-paved Main Street, Winfield, Vermont.

Rube drove slowly through a block, head ducked to stare ahead through the windshield, then swung into an angled parking space. He got out, feeling in his pocket for meter change, but every meter flag in the block showed red, no other car parked; and on ahead for three blocks, only two cars, both pickups. *Hell with it,* he thought, *probably don't even bother collecting anymore.*

On the sidewalk he stood glancing both ways. Nothing moved in the entire five-block length of Main Street, no one in sight. The walk lay silent in the morning sun, his foreshortened shadow slanted toward the curb; he turned to walk on, hearing no sound but his own footsteps.

In the block ahead, a man in blue jeans, dark plaid shirt, and a yellow good-old-boy visored cap walked out from a storefront, and on across the walk. He was young, big, wore a thick Zapata mustache, was heavy and big-bellied. He climbed up into a red pickup with enormous tires, and when he slammed his door the tinny crash bounced between the storefront walls, the only sound in the street till he started his engine and drove off.

Rube walked on past a men's clothing store, one of its two display windows paved with work shoes, cowboy and pull-on boots. Past two bars into which he could not see. Past storefronts boarded over with plywood sheets so weathered the outer layers were separating in narrow swollen bulges. Most of the buildings he passed were two stories, a few three. Some of the upper windows were labeled: a doctor, a lawyer, a chiropractor. Rounded bay windows hung out over the walk at some corners, their separate roofs steeply conical. He glanced down the side streets as he crossed them: houses, wooden and old. Many had porches elaborately ornamented at the eaves, but the ornamentation was often broken, pieces missing. None of the houses had been painted in a long time, and a few were covered over with green asphalt shingling. The front windows of one were curtained with a gray blanket and a sun-faded quilt. The lawns were gone, only chopped-down weeds and winter mud marks, often tracked by car wheels. Cars stood on a few of these former lawns, others on dirt or cinder driveways. All were old, big, American. All sun-faded, dented, some listing. A new high-wheels pickup stood parked in the street, one set of wheels up over the curb.

On past a little stucco movie theater, its shallow poster-display cases empty, the glass broken, its marquee letters reading, *Closed*. At a corner, a small grocery store, door open. Just inside, a low showcase crowded with bottles: dozens of brands of whiskey, gin, vodka, brandy. All were half-pints, and the sliding glass doors of the case were padlocked. Rube walked in, nodding at the middle-aged clerk. "Do you have a city directory?"

The man shook his head, eyes amused. "Isn't any."

"Is there a city hall?"

"Nope. No more. No city anymore, friend. We're just county now. Who you lookin' for?"

"John McNaughton."

The man shook his head. "Nope."

Out on the street corner, Rube stood glancing around again. Just ahead the street divided to angle right and left around a little square slightly higher than the street, its cut-stone curbing angled outward by frost, pieces missing. The square had been paved over, the asphalt now broken, patches of dirt showing, remnants of white-painted striping still visible, the ghosts of old parking spaces.

What now? Coffee. Just ahead, *Larry's Place*, and he walked on to it, looked in. It was open: aproned proprietor behind the counter, a counter customer hunched over his coffee. Rube went in, ordering coffee as he sat down at the counter, glancing at the other customer as the man turned to look at him. *"Major! Major Prien! My God, how are you!"*

"Why, I'm fine, John, just fine," Rube said easily, but — did he really know this man?

Who smiled and said, "Not quite sure about me, are you, Major?" He was big, broad-backed, maybe forty, wearing a threadbare brown suitcoat over a gray flannel shirt. Sliding his coffee cup on in advance, he moved to the stool beside Rube, saying, "Take a good look."

An old-fashioned face, Rube thought, thin, tight-skinned, permanently weathered. The way Americans used to look, with haircut to match, no sissy sideburns but economically clipped high on the sides, a real last-a-month whitewall. "You look like a World War One doughboy."

"Feel like one sometimes. Well? You know me?"

"I don't know. Maybe. You look like a hick; are you?"

"Depends. On occasion and within limits I can be a kind of rural Noel Coward. But yeah, by inclination I'm a hick. The haircut's no disguise, it's me."

"You're smart, though."

"Well, yes, though I wouldn't call for a new deal if I were dumb. Because it wouldn't matter; I'd go along just about the way I do anyway.

71

I'm a simple man, I like the simple life, so there's no real need to be smart. Kind of a waste, actually. I have to be smart enough to stay simple and not get all dissatisfied. The way I'd be anyway if I were dumb. You follow me?"

"I'm not sure. Maybe I'm not smart enough."

"And what are your hobbies and favorite sports, Major?"

"Well, John, I like things to go my way. And I work at it harder and longer than most. What I don't like is anyone trying to jerk me around. So just tell me; I think maybe I know you, but I'm not sure: jog my memory."

"Remember Kay Veach? Thin, black-haired girl?"

Rube shook his head.

"From the Project. I phoned her; lives in Wyoming. But she didn't remember me or the Project. How about Nate Dempster? Around thirty? Bald. Wore glasses." Rube shook his head again. "Also from the Project, and also didn't remember it or me. Oscar Rossoff?"

"Oscar, yeah. I phoned him. He said you'd called. And gave me your name."

"Did he now?" McNaughton smiled. "Oscar was a little unhappy with me. Couldn't quite remember me. Or the Project. Almost! But — no. Got mad when I pushed him about the Project."

"The *Project*, the *Project*. What the hell is the Project!"

"Well." McNaughton tasted his coffee, made a face, setting it down. "You never quite get

72

used to how bad this stuff really is. Picture a big building, Major Prien. Fills a whole city block. Made of brick, no windows. On the outside says, *Beekey's Moving and Storage,* phone number, stuff like that. But that's only a front: inside, the building is gutted. Every floor but the top one ripped out, and the top one turned into offices. Underneath, just a hollow shell of brick walls, a block square. And down on the floor —"

"The Big Floor."

"Yeah! You're doing good! Down on the Big Floor, something like movie sets. Separated by walls. An Indian tepee on a stretch of prairie, walls painted to look like more. World War One trenches in another, a barbed-wire no-man's-land stretching away in front. An actual house in another. An exact replica of a house right here in Winfield, but the way it was in the twenties. And a man living in it: me." He sat grinning at Rube.

"Yeah, yeah, I'm all ears."

"Real Crow Indians living in the tepee; had to be taught the language, though. Guys in the trenches wearing 1917 U.S. Army uniforms. All of us getting the feel of how it was, you see. Before we moved out into the real thing. Indians out onto an enormous stretch of real prairie. Doughboys in France in genuine World War One trenches restored. Because the Project, Major, was a search for a way to move back in time."

He sat waiting but Rube outwaited him, looking at him expressionlessly, and McNaughton smiled, leaning closer. "It was you, Major, who first told me all this, the first day I joined the Project. Standing up on the catwalk over the Big Floor; you could walk anywhere on the catwalks and look down on the sets. Big banks of lights up there to imitate day, night, cloudy, sunny, rain, anything. Machinery to control temperatures: winter on one set, heat wave on another. You and I stood up there looking down, me brand-new to the Project. You said that according to Einstein, time is like a narrow winding river. And we're all in a boat. All we can see around us is the present. But back in the bends behind us the past still exists. Can't see it, but it's there; *really there*, Einstein said. And meant it. Well, Dr. Danziger —"

"What were his initials?"

"E. E."

"Right! Right: E. E. Danziger."

"Major, let's get out of here, the guy's starting to listen. Pay him for — what does he call this stuff? Coffee, I think."

Outside they crossed the street to a lone bench in the little paved-over square. "Danziger said that if the past really exists — and Einstein says it does — there ought to be a way to reach it. Took him two years but he got money for the Project. From the federal government."

"Where else?"

"Well, who pays you?"

Rube smiled.

"He got, must have been a few million. Built

74

the Project, and, Major, they bought this town, the whole town. Couldn't have been many hold-outs, because look at this garbage dump. Out here in the middle of nothing but played-out farmland going back to brush. Nobody here anymore but drunks, druggies, and dropouts. Can't make it anywhere else, come up here, get on welfare, and drink. Or raise marijuana on land don't belong to them. Misfits. No-goods."

"Including you?"

"Why not? But the Project restored this whole town to the way it was in the twenties." He sat watching Rube make a show of looking around at the dilapidated town, and smiled. "Oh, it doesn't look like it now, I know. Kind of a mystery here, Major, but one thing at a time. Take my word for it, they restored this place, made it a 'Gateway' — as Dr. D called them. Makes it easier to slip from the simulation into the real thing. I did it. Made the transition to the real Winfield of the twenties. Damn few can do it, Major. You couldn't. Tried, but couldn't do it. But a few of us could, and I was one, and Major . . . it took me where I'd wanted to be all my life. You should see this little town in the twenties. Beautiful, so beautiful. Quiet dirt roads, trees, trees everywhere. And a drugstore that —"

"Spare me the nostalgia."

"I hate that word. You know who uses it mostly? Time patriots. Same people who live in the best country in the world. Must be the best because that's where *they* live. And they live in

75

the best of times; has to be best because it's their lifetime. You even suggest there just might have been better times than here and now, and it's 'nostalgia, nostalgia.' Don't even know what the word means. Means *overly* sentimental, for crysakes."

"Give 'em hell, John."

"What I'll give you is the present — *look* at this street. But you should see it — oh Lord, you should see it in the twenties. Saturday night, say; in the summertime. Main Street here jammed; townspeople, farmers in from the country. They *knew* each other, stopped to talk. Someone else would come along and join in, and there'd be a little group on the walk. Not like the damn shopping malls. Go to a shopping mall a hundred times, and it's always mostly strangers you never saw before, and never see again. In the twenties this miserable dead little square was beautiful; trees, grass, shrubbery, paths, green benches, and *people*. Some of the farmers came in buggies or wagons. Hitching posts along the curbs, not parking meters. There were cars, sure. Mostly Model Ts. But I had a job, mechanic at Pierce-Arrow."

"Surprised you could stand the cars, John. All those nasty exhaust fumes."

"Maybe so. Maybe twenty, thirty years earlier Winfield is even better. Be happy to go see. Major, I have got to get back, got to."

"Why the hell did you leave?"

"The stuff that killed the cat, if you can believe it. I came back to the present, just for a day

76

or so, I thought, to see what was happening at the Project. You took the Project over, you know. Once it succeeded. You and Esterhazy. Forced Danziger out. Too cautious for you: he worried about altering events in the past because you couldn't tell, he said, how the change might affect the present. Dangerous. But you and Esterhazy were rubbing your hands! Couldn't wait to try it, and find out what would happen. But what I came back to, Major, was this. It's no Gateway anymore. I can't get back from this!"

"John, it's sure interesting, all this stuff. And you tell it so well! But I've *been* to your Project. Yesterday. And Beekey's Moving and Storage warehouse is a moving and storage warehouse. And always has been. You can see that with one look!"

"That's true. In a way."

"And it took fifty years for this stinking town to get like this; it's never been restored!"

"Also true. In a way."

"Pretty good way!"

McNaughton nodded several times, then said, "Major, four, five weeks ago I took the bus to Montpelier. State capital. Walked to the state library, and they got out a back file of the *Winfield Messenger* for me. They've got it all, 1851 to 1950; paper couldn't quite last out the full century. I got the volume for 1920 through 1926, and stole something from it, cut it out of the paper. And I keep it with me all the time. Because it's all I've got left now." From his inside coat pocket he brought out a trimmed-down manila folder, and handed it to Rube.

Rube opened it. Taped to the inside lay a three-column-wide section of newspaper. A portion of the masthead across the top read, *essenger*, and just below that, between two rules, the date, June 1, 1923. Below this, the caption over a photograph, which Rube read aloud, " 'Crowd Throngs Parade Route.' " He bent over the photograph, examining it: several ranks and files of marching young men, rifles on shoulders, all wearing shallow metal helmets and high-necked uniform blouses. Preceding them, two more uniformed men carrying the American flag and a banner. Rube read aloud the banner's inscription, " 'American Legion Post —' "

"Not the parade, the spectators."

He saw it immediately: along the curb between the thick trunks of old trees stood a lineup of men, women, children, dogs. Among them a tall man wearing a flat, black-ribboned straw hat. And under its stiff brim, smiling at the camera — sharp, clear, unmistakable — the face of the man beside him.

Who nodded, reaching for his folder. "Yep. Me. Right here in Winfield. On this very street. Watching the Memorial Day parade in the spring of 1923. There's no Project now, Major; it doesn't exist. But there was. It did."

"Fine. Then why don't I remember it? You do, you say."

"Something happened, Major. Something happened back in the past that altered the present."

"Like what?"

"I don't know. Anything. When it happened, I was back in the past where it didn't touch me. I took my memories with me, and brought them back. But they didn't match the present anymore. I came back, but not to the restored Winfield. I came back to this untouched garbage dump. And went crazy. Got myself to New York, and *ran* the last block to the Project. And found Beekey's Moving and Storage, nothing else. And worst of all" — he leaned toward Rube, lowering his voice — "worst of all, Danziger didn't exist. Wasn't in the phone book. And at the library I looked through their old phone book file back to 1939. No E. E. Danziger. Ever. No record of his birth at City Hall. And no one ever heard of him at Harvard. He didn't exist!"

"He did it . . ." Rube was slowly standing, his face turning red. "Oh, that son of a bitch. He *did* it!"

"Who?"

"Why . . . Marley? *Morley!* Simon Morley! We sent him back, didn't we? Into the nineteenth century on a . . . mission. And he did this!"

"Did what?"

"Why . . . I don't know." He stood looking helplessly at McNaughton. "Something. Did something, back in the past, so that . . . Danziger was never born. No Project now. And never was." He sat down, and the two men stared at the deserted street ahead. Then Rube said, "John, what keeps you here in this nothing place?"

"My job. Part-time mechanic. At subscale pay. And the cheapest room this side of Calcutta."

"You ever do any fighting? Boxing, I mean?"

"Some. In the Army."

"Heavyweight?"

"Mostly. I pared down to light-heavy once, but I was young and could do it. Won easy. A supply sergeant, and soft. We showed the same on the scales but I outweighed him in the bones."

"Pretty good, were you?"

"Not bad. Won more than I lost, but I lost some too. Knocked out twice, and I quit. Wanted to keep what brains I got."

"You ever kill anybody?"

"Never actually did. I was going to once but the situation changed. I would have done it, though. I had it all thought out."

"This in the Army?"

"Yeah. But he got promoted, and transferred. Lucky for him. And me too, no doubt."

"Is there anything you wouldn't do, John, to get back? To the other Winfield?"

"Nothing. There is nothing I wouldn't do."

"Do you know how Simon Morley got back to the nineteenth century?"

"He was tutored. Learned all about it, got the feel of it. Then used the Dakota as his Gateway."

"The Dakota?"

"A New York apartment building. It was there in the nineteenth century, and it's there today. The Project furnished an apartment in the Dakota, got him the right wardrobe, made it a Gateway —"

"Could you do it? Get back there where Morley is?"

"Sure." He grinned. "If you can do the thing, you can do it, Major. That your car up the street, the Toyota?" Rube nodded. "Looks a little snug for me."

"They fit the Japanese, John."

"I'll manage." He stood up, inches taller than Rube. "Run me over to my place. Give me five minutes to pack my stuff. Three, if I hurry. And I'll hurry. Believe me, I'll hurry."

5

ALTHOUGH THIS was winter and well after dark, the air wetly cold, a man sat on a Central Park bench near Fifth Avenue, watching the path to his left. The light from a streetlamp just touched him, a dark motionless lump. The turned-up collar of his overcoat covered his chin, his cap pulled low over his forehead. Hands pushed into the overcoat pockets, he watched the path, and when he saw the man he was waiting for walking quickly toward him — "Right on time," he said to himself — he lowered his face and sat staring down at the path apparently in thought.

The man walked by; he was wearing an ankle-length dark overcoat and a brown fur cap, and when he'd walked on a dozen steps, the seated man stood up — tall now — and followed Simon Morley.

. . . *I walked out onto Fifth Avenue, a light delivery wagon rattled slowly by, the horse tired, his neck slumped, a kerosene lantern swaying under the rear axle. On the walk a woman in a feathered black hat, a fur cape over her shoulders, walked by, holding her long dark skirt an inch above the wet paving stones.*

I turned south, down narrow, quiet residential Fifth Avenue (the tall man, twenty yards behind him, turned too), *glancing into yellow-lighted windows as I walked, catching glimpses: of a bald bearded man reading a newspaper, the light from a fireplace I couldn't see reflected redly on the windowpane; of a white-aproned, white-capped maid passing through a room; of a month-old Christmas tree, a woman touching a lighted taper to its candles for the pleasure of the five-year-old boy beside her.*

. . . north on Broadway from Madison Square, I walked along the Rialto, the theatrical section of New York when Broadway was Broadway. The street was jammed with newly washed and polished carriages. The sidewalks were alive with people, at least half of them in evening dress, the night filled with the sound of them, and the feel of excitement and imminent pleasure hung in the air.

Following only a few steps behind now, the tall man looked at the passing faces, and glanced into carriages, sometimes stooping momentarily to do so, smiling with the pleasure of being here.

. . . I hurried past the lighted theaters, restaurants, and great hotels, until I reached the Gilsey House between Twenty-ninth and Thirtieth. There, at the lobby cigar counter, I bought a cigar, a long thin cheroot, and tucked it carefully into the breast pocket of my inner coat. Outside —

Outside on the crowded evening sidewalk the tall man sauntered now, taking his time, toward the Gilsey House . . . until Simon Morley walked out again and down the steps, tucking his cigar into an inside coat pocket, and went on. The tall man walked faster until he'd nearly caught up. Then, hanging only a step or two behind, he kept pace, one or two pedestrians between them.

Waiting for an opportunity to present itself, he saw it presently, twenty-odd yards ahead. A short brass-railed flight of stone stairs led up from the sidewalk to the first-floor double doors; *Wellman & Co., Insurance Brokers*, said the gold-leaf letters on the dark windows. Directly beside those stairs another, steeper flight led down to a below-street-level barbershop: its striped pole stood at the curb.

In the moment, in the half-step before Simon Morley reached that second staircase, the tall man just behind stepped up beside him, walked the half-step with him, then slammed the full weight of his big body sideways into Morley, thrusting his hip hard into him for good measure. He literally lifted the smaller man from his feet, shooting him into the staircase, and Morley dropped to strike the sharp stone edges of the stairs, tumbling hard down the flight until his body slammed into the locked door of the barbershop. The tall man walked on, not hurrying, and at Thirtieth Street turned the corner. Several men looked at him, and he looked back, meeting their eyes, and no one stopped him.

For half a minute Simon Morley lay almost

unmoving, his mind not truly functioning. Then the pain came into his shinbones, his right shoulder and right hip, and the palms of his hands, and he moaned. He got himself up slowly, afraid of discovering a bone had broken. Then he stood, both hands bracing against the wall beside him, his head low between them. Now he pushed himself upright, and in the weak light from the street above, looked down at the scraped-bloody, dirt-smeared palms of his hands, then at the torn trouser legs and the bleeding skin showing through. He turned and, using the black metal handrail, made himself climb the stairs to the sidewalk. On the walk again, he moved on in not quite a run but a frantic hobble.

I saw the theater ahead, saw its sign, Wallack's, *and the posters beside its entrance reading,* The Money Spinners. *I saw Apple Mary herself, the old lady who sold apples before the theaters, and tried to sprint, desperate to move faster, squeezing, sidling, bumping past baffled angry pedestrians — because Apple Mary stood facing the tall young man in evening dress. She was speaking to him, and — did I really see it? I thought so! — I saw the wink of gold from a coin dropping from his hand to hers, a dozen yards and two or three people between us. He turned, someone just ahead pausing to hold the lobby door open for him, and skipped inside.*

I walked now, only a dozen yards, walked past Apple Mary calling, "Apples, apples! Get your apples, get Apple Mary's best!" *shoving one at me. But I shook my head, and stood staring in at the busy lobby, and across the tiled floor saw the group I knew would be there: the bearded father, a ruby stud in his stiff white shirtfront; the smiling gowned mother, and their daughters, the younger in a mar- velous gown of unadorned spring-green velvet. When she smiled, as she did now at the tall young man who had given the gold coin to Apple Mary, she looked lovely. I had to hear, had to, and walked in to stand close, hiding my bloody hands at my sides.*

"My dear, may I present my young friend," her father was saying, "Mr. Otto Danziger," and I watched the tall young man bow, knowing that what had happened had happened, and that I was too late. Now they'd met, these two young people. I hadn't quite been able to prevent it. And now, in time, they would marry, and have a son. And I knew that far ahead, in the twentieth century I'd left, that son was a man long since grown, Dr. E. E. Danziger — the Project he'd begun in the old Beekey warehouse still functioning under the control of Major Ruben Prien and Colonel Esterhazy, and whatever it was they represented.

But now these were thoughts of a far-off future I no longer belonged in, and I looked again at the handsome new couple, and, not knowing I was going to, found myself smiling. Then I turned and walked out.

The tall man swung in behind Morley as he walked back to Thirtieth Street and turned east. Watching closely, he saw from the slow, painful walk that Morley's urgency was gone. And now he knew it was over; that whatever it was that Morley was attempting had been prevented. He followed for a long block, however, and for half of the next, making sure. Then — he did not know what had happened, didn't know what Morley had intended, but knew he'd done what he'd come for. And at the next corner, Morley walking slowly on ahead, the tall man turned away, and began hunting for a cab.

Walking down toward Gramercy Park, I looked around me at the world I was in. At the gaslighted brownstones beside me. At the nighttime winter sky. This too was an imperfect world, and I knew it, did not need to be told. But — I drew a deep breath, sharply chilling my lungs — the air was still clean. The rivers flowed fresh, as they had since time began. And the first of the terrible corrupting great wars still lay decades ahead. I reached Lexington Avenue, turned south, and then, the yellow lights of Gramercy Park waiting at the end of the street, I walked on toward Number 19.

At a ticket window in the small red brick Grand Central station, John McNaughton leaned toward the row of vertical brass rods between him and the waiting clerk. "Winfield," he said. "Ticket to Winfield, Vermont."

"Round trip?"

"No." McNaughton smiled with the pleasure of saying it: "No, I won't be coming back from Winfield. Not ever again."

6

JULIA WALKED into the dining room, set down the big blue-and-white platter of waffles, then walked around to her side of the table. She didn't speak, though I knew she was going to and what she would say. She pulled out her chair first, sat down, managing her long skirts, inched her chair in, slid her napkin from its carved-bone ring, unrolled it on her lap, then placed her bare forearms on the white cloth, wedding ring catching the light for a moment. Watching me, hunting for signs of my mood, she pushed the syrup in its cut-glass flask closer to my reach.

Finally, voice gentle so as not to rile me, she said, "Si. It's so far away now. And doesn't really concern you. Not anymore. Your Major Prien has had his Project to himself now for — is it three years? Or more. And whatever he's done with it is done."

I nodded, knowing I ought not be irritable — because I'd had the same guilty thoughts. For months at a time I'd forget the Project, then it would come sneaking back into my mind. I glanced irritably around the room; I didn't like breakfast in here. Too damn dark. Fine at night, winter especially, when we used the fireplace; this was a different room then. But a house stood wall-to-wall on each side of ours, no light in here except for the chandelier over the table. I preferred the big round wood table in the kitchen, the room full of daylight from two tall, round-topped windows overlooking Julia's little garden. But eating in the kitchen was unseemly to Julia, and I understood that.

I said, "Julia, I'd like nothing more than to just forget the Project. If I'd only been able to do what I tried to do." I sat thinking about that. "As I almost *did*, God damn it."

"Do not take the Lord's name in vain," she said automatically.

"If I'd done it. If I'd got to the theater just minutes earlier . . ." I smiled at her, and shrugged. "I could have stayed right here then, content forever. But it keeps coming up in my mind, Jule: What is Rube *doing* with the Project? What is he *up* to! It may be a kind of duty to go and find out."

She leaned toward me over the table. "Then *go*. Get it over with." She sat back, keeping her face pleasant, and said gently, "But come back."

"House," said Willy on the floor. He was sitting, his back against the wall, legs straight out, turning the linen pages of one of his picture books, touching each and every picture with a fat little

89

forefinger and saying or trying to say its name. He was over three now; talking and edging toward reading as fast as he could go. He was fun, and of course Julia and I looked over at him now, then at each other to smile: we'd made this little man.

"I might not be able to go back."

"Oh? Why?" She sliced into her waffle with a fork.

"I was in the Central Park a couple weeks ago. Sketching the swan boats for last week's issue."

"Yes. I believe I'd like to frame that one."

"Yeah, it's a good one. But while I was there, walking along near the Dakota, it got dark, and I glanced up at my old apartment. I always do."

"So do I. I had Willy there a week or so ago, and I showed it to him."

"You didn't tell him —"

"Of course not. Just said Daddy once lived there."

"Well, when I looked up at it, the windows were lighted. People living there. I couldn't use it to go back."

"Is there no other vacant?"

"Wouldn't help; it might be occupied in the twentieth century, no way to tell. To go back, I'd need a new Gateway, Jule, a place that exists in both times, so that —"

"I know, Si, I know."

"Well, Einstein said —"

"I do not want to hear about Einstein again. Or Gateways, or anything el—"

"He's alive, you know."

"Who?"

"Einstein." She put both hands over her ears, and I smiled. "Just think, he's alive at this very moment. Still a little kid, I think. Maybe about Willy's age. Playing somewhere in Germany right now, and already thinking thoughts beyond me. Maybe looking at a book and saying, 'Haus.' "

"Would you like another waffle?"

"Gotta leave." I pushed back my chair, and Julia stood, turning to scoop up Willy and carry him to the front windows to wave goodbye, important to him and to me.

Today I didn't walk to work; coming down the front steps, I saw a cab waiting across the Park and decided to take it, turning to wave to Willy, grinning at me behind the window, flapping his hand. Then I walked over to the cab. I wore a derby, and my brown suit.

At the cab I said, *"Leslie's,"* waiting to see if he knew where it was. He did, and I climbed in as he got down to take away the horse's leather feed bag. "Take Broadway," I called to him, and settled back.

I liked the cabs. They weren't quite comfortable; big leaf springs, very stiff, and you moved along steadily but in a just barely perceptible series of jerks from the slow trot of the horse. Some people didn't like that, but it didn't bother me. They were likely to be dirty, too, and even smell a little. Julia and I once piled into one after the theater, and got right out again. But this one

91

was okay, and I liked the snug way the double doors closed down over your lap.

The day was sunless, no sky, just an even grayness, almost whiteness, a light fall of snow on the ground. Been gray like this for a week, not cold. We turned west on Twentieth Street, and I sat back. I knew it was true, that I was afraid of returning to my own time. Afraid of what I'd find happening at the Project, what dreadful thing I'd be helpless to stop. *Stay here, stay here,* my mind told me; *what you don't know won't hurt you.*

Down Fourth Avenue . . . past Union Square . . . west on Fourteenth . . . then onto Broadway. Not the quickest route on a weekday morning, but I needed this time to myself. We jiggled along further downtown, and Broadway became more and more crowded in the morning rush until finally, down near Trinity Church, it got too much.

This is where we were, the traffic even worse today because of a little snow and because the new horse-drawn streetcars — now added to the Broadway omnibuses — stood in several motionless little strings of three or four cars, their horses standing dumbly, tails switching, the drivers clanging their bells at the stalled traffic blocking them. This happened a lot now, because the cars, confined to their tracks, couldn't turn out like the little buses. The old street was too narrow now: I'd seen buses simply turn off Broadway and go around a block to circumnavigate some snarl, reentering Broadway beyond it. Leaning out at the side of my cab, I could see that up ahead a dray loaded with empty barrels had tried to pull around a string of blocked streetcars, and met with a light delivery wagon trying the same thing from the opposite direction. The two drivers, standing before their seats, were doing the usual — yelling and waving their whips at each other. It's not easy to back a wagon or dray, and neither one wanted to. A big mess, made a lot worse by the snow and stalled cars. I'd liked them at first; now I thought that on Broadway they were a nuisance.

93

I couldn't just sit here waiting: I was due at work in eight minutes, and I pushed up the doors from over my lap and climbed down. I knew the fare from Gramercy Park to *Leslie's*, and handed up the full amount plus a ten-cent tip, which was a proper one. But he didn't thank me, and I understood; he was stuck here now without a fare, nobody would hail him till he got himself clear. So I got out my change, found another ten-cent piece for him, and this time got thanked. I had a couple of blocks to walk, and I set out.

Walking along through the morning crowd, I recognized again what I had slowly and reluctantly realized over the past year or so: that Broadway down here was just plain ugly. I couldn't see that, when I first came to this place and time. Everything then, every sight and person I saw, every sound I heard, thrilled me. And I walked Lower Broadway, as everywhere else, in an ecstatic trance at simply being here. Pretty soon — this is what happened to me first — the buildings lining the street no longer looked *old* to my eyes. From my own time I could remember one or two of them, I'm certain, still existing on twentieth-century Lower Broadway, truly old to my eye and mind then, out of place in time. But here I'd watched some of these being built, watched the Irish hod carriers climbing their ladders in the mornings as I passed, seen the new bricks rising, finally, to five or six stories of new construction smelling of wet plaster. Many others of these were no more than five or ten years old. And now to my eyes they looked right, looked modern and were. And looked ugly, I also saw now, crammed together wall against wall, too high for their widths on the old narrow lots bought and built on one at a time, their uncoordinated rooflines jagged as broken teeth. And the street itself too narrow and now narrowed still more by the inflexible new car tracks. One morning last spring I'd walked by an impossible snarl of stalled traffic, the intersection a tangled struggling chaos, and seen an infuriated driver suddenly stand up before his seat and with his whip lash out and slash open the cheek of another driver, sending him to his knees at his wagon seat. The street was badly cobbled, City Hall graft, you heard. It was potholed. And the endless, endless banging ring of the iron-tired wheels against those uneven stones could drive you crazy. And always, always, Broadway was dusty or muddy or both. And always with plenty of horse manure, which dried and turned to gritty dust so that on a breezy day you had to carefully inhale through your nose and keep your eyes slitted. The sidewalks were an obstacle course from the wooden posts of rival telegraph lines, their overhead crossarms heavy with wire. Big black-and-white painted advertising signs defaced nearly every blank sidewall, other signs hung out over the walks. Now, and long since, I saw Broadway along there as it truly was, a drably, crudely utilitarian commercial street, not even attempting to be anything but what it so purely was: ugly. And I liked it. I loved it.

Walking along that Broadway, the sidewalks busy with men going to work — hardly any women — I thought, or tried to: *What to do, what should I do, what did I want to do?* Well, I knew what I wanted to do. Stay right here, back deep in the nineteenth century. But far ahead in time the Project was still functioning because of my failure to prevent it. So now wasn't it my duty to see what Rube and Esterhazy were up to? The debate in my mind, I understood walking along the street, was repetitive, the question not answering itself. And I saw that all I could decide was simply that I had to decide — one way or the other, yes or no.

Then, up ahead I saw the Bird Lady. You'd see her now and then around town, on or near various busy street corners. This is a drawing of the Bird Lady, made a few months earlier by Pruett Share, one of our people at *Leslie's*. For five cents she'd have one of her canaries dip his beak into an open box and pull out a small envelope for you. In it, printed not very well — on her own little handpress, I suspect — would be your fortune, reading about as you'd expect. Or, if you wished, she'd have the bird peck out from a back portion of the box a yes or no answer to whatever question you silently asked. People said she did good business with racetrack and other bettors.

I walked past her; today she stood at the doorway of a little dry goods store not yet open. No one took her fortunes or answers seriously, or wouldn't say so, anyway. The Bird Lady was for fun, and I'd never seen anyone accept an envelope without grinning to show the world they weren't serious. But I believe that underneath the newly evolved  reasoning portion of our human minds, the old primitive way by which we actually reach our opinions and decisions still exists powerfully as ever. And no matter what common sense had to say to me about this, I slowed, hesitating, then turned back in the sudden, absolute knowledge that the Bird Lady was, really was, going to give me the proper decision.

I stopped on the walk before her as she smiled; then I pulled out a little handful of change and found a nickel: a nickel with a stars-and-stripes shield on its face and a big V on the reverse, which, I remembered every time I spent one, would one day be valuable. But it was only a commonplace nickel now, and I handed it over.

She smiled again, inquiringly, and I said, "A question, please." She moved the stick on which her bird perched to the back of the box, and waited a moment while I spoke my silent question: *Should I visit my own time, if I can?* Then I nodded at the Bird Lady. Her stick lowered, twitched its signal, and the little round yellow head instantly ducked and lifted a tiny envelope in its beak. Smiling, the Bird Lady handed it to me.

I took it, thanking her, and walked on, postponing because my heart was pounding. I made a smile, trying to laugh away my superstitious fear, but couldn't. A dozen more yards, then suddenly I had to know, and stepped out of the pedestrian stream to stand with my back against a cigar store window. Beside me, a nearly life-sized enameled wooden figure of a kilted Scotchman holding out his wooden bundle of painted cigars. The little envelope flap was ungummed, tucked in, and I pulled it out, took the little fold of pinkish-gray paper, and hesitated. I glanced away, at the red cheek of the empty-eyed wooden face beside me. Then I silently spoke the question: *Should I go back, if I can?* I opened the slip, and it said: *Yes.*

I believed it. That coarse-fibered slip of cheap paper with its poorly imprinted three letters not quite aligned . . . pressed into this paper long before . . . told me what now I knew I would at least try. And I walked on to the office in the calm of quiet certainty, rolling the little paper to a pebble, then flicking it away to drop into the dirty Broadway gutter of 1886.

At noon I walked down the wooden interior staircase to our cashier's office on the ground floor. He sat behind a black-painted metal grill on a high stool at a high desk where he received and paid out money. When I stopped at his window, he made a quarter-turn to face me, inquiringly. He did, in fact, wear a green eyeshade and black sleeve protectors to the elbows. I knew his name: Ben.

Ben counted out an advance, two days early, of my weekly salary, had me sign for it, then pushed it at me through the little opening — a small stack of bills, the top one a ten on the First National Bank of Galesburg, Illinois. I'd seen Ben count them, and didn't bother to recount, just thanked him, then folded and shoved the bills deep into my pants pocket. These were big bills, seven inches long, a lot of paper, and made a fairly substantial wad, felt like real money.

Down on the street in the little dry goods store, the Bird Lady gone from its doorway, I bought a money belt. The proprietor, a short, bald, eager little European who didn't really speak English yet, spread out a choice of belts on the countertop, some of leather, others of various kinds of cloth, including silk. They were widely used; few men traveled any distance without one. I took one of good lightweight canvas.

Lunch standing up in a saloon just east of Broadway, with half a glass of beer, leaving the rest; too foamy, the keg newly opened. A walk of a block and a half to my bank, where I withdrew almost half our savings, taking it in gold as many travelers did to save bulk, changing my pay advance to gold, too. Then back to the office to finish out the day, sketching from a photograph, then inking it in — another train wreck, this one near Philadelphia.

7

AT HOME in our bedroom, a little before midnight,
I dressed, Julia and I consulting about it in
whispers. No overcoat, but a wool suit, we decided; if I needed an overcoat I'd buy a modern
one. My suit was okay, I thought: single-breasted,
the lapels very small, but acceptable. One button
too many, but I could leave my coat open. Winter
underwear, and pull-on boots. I owned a derby,
a silk topper, a summer straw hat, my brimless
winter cap, so we decided on no hat at all. My
hair is straight, not quite black, fairly long and
thick — thinning a little but hardly noticeable,
Julia says. My ties were all wrong, but Julia got
a wool scarf from my wardrobe and I put it on
under my coat, crossed over my chest, concealing
the absence of a tie. I checked my money belt,
knowing I was wearing it, but checking anyway.

We had a full-length oval mirror by the window
on its stand, and I walked over. Julia lighted a
jet on the wall beside it, and we stood studying
my costume, Julia in her long blue robe. I was
wearing a full beard these days, close-cropped,

and as always, examining myself in a mirror, I thought: *Not handsome, but not too awful.* I tried to picture myself walking along a late-twentieth-century street, and when Julia said, "Well?" I said, "Walk a block in twentieth-century Manhattan and you'll pass plenty who look a lot freakier," and Julia shook her head a little at the thought of the New York I was talking about.

Down in our hallway entrance at eleven-forty by our big standing clock, the hall light very low, as we always left it at night, Julia said quietly, "Now don't worry about us; we'll be fine," and I kissed her goodbye, turned to leave, then swung back to hold and kiss her again. I'd suddenly felt as though I were leaving on a long and dangerous journey. And it was true that where I was going, if I could, was far, far away.

Then I reached for the door handle, and Julia said, "Wait!" and half ran a few steps to the big hall closet, felt around in a pocket of her winter coat, then turned to me, smiling, and handed me a copper one-cent piece. For an instant I thought she meant it as a kind of good-luck token; then I remembered. "Thanks, I forgot." And now I did leave, out, down the front steps and into the silent night.

It wasn't too far, and I walked along the dimly lighted, late-at-night, nineteenth-century streets, my boot heels too loud on the sidewalks. Through all of a long crosstown block I passed between two solid rows of brownstone houses, built side by side, walls touching, all identical on both sides of the street. Glancing now and then at a lighted upstairs window, I wondered about it, thinking of the people who lived in these streets now when these houses were new.

I turned a corner, passing a battered wagon parked at the curb, its empty single-horse shafts tipped up to lie angled back across the driver's seat. Near the middle of the block, under the streetlamp, kids had been playing, the stone sidewalks scattered with chalked inscriptions. They didn't say what I thought they would in the time I'd soon be trying to reach. Several simply announced that one first name loved another first name, and the most shocking among them told me only that *Mildred stinks*. Near the end of the block a man came walking in the opposite direction on the other side of the street. I could see that he was bent over, something big and bulky strapped to his back: a grindstone in a wooden cradle with a foot pedal. He was a street knife-sharpener; why he was out so late, I had no idea.

Then, rounding a corner, I saw it ahead, rising up against a sky luminous from the not-quite-full moon. Half a block further on, I stepped from stone walk onto wooden planking — a walkway, gradually ascending. I'd thought the little wooden booth just ahead might be closed, but it was still open, possibly to be closed in a few minutes, at twelve. Inside the tall booth, as I stopped before the little grilled window, sat a mustached man wearing a derby and smoking a pipe. I slid the

103

one-cent piece, the toll Julia had remembered, across the wooden counter, polished and hollowed from use, and he said, "Thank you, sir." A hundred yards or so further on, still climbing, I passed over the shoreline well below me now, and walked on out onto and up the long slow glorious curve of the new East River Bridge.

Far ahead, the immense, Gothic-arched stone wall of the Brooklyn tower stood black against the lighter dark of the sky, but beside me, widening out into their lovely fanlike pattern, each of the supporting cable strands stood clear and clean, stripes of moonlight. Walking steadily along beside the railing, my steps sounding on the wooden planking, I could see the river far below, blackness sprinkled with yellowed twistings of light. I couldn't really see the water, but in my mind I could — the East River, always the same, opaque and soiled, no color, dull and sluggish. In the distance to the south I could make out a black bulk dimly lighted: a tug or barge.

Near the center of the long, long bridge, the massive supporting cable beside me at something near its lowest point, I sat down on the end of a bench, and turned to look out through the railings at the river. In the day just past, streetcars and other horse-drawn traffic had crossed this bridge endlessly. Pedestrians had moved ceaselessly along this very walkway, each paying his one-penny toll. This is a drawing I'd made for the paper a few months earlier, and while there were fewer boats, it is very much the place I saw now. Looking out at the river, I thought about other times, on nights and evenings, when I'd been here looking at this same river, the same great bridge towers, these very same cables beside me. This place, and all I looked at of its immediate surroundings, existed here now . . . just as they existed decades ahead, a true Gateway, equally a part of both times, belonging in and existing in each. And so, here on my bench in the quiet darkness, I began to think of the time ahead, working to remember, to get the feeling and the sense of the time I wanted to move into.

This was easier than trying to visualize and feel a past I had never seen, as I'd had to do the first time I tried to reach the nineteenth century. Now I knew the future I wanted to rejoin. Had seen and been part of it, knew it was there. From the roadway beside and below my walkway, I heard the steady approaching beat of hooves, then watched a roofed delivery wagon approach, the little flames of its sidelights jiggling, watched the roof slide away under my view, heard the wagon rattle and hoofbeats diminish. Then I sat, seeing nothing really, just staring down at the boards at my feet, and allowing scenes and pictures, memories, of late-twentieth-century New York to form in my mind, regaining the feel of my own time. Not forcing, just allowing it to form. And saw myself on the run through the rain one morning from bus stop to the ad agency where I worked. Which brought my drawing board there to mind, and the familiar view down onto Fifty-fourth Street from the window beside me. Leading to more thoughts of days and people of my time. To my little apartment on Lexington Avenue; small, noisy, and not enough daylight, I remembered too well. To the little lunchroom across the street where I usually had breakfast. And the laundromat. Movies . . .

It was there, my own time, the feel of it; I hadn't forgotten. And now I began the almost effortless technique I'd learned so well. For many people self-hypnosis is impossible, but for others it isn't hard; it's used effectively for a lot of purposes. And I was far more than ordinarily skilled at it. Sitting here on my bench, entirely relaxed, simply staring, wide-eyed and hardly thinking, out at the river, I used my familiar skill to make this time, my life here in the nineteenth century . . . go still. Go silent, and contract. Go all *tiny*, and then into motionlessness. And presently I felt the strange indescribable *drift*, the familiar long moment of limbo between two times.

I stood, turning to face Manhattan, eyes not quite closed but looking down at the darkness of the wooden planks. Even before lifting my eyes I could already see in my mind the great rising, impossibly shining *bulk* of twentieth-century New York. Then I raised my head fast, eyes blinking to clear them, and stood stupidly bewildered.

I'd *failed!* There out before me in the moonlight lay the low-roofed old city I'd come from tonight, black dark now except for a speckling of dim pinpricks of light from gas or kerosene lamps, the church spires sharp black against the yellowed sky. And across the low roofs, across the entire width of the island, I saw the reflection of that sky lying on the water of the Hudson. And I felt — elation! I couldn't *do* it, not anymore, I'd lost the ability! And was free to walk back down into that city, to Julia, Willy, Rover, back into the place and life I loved and wanted to stay in forever.

But didn't. Because I knew. I knew what I'd done. Knew I'd sabotaged my own attempt, thinking of the drabbest aspects of my old life, of things I didn't like, didn't want to return to. And then sat watching myself, watching one part of my mind with another, refusing to let that time take hold, only pretending I'd felt it. I'd *willed* failure because I didn't want to go, was afraid. Of . . . I didn't know what. Of whatever I might find in the twentieth century. At the Project.

But I couldn't let myself sneak back home knowing what I'd done. And I walked to the bridge rail, set my forearms on it comfortably, hands folded, staring down at the black of the river. And now I began allowing memories to rise and sharpen and come to life — not of a dingy apartment or a job I hadn't liked, and the lonely times, but the memories I had just suppressed.

They came without volition, simply appeared as though I were watching a film. I saw four of us sitting on the great wide Fifth Avenue staircase of — yes, the Metropolitan Museum. Saw the enormous blue-and-white banner hung fifty feet above us across the facade. We sat far below it, lounging back on those steps in the late morning of a summer Sunday waiting for opening time. Sat casually talking with a lot of easy joking, no hurry about anything, aware of our pleasure in the feel of the sun and of the day itself. Yes.

And — well, of course the Village. Just wandering through the fine balmy night with — Grace Wunderlich? Yes, it was — the pair of us walking aimlessly, a part of the slow crowd flowing into and out of the open-doored, open-windowed places — the bars, the art shops, the cafes — the air murmuring and alive with voices.

Then a surprise: myself moving fast along a Second Avenue sidewalk at noon, a little warm and humid, the sidewalks jammed. But me moving swiftly along that walk through the crowd like a fish darting through weeds, my shoulders swing-

108

ing sideways, hips twisting, slipping between, sliding past, darting around. Why was I standing here in the dark smiling at that? Because that had been fun: I was using a skill, the special acquired skill of moving fast through a New York crowd. Crazy, but I was smiling.

Standing in a line along the sidewalk outside the 8th Street Playhouse with Lennie Hindsmith, a fellow artist. We stood hands in pockets, shoulders hunched against a raw, partly rainy, partly misty evening with twenty minutes yet to wait, complaining to each other. This was boring, not worth it, maybe we ought to leave. But staying. Waiting to see a revival of a picture I'd heard and read about all my life, filmed before I was born. And complaining, I nevertheless continued to stand, inwardly and smugly happy with the knowledge that there was no other place in the world where I could be doing just this.

Strolling around the great plaza of Lincoln Center at intermission time with a girl I knew for a while, out in the open there looking up at the people, some in formal evening clothes, behind the glass on the chandelier-lighted staircase, aware that in this particular moment this was the best place in the world to be. Followed instantly by the memory of an Off-Off-Broadway play, or maybe even further off than that, in a moldering building deep in an East Side slum. And to get to it from the street we were finding a way through a nearly solid curbside wall of stuffed black garbage sacks. And the play was dreadful, awful. But . . . you could see a pretty good play in a pretty good theater most anywhere. Where else could you see a glorious mess like this?

Ducking across Forty-second Street through a squall of rain, trotting under the canopy into Grand Central Station, down the ramp, across the big marble interior, down a stairway, into a long twisting tunnel, up into an office building lobby, out the doors, and across the street into the building I was heading for, almost bone-dry. *Coping.* Coping with the place, *beating* it! Standing in a subway car, hating the graffiti and the word itself, but right there at the door, hip pocket tight against the pole so my wallet couldn't be yanked, knowing my stop without having to duck and look out the window for the sign, first out of the car and up the steps.

A big rat trotting along a gutter late at night, ignoring me, owning the place. Midnight and the asphalt soft under my shoes because it had been hot for a month, even the white twists of dead vapor rising from the manhole cover looking enervated. Howls and screams late at night in the street somewhere far below my windows, never to be explained. What were such memories? Some kind of perversity? Did I *like* rats? Couldn't say, there at my bridge rail. But I thought of the time I'd flown to San Francisco to see it on a one-week vacation during my first year in New York. On the balcony of a college friend's apartment we sat looking out at that spectacular bay,

110

the day sunny, a little breezy, lots of sailboats. And me nodding, agreeing with what he was telling me: that this was the best place in the United States to live. That the Bay Area was charming, lively yet laid back, and that North Beach was great. That there was plenty to do here, and some very good experimental theater. And that New York was sick, squirming with crime, side by side with truly depraved ostentation; and that it was actually, truly, finished at last. And I nodded and said yeah, and how I envied him his life here. And flew back a day early to the land of the all-night bookstore.

Young in New York, and feeling that you're beginning to know it fairly well; feeling its pull, its growing hold, finding and appreciating — oh, so much — that can't be found anywhere else because it doesn't exist anywhere else. And oh, how smug, yes, but I didn't care, and standing there on the bridge feeling more knowing about that city than I'd ever really been, enjoying the secret patronizing superiority over everyone else who didn't know and didn't understand the infinite variety and excitement of this strange place — I knew I was ready. I wanted back, now; had to see it once again.

The fear, the wanting to stay where it was safe, wasn't gone but quiescent, ignored and overwhelmed by the pull of wanting to be there one more time. And at my bridge rail I again began the process of return, but with more power; confident and willing it; knowing what I needed to

111

do, and doing it swiftly. I felt it begin, the actual little movement, the queer feeling of the shift into drifting-time. Standing motionless, looking down into the black water, releasing myself from my own hypnosis, I felt the drifting-time ending — and then, abruptly, the sudden, swift, exciting, and unmistakable sense of new place.

I knew where I was, really knew, feeling no surprise as I turned, feeling only a rush of elation at the great sparkling walls of light rising in tiers like a strange mountain range, and glittering to make your heart stop. There it stood, nothing else like it, nothing, nothing, Manhattan Island in the last of the twentieth century.

The sudden sight of other bridges startled me for a beat; I'd forgotten. In my mind I can dance as well as Gene Kelly, but I began walking sedately enough down toward the shining city. Then — I really *can* sing as well as Gene Kelly — I very softly began my favorite of all the New York songs. "I'll take Manhattan . . ." and my all-time favorite rhyme, "the Bronx and Staten . . . Island, too." I was out of words already, but I knew the tune: "Dah, dah, dah, *dee* . . . *dah*, dee!" I'd walked onto the East River Bridge, and now, feeling good, I walked down off the Brooklyn Bridge.

Manhattan smelled a little, not much; I'd simply lost my immunity to exhaust fumes. A cab sat waiting, roof light on, just beyond the bridge roadway, I don't know why. Maybe people did come walking off the bridge at one in the morning, or maybe he didn't really want a fare. I took the door handle, not opening it: "You free?" And he turned off the roof light, and leaned back a little to catch my destination before he would say he was free. "Plaza Hotel," I said, getting in, and he surprised me: "Yes, sar," he said politely, pushing the meter flag down. When we started up and passed under a streetlamp, I saw he was truly black, Jamaican, I think.

I sat leaning out the open cab window a little to look both out and up at the city I was returning to, when the cab slowed to pull in at the Fifth Avenue entrance, and I was pleased to see the old hotel again. I'd been in and out of the Plaza often enough, but in the nineteenth century it was — for me — gone. Not yet built, of course, only the plaza here. Now — for me — here it was back again.

I had my exit planned. Before the cab was fully stopped I was hopping out, beckoning to the cabby: "Come on in!" And you can bet he did, parking brake snarling, ignition off, and out fast and right on my heels.

The man at the desk was tall, lean — an athlete's build — and remarkably handsome; his nameplate on the desk said, *Michael Stumpf, Manager*. When I said hello, I included my best smile, and said, "My plane was late, so I'm late too, but I hope you have a room for me."

"Do you have a reservation?"

"I'm sorry, I don't."

His fingers moved through some cards. "A sin-

113

gle?" he said dead-pan, not a glance at the big cabby just behind me, and I had to smile: he could do "imperturbable" very well.

"Yep."

"Well," Mike said, smiling a little too now, winking at the cabby, who grinned — we were a happy bunch all of a sudden — "I can give you a nice single on the Park side." I didn't ask the room rate, I wasn't interested, just said that would be great. He waited while I printed my name on the registration card, then read it upside down. "And how will you be paying for this, Mr. Morley? Check or credit card?"

I was all set for him, my left hand lying on the counter, loosely clenched. "Neither," I said, "in gold," opening my hand to let a dozen gold coins spill onto the marble. It was fun, and his eyes widened. Then Mike Stumpf topped me.

He reached out, fingers spreading like a spider's legs, and drew the scattered coins together, lifting his hand, fingers closing, and the coins followed to rise into a neat stack. Like cutting a deck of cards, he split the stack into two equal smaller stacks side by side, then again drew them up between his fingers, the coins magically interleaving, into a single stack once more. I said, "I've tried that all my life. Never did it even once, and never will."

"Just takes a little practice," he said easily, and the hotel manager was gone: without a change in a thread of his suit or hair of his head, it

114

was Get-Rich-Quick Wallingford who stood smiling at me now, and I knew this man had played a lot of cards in his time and knew his way around more than this lobby.

I had my story ready; wallet, checks, credit cards stolen at the airport. But I was a coin dealer: gold only, U.S. and Edwardian English coins. Here from Chicago a couple times a year, usually staying here or at the Algonquin. Something that bothers me a little is that I enjoy lying. Once I start, the convincing details flow out effortlessly; I don't even have to think. Tomorrow, I went on, bringing my folded money belt from my coat pocket and setting it on the counter to let the other coins inside it clink, I'd be selling each of my coins for — I wasn't sure of this — several hundred dollars apiece. Take as many as you like for security and, please — so this cabdriver doesn't kill me — advance me a hundred in cash.

G.R.Q. Wallingford Stumpf knew what these coins were, and he simply nipped the top coin off the stack, saying, "One is more than enough," and now the coin appeared on the back of his hand between knuckle and finger joints. And by slightly moving his fingers as though playing a piano, he made the coin walk back and forth across the backs of his fingers, flip-flopping heads to tails, tails to heads, back and forth so easily. I'd have given him the gold piece to be able to do that. "I'll give you a receipt for this," he said, the coin disappearing into his closing palm,

115

"and you can sign for the hundred."

I felt marvelous signing the receipt. Each of my hard-earned nineteenth-century dollars had become worth about forty here. I had over twenty-five thousand dollars, and from my hundred dollars' cash I gave the cabby a ten for the six-dollar fare, and added another ten. "That's for being a good boy."

"Welcome to New York, boss," he said. Then Michael Stumpf accepted my invitation, and we went into the Oak Bar for a nightcap.

In my room I turned on the television, clicking slowly through the channels just to enjoy the novelty of it again; what I saw had not improved. Then I got out the Manhattan phone book, looking at the new cover with some interest. Sitting on the bed, the phone book on my lap, I opened it, and found the *Danziger* listing, a fairly long one. I hesitated, then moved my finger down the column . . . and found it — *Danziger, E. E.* — and smiled. Should I call him right now? I wanted to, but it was far too late. I'd phone in the morning and invite him to lunch; I'd be glad to see Dr. D, and knew he'd be glad to see me. I was tired, as though I'd traveled for hours, the two drinks I'd had downstairs helping the feeling along. I switched on the air-conditioning, mostly for the pleasure of being able to, and got to bed.

The light out, I waited, knowing sleep would be along quickly. A police car or ambulance howled down in the streets somewhere. Should

116

I have come back? Was it wise? A car drove over a manhole cover, *wump-wump*, and I smiled, and in my head sang, *I'll take Manhattan, the Bronx and Staten . . .*

8

RUBE PRIEN sat in the windowless little street-level office of the Project; sat on the edge of the worn oak desk, swinging a foot, looking around: at the out-of-date wall calendar still reading *Beekey's*, at the framed photographs of long-gone moving crews. He was nervous, therefore irritable; hated waiting. He stood, walked a step or two to the street door, and opened it wide, turning back to the desk. He sat down and hopped right up again, back to the door to almost close it, leaving it ajar by an inch. He studied this narrow gap of daylight, then opened the door perhaps half an inch more, and returned to his desk.

Outside, approaching along the walk on the same side of the street, Dr. E. E. Danziger walked toward this door fairly rapidly, a tall, thin, elderly but not-quite-old man in a dark topcoat and tan felt hat. This was late morning, temperature around fifty, the sky a high-up even gray. He glanced at a band of faded black-and-white lettering — BEEKEY BROTHERS, MOVING

AND STORAGE — running around the roofline edge of the great blank-walled brick building that filled the block just ahead. It looked the same: Was it possible that it was? That for the past three years the Project had gone on very well without him?

Now he stopped at the corner of the building to look at the weathered gray door there, and thought he knew why it stood invitingly ajar. Thought he knew that if he accepted this tacit invitation, pushing the door open and stepping in, he would seem to have agreed that he belonged here still, still had the right to walk in. But he was not going to make this meeting so easy for Ruben Prien; the major had some crow to eat.

Without stepping closer he reached forward and with a big blunt forefinger pushed the door hard enough to swing it wide, but he stood where he was, looking in at Rube hopping quickly from the desk, smiling that sudden fine Rube Prien smile, mouth opening to welcome him. But Dr. Danziger, face blankly unresponsive, spoke first. "May I come in?"

It flustered Rube; Danziger saw him blink. "Of course, of course! Come in!"

Walking in slowly, Danziger said, "Oh no; there's no of course anymore about me coming in here uninvited. You threw me out, didn't you?" Then, voice neutral: "How are you, Rube?"

"I'm fine, Dr. Danziger. And you're looking good."

"No I'm not. I was old when you saw me last,

and now I'm older." He looked carefully around the little anteroom. "Looks the same. No change."

"Oh, it is, it is. Dr. D, we could still go have lunch somewhere. Be a lot pleasanter to talk."

"No. I'm not ready to break bread with you, Rube: I'm still puzzling out my feelings."

"Oh?" Face uncomfortable, Rube stood wanting to ask his guest to sit down, wanting to be hospitable, to get this off dead center, but not quite daring.

"Of course. I felt confused when you phoned. Wondering as I heard your voice whether I hated you. Should I refuse right then and there to ever even look at you again? Or come here and look my fill, indulging my hatred, feeding it. And thinking of revenge." He smiled. "Or vengeance; I like that form better, don't you? And yet as we spoke, I thought maybe what I felt wasn't hate but only powerful dislike. So unforgiving I wouldn't be able to take the sight of you. Or, if I could stand it, would still rather not. Or maybe, as you continued, your voice so happy to be speaking to me again, I wondered if perhaps the passage of time had only left a permanent but healed-over scar. The pain finally gone so now I could — what? — tolerate the sight of you? Come here and look at you with only simple distaste now? Curiosity with the lip curled?" Rube's courteous smile remained and — he managed this — seemed without strain. "Or maybe none of those. When I thought of Rube Prien these days was it, I asked myself, with only a kind of mental shrug? A feeling of: Oh well, it was all some time ago, so what the hell."

"And what did you decide?" Now Rube indicated a wooden upright chair. "Sit down, please, Doctor."

"No, I want to go upstairs and look around. See the Project again. It's why I decided to come. And therefore decided also on an attitude of tolerant curiosity, Rube. On viewing you with an air of faint cold amusement. That's what I'm doing now, if you can't tell. Looking you over, a little amused at your presumption. Wondering how the hell you could possibly have the nerve to speak to me even by phone. Let alone ask me to lunch! So — speaking calmly, Rube, tolerantly amused at your presumption — what the hell do you want?"

"Your help. And, if it's possible . . . to make a beginning at restoring a friendship that at least I still feel."

"You know, maybe I really *am* amused. The nerve. The fucking nerve of you. Now, once again — what do you want?"

For a moment, eyes pleasant, Rube stood looking at Danziger. Then, on apparent impulse, he put out his hand. "To make a new start."

Danziger stood shaking his head incredulously. Then, continuing to shake his head, began to grin reluctantly. "The *nerve*," he said, but took Rube's hand. "Come on." He turned away toward a metal-sheathed door in the wall opposite the street-side wall. "Let's go up." Rube moved ahead

121

to pull the door open, holding it for Danziger, who stepped through to stand glancing curiously around the tiny, concrete-floored space before the closed elevator doors. Grinning now, Rube stepped in, and Danziger said, "You treacherous bastard: something I didn't quite anticipate in all my ruminations, but it seems I still retain some sort of senile liking for you. Who'da thunk it." He poked the elevator button, and the doors slipped open.

On the top floor, the sixth, they walked along a vinyl-tiled corridor, the tall older man glancing around, eyes sharp with interest. He carried his hat in his hand now, was bald, the top of his head freckled, his side hair dyed black. This looked like a floor of an office building, directional arrows stenciled on the walls indicating groups of office numbers; black-and-white plastic nameplates beside some of the closed doors. Danziger nodded at one that read: *K. Veach.* "Katherine Veach. Katie," he said, "nice girl," and stopped. "I'll just step in for a moment, say hello."

" 'Fraid she's not here today, Doctor."

Just ahead Danziger stopped again, at an unmarked door. "This leads to the catwalks, I believe. I'd like to go in again, Rube, look down at the Big Floor."

"Well —"

But Danziger stood stubbornly shaking his head with something of the old authority he had once held here. "Rube, I want to see it. It won't take long."

"What I was going to say, Dr. D, is that I didn't bring my keys today."

For a moment Danziger stood looking at Rube; then they walked on, turned a corner, and stopped at the conference room door. Danziger would not open it, and Rube Prien reached past him to turn the knob, and gestured him in. For a moment longer Danziger stood looking up and down the long corridor, then walked in saying, "Rube, where *is* everybody today?"

"Well" — Rube followed him, closing the door — "it's the weekend, Doctor. So I expect they're home. Sleeping late. Reading the paper. Whatever." He stepped toward a chair at the long table, on which an attaché case lay, motioning Danziger to a place opposite.

Walking around the end of the table, taking off his coat, Danziger looked at the walls, overhead skylights, the carpeting. He said, "Weekends didn't mean that much when I was here, Rube." He placed hat and coat on a chair, and sat down on the chair beside them; he wore a blue suit, white shirt, and blue-and-white-striped tie. "I was here every day for at least a few hours even on Sundays, usually a lot longer. So were you. And Oscar. Most everyone on the staff. Here at the Project because it was where we wanted to be." Facing Rube, he sat back comfortably, one long arm extended on the tabletop — a posture familiar to Rube.

"Well, it's been several years since you left. And since Si left." Rube shoved his attaché case aside and lay his forearms, hands folding, on the tabletop. "And things have settled down. Fallen into place. So that we've all gotten pretty much used to . . ." His voice trailed off because Danziger, arm still lying on the table, was writing in the dust with the forefinger of his speckled old hand.

Rube had to lean to one side, finding the angle; then the word Dr. Danziger had printed popped up for him, clearly defined against the dust: *Bullshit*. Their eyes met, and the big old man said, "You're going to have to tell me eventually, Rube. Eventually, why not now? as the old ads used to say — remember? Maybe you don't. Pillsbury flour, I think."

"Okay." Rube sat nodding. "Okay. I didn't really hope to fool you, Dr. D. Or even intend to. I just put it off because I'm embarrassed. Humiliated. If you wanted vengeance, then maybe you've got it." In sudden decision, he shoved back his chair to stand. "You want to see the Big Floor? All right: I'll show you the Big Floor!"

Down on the main floor again, they walked along a narrow concrete-floored tunnel-like corridor lighted by ceiling bulbs in wire cages. At a metal door labeled, *Keep Out. Absolutely Keep Out*, they stopped; Rube brought out a key, unlocked the door, and stepped in, holding the door open with a foot while stooping to pick something up from the floor just inside. Following, Danziger had immediately stopped to wait because the interior stood dark — solid unrelieved blackness.

124

Then Rube switched on the big five-cell flashlight which had been standing on its wide lens-end on the floor by the door. Swinging the hard solid beam, searching, Rube said, "This is how we have to look at the Big Floor these days. If at all." His light found a small frame house, clapboard sides, wooden-shingled, an old house of the twenties, and Danziger said, "McNaughton's hou—" He went silent because the trembling white circle had steadied on the low porch roof, caved in, broken-backed over the stump of the post that had once helped support it. Then the light swung on along the side of the house across the windows glinting black and mirrorlike, then held on a smashed pane, the window frame jagged with glass shards.

Neither spoke. Rube lowered his flash to make a rhythmically skipping oval of light on the floor ahead as they walked on. He stopped again, playing his light over an Indian tepee, painted with buffalo silhouettes and sticklike figures of men, and torn to long ragged tongues of hanging cloth. Inside it the chromed wire basket of a tipped-over shopping cart reflected dully. The flash swung away to play over another tepee, collapsed on its side. "Rube, I hate this," Danziger said, his voice thinned and echoless in the great space they stood in. "Hate it. Turn that damn thing off."

The light vanished, and in the utter blackness Danziger said, "All right. What happened?"

"We went broke. Our funding cut off. Every dime. And the Project canceled. We're out of

125

business, Doctor. There is no Project. I'm just kind of a squatter here now; I can't keep away. I expect they know I come in sometimes. At least they haven't changed the front-door lock. But they've cut off most of the electricity, all the big lines. And the whole place is on a government surplus list. They just haven't found a buyer for a gutted warehouse with no interior floors."

"Rube, this is worse; turn the thing back on." Rube switched on the flash, and swung the beam upward. With it he searched for and found the catwalk five stories above, then slid the beam along till it reached a section with a gap of a dozen feet. "That came loose. A bolt rusted or worked loose, there've been no inspections, it dropped a little, and other bolts yanked out, I suppose. And the section fell, grazing our Denver storefront. Smashed it up good. There's no maintenance at all, and now the catwalks are permanently locked." He sent the beam along the floor before them, and they walked on. They passed without stopping what looked like a section of farmland with split-rail fencing, and a tree, but in places the soil was gone, exposing the concrete floor underneath. Two beer cans lay in the no-man's-land before a World War I trench. "Okay, Rube, enough. Let's get out."

In the conference room Dr. Danziger said, "All right, tell me."

"They started saying we'd had no results."

"No results!"

"That's right. That we'd spent a lot of mon—"

"No *results!* What the hell do they mean!"

"They said we didn't. I don't know who said it first: somebody. And it was like the kid saying the emperor has no clothes — they all joined in. Yeah, look! No clothes! Hell, they're mostly politicians, Dr. D, what do you expect! The kind who beat the rats off the ship! Remember Si? Simon Morley?"

"Of course."

"Well, he never came back, God damn him. Just *stayed* there back in the fucking nineteenth century. If he'd only come *back!* The way he was supposed to. The way he said he would. He was committed to it! Dr. D, if he had come back with proof, as only he could, why, hell — they'd have given us everything but the Washington Monument."

"Instead . . ."

"Instead, it was how did we know where Si was? Or McNaughton? Maybe all Si ever did was hole up in the Dakota apartment building for a while — at taxpayers' expense — going through the motions, lying to us, pretending he was about to make the transition. Then he ducks out one night, shows up at the Project a few days later, and says, Hooray for me, I did it! And we fell for it. In an access of wishful thinking. This senator, this guy got wind of the Project, and for a while it looked like he was going to give us that stupid Golden Fleece award. A Pentagon major general career man saw his third star fading away, and covered his ass fast, said he never had believed us and told us so, the lying son of a bitch. Oh, they came after us good and fast. Even the academics. Prove it, prove it! God, I got sick of that word. And we couldn't. At our very last board meeting — they shut us down a day and a half later — this wormy little congressman, you remember him, really got on me. Si was supposed to go back and — well, of course you know what Si was supposed to do."

"Know? I hated it."

"Yeah, well, I'm sorry. But the thing is, we had to brief the congressman. Had to. So he knew Si was supposed to go back and . . ." Rube glanced at the old man. "Go back and very slightly alter one past event, and damn it, Dr. D, it *was* small."

"Yes, well, let it go, let it go. Alter the past just enough so that Cuba would have become an American possession. Wonderful. As though you could predict the consequences of *that*. Ridiculous. Ridiculous and almighty dangerous. But go on."

"This little congressman kept saying stuff like, 'Major, what's Cuba now? The fifty-first state? Yuk, yuk. And where's Fidel these days? Pitching for the Mets?' "

Danziger sat grinning at him. "Served you right."

"Yeah, well, the thing is, we had no proof. No nothin'."

"What about our Denver man? He made it. And came back."

128

"Didn't help. Never happened either, you see, same as Si. Where's the proof, where's the proof? Goddamn bunch of parrots. As for our boy made it to medieval Paris for — what? Ten seconds? — they laughed in our faces at that one. Make a politician look even slightly wrong, and believe me, you have not gained a friend."

"Yep. Well, Rube" — he began gathering up his hat and folded topcoat from the chair beside him — "that's that, then. It was great while it last—"

"Wait."

"Oh, Rube, Rube, Rube. The Project is finished. Forever. Can you possibly wander around it with your flashlight and see it all rebuilt? The Big Floor restored? The School back in business, Oscar Rossoff back, a new batch of candidates arriving? It's dead! With a stake through its heart."

"Sure. I know that. But we don't need the Project."

" 'We'?"

"It'll be 'we' when you find out why."

"Oh? And if 'we' don't need the Project, what *do* we need?"

Rube leaned forward over the tabletop, holding Dr. Danziger's eyes. "Si."

"Si Morley?"

Rube sat back, nodding. "Yep. Si Morley, the best we ever had. That's who we need, and that's *all* we need. Can you reach him, Dr. D? *Can* you?"

"*Reach* him? *How? How* reach him back in the nineteenth century?"

"I don't know." Rube sat looking at him. "I don't *know*, damn it! You thought up the whole Project! It was your theory. If anyone can figure out how to reach Si Morley, it has to be you."

"Rube," he said gently. "Short of actually going back myself, how could I reach him?"

"You've tried going back?"

"Of course. And so have you, I'm certain."

"More than once. I'd give anything I have or ever will have to be able to do it. Just once. Even for only a minute." He sat looking across the table at the old man, then said, "It's funny; you and I *made* the Project. Made it work. Yet we can't do it: we need Si." With his clenched fist he softly, soundlessly pounded the tabletop. "*We need Si.* You can't reach him? No way at all?"

The old man looked away, moving a shoulder in almost but not quite a shrug. He looked uncomfortable, frowning a little, arranging his topcoat over one arm, and Rube Prien leaned forward, watching him intently. Then, his voice very soft now, and beginning to smile, Rube Prien said, "Oh, Doctor, Doctor: you can't quite lie, can you? You don't really know how. You know you ought to. You'd like to. And you try, but you can't fool me. You *can* reach Si Morley!"

"If I can, it won't help you." Danziger glanced around the room. "The Project actually succeeded; I'll always know that. But then the troublemakers took over. You. Esterhazy. And whoever else was behind you, I never did know who: I *am* an innocent. But the Project is gone now, and if I can't quite say I'm glad, I'm close." He stood up, coat over an arm, hat in hand. "I'll never help you. I like you, Rube, God knows why. But you'd alter the past. In order to alter the present according to your own godlike understanding of what's best for the rest of us. Well, if there can be an idiot savant, there can be a sane madman. And there are always some around. Quite often brave men in uniform. Patriots. But still the enemy." He leaned toward Rube, extending his hand. "So I'll just say goodbye, thanking you for an interesting morning."

Rube stood up, face genial, shook Dr. Danziger's extended hand, and said, "Sit down, Dr. D. Because you *are* going to help me. You're going to get me in touch with Si Morley because you'll *want* to." He pulled over his attaché case, Dr. Danziger, still standing, watching him. Rube snapped up the two brass fasteners, lifted the lid, and began removing the contents, tossing them to the table before Danziger: a glossy black-and-white photograph of what appeared to be a small-town Main Street; an old newspaper, edges browned; a campaign button; a sheaf of letters clipped together; an envelope with a triangular stamp; a tape cassette; an old book with a loose binding; a rubber-banded coil of black-and-white film. "Look at this stuff, Doctor. The photograph, take a look at that."

Face and movement reluctant, Dr. Danziger put down his coat and picked up the photograph. "Yes?"

"Well, look at it. A small-town Main Street, right? And taken in the forties, wouldn't you say? Look at the cars."

"Yes. There's a '42 Plymouth roadster; I once had one."

"Now look at the movie marquee: can you read it?"

"Of course; I'm not quite —"

"Okay. Read the title of the movie they're showing."

Twenty minutes later, Dr. Danziger — standing with a coil of movie film held up to the overhead fluorescent light, examining the frames of the final foot — finished, and tossed the film onto the table with the other things. "All right," he said irritably, sitting down. "These all say the same thing. In different ways. Events that apparently once happened one way seem now to have happened in another. Where'd you get them?" he asked curiously.

Rube shrugged. "A friend, a young army friend; they're more or less on loan."

"And what've they got to do with Si Morley?"

"Isn't that obvious?"

"No."

Rube nodded at the objects on the table. "He's *doing* this. He and maybe McNaughton — one more guy who broke his word and didn't come back! They're back there in the past, trampling

132

around, *changing* things, aren't they? They don't know it. They're just living their happy lives, but changing small events. Mostly trivial, with no important effects. But every once in a while the effect of some small changed event moves on down to the —" He stood, frowning: Dr. Danziger was shaking his head, smiling. "Why not!? What the hell, I'm quoting *you!*"

"Misquoting. It takes more than a trivial event. It isn't Si. Or McNaughton. *Look* at these things."

"I have. Most of last night. Looked till —"

"Well, look again. You shouldn't need this spelled out by a senile old man."

"You? That'll be the day." Rube Prien picked up the white campaign button and looked at the printed faces of John Kennedy and Estes Kefauver; looked at the front page of the old newspaper. Touched the tape cassette, the old film, the packet of letters, his expression growing irritable. Then he sat back, hooking an arm over the back of his chair. "Dr. D. You know I was never in your league. Just tell me."

"Not one of these artifacts predates the early years of the century. That didn't occur to you? If Si, back in the 1880s, were causing this" — he gestured at the scattered things on the table — "some, at least, should have occurred much earlier. And if McNaughton, then none could predate the twenties." His face and voice had grown interested. "Something happened, sometime around 1912, it appears. Some kind of . . . what? Some very important event, a kind of Big Bang,

133

to steal a term. Something that altered the course of many subsequent events; these and undoubtedly others."

"What kind of Big Bang?"

"Who can say? You've read Si Morley's published account, his book?"

"Twice. Making notes. And cursing him out at least once a page."

"Yet an accurate account, wouldn't you say?"

"Oh, I don't know. What about that last chapter?"

Danziger laughed. "Oh, you're right, you're right! Not quite accurate there, thank the Lord. Keep my parents from ever meeting! Thus effectively preventing the Project itself. I enjoyed that. But everything else was accurate, including your own grandiose ideas. So why do you suppose he wrote that final chap—"

"Wishful thinking. The way he'd have *liked* it to happen."

"I don't know: if he'd really wanted to do that, what could possibly have stopped him?"

Rube shook his head. "I have no way of knowing." They sat silent, reflecting; then Rube said, "Okay. But who did cause your Big Bang?"

"Anyone who read Si's account of how he succeeded. And who then tried it himself. Or herself, as we are obliged to add now. Tried and, unlike you and me . . . succeeded."

"Oh, come on! Are you serious? Just from reading his account?"

"Oh, I know the difficulties. And how few ever

managed even with the facilities we once had here: the School, the researchers, the Big Floor mockups. Virtually re-creating the whole town for McNaughton. And yet just possibly, some reader, absolute amateur, was actually able —" He couldn't finish, breaking into laughter. "Of course I'm not serious! I'm teasing you, Rube!" Still amused, he turned to gather up his coat and hat. "Well, it's been fascinating." He pushed back his chair to stand. "But now — so long, Rube. Thanks for everything, as we say."

"I can't believe you're walking out on this. You, the fanatic about any least change in the past." He swept his hand over the scattered objects on the table. "What about *these* changes!"

"You've never really understood, have you? Yes, these things seem to indicate a past that has been changed. Thus altering our present. And if I could have prevented it, no doubt I would have." He set the palms of his hands flat on the table edge to lean forward, stiff-armed, toward Rube. "But now that altered order of events is our present. Would you change it again? Send Si Morley back if you could to . . . do something, you don't even know what, and produce some new order of events? Whose consequences you can't possibly foresee?"

Rube picked up the campaign button, saying, "What about *this?*" and tossed it to slide across the tabletop and stop faceup before Danziger.

Danziger glanced down at the two pictured faces, and took his hands from the table. "Yes.

135

I liked that young man. It was a pleasure having a President who could speak his own language. Fluently and properly. Often with grace and wit. When he stood speaking somewhere representing the United States, it was possible to feel proud. We haven't had many like that since Franklin Roosevelt. Yet in a fairly short time this charming young man took us closer to nuclear war than we've ever been before or since. And did it on defective information. Took us into the most foolish, badly planned venture, in Cuba, that I can easily conceive of. So what next, Rube? If he'd lived out his first term and had a second? Would he have improved? Maybe. He might have grown into that enormous job. And the present we'd be living in now would have been something glorious. Or catastrophic. You can't *say,* you see, you can't *say!* But you want to gamble? Reach into the grab bag and find out?" He gestured at the photograph, the letters, the old newspaper, all the things on the table between them. "I'd love to know the cause of these: what event, what Big Bang, back in the early years of this century brought these changes about. And others undiscovered, no doubt. I'd love to know, but never will. And I won't help *you* to know. You're a lovely man, Rube, as the Irish are supposed to say. But a troublemaker, a shit-disturber." He began getting himself into his coat, movements stiff. "So pick up your marvels, Rube, and go home. Let well enough alone. The Project is over."

"Okay." Rube smiled as he stood, so genuinely

that Danziger smiled back in equal friendship. Rube began gathering the things on the table, dropping them into his leather case. "I'll walk down with you."

In the little street-level office Dr. Danziger, hat on now, stood buttoning his coat, glancing around. "Well. The Project's finished and I'll never be back. But whatever I ought to feel, mostly I'm just relieved." He looked questioningly at Rube, who stood waiting, his tan cloth cap in hand, but Rube merely shrugged, and Danziger nodded. "Yes," he said. "It actually meant more to you than even to me. A very great deal more, I think. Ready?"

Rube nodded, pulled on his cap, but continued to stand looking around, unable, it seemed to Danziger, to take the last steps. He reached forward to a wall and lifted off a small framed photograph of a mustached crew standing or squatting beside an old chaindrive moving truck; the photo was labeled *The Gang* in white ink. "Here" — he offered it to Danziger. "You want a souvenir?"

Danziger hesitated, then nodded. "Yes. Thank you." He took the photograph and slid it into his overcoat pocket. Rube took another framed photograph for himself, walked to the door, and when Danziger stepped out, switched off the light. Outside on the walk, he pulled the door closed, then locked it with a key he brought out from the breast pocket of his coat. "Which way you headed, Dr. D?"

"East, then a bus to home."

"Well, I hope to see you again sometime, Dr. Danziger."

"Yes, I hope to see you, Rube. I do. But let's just leave that to fate, all right?"

"Right. Okay." They shook hands, said goodbye, and turned away. After half a dozen steps Rube stopped to look down at the key in his hand. He glanced back to see Danziger walking away, then looked up the blank brick wall beside him to the weathered lettering painted around the roofline. He tightened his fingers on the key in his palm, turned and threw it, high and hard as he could, across the street. Stood listening, then heard it strike metal somewhere within the tall rows of stacked squashed car bodies behind the chain fence across the street. Then he walked away.

9

WHEN HIS phone rang at 3:51 in the morning, Rube Prien's eyes immediately opened and he glanced at his clock as he picked up the phone. Speaking before it could ring again — pleased with himself and his swift response, annoyed at knowing he was as sleepily confused as anyone else might be.

"Rube, it's Danz—"

"Hello, Dr. Danziger."

"I'm terribly sorry to c—"

"It's all right. I know you have a reason."

"Believe me, I do. Rube: the newspaper you showed me at the Project, the old paper."

"The New-York Courier."

"Yes. Rube, please. Get dressed. And bring it over. I'd come to your place, but —"

"I'll be dressed and out the door in four minutes."

"I'm slow, you see, so slow. At my age it takes me forever to get up and get started. And this can't wait."

"I'm on my way."

"With the paper?"

"Oh, you bet."

In the high-ceilinged dining room overlooking West End Avenue, Rube pulled out a chair at Dr. Danziger's gesture, and sat down at the table. He wore tan wash pants and a black pullover sweater. Standing across from him in pajamas, maroon robe, slippers, wearing glasses, the dyed hair at the sides of his bald head disorderly, Danziger spread the old newspaper, very slightly browned at the edges, on the table. He began scanning the columns of the front page, down and up, down and up, the shiny top of his head catching light from the overhead chandelier. "This'll take a little time. I have to be certain."

Presently he turned the front page, opening the paper fully, the page a little larger than modern newspapers, Rube thought. Still scanning the pages column by column, Danziger absently pulled out a chair and sat down slowly, never stopping his scanning, head bobbing in slow motion. His glasses were magnifiers, and each time his head lowered they slid down a trifle, and each time he raised his head for the next column, his big forefinger lifted too, to poke them back into place.

Minutes passed, the street outside, five stories below, remaining silent, the city as quiet as it ever got. Rube glanced around; he had never been here before. The windows were dark, touched by the light of a streetlamp. He didn't feel tired and his mind waited easy and alert, yet his body told him it was unnatural to be awake. The old man, he thought, was doing a kind of speed reading, eyes moving at an even rate down the center of each narrow strip of type.

Danziger turned a page, this time to a double spread of classified ads, and Rube leaned forward to read the upside-down headings: *Flats and Apartments . . . Furnished Rooms . . . Boarders Wanted*. Another page: *For Sale . . . Horses, Carriages, &c . . .* Two pages of *Help Wanted — Female* and *Help Wanted — Male*, Danziger apparently looking at every ad for an instant. "Sorry," he said, glancing up as he turned yet another page. "Highly unlikely to find anything in these, but we must be sure." His head resumed its slow up-and-down nodding. Two pages of *Society . . .* then *Sports*, Rube waiting, hands quiet on the tabletop, face patient, eyes curious.

The final, back page now, examined slowly from upper left to lower right. Then Danziger picked up the paper and, shaking it gently, restored it to its old creases and pushed it over the table to Rube. He took off his glasses and slipped them into the breast pocket of his robe. "You've read this, have you? All of it?"

"After a fashion."

"And found?"

"Well." Rube revolved the paper on the tabletop to look at the front-page headings. "The main news story is 'President Urges Trade Reciprocity' " — he smiled — "and I may pos-

sibly have skipped a word or two of that. And
. . . news from Europe. Not a hell of a lot,
and I'm afraid I didn't read too much of that
either. There's a local story: Cab ran up over
the sidewalk on Fourteenth Str—"

"Yes: anything else?"

Rube shrugged a shoulder. "Glanced at the ads.
Theater stuff. Fashions, cartoons. Sports. I did
read the sports stuff pretty well; kind of interesting. Skipped the editorials."

"Yes." Danziger was nodding, eyes pleased with
himself. "About the way we all read old newspapers. As curiosities. And that's why we both
missed Sherlock Holmes' dog."

"Did we really do that? Pray continue."

Danziger hunched comfortably over the table
on his forearms, a big forefinger hooking out to
tap the newspaper's masthead as he read it aloud.
" 'The New-York Courier. Evening Edition.
Sports Final.' " He looked up at Rube, and sat
back again, one arm lifting to dangle from the
back of his chair. "An old forgotten paper, one
of many from New York's glory days of newspapers by the dozens. Well, the *Courier* stopped
publishing, you tell me, in 1909; records confirm
it. And yet there lies an issue of February 22,
1916" — his forefinger moved out to touch the
dateline. "You saw that. And so did I, so did
I, missing the point completely. We all missed
the dog, the clue, said Sherlock Holmes, of the
dog who should have barked . . . but did not.
Look at that date one more time."

142

Rube obeyed, staring down at the printed dateline through a second or two, then lifted his head. "Oh my God," he said very softly, eyes brightening with excitement. "The battle of Verdun. The battle of Verdun had started . . ."

Danziger sat grinning at him. "Yes. So what we have here is a published newspaper of — what would you call it? A paper from a *different order of time and event.* Oh Lord," he said softly, "oh Lord, Lord, a newspaper of 1916 without a word about World War One. Rube — damn it, Rube! — the paper lying under your hand . . . is a remnant of a different path the world once took. Where there was no World War."

The two men sat looking at each other, eyes happy with wonder. Then Danziger leaned forward. "You're the historian. Is it *possible?* Could such a . . . stupendous thing, Rube, could such a stupendous happening as the first World War actually have been avoided?"

"You're goddamned right: it almost was!" Simultaneously, unable to sit, both men pushed back their chairs and stood. Rube shoved both hands into his back pockets, glancing down at the yellow-edged newspaper, then looking up to nod. "It's a fact all right. Long accepted. The first World War not only could have been avoided but should have been. *Should* have been, Dr. D: it can break your heart sometimes when you sit and read about the men and times and events just before that war. When you're into primary sources, sometimes reading the actual scribbled handwriting of men deeply involved, and then you sit back and just think about that fucking war. *So close,* it came so goddamned close to never happening at all."

Out of physical need to move, both men turned from the table, Rube picking up the paper, and they walked into the shadowed living room. At the front windows they stopped to stand looking down at the two rows of automobile roofs lining the motionless street five stories below. Softly, Rube said, "World War One, 'the Great War,' the English called it. There was no powerful reason for it. It wasn't necessary. It wasn't to anyone's real interest. Right now I could give you eight or ten names, qualified people who've spent important hunks of their lives studying that war. Reading, reading. Studying. Walking the old battlefields. Thinking. Who could describe specific ways — the very times and places — in which that war very nearly didn't begin. Ludendorff could have stopped it dead with a word. And would have if he'd only understood a certain truth: that the United States truly *did* have the ability to mobilize, equip, train, and transport an army to Europe within months."

"Surely, though, an event of enormous complexity, that war? Four years that altered the nature of the world?"

"Complex after it began, not before." They stood staring down at the car roofs through several moments; then Rube said, "World War One began almost casually. For no big reason. Dis-

144

sensions between nations, you read. Well, yeah, they existed all right. Always do. But trivial in 1914. Even more so in '13 and '12. A lot of talk about colonies, but who really needed or even wanted them anymore? Their day was over, they all knew that. A lot of bluster for the hell of it, really. Ignorant men in high places. Without much understanding of historical cause and effect. Issuing stupid ultimatums out of no real necessity. A foolish war. Blundered into, no one actually wanting it or truly believing it would even happen. Some wars have to happen, no stopping them. Our own Civil —"

"Rube." Danziger stood smiling at him. "I'd like nothing more than to hear the full lecture. With lantern slides. But at this time of night I'm afraid I'd flunk the exam."

Rube smiled, glancing at his watch. "Right. Time to go home. But you can't help thinking: Without that war, this might have been a remarkable century. Quite possibly even a happy one, Dr. D."

"Rube, Rube" — Danziger laughed, clapping Rube lightly on the shoulder — "you never change, do you? What's it been, three minutes, four? Since you learned what the old newspaper meant? Yet you're off and running, aren't you?"

Rube smiled again. "No. Because I don't know where to turn. If Si were standing here right now, I wouldn't know what to tell him. I'm not a full-fledged historian, you know. Only got into it after I joined the Army. And my specialty is

145

military history, specifically the two World Wars in Europe, *after* they began. I don't know any more about purely domestic American history than the average high school senior. But we have people who do. People who might know, and probably do know, how that war might have been prevented. Maybe almost *was* prevented. Dr. Danziger, I'm not thinking about some little experiment cooked up by Esterhazy and me. Some tiny change in the past that might affect the present in an equally tiny way. I'm thinking about the actual possibility of preventing World War One. I know that you can reach Si Morley; well, it's time to do it."

"Is it? Why?"

"Jesus. Prevent World War One — *if* that's possible. And you ask why?"

"Sure." Danziger reached out to touch the old newspaper in Rube's hand. "Because *show me the next day's issue.* And the issue of a month after that. And a year. Then a decade later. What would those newspapers have to tell us? Of the nature of the world? Who can assure us that if World War One had never happened, the world would now be a rose garden?"

Rube stood staring down at the unmoving street. "Certainty," he murmured. "Certainty. You're obsessed with it!" He swung to face Danziger again. "Who the hell is ever certain about anything? Including his own next breath! We're affecting the future right now just *standing* here. Some loony insomniac across the way may be

146

watching us, starting a train of loony thought, and blow up the fucking world!"

"That we can't help. But we don't have to make the risk retroactive."

"*Yes we do*. If we can, we've *got* to."

"Minutes. Only *minutes* have passed, and listen to you. Well, I'll never help you, Rube. Ever."

Rube nodded several times, then smiled, the deep smile, utterly friendly and without guile, that made most people like him very much. "Okay," he said, then impulsively offered the old newspaper in his hand to the older man. "Here you are, Dr. D, a souvenir. You might as well have it."

"No, no, Rube, you must keep it; it belongs with —"

"You're the only one saw what it meant; I want you to have it. My lieutenant friend can explain not bringing it back; she likes me." He looked around the room for a place to lay it, then walked to Danziger's pigeonholed desk, cluttered but orderly. Eyes skimming the desktop, he pushed the phone and its attached notepad aside, clearing a space, and set the paper down, memorizing in the instant of seeing them ten digits penciled on the pad.

He walked home, twenty-odd blocks including five long crosstown. He liked being out now, watching the occasional car or early pedestrian. Idly wondering about them, seeing their numbers begin to increase. Seeing the nighttime sky begin to alter, trying to sense the very moment that

147

last night ended and tomorrow began. Thinking idly about time itself, wondering if it was ever to be understood.

When his alarm rang two hours and twenty minutes after he got home, the city noisy and fully alive down on the daylight streets, Rube rolled to the phone and dialed seven of the ten digits — 759–3000 — he had seen on Dr. Danziger's phone pad.

"Plaza Hotel, good morning."

"Good morning." He spoke the last three digits: "Four-oh-nine, please."

"Hello?"

"Hello, Si. Welcome back to the present. This is Rube Prien."

10

I SAT playing with table crumbs, herding them around the cloth with a finger, listening. Rube and I had been here in the Oak Room of the Plaza Hotel for a while now, the breakfast crowd thinning, on our second and third cups of coffee. Finally I reached over to put a hand on Rube's arm, shutting him up. "Okay, Rube, *okay*. Go back and prevent World War One. Sure. Any old time. Who wouldn't? But say it out loud —'Prevent World War One' — and doesn't it sound a little bit silly?

"Listen. What is that war? To you it's old black-and-white film on TV. Plus whatever you've read, been taught and told all your life. An enormous thing, millions killed, a million men killed at the battle of Verdun alone. Prevent all that? Ridiculous."

"But Si. Before it started? Summer of 1914, maybe? Too late even then, I think. But 1913? Maybe. Because as you go back the thing shrinks. Into beginning causes. Smaller, more individual, more manageable. And in 1912 only a handful of men are even thinking about war. You're back there, God damn it, to *when events are small, and can be changed.*"

"So I go back and do what? Shoot the Kaiser?"

"It could work. You think it couldn't? But if you try it, Si, sneak up on his left side; that's the bad arm. I have no idea what you could do. I couldn't pass a high school exam in American history. I could in European. Right now I could describe to you a certain specific time and place in which a meeting occurred. Between three men whose names I could give you, including middle initials. Anyone else in my field could do the same. Three men who met in 1913 in a Swiss restaurant. Which is still there, incidentally. In Berne — I made a point of eating there once just to see it. And, Si, if someone had — well, what? If someone had done nothing more complicated than stall a car, say, before the old limousine taking two of those men to that meeting . . . and had simply gotten out, apologized, and then spoken a few sentences — which I could dictate right now — they would absolutely not have gone on to their meeting. Altering the course of subsequent events just enough to send them down a little different path. And" — Rube softly and noiselessly pounded the cloth with his fist — "there'd have *been no war.*"

"So if I could get myself to Switzerland —"

"No." He grinned. "You'd have to speak German. But if you picked up a phone on July 14, 1911, in Paris, all government offices closed, and

150

made a certain phone call" — he grinned again — "in good idiomatic French, of course, you'd have accomplished the same thing in quite a different way and for different reasons. Hell, if you could even speak English the way the English do, and could hang around on the public sidewalk outside the House of Commons between noon and twelve-forty on May nineteenth, twentieth, twenty-first, or twenty-second — it wouldn't matter which — in 1912, a certain young aide of Joseph Chamberlain would come along. I could supply you with two good photographs as he looked then. And if you simply stepped forward and spoke about forty-five words in a nice fluty English accent, an event of that session of Parliament would have turned out differently. And would almost certainly have altered the position of England in a system of European alliances that did lead directly to war. But like most of your semiliterate countrymen, all you can do is speak plain vanilla American."

"Oh, yeah, as they say in the old movies. And how about you?"

"I read German, French, and Italian. And can get along speaking them if you don't mind a foot-in-the-mouth accent. Didn't speak anything but good old 'Murcan till I joined the service and got into army history. Now I can also do fairly well reading Russian, and even printed Japanese. But for you we'll have to have something involving only Americans, and prewar U.S. isn't my specialty. I'd have to get to Washington, pick

151

some brains." He sat watching me, waiting.

"And what do you think Dr. D would say about this?"

"Oh, we both know what he'd say; I can quote from the little red book, the wise, wise sayings of the cautious Dr. D. Supercautious — I believe he carries a spare set of shoelaces. But we're not talking about *changing* the past, Si; it would be a *restoration*. The old newspaper tells us that." He hunched forward over the table toward me. "The twentieth century, Si, should have been the best, the happiest, the human race ever knew. We were on our way in those first early years! And then the great change occurred. Something that sent us down another path. Into a war nobody needed. What we can do, Si, would not be a change but a restoration to the path the world was already on."

"I came here for a few days. Not to see anyone, except Dr. D. Least of all you. Just a final visit, mostly to walk around. Storing up images. Like a man visiting his old hometown for the last time. Now instead" — I shook my head, laughing a little — "instead you want me to prevent —"

"Give me a week, Si. That's all. Meet me at noon a week from today. At the old place. In the Park where we talked the very first time."

He waited, watching me, but what rushed through my mind was not what Rube thought. My mind was screaming, *Tessie and Ted. Do this, and you'll be where Tessie and Ted are!* But that's a forbidden thing, isn't it? Not if I *have* to do what Rube is asking. Not my fault then, is it?

"Well? You'll meet me in a week?"

I nodded: scared and terribly excited. Tessie and Ted . . .

Rube said, "You going to talk to Danziger?"

"I think so."

"You're not going to let him talk you out of —"

"No. It was different when you and Esterhazy only wanted to fool around with the past. Just to see what would happen. Then I was with Danziger. But this: yeah, sure; I'll meet you in a week." *Tessie and Ted . . .*

11

THROUGH THE revolving doors of the Plaza, down the stone steps, and north to the Fifty-ninth Street corner, where I stopped to wait for the light. I was wearing gray pants and a navy-blue zipper jacket I'd bought a few days ago, no hat. The light changed, I crossed to Central Park, then turned onto a dirt-and-gravel path. On a bit, feeling a little excited, curious about what Rube might have. Off the path then, to walk across a dozen yards of weedy grass or something like grass toward a big outcropping of black rock.

Rube sat waiting, in tan army shirt and pants, tan shoes, an old leather jacket, and an odd-looking blue knitted cap with a fuzzy little tassel. He sat leaning back against the rock, eyes closed, face tipped up into the sun, a brown paper sack on his lap.

He heard me and opened his eyes, grinning, and gestured at the area around us as I sat down, the same place where he had first told me about the Project. "Symbolic, isn't it? Meaningful."

"Or something."

"Well, you made a hard decision then, but the right one. Now do it again. But first . . ." He opened the paper sack, and took out a wax-paper-wrapped sandwich, and handed it to me. "What you ordered, I believe? The first time we sat here?" I smiled, knowing what was coming: a roast pork sandwich. "Also symbolic. Of the pig in the poke you bought then. Well, Si, I'm afraid it's another one now. A bigger pig and a far worse poke. But first to the feast!" Rube brought out a pair of apples; they too, I remembered, were what we'd had here for lunch once before.

We ate, no hurry. Sitting back against the sun-warmed rock, it wasn't too bad here. On the path a pair of more than usually nice-looking young women walked by, glancing over at us, then walking on with just a tiny bit of extra hip-sway, maybe three eighths of an inch. Rube said, "Those are called girls, I think. Or used to be. And someone once told me — but I've never believed it."

"Good you're in the Army, Rube: the outside world would only confuse you."

"It does, it does. If only they'd let the Army run it." He glanced at me. "But that's not the right thing to say, is it? You already think I'm some kind of homegrown Hitler."

"No, I don't think that, Rube. Napoleon, maybe. Except for the hat."

He reached up and touched it. "Comes to protecting my old bald head, I have no shame. A friend made it; I have to wear it occasionally."

155

We finished our sandwiches, I dusted crumbs from my hands, took an apple, bit into it — it was tart — and said, "Okay, Rube, I'm all ears."

He reached around to the side of the rock face we were sitting against, and picked up a tan leather carrying case. "What do you know," he said, unzipping it, "about William Howard Taft and Theodore Roosevelt?"

"Taft was fat, and Roosevelt wore funny glasses."

"More than I knew. I wasn't even sure which was which." He brought out a blue-lined yellow sheet of penciled notes. "But apparently they were friends. Good ones. Roosevelt was President first, then he got the job for Taft. Naturally, after that they fought over who'd be President the next time around. In 1912. But here's the thing: According to our U.S.A. specialists, there's something they stuck together on. They both wanted peace. I mean really did, no political bullshit, or not too much anyway. Roosevelt had already won the Nobel Peace Prize. Taft's father" — Rube tilted his yellow sheet of notes to read a line along the side — "had been minister to Austria-Hungary. And Ruman— no, Russia; can't read my own scrawl. Taft himself had been Secretary of War. Roosevelt had brought Japan and Russia together to end their war. And so on. And they were both smart, they knew how things worked, they knew what other smart men all over the world knew, that things were beginning to shape up so that the world just might eventually

156

trip and stumble into a war that made no sense."

Rube folded his yellow sheet, shoved it back into the case, but didn't withdraw his hand. Grinning at me, he said, "I've got something here that's classified, Si. It's army stuff: our people found this, it's ours, and still secret. They think Roosevelt and Taft had an agreement. Whichever was elected in 1912 would implement something they'd already started together. And in the unlikely event that the Democrat was elected, they'd brief him on this, and hope for the best. Sometimes our people are pretty good, Si; take a look at this." He brought out a letter-size sheet, and handed it to me.

It was a xeroxed copy of a smaller sheet, blackened all around the edges for a couple inches surrounding a slightly tilted memo-size rectangle of white. Printed at the top of the memo: *The White House.* Below that in three penciled lines of fairly good handwriting: *Lunch D.S.;* under that, *wrp gft;* below that, *Detail Z on G, B, V.E.*

"Cute, eh?" said Rube. "Our people tell me that Presidents save bales of stuff. And that it's getting worse. Not much from George Washington, carloads from Gerald Ford." He touched the paper in my hand. "So what does that thing mean? — it's Taft's handwriting. Probably nothing, and who cares. Except that anything a President writes is of some interest, so eventually somebody — I don't know who, it was years ago — at least worked out the date. D. S. was probably Douglas Selbst, senator from Ohio, Taft's state. So check out the senator's journal in the Library of Congress, and yep, it mentions his lunch with the President all right, at some length. On August 14, 1911. So now the memo is dated, and our people note that fact. Not on the original memo, though. It's our information, and to hell with anyone else — right? Don't ever let the Navy find out that Taft had lunch with Senator Selbst in 1911.

"Twenty-five years later — I'm not fooling, Si — another one of our people, an ambitious young girl, if you'll excuse the ugly word, a lieutenant, who hadn't been born when the memo got dated, came across our file copy. And got interested in the other items. What was 'rupp guft'? All she could think of was 'wrap gift,' so she checked out Taft's wife's birth date — not the easiest thing in the world to find out, incidentally. But sure enough, it was August fifteenth, so now the United States Army History Section knew that 'rupp guft' did indeed mean 'wrap gift' — terrific! Apparently Taft did his own gift wrapping; those were leisurely days even for Presidents. That information, by the way, is also classified. Swear you'll never tell."

I crossed my heart.

"Okay. Our people earn their pensions. Eventually. And a lifetime after Taft scribbled his memo, one of our guys going through some stuff that included this glanced at the third item, and the initials translated themselves for him. On sight. That happens. 'Detail Z,' said the memo, and then — G for George, B for Briand, and V. E. for Victor Emmanuel. George Fifth of England; Briand, the premier of France; and the king of Italy, Victor Emmanuel. Three heads of state! And so a lifetime after this thing was written, our people got interested. Sort of. And went to work. Also sort of. Who was Z? they wondered. That was three years ago, and at first —"

"Rube. In only five or six hours it's going to get dark."

"All right. I get carried away. Who was Z? Well, Z was a guy Taft and Roosevelt sent to Europe. To extend greetings from the President to various heads of state: that sort of thing. But also to — well, to chat. And reach a few informal agreements. Form a sort of unofficial alliance. Whoever was elected in 1912 — and also including the Democrat, if possible — would commit himself to actively work, to do everything in his considerable power, to float the idea that we would enter any European war on the side of the Allies. And precede even that with Atlantic submarine patrol."

"They couldn't promise that, could they?"

"Of course not. Congress would have to declare war; this was back in the old-fashioned days when Presidents felt they had to honor their oath to abide by the Constitution. Only Congress could declare war then, and undoubtedly would not have done so. Everyone knew that. All over the world. But this is the point, Si: While I'm an ignoramus about U.S. history, we now move into a historical

159

field I do understand. If there were even the slimmest possibility that America would come into a European war . . . that war immediately becomes impossible. Don't need Congress, formal treaties, don't need even the least certainty about it. Because no nation begins a war, Clausewitz tells us, that it does not believe it will win. And that's true. That war, Si, unnecessary to anyone, would simply not have begun. No idiotic ultimatums, no declarations. Believe me, Si, it would have worked! The war would have been made impossible. Dig up Ludendorff and Hindenburg and ask them. They'll tell you."

"But Z didn't get his agreements."

"Oh, he got them. So our people believe. What he got was letters, informal exchanges. No acts of Parliament or anything like that. But signed. By heads of state. So they counted. They had power and magic."

"And that's how World War One never happened?"

"It happened."

"How come?"

"Z never got home."

"What?"

"No sign of it in anything our people came across. On his way back, all finished, had what he came for: they have cablegrams on that. But then . . . he just seems to vanish. Thin air. We know because there are references to it. Maybe they knew why at the time. Probably did. But we don't."

"Well, who was Z?"

Rube sat slowly shaking his head. "Our people don't know. His actual name never shows up. He is always just 'Z.' And damn it, Si, our people here don't really care. They're not that interested. This stuff is all just a favor to me. Can't blame them: it's nothing they're *on*, you see. To them this is just one more failed mission, and there are dozens and dozens of those in any country's history. It happened a lifetime ago, is very little documented, so — it's a case of so-what."

"Can't you tell your people why you —"

"No. I've been able to form a new unit on this. Very small, need-to-know. Esterhazy heads it, nominally; I'm second in line, and the rest of the unit is mostly the sergeant who brings us coffee."

"Esterhazy."

"Yep. Brigadier now. Si, you know we can't tell people what we're doing. Most of our people never even heard of the original Project in the first place. How could we explain what we hope to do? Show them the Project, a junk heap? I've had to accept what they've offered, which is mostly what they already had at hand. Anyway, I doubt that there's much of anything else. We're talking history of the U.S.A. well before 1914, hardly anyone even thinking about a coming war. Wasn't like Europe; I've told you the kind of stuff I could give you for Europe. But here? I think what I've got is about all there is to get." Rube grinned at me suddenly, reaching over to clap me on the forearm. "But an old dog doesn't forget his old tricks! What do you do when a trail peters out? You run around in circles! Till you pick up the scent again. Look, let's get us some coffee or something." He hopped up, the old athlete, offered me a hand, and I let him help pull me up, and we turned to walk over to the path.

We reached it, turning south toward Fifty-ninth Street and the Plaza Hotel. Rube said, "You ever hear of Alice Longworth?"

"Yeah, I think so. Old lady? Dead now? The one who said Thomas Dewey looked like the little man on a wedding cake?"

"That's her. She also said, 'If you can't speak well of someone, come sit by me.' That last is the reason I thought of her. She was real bright. Clever, witty. Had a tongue in her head, as they say. A gossip. Married to a socialite congressman And she wasn't always an old lady. Once she was young, and very much the leader of the young Washington set. Knew everybody who was anybody in Washington. Did you know she was Theodore Roosevelt's daughter?"

"I don't know. I guess so."

"Well, I remembered, and began reading a little bit about her. Two, three books from the library. And I put together a list of her friends, many as I could. And, figuratively speaking, I began ringing doorbells. I wrote, I phoned, and in one case, in Washington, I actually did ring a doorbell. What I did, Si, was get in touch with people

162

who'd had some connection with Alice; grandchildren of her friends, great-grandchildren, great-greats, anyone I could find who just might have some letters of hers. That's something a family might save, a letter from Alice Longworth. I reached maybe one out of five on my list. Some of them didn't even know who she was." We came out onto the Fifth Avenue sidewalk beside the Park, walking on toward Fifty-ninth Street ahead. "It was tedious work, and I'd get bored, irritated. One day on the phone I said, 'What! You never heard of Alice Longworth! Your life is a wasteland! Why, she's the one they wrote the song about!' What song? he wants to know, of course, so I sang it to him. Over the phone." Rube began singing, softly and in not a bad voice, hitting the notes right: "In her sweet lid-ull Al-liss blue gown!" It's a nice old song really; I'd always known it, but never knew the words referred to an actual Alice. I joined in, and we walked along Fifth toward the Plaza across the street, singing softly. I felt pretty good after that, walking into the little bar off the lobby, picking a table. I knew Rube hadn't planned it; he could be devious, but also impulsive, even reckless, and I knew his singing had been spontaneous. But when the waitress arrived, Rube smiled up at her and said, "What the hell; I'll have a martini. First in a million years." And instead of the Coke I'd thought I was going to order, I said I'd have one too. And thought later that maybe Rube had recognized a spur-of-the-moment opportunity to

163

get a little booze in me as an aid toward the right decision.

There were maybe twenty tables in here but only one other occupied, by a pair of Japanese men. Rube had picked a table well away from them, taking the chair by the wall where he could see the whole room.

Waiting for our drinks, still smiling a little at our singing, Rube unzipped his case, saying, "What I got for my efforts was a couple Alice Longworth letters mentioning Z. I thought people would send me xeroxes" — he brought them out — "but they both sent the actual letters."

"Is that stationery 'Alice Blue'?"

"I think so. And so does the Library of Congress. She was a little vain at having a color named for her." He brought out two xeroxes. "The Library of Congress has some AL stuff in their Roosevelt file, which got me a pair of notes from Z to her." Rube started to pass me a letter, but our drinks came and he waited, didn't want anything spilled or dripped on them. We tasted our drinks; then I nodded at his letters. "These all say 'Z'? Don't mention his name?" Still trying his drink, Rube nodded. I said, "How come? Alice knew who he was, didn't she?"

"Sure. He was a friend of the Longworths, but he still signed his notes 'Z,' and she said 'Z.' No secret to any of them, but here was a President edging into what was really congressional business, the way Presidents like to do. Those were pretty easy days though, long before C.I.A. time,

164

so about all they did was keep their man's name off paper. If Taft writes himself a memo, he can just say 'Z,' case anybody happens to see it. And Z briefs his friends: Call me Z! Which Alice loved, thought it was hilarious. Pretty jokey bunch. The smart young set of Washington."

I put my hand out for a letter, and Rube handed me a blue sheet; the ink was blue too. In a slapdash but legible handwriting it was dated February 22, 1912, and began, *Laurie, dear!* Rube said, "You can skip most of that; pick up near the bottom." I did, and it said, *And of course Z — and we simply must say Z — isn't it delicious? — will at last have his fill, and we shall hear of nothing but the two-a-day. At least he'll see over the ladies' hats! Nicky and I may just run up to see him, if only for a day. But I must tell you of Evie's famous party, or shall I say soiree? Of course we arrived late. Nicky had a tiresome —* I turned the page, but Rube said, "That's all on Z in that one."

I said, "Just what does this do for the cause, Rube?"

"Well. It tells us something. 'Two-a-day' means vaudeville; he must like vaudeville. And he can see over ladies' hats in front of him, so he's tall. It's quite useful."

"Sure. Beats 'rupp guft.' What else?"

He handed me the second letter in the vigorous blue handwriting, this with the numeral 2 at the top, and Rube said, "That's all these people could find; first page is missing." It began: *insists she couldn't possibly have known, yet she knew the name*

165

was Clara! And even his watch number! Which he actually gave me: 21877971. Doesn't that beat the Dutch! Z is simply darling, and we shall miss him when he leaves. The next paragraph began describing a dance, and I looked up at Rube, but before I could speak he said quickly, "Here's the envelope it came in," and handed it to me.

It was addressed to Mrs. Robert O. Parsons in Wilmette, Illinois, and Rube said, "Look at the postmark." I did, a slightly smudged black circle stamped at the left of a canceled two-cent red stamp with a profile of Washington; it read, *March 6, 1912,* at the top, *Washington, D.C.* at the bottom. I didn't know what to say about that or the letter either, so I just nodded and passed it back to Rube.

"It's true," he said, as though I'd made some spoken criticism, "that those are just . . . small clues. But here's the real find!" and he grinned with forced enthusiasm. "Here's where we actually pick him up, as we say in the trade. I think. I heard it on television." He brought out a folded white sheet. "They found the original of this in a book from AL's library, probably tucked in as a place mark."

I unfolded the little sheet, a xerox copy. *Plaza Hotel,* it said at the top in elaborate script, the *P* especially fancy. Beside it an old-style engraving of the hotel. Handwritten at the top, *March 1.* Then: *From Z to A! Always and ever an enchanting city! And a splendid time of it thus far. Even my obligatory presence at Madam Israel's Delmonico lec-*

ture an unexpected pleasure, for the ever-smiling, ever-nimble Al himself made a surprising and very welcome appearance. Missed Knabenshue yesterday. Immediately following The Greyhound, however, I saw — actually saw! — the Dove Lady herself! Would have followed but stood dumfounded instead, though I must say city-wise Broadwayites simply ignored her.

Tonight, my dear, something that should thrill your usually unthrillable soul, I am to meet that man whom of all the world I most admire, at — but no, I will not use so ugly and utilitarian a name. Too much like calling a lovely woman Tillie! Rather, her prow sharp and straight as that of the Mauretania *herself, I say she is a ship! Of stone and steel, true, yet seated within her, a wheel and tiller in hand, I do believe one might sail her up Broadway or the Fifth Avenue to the delight of all. We meet tonight, not, I regret to inform you, at the stroke of midnight, but a drab hour earlier. And then, finally, I will have — The Papers!*

Of course, dear girl, this is serious business, and I do assure you that in practice I am in deadly earnest. But not with you and Nickie; no fun in that! Wish me luck, my dear, wish very hard. love, Z.

I handed his letter back to Rube, and sat nodding thoughtfully; I didn't know what to say. "Did people really write that way?"

"Yeah. Talked that way too, I think. It was obligatory, everything light and jokey."

"I don't suppose 'The Greyhound' was a bus."

167

"It was a play. By Wilson Mizner and somebody else. Opened at the Knickerbocker Theatre, Broadway and Thirty-eighth. I checked out the old theater ads."

"And what's the Dove Lady?"

"Don't know."

I sat forward toward Rube, and spoke very carefully; I knew he'd worked hard on this. "Rube," I said quietly, "what would I do with this stuff? I get there, if I can —"

"You can, I know you can."

"Yeah, well, maybe. I get there, go to this lecture, and he's there, we know that. But how do I pick him out, Rube, how? And this other stuff —"

"Well, God damn it, Si, I'd give you his photograph if I could. In 3D and color. Plus his fingerprints and a letter of introduction. Si, it's all we've *got*."

"Okay. Not trying to give you a hard time, Rube." I reached over and with a forefinger sort of stirred his pathetic little stack of letters around a little. "But these are nothing. They tell us nothing. The Dove Lady. Somebody in a large crowd sees her. Well, the whole crowd sees her, don't they? And sees what? A lady in a dove-gray dress? Or who flaps her arms and coos like a dove? Or wears a dove on her head? And what is this building like a ship? Christ Almighty."

"Oh, you're right. Absolutely right. Face the facts, and this is hopeless. All you actually *know* is his goddamn watch number!" He reached out,

168

and with a hooked forefinger began tapping his papers. "But Si, right now these things are dead. Connected to nothing anymore. The people who wrote and read them gone. The very buildings they were sent to gone. The mailman who delivered them and the clerk who sold this stamp, dead. Read these, and it's like staring at an anonymous nineteenth-century sepia photograph you pick up in a junk store, wondering at the face looking out at you from under the funny hairdo. To ask who she was is hopeless now because all the connections, every friend, every relative, even every acquaintance is dead and gone. But when that face was alive and smiling at the camera, so were her friends alive, her relatives, her neighbors. And you just might find out who she was because the connections are still there. Well" — he tapped his letters again — "you and only you can return to the time when this ink was still wet. The people alive, the events happening, the connections all there!"

I nodded. "Okay, and if I found Z, what then?"

Rube just shook his head. "I don't know. You'd . . . stick with him, I suppose. Try to — protect him, maybe. Hang on to him, get him back okay. *I don't know*, Si! But I'll tell you something I've never told anyone else in my life. I won a medal once. I was a kid in Vietnam. I don't wear it, don't show it. But I can tell you I value it. And I won it in a hopeless situation in which I *acted anyway*. And succeeded in the only way there was to succeed. By luck. That's all. If something

169

is truly hopeless, Si, then luck becomes your only hope. Because it exists. Luck happens. But you have to give it a chance to happen."

"Is that true, Rube? About your medal?"

"No, hell no. I was never in Vietnam. But it's *basically* true, and you know it! It's the way I'd have thought and acted. It's what I'd have *done!* If the situation had ever come up."

I nodded. It was true.

"So I don't know how you find a man in New York in 1912 or any other time, when you don't know who he is or what he looks like. Or what you do if you find him. But you know what's at stake. So you have to try. Give luck a chance."

"Go in and win one for the Gipper."

"Sure."

"When I was a kid I thought it was pronounced *gypper.*"

"It often should be."

"So I've got what — two, three days? In New York, 1912? *If* I can make it. *If.* In and out fast. Make or break. Find Z or not."

"That's about it."

"Well, okay, no use blathering away about it, because we both know I'm going."

He smiled, that fine Rube Prien smile you could not resist, and beckoned to the waitress. When she arrived with her little silver tray he said, "Keep 'em coming! Till you close!" Smiling to show he didn't actually mean it. Then he nodded toward the two Japanese. "And see what the boys in the front room will have."

She returned first to the Japanese table to unload two of her drinks, and when we had ours, all four of us lifted our glasses, smiling, nodding, bowing, Rube murmuring, "Remember Pearl Harbor!" And then to me: "They're probably saying the very same thing."

12

I PHONED Dr. Danziger that evening, out of courtesy and respect, trying to explain why I was going to do what I was, or try to. He listened, always polite, and as a kind of consolation I told him how unlikely it was that I could even find Z, and how little I had to go on. He asked about that, pleased, I suppose, at how slim my chances were. I knew he regarded that as interfering with the past, the great sin, but he didn't preach at me. And finally, all he said was, "All right, Si; we all have to do what we must. Thank you for phoning."

When I first joined the Project long ago, the struggle for me was to believe that Albert Einstein meant exactly what he said. And what he said, Dr. D assured me, was that the past existed. And he meant that literally: the past was truly there . . . somewhere. Therefore, Dr. D believed, it just might be reached.

I hardly knew what it meant to say the past existed. How? Where? And whenever disbelief washed over me and I was suddenly certain that this strange project was only an old man's delusion, I would hang on to — like a monk gripping his cross as he struggled to hold on to his faith — Einstein's Twin Brothers.

Think of two brothers, he said, as I recall what I was taught at the Project. They're twins, thirty years old, and one is shot into space in a rocket traveling at nearly the speed of light. The round trip takes him five years, so he returns to earth thirty-five years old. But his twin, left on earth, is now ninety, because time itself isn't fixed but is only relative to other aspects of the universe, and moves differently for each. The very idea seems absurd — but Einstein said it, and meant every word.

And proved it. An atomic clock, whatever that is, is perfect; neither loses nor gains even the tiniest fraction of a second. Two such clocks — costing millions each, naturally — were made, each keeping precisely the same time to the billionth, or maybe it was the zillionth of a second, I don't know. One stayed on earth, the other was shot into space in a rocket traveling as fast as man could make it go. And when the rocket returned — this is actually a demonstrated fact; it happened — those clocks no longer showed the same time. The clock kept on earth was a fraction faster, only a tiny fraction of a second but a fraction with a world of meaning. Time, for the clock in the speeding rocket, had moved slower. Impossible. *Impossible.* Except that it truly happened. Each had briefly existed in a different order of time. And when I sat in a Project class-room listening to Martin Lastvogel as he taught me what the New York City of 1882 was like . . . I hung on to the twin brothers like a talisman. If there was such a thing as two orders of time — and *there was,* the two clocks proved it — then the rest of Albert Einstein's theory was also true . . . and the past truly and actually exists, I didn't have to understand how. What I did have to do was find it.

So now, on a Monday morning, I sat down at an old wooden table in the newspaper room of the New York Public Library and began to look for it. I was comfortable, in new blue denims and a gray crew-neck sweater, and I began scanning the front page of a newspaper. Printed in the upper right-hand corner was not *60 CENTS* but *ONE CENT*. And the printed date was January 12, 1912. The masthead, though, reading, *The New York Times,* looked identical — the same familiar Gothic lettering — to that of the paper I'd read with my room service breakfast. So was the little box that said, *"All the News That's Fit to Print."*

And so was the news, really. *Political Chaos France's Peril,* said one front-page heading, which I had no trouble skipping. *Hold Up Aged Merchant,* said another, and I read that "four men sprang out of a doorway in Water Street yesterday," and "grabbed George Abeel, an iron merchant." "The four men throttled him, while one of them went through his pockets and took his gold watch worth $150 and $50 in cash. Then

174

they beat the aged merchant, who is 72 years old, about the head and face . . ." Ho hum.

I read that Andrew Carnegie had stonewalled a congressional committee. Saw nothing wrong with inducing the President of the United States to appoint one of Carnegie's steel company lawyers secretary of state. Said that "his personal contributions to various Republican campaign funds" had nothing at all to do with the alleged violations of the Sherman antitrust laws by the U.S. Steel Corporation. Didn't seem to understand, in fact, just what this antitrust law was. Denied that he was head of the company: he was only a stockholder who happened to own fifty-eight percent. Didn't even know what his lawyers did or what their duties were. The editorial page ran a verse:

> If asked your age,
>   Or name,
>   Or views,
> On anything in life,
> Or "Where's your home?"
> Or "How's your health?"
> Or "Have you got a wife?"
> Or, "Tell me do,
>   What's two plus two?"
> Don't answer.
>   Simply chant:
> "I'm fully,
> Quite fully,
> Blissfully ignorant." Ho hum.

Jack Dorman had knocked out Young Cashman last night, a society couple was divorcing, and Wall Street was "shocked" at a stock exchange scandal. So ho hum again. Was 1912 just like today? Couldn't be. The news people make, the things they do, Dr. Danziger had once taught me, remain essentially the same in every time. But in the ways people think, feel, and believe . . . every time is different. So I began to hunt for the people of 1912 between the lines of the routine news they made.

And began to find them. A first hint, I thought, of the way people once felt and believed showed up in a Saks ad headed, *Resolutions for You and for Us*. Below that, a long column of sentiments like these: "To bear failure with courage, and success with humility . . . To whine a little less and work a little more . . . To speak in small type and think in capitals . . . To remember that the echo of a knock reacts on the knocker." And so on and so on, a column of stuff like that, almost unbearably trite to our eyes, followed only by the Saks signature.

And yet, I sat thinking, a copywriter in an early ad agency, and a business firm that okayed and paid for that ad must have thought they knew their fellow New Yorkers. So — a first hint? — wasn't this ad published for a people who were ambitious? Hopeful? Cheerful? Optimistic? Certainly not cynical.

And so I began, in this and many another paper,

to look for what the people of 1912 had to tell me about themselves. Skipping crime, divorce, and liars under oath, I read the classified ads, and learned that three 1912 people had lost their dogs, whose names were Tammy, Sport, and Bubbles, and whose breeds were "a French bull dog," a "Schipperke," and a "Pug." And when, later that afternoon on my way out from the library, I stopped in Reference to look up *Dog* in the *Encyclopaedia Britannica* for 1911, I found that photographs of those breeds didn't really look the same as even those same breeds today. And I walked down the library steps onto present-day Fifth Avenue, wondering where to have dinner, with the first beginnings in my mind — knowing what you might see at the end of the leash — of what the sidewalks of New York might be like in 1912.

Every day that week, all day except for lunch and one or two coffee breaks, I sat reading — trying not to think too much of home — the *Times*, the *Herald*, the *World*, the *Telegram*, the *Express*. Of 1909 . . . 1910 . . . 1911, '12, and '13. And found stories I should have passed by, but didn't have the willpower. And so I learned that Thomas Edison had just invented a way to make furniture out of concrete. Including phonographs. With a photo of one that looked fine to me. But I was also becoming aware of how often I came across references to sheet music. And how often pianos were advertised. Looked like these people made their own music.

177

A brief account of an accident in which "A Second Avenue trolley car crashed into an Avenue C horsecar at Houston Street and Second Avenue" told me that the nineteenth century in which Julia and I lived was colliding with the beginnings of the twentieth.

The Pennsylvania Railroad train to Cleveland carried a library car. Office supply ads illustrating new rolltop desks helped me peek into a 1912 office. An ad headed, "A Demi Unit filing cabinet is a genuine *multum in parvo* for the private office . . ." said to me that an advertiser felt he could count on 1912 businessmen knowing some Latin. And suggested a vanished kind of schooling which graduated people who knew geography, arithmetic, spelling, American history, some Latin, and maybe even some Greek.

I discovered how the Brooklyn Rapid Transit, Surface and Elevated, thought their 1912 patrons ought to be treated, because they regularly ran ads to tell them what they had left behind. Giving me a glimpse of empty El and streetcar seats on which lay "eyeglasses, small music roll, suitcase, stationery, baby's bottle, derby hats, velvet handbag." Told me they walked out of the cars in their 1912 clothes leaving "a letter file, muff, man's coat, pocketbook, handbags, rubbers, purse, book, knife . . ." And I wondered why champagne was advertised so incessantly. Was it the Coca-Cola of 1912? All of February 1912, I learned from the weather reports, was "unseasonably mild; spring- and almost summerlike, unusual for New York."

Newspapers, magazines, even trade journals. And after a while I got tired of them and of the library, and began bringing books back home. Up to my room in the Plaza elevator with *A Girl of the Limberlost*, by Gene Stratton-Porter . . . or *Cap'n Warren's Wards*, by Joseph C. Lincoln . . . *Truxton King: A Story of Graustark*, by George Barr McCutcheon . . . *The House of Mirth*, by Edith Wharton . . . All with color illustrations on their covers.

And then for a while — mornings after breakfast in the armchair in my room, or on a Central Park bench in the warm part of an afternoon, or sitting up in bed leaning toward the lamp cleverly shaded to keep light from reaching my book — I read things like:

"He was a tall, rawboned, rangy young fellow with a face so tanned by wind and sun you had the impression that his skin would feel like leather if you could affect the impertinence to test it by the sense of touch." Further down the page: "This tall young man in the panama hat and grey flannels was Truxton King, embryo globe-trotter and searcher after the treasures of Romance. Somewhere up near Central Park, in one of the fashionable cross streets, was the home of his father and his father's father before him: a home which Truxton had not seen in two years or more."

Where had he been? "We come upon him at last — luckily for us we were not actually following him — after two years of wonderful but rather disillusioning adventures in mid-Asia and all Africa. He had seen the Congo and the Euphrates, the Ganges and the Nile, the Yang-tse-kiang and the Yenisei; he had climbed mountains in Abyssinia, in Siam, in Thibet and Afghanistan; he had shot big game in more than one jungle, and had been shot at by small brown men in more than one forest, to say nothing of the little encounters he had had in more un-Occidental towns and cities . . ." But: "He had found no sign of Romance."

However: "Somewhere out in the shimmering east, he had learned, to his honest amazement, that there was such a land as Graustark." And reaching Graustark, he was soon talking to an old man who "straightened his bent figure with sudden pride. 'I am an armorer to the crown, sir. My blades are used by the nobility — not by the army, I am happy to say . . .'

" 'I see. Tradition, I suppose.'

" 'My great-grandfather wrought blades for the princes a hundred years ago. My son will make them after I am gone, and his son after him. I, sir, have made the wonderful blade with the golden hilt and scabbard which the little Prince carries on days of state. It was two years in the making. There is no other blade so fine . . . There are diamonds and rubies worth 50,000 gavvos set in the handle . . .' "

A page or so later Truxton King met "a young woman of most astounding beauty," and "Somewhere back in his impressionable brain there was growing a distinct hope that this beautiful young creature with the dreamy eyes was something more than a mere shopgirl. It had occurred to him in that one brief moment of contact that she had the air, the poise, of a true aristocrat."

Well, I didn't read too much more of that, but what about such a story? Not much like those we watch on television, but is it less believable? Do automobiles, after all, really soar over the crests of hills ten feet above the pavement, landing on their wheels without any problem? The Graustark novels were wildly popular, one after another, in the first years of this century, but I don't suppose the people who read them took them any more seriously than we take most of our entertainment. And when I closed this one — I was sitting on a Central Park bench within sight of the Plaza — I was smiling, but I was also inclined to like the kind of people who liked Truxton King. But are "mere shopgirls" really inferior to "true aristocrats"? Was 1912 also a time of easy social prejudice? Unconcerned and unrebuked?

The people I was looking for read more than easy junk: they read Edith Wharton. And in *The House of Mirth*, which I began back in my room one morning after a coffee shop breakfast, a woman of twenty-nine is waiting in Grand Central Station (I had to stop and think: that was the little brick Grand Central Julia and I knew, not today's) for a train not due for some time. She meets a young man she knows, and accepts his invitation to have tea at his apartment nearby. In the apartment, "Lily sank with a sigh into one of the shabby leather chairs.

" 'How delicious to have a place like this all to one's self. What a miserable thing it is to be a woman.' "

The young man replies, " 'Even women have been known to enjoy the privileges of a flat.'

" 'Oh, governesses — or widows. But not girls — not poor, miserable, marriageable girls!' "

She leaves the apartment, ". . . but as she reached the sidewalk she ran against a small glossy-looking man with a gardenia in his coat, who raised his hat with a surprised exclamation.

" 'Miss Bart? Well — of all people! This *is* luck,' he declared, and she caught a twinkle of amused curiosity between his screwed-up lids."

She replies — he is a Mr. Rosedale — and "Mr. Rosedale stood scanning her with interest and approval. He was a plump rosy man of the blond Jewish type, with smart London clothes . . ."

She feels she mustn't say she was visiting a young man's apartment, and says she was here to visit her dressmaker. But it turns out that he knows there is no dressmaker in the building: he owns the building, and knows that all its tenants are young bachelors.

She hails a cab, and on her way back to the station wonders, "Why must a girl pay so dearly for her least escape from routine? Why could one never do a natural thing without having to screen it behind a structure of artifice?" She is "vexed" with herself because ". . . it would have been so simple to tell Rosedale that she had been taking tea with Selden! The mere statement of the fact would have rendered it innocuous." She should also have accepted his offer to take her to the station because "the concession might have purchased his silence. He had his race's accuracy in the appraisal of values, and to be seen walking down the platform at the crowded afternoon hour in [her] company would have been money in his pocket, as he might himself have phrased it. He knew, of course, that there would be a large houseparty at Bellomont, and the possibility of being taken for one of Mrs. Trenor's guests was doubtless included in his calculation. Mr. Rosedale was still at a stage in his social ascent when it was of importance to produce such impressions."

Did that tell me something more of how 1912 believed, felt, thought? Even the author herself? I thought so.

Books, newspapers, until finally, late one morning, I understood that they no longer had much left to tell me. Magazines, for a while, then on to old film, projected for me one morning and again the next in the little theater in the Museum of Modern Art; Rube had arranged this for me. And I sat, comfortably slouched, looking up at the old images, seldom very sharp, some being copies of copies. But in the old film the people of 1909, '10, '11, 1912, and '13 actually moved.

I sat watching a vanished streetcar roll down a strange Broadway, saw it stop, watched a step unfold, watched women delicately lifting their ankle-length skirts just enough to manage the step. I saw horses trot, and saw them plod tiredly. Watched pedestrians cross the street, saw one man actually running a little, hurrying off the screen on an errand lost to all memory. In the silent dark I reminded myself that what I watched, moving up there on the screen, had once had its precise duplication in actuality. And I tried to supply the missing sounds and colors: that streetcar had been red.

Stereo views at the Museum of the City of New York, most of these sharply focused, clear, finely detailed. And with them I looked out over the city a lot — at aerial views from various tall buildings looking over the length of the 1912 city toward Central Park; or toward the harbor; or overlooking a river. And saw the city — of tall buildings, yes, but not so very tall. And mostly scattered, New York still open and airy, still full of sun and daylight. Occasionally, here and there in some of the views, I'd spot a puff of steam or vapor rising from a roof vent, and that — the frozen instant — would suddenly make the lost city real.

Rube phoned me two or three times, in the late afternoon when I was likely to be in my room. The first time, he suggested dinner, but I said no, I was in the process of separating myself from this time, it was best to be alone. Once he phoned in the morning before I'd gone down for breakfast, wanting a list of my clothing sizes.

One morning — it was drizzling, and I walked along the west side of Fifth Avenue edging as close as I could to the partial protection of Central Park trees — I went up to the Metropolitan Museum for the opening of a new exhibit. And for the rest of the morning and for three more hours, after lunch in the museum restaurant, I moved from one tall glass case to another staring in at models dressed in clothing surviving from 1910–1915. There, tantalizingly just behind the glass, stood some of the absolute reality of those early years — the visible threads and buttons and actual weave of the cloth; the dull gloss of fur; the hard glitter of jewel-like ornamentation; the actuality of feathers, the reality of dye. I knew already from photographs, sketches, and film what kinds of hats women wore in 1912. But now here they really *were*. Huge cartwheels wide as a woman's shoulders: made of cloth, of woven straw and even fur; plain and decorated with artfully folded and twisted cloth or speckled with jewel-like stones or artificial flowers or fruit. Still other hats without brims, but the crowns oversize, huge, one of them with a pair of actual bird wings cupping the sides. Once the Dove Lady's?

I couldn't get enough of the realness of what I stood staring at. There in case after case hung their very clothes, touchable except for the glass. There hung the blue serge of a skirt once actually worn by a living *girl,* as they were then, the hem narrowing in just above the ankles. Beside it — surely this had really moved through the lobby of a New York theater at some forgotten play — an evening wraparound cloak of peach-colored satin trimmed with white fur, and it wasn't hard to catch glimpses of it in my mind, moving through a crowded, buzzing lobby. The high-heeled white shoes just below the furred hem of that cloak were like today's except not quite; I think it was something about the heels: they looked — well, funny. And the men's suits — the left shoulder of one almost touched the glass, and I could see the faint fuzz of the tweed — were like today's except that, no, they weren't, everything a little different, the pants cuffs narrower, the lapels . . . different; smaller, I think. And the cloth seemed heavier, and there were more browns than I'd have expected. And the men's hats: the brims of the felt hats were wider but that wasn't all. I didn't know what the other differences were, though I could see them. I wore a derby once in a while, going out with Julia, but these derbies behind the glass here weren't the same. And there were a lot of caps.

I spent the day looking at these old clothes, and thinking about them. Most of the next day I spent back at the exhibit, and most of the morning of the third. I did what Martin Lastvogel had once taught me at the Project school: I stared at the closeness of these dresses and cloaks and shoes and parasols; at the hats and caps, overcoats and suits and Norfolk jackets, and the shoes and

186

boots and galoshes, until . . . finally the strangeness left them. It took work: Other visitors came and looked and commented and left, but I walked up and down the aisles between cases, and stopped and stood working at seeing these things on city streets. Worked at seeing them, in my mind, passing by on a sidewalk. Worked at seeing them not here on display but in use . . . until sometime during the third day they had turned no longer strange but ordinary. And when I left, and walked out and down the steps of the museum into modern-day New York . . . I knew I'd come closer to, could truly sense all around me now, somehow just behind and under what I could see — the actuality of Albert Einstein's simultaneously existing past, the New York of the younger century, now very nearly attainable.

13

ONE DAY in my room, leafing through *The American Boy* magazine of January 1912, I understood that I was ready. I sat slouched in a big upholstered chair by my windows to bring the afternoon light onto the pages, wearing jeans and a plaid cotton shirt. And understood that my preparations were finished. I didn't begin to know all about the New York City of 1912, but neither does a man of today fully know his own time and place. I knew enough. In this moment of the present, I knew what you always have to know, have to believe, and above all have to feel: that another New York was here too, lying invisibly all around me.

Below my window, and just across the street, lay Central Park. Looking out now across its treetops, I could see in my mind its paths, bridges, rocks, water, all virtually unchanged from century to century. It existed out there now just as it existed for Julia and Willy. And existed in a moment like this of the late winter of 1912. The Park, little changed, was part of each day in New

York for more than a century past, a Gateway to each. And I stood up, and began to get dressed.

The clothes had been hanging in my closet for nearly a week; I'd found the package in my room one night in a Brooks Brothers suit box sent up by Rube: a complete outfit, including underwear, a wallet, even a handkerchief. Now I stripped down and got into the underwear, an odd one-piece affair that actually buttoned up the front. Then socks, which had a pair of Paris garters already attached. Money belt of lightweight tan canvas, packed and heavy, gold and the old-style large bills in big denominations, some of them one-thousands. I took out a hundred dollars for my wallet, then strapped on the belt; it made me a little nervous. Then a green-and-white-striped shirt, and a stiff detached collar. Two gold-plated studs already in the shirt band. Attaching the collar was something I knew all about: First tuck the tie up into the fold of the collar all around. Fasten the collar to the shirt at the back stud. Put on shirt and collar, and close collar at front with the stud there. Then tie the tie.

In the bathroom I looked at myself in the mirror. The collar was higher than I was used to; it actually touched my jaw at both sides, a little uncomfortable and looked it.

Shoes now: light brown, almost yellow oxfords with funny wide shoestrings, widening out like little ribbons near the tips; blunt toes bulging upward. My size and width; Rube had asked me. And not quite new: broken in, and I wondered

189

where he'd gotten them. Pants next, the cuffs so narrow I had to take off the shoes to pull on the pants. Vest and jacket finally, the suit a nice shade of tan. Tan porkpie hat. Then to the bathroom mirror again.

Not bad. I liked it, and knew it was right for the time. The pants had a watch pocket for the gold watch Rube had supplied, wrapped and labeled *Careful*, in the Brooks Brothers box. I put the handkerchief, white with a blue border, in my back pocket. And finally, into the right-hand pants pocket, a little handful of coins from the plastic sack Rube had wrapped them in. I checked; none was dated after 1911.

Everything else I owned went into my modern soft-sided bag. I'd already arranged with the hotel to check it when I was ready, until I "returned from a trip." At the mirror a last grin at the stranger with my face; then I picked up my room key and bag.

Across Fifty-ninth Street and into Central Park. Then I walked not quite aimlessly but not quite knowing where I was going either, turning at whim onto branching-off pathways, deliberately losing myself. Behind me on the asphalt-paved path, the fast click of high heels, and a young woman hurried past me; getting a bit late to be caught alone in Central Park.

Presently, wandering, I came to what I was looking for, a bench deep in the Park so surrounded by heavy-leafed, late-summer trees and shrubbery, and with a long gently rising hillock before me, that the city was gone. Directly ahead through a high gap in the trees, I could see the western sky, and a very few thinned-out fragmenting clouds tinged by the lowering sun.

I didn't work at what I had come here to do. Just sat there on my bench, legs stretched out, ankles crossed; not thinking really, but not trying not to either. Just sat staring absently down at my bulge-toed shoes. At the Project we'd been trained in self-hypnosis, necessary, Danziger believed, in order to break the billions of tiny mental threads, as he called them, that hold the mind and consciousness to its own present. They are in truly countless things, the endless facts, large and trivial, the truths and illusions and thoughts that tell us that this is what for us is *now*.

But long since, I'd learned that I no longer needed hypnosis. I did — well, what was it I did? I'd learned the almost indescribable mental trick of allowing that immense body of knowledge that means and *is* the present . . . to go still in my mind. Just sat there deep in the Park waiting — in the way I had learned — to feel it all finally go quiescent. Sitting there, elbows comfortably winged out on the back of the bench, watching the first hint of evening begin to gather at ground level, still afternoon in the sky, I may have drifted into a kind of trance. But still, I heard the present hidden around me; heard a cab horn scream; heard a whispering jet very high and distant.

But then no more, and I sat letting thoughts

and impressions move through my mind of an earlier New York of this century, the New York of early 1912. I knew as simple fact that all around me 1912 truly existed, was there to be found. And didn't force. Just waited to begin feeling it in strength.

I watched the sky, saw the treetops lose all but the very last of the sun, the high-up blue darkening toward evening. An old phrase from somewhere spoke itself in my mind, and I murmured it to myself — *"l'heure bleu,"* the blue hour. I'd never seen it before but now the sky and, truly, the air itself as I sat here watching had acquired a lovely haunting blueness. And with this blue dusk there had come, strangely and thrillingly, a kind of pleasurable melancholy. To me at least, it's what the blue hour meant, the exciting sad-sweet knowledge that all over the city that lay somewhere around me, lights were coming on in 1912 in high-up windows, city people beginning to prepare for gathering in special places for the special times the blue hour promises. *L'heure bleu:* not every night anywhere. And in most places never. But now in this beginning Manhattan evening I could feel it powerfully present, a lovely lonely joy with a promise possible only just here and just now and in the moments to follow, all around and close by, just ahead somewhere if I would simply rise and walk through the cooling blue dusk out into it.

I didn't hurry, just stood and began to walk, following the windings of the path, moving more or less toward Fifth Avenue and Fifty-ninth Street. Before I reached them I heard what for me became forever the sound of the blue hour. A gay brassy sound, not electronic but — my ears knew this — a real sound made by the actual squeezing of a fat rubber bulb mounted on a wide running board beside an out-in-the-open driver. *Hohn-nk!* it said like a trumpet call, then gloriously sounded again, and I grinned and began to hurry.

No surprise to turn a last curve of the path and suddenly see the Plaza standing alone once again against the blue-hour sky. No surprise to walk out onto Fifth Avenue and see the street lying once more in its old narrow width. No surprise as I walked ahead toward Fifty-ninth Street to see all traffic lights vanished. And then to stop on the curb and see the big boxy taxicabs — passenger seats enclosed, drivers out alone under a little canopy — parked down at the Plaza's Fifty-ninth Street entrance. It did startle me to look across the street and see that the fountain before the Plaza didn't yet exist. But to my left directly across the street General Sherman sat in the blue dusk unchanged on his big gilded horse.

The hotel looked the same, I thought standing there at the curb, my eyes moving up along its sides — except that now nothing around it stood higher than the Plaza. I stood looking up at the scatter of room lights across its side, more coming on as I watched. Directly across Fifth from the Plaza, the room lights of another great hotel, and of still a third catercorner across from the Plaza. This cluster of great hotels coming to life here in the new dusk seemed thrilling to me, and I stood watching more and more of their rooms spring into yellow squares against the slowly darkening sky of Manhattan. In the almost spring of 1912. In *l'heure bleu.* Then three wonderful things happened almost simultaneously.

I saw a cab — a tall red box behind a driver at a nearly upright wheel — pull into the curb at the Plaza's Fifty-ninth Street entrance. Before it had fully stopped, its rear door opened over the curb, and a girl — hardly having to stoop, the cab roof was so high — walked out; ran out, really, and across the walk. A smiling happy girl in a wide, wide hat and a long slim pale dress, a hand reaching down to pluck up its hem as her foot touched the stairs.

As this excited girl reached the top of the stairs someone inside opened and held the door for her, and I heard music from inside, a strange-sounding orchestra, piano and violin very strong — music with a fast, almost modern beat. And in the moment of hearing this sudden music and of seeing the girl step into the hotel, another thing happened. The red cab chugging out into the street again, I saw the driver's gauntleted hand squeeze the plump bulb beside him, heard the happy *hohnnk!* . . . and precisely in that instant, the brassy sound still sounding through the blue dusk, all the streetlamps along Fifty-ninth and down Fifth

silently blossomed into light, and a rush of diz-
zying pleasure moved up through me, and I
stepped out to cross the street toward the Plaza,
toward the music, toward whatever waited for
me now.

14

I CROSSED Fifty-ninth Street, only three slow-
moving automobiles chugging harmlessly toward
me, and the distant electric eye of a cable car.
No Fifth Avenue entrance to the Plaza that I
could see; the familiar pillars, yes, but plate glass
between them, behind them a glittering restaurant, everyone in evening dress.

So into the Plaza at Fifty-ninth Street; then
I followed the music down a carpeted corridor
to *The Tea Room*, and my sketch here is my
memory of what I saw. It was wild, a quartet
somewhere back there pounding out the ragtime
beat: piano, trumpet, violin, and a harp plucked
and swiped at by a shoulder-swaying lady in a
long lavender dress. The men in suits, ties, vests,
and nearly every woman wore a hat — big hats
with big brims, or headbands, one of them sport-
ing a two-foot-high ostrich feather rising straight
up from the woman's forehead, jiggling steadily
— I could follow it moving around the floor.

Standing there watching, listening, grinning, I
knew the words of this music, but . . . what

were these people *doing?* Because they were moving to the beat all right, really moving, shoulders, arms, hips, feet, and wagging heads. But in my sketch I've tried to show how some women — like the one in the foreground — held their left arms oddly, hand on hip but with the elbow swung around to point straight forward. Others, like the woman at the left, let their forearms dangle limp. Occasionally a man bent his partner far back, nearly horizontal.

Abruptly the music ended: *See that ragtime couple over there,* I stood mentally singing along, *see them throw their feet* — and they did everyone abruptly kicking one foot back — *up in the air!* Suddenly everyone joined in singing the final words aloud: "It's a bear, it's a bear," and now they yelled it, "IT'S A BEAR!" The music stopped, and every dancer out there hunched shoulders and, feet shuffling, waddled off the floor, grinning, in imitation, I realized, of a walking bear. It was something.

A waiter in dark green trimmed with gilt braid stopped before me. "One, sir?" I said yes, and he glanced around worriedly, frowning, but it was a token gesture. "I'm afraid we have no empty tables, sir. Would you care to share one?" He turned, nodding toward a table at which a young woman sat alone. She smiled and nodded tolerantly. I said fine, and he took me there. She wore a headband with a plume of some kind, and sat fixing an earring as I arrived. "Tea for two?" said the waiter to me, and I glanced at her, saying, "You sure this is all right?" and she nodded, saying, "I'm not usually so bold, but I do dislike sitting alone at a *thé dansant*. Tea dance."

"Oh, I know what *thé dansant* means," I said, pulling out my chair. "I speak impeccable French. *L'heure bleu!*"

She said, *"Tiens. Croissant!"*

I was running out of French, wondered if I could risk this, and did. *"Merde!"* But she laughed, and we sat smiling, and were okay, and I was glad to be exactly here because I was remembering something. I remembered the occasional somber loneliness, like no other kind, of entering a time in which you know not one single human being on earth. So that to sit here and be able to talk and laugh a little was nice.

The waiter was back with a tray that looked silver and maybe was. He set out cups, saucers, two teapots, cream jugs, all of thin white china, and a silver sugar bowl, tiny spoons, cloth napkins. And I sat, during this ceremony, looking at the girl across the table, and — it was the headband — a phrase, a name, rose up in my mind: *the Jotta Girl*. Because when I was a five-year-old, I lived for some months with an aunt who, in the 1920s, had been what she called a flapper. And one day in a drawer she came upon something she'd worn then, a kind of elaborate headband with tall feathers and a lot of glass jewels, not much different from the one across the table from me now. My aunt put on her old headband and did a dance, expertly it seemed to me, which she called the Charleston, singing a song of her youth called "Ja Da." I loved that dance and song, and occasionally when I asked, she'd do it again while I tried to imitate it, to her amusement. And I loved the song for its nonsense words. We'd both dance and sing, a staccato "Jotta . . ." a beat, then again, "Jotta!" Another beat, then the part that delighted my primitive five-year-old soul, "Jotta, jotta, jink-jink-jing!"

So now the girl across from me, pouring our tea, became in my mind the Jotta Girl.

She said, "My name is Helen Metzner," and I said, "I'm Simon Morley." But she didn't look like a Helen to me. She looked faintly familiar, like someone I'd known, so she remained the Jotta Girl for me. We fussed with our tea, she added sugar, intent on the stirring. Then, retreating to our earlier joke for something to say, she said, "Your accent is a bit different from many French. Better, of course!"

"Of course. Because they're the ones who fail the accent test." She smiled, waiting; she was good-looking. "Even if you're born French that accent can be too much. So at eighteen you have to take the accent test. And even with coaching and special gargling practice, eleven percent fail, and are exiled forever."

"Given the dreaded red passport," she said.

"Allowed home for a brief visit only once every ten years."

" *'Allo, Maman!* I am 'ome!"

"*Sacre bleu!* For 'ow long!"

We relaxed then, we'd made it over the hump. The musicians were back, and now they began something I didn't know, but with the same nice ragtime beat. "Well," said the Jotta Girl, "it's a tea dance. We have our tea, so now — shall we dance?"

I wear a wedding ring, and had my left hand lying on the table where she could see it; I didn't want any misunderstanding. "I'm sorry," I said, and was able to add truthfully, "I don't know how."

"Oh, of course you do; it's easy; look at them." We watched them, dancing as they had before. Then the little musical group swung into an old friend, "Alexander's Ragtime Band," and I grinned and began singing the few words I knew, "Come on along! . . . Come on along!" and the Jotta Girl jumped up. "Yeah! Come on along!" she sang, holding out both hands, "to Alexander's Ragtime Band!" and I had to stand, and walk out onto that wild dance floor with her.

I was right; I couldn't dance to this. But so was she: Yes I could. Sort of. She more or less led me, guiding, keeping me out of harm's way. And I imitated what I saw all around me, swaying my shoulders, kicking out when everyone else did, whirling, doing the best I could — and it was fun, exciting, even hilarious; we were laughing. But when the little musical group under the arches paused, leaning forward to turn their pages, I had the good sense to turn toward the edge of the floor.

Back at the table, we sipped a little tea, which was getting cold. I liked being here in this busy room, all a-murmur with talk and laughing and the happy chink of china. I sat back, looking around at the marvelous big hats; looked for the girl who'd come running in from the red taxi, and couldn't find her; looked for the two-foot ostrich feather, and spotted it immediately, swaying over the dance floor. Then the musicians swung into "Oh, You Beautiful Doll!" and I didn't want to be anywhere but here. But I made myself lean forward toward the Jotta Girl to say, "This is fun, a lot of fun. But I've only just arrived. From a long way off," I said truthfully. "And" — this suddenly turned true with saying it — "I'm worn out."

"Of course. So was I the first day I arrived; New York is so exciting. Are you staying at the Plaza?"

"Yes." I'd picked up the check — two dollars — and I put down three.

"So am I. Thank you for the tea," she said, and released me gracefully by adding, "I'll just stay and finish mine. *Bonne nuit, monsieur.*"

I'd thought I was going straight up to my room, but — I was too excited — in the lobby I walked on past the elevators, and out of the hotel into this night of early 1912. On the curb, there in the new darkness, I stood facing Central Park just across the street. Was *l'heure bleu* over? Yes. The trees and shrubbery of the Park stood night-black and formless now. At regular intervals under the streetlamps, circles of weak orange light silvered the streetcar rails and nicked into the curb. I glanced up at the sky; the air still clear here in these early years of the century, the stars hung as low and sharp as they did back in my time with Julia. Across the street a man and a woman, his hat in his hand — it was still daytime warm — stepped down off the curb and crossed at a long leisurely angle toward an enticing row of lighted globes along the front of the Savoy Hotel.

From the street came the steady clattering grumble of the cable down in its slot between the cable car rails, tugging a car toward me from my left. I stood watching the car's round electric eye flitter its light along the uneven brick pavement ahead. Something puzzled me: on each side a rectangle of light accompanied the car, sliding along the bricks beside it. Then I saw that the car was open, without sides, and now I could see its passengers on benches extending across the width of the car, no aisle. A couple dozen teenagers, high schoolers, sat there under the ceiling lights, talking, laughing a lot, the girls all with long hair, some in long braids down the back, the boys all in suits, ties, and stiff collars. This was an open-sided summertime streetcar chartered for tonight, I supposed, in this spring-like weather. Now I could see the overhead lighted bulbs — of clear glass with spike tips just as the glassblowers had left them. A blue-uniformed conductor stood casually on an outside running board the length of the car. A pair of girls, one with a big pink bow on her hair, sat, one busily talking, gesturing, the other listening, nodding, smiling. This wonderful open streetcar trundled past me now, the moving rectangle of light beside it sliding along, reaching just over the curb, to momentarily brush a wavering polish onto the rounded tips of my shoes. The listening girl, still nodding at whatever the other was saying, glanced casually out toward me, and — elated with this glorious sight — I lifted my arm on impulse and waved.

She saw me, and even in this fractional moment I had time to wonder: Would a young woman of the 1880s wave back? No, she surely would not. Or a young woman of the latter part of the twentieth century — would she wave from the window of a bus on this very same street? No, she wouldn't risk being misunderstood. But the girl of this New York here on a fine evening in this early year of this fresh new century saw my little wave, smiled immediately, and without thought or pause waved back. Just a little flutter of the fingers as she rolled on by, but it told me I was visible, told me I was truly here standing on this sidewalk in this moment of her passing. And to me it said — this immediate, unconsidered, open response — that I had come into a time worth protecting.

The little island of light, slowing for Fifth Avenue just ahead, rolled on by, and I'd had enough for this night. All around me in the darkness the new city and whatever it might hold for me lay waiting. But for the moment I was content, and an almost welcome tiredness liberated itself to move through my mind and body. And I turned back to the hotel, to register and go up to my room and a room service dinner. And finally to bed and — I'd brought no wardrobe — to sleep in my funny new underwear.

15

THIS IS my room, the photo from a hotel brochure I picked up at the desk when I registered — the room I dressed in next morning looking down at Central Park to take my mind off the soiled linen I had to put on. I hate putting on dirty clothes, socks especially, so after a fast breakfast, out to a Sixth Avenue haberdashery. And at a shop next door, on impulse, bought a red leather box Kodak. Thought about a topcoat, but gambled it would warm up. Back for a shower, then a leisurely walk down Fifth Avenue with my new camera.

I snapped this first, the Plaza Hotel there at the right. And at the left, the Savoy. Both would be new to Julia, and astonishingly tall. Directly

ahead, the peaked roof of an old friend; the Vanderbilt mansion. But what were the two tall buildings up ahead there? I snapped this scene, then stood a moment or so longer looking down Fifth. Was this the look of 1912 New York? If so, I liked it. There's no escaping that nineteenth-century New York is — well, ugly. The buildings have a squeezed-down, huddled look; cramped

— I like it for reasons other than its look. But this — tall buildings but not inhumanely tall, and well separated — this was an open, airy, sunny city; it occurred to me that this was how Paris still looked in the years up ahead.

I set out to walk down Fifth for a way; too early to go down Broadway hunting for what I hoped and was afraid to find. My new camera, like the city around me, was a novelty, so for a time it was *clickety-click,* snap, snap, snap. I crossed Fifty-ninth to head on down Fifth, turned to glance back, and saw a double-decker bus rumbling toward me. I'd heard of them but never seen one, and had to snap this. Watching the bus roll toward me in the little viewfinder, I was surprised to see that it was green; I'd always thought they were red. There at the right, the Netherland. This whole new corner would amaze Julia.

I snapped the bus as I stood beside the Van-

derbilt mansion, and now I walked across Fifth Avenue for a better look, then quickly raised my camera in time to snap the girl watcher — see him there on the walk? Hoping, I suppose, for a glimpse of ankle. And I accidentally caught

something else I'd see a lot of in this New York — the street-corner loafer there by the lamppost. A moment later, he leaned his shoulder against it. Julia would be pleased when I told her the Vanderbilt mansion still looked just as we so often saw it walking up Fifth Avenue toward the Park of a Sunday — Julia never failing to wonder what it looked like inside, and I never failing to suggest that we drop in and see, explaining to the Vanderbilts that we were just passing by.

A car came rolling into the mansion grounds through the Fifty-eighth Street gate, and I strolled over and tried to sneak this, but got caught, as you see. It was a fairly big camera, hard to hide, and at Fifty-seventh Street as I stood waiting to

cross, an open car came chugging along toward
Fifth. I could easily have skipped across in front
of it, but instead I raised my camera, pretending

to take something up ahead. And I snapped this
as it rolled past, the beauty inside giving me the
haughty eye. The young guy at the wheel was

singing "Turkey Trot," and as I walked on behind their car I sang softly: "Everybody's doin' it, doin' it!" This was fun, walking — strolling, really — along this sunny, leisurely street. Some kids were playing up ahead on the walk, and when I stopped

to take this, I got caught once more, by the tow-head there, and as I passed he said, "Juh take my pitcha, Mista?" I said, "No, you broke the camera." There's a first time for everyone to hear

this ancient joke, and he stared, then grinned
and whirled to inflict it on the girl playing behind
him. "D'man says you broke duh camera!"

I'd suddenly recognized the building up ahead
with the awning, the St. Regis Hotel. I walked
on a block, and near the corner I took this. From
under the awning and behind the hedge I heard

voices and the cheerful clink of china. Lunch?
I pulled out my watch; only a bit after eleven
— they were serving breakfast and I wished I'd
known and sat here too, under that awning watching the easy leisurely traffic move by.

Onward, watching, happy, I saw this approaching, turned and caught the bride inside smiling
out at me, at my camera, and at the world.

Then I stood winding my film, and a couple
strolled by me, her face merry and beautiful. She
was young, not more than thirty, and it occurred
to me that she'd been born about the time I met

Julia. And that by my own time far ahead she'd be . . .
but that wasn't a thought I wanted.

They'd gone by, but I took their picture anyway, here beside a formidable building I didn't know. Took it because they were

young here in 1912; took it for the twin spires of St. Pat's Cathedral up there ahead alone on the sky — it would have pleased Julia that at last both spires were finished. And I took this picture for the fire hydrant there at the curb, the lamppost on the corner, and to capture this quiet instant of this fine vanished day. A dozen more steps, and the couple turned into the building beside them. A moment or so later when I passed the entrance and saw the polished brass plaque reading *Gotham Hotel*, I wondered what my young couple were doing in there; then wondered if they were married, sort of hoping, too, they weren't. And walked on then, wondering why I should hope that.

Up ahead, the southwest corner at Fifty-third Street meant *Allen Dodsworth's School for Dancing*. But no longer. His sign was gone, though the building still stood. I wasn't surprised: the dancing I'd seen last night wasn't what Allen Dodsworth had taught. Was he still alive? And what stood on that corner far ahead in my own time? The Tishman Building? I wasn't quite sure.

On past one of the great old Fifth Avenue mansions I knew so well, from the outside. I turned to look back, then moved to one side, composing this view, which I'm a little bit proud of. See how the old Fifth Avenue of the foreground sort of frames the new twentieth-century Fifth Avenue of great fashionable hotels rising behind it? Must be giving the owners of the house beside it fits.

Click-click, snap, snap. Just ahead lay a stretch

of the street, this one, looking almost unchanged, one of the great old mansions serenely taking up half the sidewalk, St. Pat's over there at the left and on ahead, across the street to the south of it, an old friend (Howdy!), the Buckingham Hotel, looking as permanent as St. Pat's, but I knew

I was seeing a ghost. Because as I framed this scene in the little window of my viewfinder, I could also see, standing in the Buckingham's place far ahead of time, Saks Fifth Avenue looking just as permanent. Well, Saks became an old friend too.

At Forty-ninth Street I stopped, stepping just around the corner to watch a gray limousine, the gray-uniformed chauffeur sitting out front in the open, hunched over his wheel, as he swung off Fifth into West Forty-ninth, made a tight little U-turn, and stopped before an imposing brick building. The chauffeur hopped out and stood almost at attention by the curbside rear door. Then the doors of the building were swung open by a uniformed attendant, and out trooped this impressive bunch, to head down to their waiting

limousine, their faces certain of the world and their places in it. Then for a few minutes I stood, my back against a sun-warmed building wall, to watch other faces move past my eyes along Fifth, wishing I had the nerve to lift my camera and snap some of these faces head-on. What were they thinking, these 1912 people, their shoe leather scuffing or tapping by? Who were they? People of other times aren't simply people like us except for the funny clothes. These faces were different, even the children's, formed by the thoughts, events, and feelings of the unique experiences of their own time. So what did these passing faces tell me? I thought that they looked . . . serene. That most of them seemed cheerful, eyes fully open, aware of and enjoying this particular day. And — what else? There *was* something else. They didn't seem afraid, I decided. Or worried, most of them. And no one I saw looked angry. These people walking and strolling past my eyes along Fifth Avenue through their own time and world seemed to me secure and confident in it. I knew that they were wrong; that this pleasant peaceful world had only a few years left to it. Unless . . . but it seemed preposterous that I could possibly do anything at all about that.

Walking toward me now, here came a not-quite-elderly marvel, a boulevardier, a bona fide dandy with Kaiser Wilhelm mustache, gray, striped trousers, black coat with plush lapels and collar, heavy gold watch chain, silver-headed cane, glittering silk hat. I walked toward him, trying to make myself lift the camera and snap him, but didn't. Couldn't. A spear of lightning would have flashed down and instantly killed me.

But when he had passed, heading north there on Fifth Avenue, cane swinging beautifully, I turned around to catch him, but waited a moment, fiddling with the camera, then pretended to take my man up ahead — and instead snapped these marvelous chattering girls. Yes, *girls,* damn it. Of course they are young women, but to sometimes say "girls" was never to call them children.

The English language is hardworking; the meaning of a word can vary by context. And to compare using "girl" for "young woman" with the Southern use of "boy" for a black man is thoughtless, and just plain dumb.

Well, all right. Okay. Yes, yes, I'm fine now. The girl on the right is wearing a green-and-white-striped coat, the young woman in the middle a maroon dress, and the other — your choice now — a kind of bottle green, I think you'd call it. She caught me in the act of snapping this — and I caught another young-woman watcher behind them.

Where was *The Rev. and Mrs. C. H. Gardner's Boarding and Day School for Young Ladies and Gentlemen?* Gone. Julia sometimes talked of sending Willy there, but I didn't.

Fifth Avenue was changing more obviously now, as I walked on. I was seeing more and more storefronts. And *Apartment to Let* signs like this one, which I took because I remembered the house

there with the heraldic lions as the home of a rich family. A little depressing somehow, and then I glimpsed something just ahead at Forty-fourth Street that made me hurry on to see what it was. I walked on across Forty-fourth Street, grinning with pleasure and using my next-to-last film to take this wonderful little wedding cake of a building. What *was* this? I had to see, and I walked catercorner across Fifth Avenue past the cop. And

then, standing under the awning looking up the stairs, I saw the polished brass plate that told me this was Delmonico's, moved uptown. A hand touched my elbow, and a woman's voice behind me said, "Well, I *am* surprised! Are you here for the lecture?" I turned, and the Jotta Girl's face, framed in the cartwheel brim of a pale blue hat, smiled up at me, and I smiled back.

"Well!" I said a little stupidly. "What are you doing here?"

"Following you, of course! Are you coming in?"

At the curb women were arriving steadily, mostly middle-aged or elderly, stepping out from limousines, cabs, or carriages — more limos than cabs — car doors slamming, low-horsepower engines clunking as they pulled away.

"Well, I don't know," I said. Now here came the young women, smelling just great, laughing, looking so splendid in their enormous hats, and showing some fine ankle as they plucked up their skirt hems to climb the stairs. Accompanying a lot of them, and all the best-looking ones, were young or youngish men, nearly every damn one of them eight feet tall.

"Oh, don't be a stick!" said the Jotta Girl, her hand at my elbow urging me on. "This lecture should be very helpful to you!" and she smiled at some kind of joke.

"Okay." We walked on up. "What's going to be so helpful?"

She nodded at a large poster just inside the open doors. It stood on an easel of gilded bamboo, and read in expert lettering, the margins decorated with painted ivy leaves: *Mrs. Charles Henry Israel's Committee on Amusement and Vacation Re-*

sources for Working Girls Will Present Professor Duryea's Demonstration of the Dance Promptly at 10 A.M. I understood her joke now, and said, "I thought I'd done my share of entertaining working girls with my dancing last night," and she smiled again.

No one inside seemed to be taking tickets, and we followed the crowd up a flight of carpeted stairs at our right, the women ahead of us daintily lifting their skirt hems, and I realized how well I was adapting, already an expert ankle watcher. Down a short hallway now, the women, chattering, laughing a lot, leaving a trail of perfumed air. *Okay, Rube; I'm following orders. When do I get lucky?* A man just behind us said, "Hello there, Helen," and the Jotta Girl turned to smile and answer, "Hello, Archie," and I wondered, Helen Who? Into a ballroom now: wood floor, mirror panels inset in the walls at intervals, a small raised platform up front. Rows of gilt chairs had been set out, the crowd sidling into them, women doing that splendid skirt-smoothing motion as they sat down. Up front, before the raised platform, stood a half-circle of chairs, green ribbon strung along their backs to mark off a reserved section of floor.

I glanced around as we sat down, and saw that among the few men in the audience a couple were reporters, I thought, because they seemed to be jotting down names, and it occurred to me that this might be a pretty social crowd.

Up on the platform three men in formal morn-

221

ing dress sat waiting, music open before them: a pianist, clarinetist, and violinist. And at stage center, on a gilt chair, a large, magnificently impressive, gray-haired woman in a maroon beaded dress, pince-nez glasses hanging from a dime-size gold button fastened at her chest: Mrs. Israel herself, I had no doubt. Nodding, smiling graciously, she sat talking eagerly to the man seated at her right in a double-breasted black frock coat whose hem touched his knees. He was fifty, maybe, dark graying hair worn longer than any I'd seen anywhere else. His wife, I guessed, to whom Mrs. Israel turned now, wore a white evening dress with a gardenia pinned to one side at her waist.

Behind and around us the laughter and chatter continued, and I was certain I caught a whiff — and sneaked a look around me — of cigarette smoke. I glanced at the Jotta Girl, and she nodded. "One of the young ones sneaking a smoke," she said. "It's all the rage. Glad you came?"

"Of course. Actually I'm a big fan of Madam Israel's. Wouldn't miss a lecture."

Mrs. Israel stood up, smiling benignly out at us, one hand clasping the other on her stomach, serenely confident that the talk would quickly subside, and she was right. She began to speak, and what she said, as well as I can remember, was: "Welcome, my fellow social workers. How very pleasant to see you here this morning, so many leaders and leaders of the future of our New York Society willing to give of themselves." She paused, looking out at us, her smile fading to let us know that now came the serious part. "In the course of your committee's vigilant watch on the dance halls of New York, it has become necessary, we believe, to strike out at some of the forms of the Turkey Trot and the Grizzly Bear which have appeared even where Society dances. We are all of us, certainly, modern. But that there should be some standard of decency in social dancing we do not doubt." I gave a quick sideways glance at the Jotta Girl just as she glanced at me, and we both held on to our serious expressions, facing front again. "What is good, however, and what is bad? How are the supervisors to answer the working girl when she protests that everyone is dancing the Turkey Trot? But an innocent version of the Turkey Trot may well be preserved, if rechristened" — I leaned toward the Jotta Girl to whisper, "The Buzzard Bounce?" and she folded her lips in — "rechristened lest the dancers of the poor be misled into thinking there is high sanction for the Turkey Trot as they see it in the ill-supervised halls that are their only refuge from dark and dismal homes. We should all of us here today know just what these things are; for the girl who dances at Sherry's has just as much responsibility for the welfare of the girl who dances at the Murray Hill Lyceum as has the recreation supervisor in that district."

Mrs. Charles Henry Israel was really saying these things up there on the platform. "We are met this morning to answer this question by observing the Turkey Trot and the other newer dances performed as they ought to be danced, if at all. The demonstration will be conducted, together with his charming wife, by one who, for many of you, will require no introduction. May I present Professor Duryea, a teacher of dancing who thinks about his art." Smiling, supergracious, left hand splaying across her chest, she turned and, half bowing, nodded at the professor.

He stood up, taller than I'd thought, and thinner, his double-breasted frock coat like a tube with black silk lapels. He took a step forward, smiled for a moment, then said, "The Monkey Glide. The Lame Duck. The Turkey Trot, the Bunny Hug, the Grizzly Bear, the Bird Hop, all come hailed as 'the newest thing,' yet are only slight variations, if any, of the slow rag. Can these new dances, if properly done, offer an occasional variation of our repertoire? Perhaps. But I do not believe that Society can accept the uglier extremes of these dances. For there is no safety in retaining anything that departs from a correct position, as in the impeccable waltz, where the man has his right arm around the girl's waist, and her right hand rests in his left, which must be extended. Only last Wednesday I dropped into Terrace Garden for observation, and saw a policeman there in the middle of the floor busy barring the Turkey Trot, and he did it by two gestures, one to indicate that the man's left arm must be extended, and one that the languorous half-walk must not be substituted for the good old-fashioned twirl. These simple rules, born of the bluecoat's own experience in suppression, cannot be improved upon. Yet without the presence o a bluecoat, closer and closer the partners dance. And more and more perceptible becomes the tremor that keeps time with the ragging of the orchestra. This is the evolution so often followed, and can take place not only from season to season within the world of dancers but within a single evening." With a professional smiling nod and gracious half-turn of left hand and wrist, he beckoned to his wife, who smiled and stood.

He took her hand, and they stepped down into the little area marked off by ribboned chairs. Both holding their smiles, they turned to face each other maybe eight or ten inches apart. She set her left hand on her hip, fingers to the back, elbow swung well forward. He put his right hand through the loop of her elbowed-out arm, his palm covering the back of her hand. They clasped their other hands, raising them well above their heads. Professor Duryea nodded at the musicians, the pianist struck a chord, nodded at the other two, and the group began — sedately, the violin strong and rich — *Oh, you beautiful doll*. And the Duryeas began — truly skilled and graceful about it — a kind of equally sedate hop from one foot to the other so that they rocked from side to side, their clasped hands moving in a wide overhead arc, the distance between them rigidly maintained.

Continuing to dance, the professor said, "The Turkey Trot as it *can* be danced, should be danced; who could object? But right here on Fifth Avenue I have seen the change of which I spoke. At the start the participants would be dancing with the hop and the arms held out. Four hours later, with the room more crowded and the dancers more weary and more in the spell of the music . . ." This seemed to be a cue, the trio now speeding up the tempo and — is this the word? — slurring it a bit, and to my ears it really did sound a little lewder. "The man and his partner would dance closer and closer." And now so did the Duryeas. "And as they circle the floor, the hop becomes more of a glide." Their two raised arms had gradually lowered as the Professor talked, and now their other arms lowered to each other's waist. "Thus the Turkey Trot becomes almost indistinguishable" — both of them crouched a little, unclasping their upraised arms to bring them, too, down to the other's waist — "from The *Shiver!*" They began shuddering their shoulders to *You great big beautiful doll,* and the audience murmured; just behind me a woman gasped, a little theatrically, I thought; and I saw a woman in our row sit bolt upright to frown dramatically. But I heard a good part of the audience behind us snicker.

Above the nice rhythmic piano, swooning violin, and tootling clarinet — I had the feeling the musicians liked this — Mrs. Israel called out, "How many have seen this very thing done in the dance hall!" The Jotta Girl's hand flew up, and as I glanced around, dozens of younger

226

women were raising their hands, and an indulgent laughter moved through the room. This was an audience more young than not, looking beautiful in their cloches and wide-brimmed hats, and I understood that the young ladies weren't taking this too seriously.

And realized an instant later that they'd come for more reason than the Duryeas, because the room stirred, murmuring. I turned and now a young man and woman stood at the back of the hall. In a way I couldn't quite figure out, they looked and were different from the rest of us. They stood quietly, polite and attentive to the dancing Duryeas, but they held the eye, and for a moment or two I forgot to turn front again. She was beautiful in a very young, innocent-faced way. Wore a long pink dress to just above her white-stockinged ankles, and a wide-brimmed pink hat set way back to frame her face and light brown hair with a pink wheel of brim. His hair, shiny black, was combed straight back, his face a thin cheerful triangle, and his suit — well, his suit was checked and sharp. She smiling, he grinning, they stood looking happy to be here, and I knew — how, I don't know, but it was easy to see — that these were stage people, onstage right now, somehow far more alive and interesting, just standing there, than anyone else in this room: you wanted to go back and join them. People made themselves face front again, smiling excitedly, heads ducking to murmur or listen to quick whispering. But these were courteous, well-bred people, and they quickly silenced themselves, attentively watching the Duryeas through the final moments of their dance. Not quite final. As the last notes — *Oh . . . you . . . beautiful doll!* — plinked and tootled, the Professor "signaled to the pianist," the *Times* said next morning, though I didn't see the signal, and "the Gaby Glide strains floated out across the room and away they went with the dance at its worst. A faintly suppressed ripple of laughter could be heard" — that was true — "and there were frank chuckles when cheek touched cheek, and the languor of the movement was intensified."

They finished the Gaby Glide, not looking much different to my ignorant eyes than they had before. Then Professor Duryea and his wife joined hands — she had a great smile; I liked her — to bow together, getting a fine hand, certainly including mine. They sat down, pleased, Mrs. Israel rising to thank them, which she did very nicely. Then she smiled to say, "I think the Professor and Mrs. Duryea have shown us — in the *earlier* portion of their splendid performance," she added, getting her laugh, "that an innocent version of the Turkey Trot may well be preserved if rechristened," and the Jotta Girl winked at me.

Mrs. Israel beckoned to the new couple at the back of the ballroom, and up they came, walking around the edge of the room, smiling across it to acknowledge the polite tips-of-the-fingers preliminary applause, and suddenly I saw who he was. Of course I'd never seen him before, only in pictures, but unmistakably here, edging along the side of the room so that he continued to face us, came a very young version of him, grinning, cocky, having a great time.

"The morning was one of contrast," the *Times* reported next day, which I quote because it was true, "and the Duryeas, he in a frock coat and she in a simple evening dress of white, gave way to Al Jolson and Florence Cable of the Winter Garden, she with her hat on, young and gay . . . he in high jollity . . ."

Jolson stood facing us now, smiling and really looking at us, glad to see *us*, it seemed. We all grinned back, and he said, "I picked up the art of dancing as I saw it on the Barbary Coast where I used to sell papers as a San Francisco boy." His voice, I thought, had just barely a touch of raspiness, and seemed to fit the look on his face of a man absolutely confident in himself. Suddenly he did a fast little dance step of some kind, the patent leather of his shoes sparking light. Three seconds of that, no more; then he suddenly stopped, knees still bent, both hands thrusting downward to one side, fingers splayed, and he grinned, and had us: we loved him. He flicked a finger at the pianist who instantly began, clawed hands bouncing off the keys in rhythm with his shoulders, and even I knew we were hearing ragtime.

And then how they danced — together, then whirling apart, then together again, Florence Cable simply marvelous, Jolson with the kind of nimble effortless perfection that makes you suddenly sure, knowing better, that you could do it too. They danced close, then threw themselves apart, hands clasped at arms' length as they leaned far apart, bodies making a V. Together again, chins very nearly on each other's shoulders, feet flying, hands — I don't know how their hands were or what they were doing, but oh, they were great. They stopped, piano still going, and Jolson said, "It's all the same dance. Call it Turkey Trot, Bunny Hug, Lovers, Walk Back, Bird Hop, as you will. Strip off the variations — just watch us! — and they all come down to the same thing." Again they moved, the happy pianist bouncing from one tune to another, and I guess they moved into and out of various dances, because I heard people murmuring dance names. But — he was right — they were the same dance, and I was wishing I could do what Al Jolson was doing. They stopped again, the pianist continuing, Jolson sweating a little now. "Fifteen or twenty dance halls there on the Barbary Coast," he said, "doing most of their business on the half-drunk sailors in port. And — what do you expect! — all those ginks could *do* was half skate around the dance floor to begin with. There was a Negro cabaret there on the Barbary Coast, and they say it all started there; they called it the Texas Tommy." He grabbed Miss Cable, and they flashed around the floor in the Texas Tommy, Jolson looking comically drunk. They stopped. "And then the orchestra would hit up, and they'd rag it a bit"

— he grinned at the pianist, whose hands and shoulders took the cue — "and then strike out on the minors that are more seductive, I guess." The pianist slowed, striking out on the minors, I'm sure, and Al Jolson and Florence Cable pulled closer and closer, tightly together now, very cheek to cheek, and I glanced up at Mrs. Israel, who looked fascinated. "And get closer and closer," Jolson said, then suddenly drew back to snap the fingers of both hands, "and . . . I guess I've said enough!" Then they just flew, feet flicking, flashing, in a whirling miracle of dancing, and the audience went nuts. "He was thunderously applauded," the *Times* said next morning, "as he and Miss Cable showed how it was done."

Then it was over, the applause wild, the two of them bowing, happy, and I glanced up at the Duryeas. They were applauding too, smiling, and — he was a pro — his smile looked real. But hers, I thought, didn't quite make it. You can't really tell what people are thinking, but I had to wonder what the Professor up there in his frock coat and artistically long hair felt in this moment. His face wasn't old but you could see how it would look when it was. He'd had his way for years, I imagined as I applauded; he'd taught the waltz and the two-step to generation after generation on into this new century. Now, suddenly and out of nowhere as it may have seemed to him, there stood these bowing young-sters down on the floor, and the applause was for their kind of dancing. Finally the applause tapered off, and I sat wondering what was going to happen to the Duryeas now. Maybe they'd saved their money.

16

OUT ON the walk with the Jotta Girl, I could see she expected me to ask her to lunch, but I didn't. Wouldn't. Stood smiling, nodding, bowing, tap dancing, and howling at the moon, but not a word about lunch. Said goodbye, turned and headed west, across on Forty-fourth Street, toward Broadway — I was on my way to hunt for Tessie and Ted, and that had to be alone.

I hadn't found them listed in any of the vaudeville ads of the *Times* or *Herald* at breakfast. And yet I knew, knew, *knew,* didn't I, that this had been the famous week, the never-to-be-forgotten, endlessly talked-about week that Tessie and Ted played Broadway?

On past the Algonquin Hotel, looking about the same I guess, except for its sign: blue and white enamel with clear-glass light bulbs picking out its name. What were Robert Benchley and Dorothy Parker right now, teenagers maybe?

Here at the Hippodrome — look across the roof between the towers: that's the Algonquin — I walked into the lobby and read the posters.

Plenty going on in here, but no Tessie and Ted.

At Broadway, beside a brand-new Astor Hotel, a little theater with a cupola: Marie Dressler in *Tillie's Nightmare*. Then I wandered all the way down Broadway, the *Times* building on Times

Square up ahead there. And walked into every theater lobby I saw, not quite sure which was

legit and which vaudeville. Stood just inside one, listening through the closed lobby doors to the young voice of a Douglas Fairbanks (in *A Gentleman of Leisure*) who hadn't yet heard of a teen-aged Mary Pickford.

I reached Times Square here; that's Seventh Avenue where the horse is trotting out, Hammer-

stein's Victoria Theatre over on the corner. This *was* vaudeville, I found out. Standing in the lobby I read: *17 Big-Star Acts. William Rock & Maude Fulton in their entirely new Satirical Protean Musical Revue with Co. of 12 . . . Walter C. Kelly, "The Virginia Judge" . . . Arthur Dunn & Marion Murray in "Two Feet from Happiness" . . . The Three Keatons, the Tumblebug Family*, with a family photograph, a smiling very young Buster in the middle. Seventeen big acts: *Lane & O'Donnel, Comedy Skit . . . Van Hoven, the Dippy, Mad Musician . . . Palfrey, Barton and Brown* (the tumbling law firm?). But Tessie and Ted? Nope.

So I wandered around, into and out of the West Forty-second Street theaters, like these. . . .

Checked with a stage manager (the little fat one). Nothing.

Then on down this famous Broadway of theaters: the New Amsterdam, Liberty, New York, Empire, Criterion, Lyceum, Knickerbocker, Garrick, Hudson, Harris, Gaiety, Park, Fulton, George

M. Cohan, Grand, Wallack's, Fifth Avenue, Winter Garden, Maxine Elliott's, Playhouse, Broadway, Casino, Lyric, Herald Square, Lew Fields . . . and more. A sophisticated Broadway of world-famous Rector's and Shanley's. Of opulent hotels: the Normandie, Marlborough, Knickerbocker . . .

But now also this leisurely daytime street of corner loafers and the Horatio Alger shoeshine boy. A street of barbershops, pool halls, and (I heard the sudden hollow clatter of wooden pins

from somewhere) bowling alleys. And a street of sidewalk fruit stands, and even a movie house. No fake glamour or glitz, but an almost homely street, this easy, comfortable daytime Broadway. I climbed a few steps of a lowered fire escape to take this. Across the street there, the Knickerbocker Theatre where tomorrow *The*

Greyhound would open . . . where tomorrow the Dove Lady would walk by — right *there,* right across the street. And standing on the walk to stare after her would be Z. Who next day would write a letter to say so. And which I had already read.

But Tessie and Ted? I walked on, clear down to Twenty-eighth Street here, the end of the

theatrical district. Checked out Daly's. And Joe Weber's next door. And — my last hope — Proctor's Fifth Avenue Theatre down at the end of the block there. No Tessie and Ted, but . . . there was the Dove Lady.

Listed along with the others on the vaudeville bill, her photo on a big lobby easel, a bird on each shoulder, she smiling out at the world; a good friendly face. And Madam Zelda, the world-renowned mind reader, and six other acts. I stood there at the Dove Lady's photo, bemused, thinking that just maybe Rube was right: Here the connections still existed. Here the people of Rube's handful of old dead letters still lived. Was I really in some odd way going to find the lost people I was hunting?

Yes, damn it, *yes,* if not here, then somewhere — and it occurred to me that there was one last place to hunt. And back at the hotel I bought a copy of *Variety,* took it up to my room, and, shoes off, lay back against the headboard, and found . . . twenty fine trained roosters. Found Deas, Reed and Deas. Found Nadje. Found — could it be — Ed Wynn's *mother?* Found this — as it seemed to me — sad and forlorn pair.

Found endless vaudeville acts, large and small, including a monkey man. What's that? And if you were a *first-class* monkey man, would your

mother be proud? Surely Mrs. Kuhn was proud of her three boys and their clever way with words.

I lay on my bed looking through column after column of ads like these — some big, some small — wondering who these people were, these monkey men, double-voiced people, and White Kuhns.

Well, they were people with problems, just like the rest of us, problems that sometimes showed up in their ads. This inimitable trio seemed to be having trouble with imitators. Even world-renowned Eva Tanguay had problems. Just like me. Through page after page, column upon column of ads like these, not a word of Tessie and Ted.

17

IN MY hotel room in the morning, walking across the carpet buttoning my shirt, I stopped at the window to see what was going on outside today. Nothing much, the usual, except . . . were the pedestrians across the street moving a little more quickly? Yes. Then a group of three boys, heading west, came running, passing the other pedestrians, and I finished with my shirt, grabbed a jacket, and went downstairs to stand on the curb staring toward Columbus Circle three blocks to the west. Lot of people over there, mostly men, all turning north into Central Park West, all in a hurry.

"What's going on?" said the Jotta Girl at my elbow.

"Don't know."

"Well, let's go *see!*" She took my arm, and we stepped down off the curb to cross. Then I gripped her elbow, holding her back; an open roadster was tootling along toward us from the east just a shade too fast — a dark green beauty, windshield folded flat down on the hood — but it slowed and stopped beside us. "Going to see

244

knobby shoes?" the driver said — to both of us, I guess, but looking at the Jotta Girl. He was maybe thirty-five, hatless, wearing a heavy black turtleneck. "Well, hop in!" Hands on his big wooden steering wheel, his idling engine going *chunka-chunka, chunka-chunka,* he sat grinning at us, open and friendly, nodding at the seat beside him.

I said, "Well . . ." but the Jotta Girl said, "Sure. Thanks!" We walked around the back of the car; two enormous spare tires lay flat, strapped to the back. He'd leaned across to open the door for us, and for some reason I got in first, surprising the Jotta Girl a little, and me too. She pulled the door closed, he shoved the shift lever, a heavy rod with a grip handle that rose straight up from the wooden floor, and we rolled on, keeping to the car tracks for a smooth ride. Suddenly I felt good; this was a fine day, the windshield folded flat down on the long hinged hood, the air gentle on our faces. Our driver sat glancing up at the sky, almost sniffing the air, then turned toward us with a big smile and said, "Looks like old knobby picked a good day."

I didn't know what he was talking about, but the Jotta Girl said, "I'm worried about him."

"Well, he's not worried, you can bet your boots." Our driver grinned at her. "My name's Coffyn," he said then, "Frank Coffyn," and the Jotta Girl, sounding surprised and delighted, said, "The aviator?" and he nodded, looking pleased. We told him our names; then the Jotta Girl sat

245

sneaking little looks at him. He had a longish thin face, dark blondish hair, and — no, he wasn't wearing it long, I saw, just needed a haircut. The wind was ruffling his hair, and when he sort of smoothed it back, the Jotta Girl said, "I expect your hair is permanently windblown from flying so much."

"Yep." He leaned forward to smile across me at her. "Used to be curly, but years of flying straightened it out." I could tell he'd used the line before, but she laughed.

At Columbus Circle we turned north, and up ahead at Sixty-second Street saw a steady straggle of people coming out of Central Park to cross the street, others coming from the north and south, some actually running, all heading for a big vacant lot on the corner. The lot, we saw driving toward it, stood enclosed by a ten-foot-high fence of new pine but already plastered with a big poster in giant type for something called Moxie. Inside the fencing — long, tan, and rising higher than the fence by a dozen feet — stood a tent. And as Frank Coffyn parked across the street from the lot, we saw cops all over the place, but a boy was managing to climb the fence by jumping up on a friend's back, then climbing quickly to his shoulders, and finally leaping to catch the fence top, hauling himself up fast before a cop could come running over. Another boy set his foot in the stirrup of a friend's clasped hands who shot him to the fence top, where he swung around on his belly to drop, grinning, out of sight.

We walked across the street toward a wide opening on the Sixty-second Street side of the fence, but cops stood barring the entrance there. Beyond them, inside on the trampled-down weeds, stood the long, high tent, and at its entrance a young man of around thirty speaking to the crowd of boys, men, and two or three women. He wore boots laced to the knees, and a tan leather jacket. "Roy Knabenshue," Frank Coffyn said, and lifting his arm, he began waving it slowly back and forth. "And from thence, wind permitting," Knabenshue was saying, "in a southerly direction." Some of the men — reporters — were making notes.

Knabenshue saw Coffyn's arm, and called, "Frank! Come on in!" To the cops who'd turned to look back at him, he called, "Let him in, please! He's an assistant!"

The cops nodded to Frank, who took us both by the arm saying, "We're all assistants," and walked us in. I don't know if Roy Knabenshue really had been waiting for Coffyn or not, but he beckoned to us now, turning to push aside the tent flap, then stood holding it for us, and we walked into the brown light filtering in through the canvas: I had no idea what we were going to see.

It was a balloon, almost filling the tent, a long dirigible-shaped balloon, enormous, its rounded bottom well over our heads, the sides almost touching the tent walls; it was like standing in a closet with an elephant. The thing rose clear up to the far-off tent roof; sixteen feet high at its thickest part, I learned the next day from the *Times*, and sixty-two feet long. The tent seemed full of men — no other women — and the Jotta Girl left to go stand outside.

I could see better now, adjusting to the light. The balloon hung just above us covered by a snug-fitting net from which ropes led down to a flimsy-looking framework. The bottom of the framework was a pair of narrow skids; long sand-bags lay across them to hold the thing to the ground. Someone, maybe Knabenshue, yelled, "Okay!" and the men in the tent began positioning themselves along the sides of the framework. Frank stepped up with them, so I did too. Some-one on the other side yelled something, and every-one on my side grabbed a rope and began shoving or kicking the sandbags off the runners. I did the same, feeling the sudden strong upward pull of the balloon.

We walked it out of the tent, the cops waving people aside. Outside at the fence entrance, people were crowding up against the cops as we came out, trying to look past them at us, kids jumping up to look over shoulders. Men came trotting out of the tent with the sandbags and tossed them down across the skids, anchoring the thing to the ground again.

Frank and I were able to step back then, and look up at the balloon, the Jotta Girl strolling over to stand with us. It surprised me that the balloon was yellow, a sharp bright yellow there just above us against the blue sky. "Shaped like a whale," the Jotta Girl murmured, and Frank nodded, adding, "Without a tail." It was: the great thing hung up there snub-nosed at the front, widening back to the shoulders, then tapering back to a tail-less end. The framework underneath was aluminum, I could see now. Mounted in the framework stood a little gasoline engine connected by a belt to a four-bladed propeller, and I could see that the blades were *cloth* — aluminum-painted cloth — or maybe leather, stretched tight over wooden paddle-shaped frames. At the rear, a great big rudder with a pair of horizontal stabilizers. And in between these, mounted on the runners, a seat about the size and shape of a bicycle seat, but with the edges cupped upward like a tractor seat.

And that was it; no belts, no parachute, just that seat, and now damned if Roy Knabenshue didn't step up and, grinning with the sheer fun of all this, sit down on that little seat and plant his feet on those inch-wide runners. The reporters, notebooks open, pencils ready, pressed around him, sort of pushing us aside. One of them called out to ask if flying in this wasn't dangerous. Knabenshue, sitting there as though he were on a bike, looked happily amazed at the thought.

"No," he said, "once you get over the first exciting sensation, the consciousness of danger leaves your mind entirely." The way he said this made me think he'd given this answer before and often. "It becomes a habit," he said, the reporters taking this down, "to float one thousand feet above the ground, just as it does to the ordinary man to walk around on it, and the task of building an airship — well, I really prefer to call it a dirigible balloon — is as simple as the task of navigating it, once you have become aware" — he was really talking like this — "of the existence of certain natural laws that we have to conform to."

That all seemed okay to everyone, heads nodding, but I half whispered to Frank, "Is that true? Isn't this dangerous?"

"Of course it is," he said quietly, "though he half believes that himself now; he's not the least fearful. But that little insufficiently powered creation could be turned upside down in an instant by an unexpected gust. A stray wind could tear it apart. It's a foolish little thing. And its day is over. The future is in strongly powered aeroplanes. I like the man; I met him last night. But he's a boy at heart, playing at this. And one day it will kill him."

The reporters finished, Knabenshue yelled, "Ready!" and we all stepped up again to hold our ropes, kicking the sandbags aside. We held the thing, then, maybe five feet above the ground. The nose pointed down a bit, and Knabenshue reached into one of a dozen sandbags hanging from the rigging around him, brought out a handful of sand, no more, and scattered it, watching the nose. It actually lifted a bit, and he scattered another handful, leveling the thing. He was sitting above us, and I couldn't see how but he started the engine, a slow *putt-putt* sound; then it sped up into a rapid *putter-putter-putter.* I wouldn't have trusted it on a golf cart, but Knabenshue yelled, "Ready!" again and we all let go of our ropes, stepping back, and up she went, nose dipping but immediately leveling.

Straight on up into the sky she went, not fast, not slow, the kids yelling and capering, the adults making that sort of awestruck groan you hear at a fireworks exhibition. Up a hundred feet, two hundred, I didn't know, but high enough to begin looking smaller. Straight on up, and looking great, a yellow whale in the blue sky, Knabenshue looking like a skier, feet wide apart on those flimsy little aluminum yardsticks, waving one arm at us, the other hanging on to something. Up a little more, then a breeze from the west pushed him out across Eighth Avenue toward the Park. Knabenshue moved his rudder, and — still rising — putt-putted off to the south.

The crowd broke to run out or walk fast, depending on age and condition, Coffyn saying, "Come on!" Across the street, into his car, and Coffyn U-turned slowly, squeezing his horn bulb again and again, the street full of kids running south. Then we got clear of them, and following the balloon above and a little ahead of us, I understood why it was yellow, moving along so plainly against this clear blue sky. Silhouetted against that long yellow oval, Knabenshue half stood, half sat, getting smaller and smaller as he slowly moved higher and higher, chugging along behind those ridiculous low-powered cloth propellers. On he sailed, passing almost directly over the Circle Theater just north and west of Columbus Circle. Frank steered us around Columbus Circle and onto Broadway, where Knabenshue seemed to be heading.

Frank sat snatching glances upward, hunched over that big wooden wheel, and the Jotta Girl and I just sat with our mouths open, heads tipped back, following Knabenshue. Sometimes he seemed directly over our heads, and sometimes either he or the street veered, bringing him to one side of Broadway or the other. On and up — slowly shrinking, Knabenshue stood on a pair of black threads underneath his yellow whale. On over the Upper Broadway hotel district, chugging along at close to a thousand feet, I thought. Now the small wind up there pushed him east directly over Seventh Avenue, it seemed. People began appearing at windows, looking up, and we saw them coming out onto roofs. On down to Fiftieth Street he sailed, and just west of the Winter Garden — moving his rudder, I expect — Roy Knabenshue began moving right down and high above the Great White Way itself.

And Broadway had become aware, the news traveling — by phone, I suppose — faster than Knabenshue himself. Because now around us and up ahead, pedestrians were stopping on the walks, turning to look back, then looking up. And were

252

calling, pointing, beckoning. Beside us and up ahead, office windows were raising, heads appearing, to lean out and look up. More people on rooftops, and a block ahead, a little red Broadway streetcar had stopped, and everyone on it including the uniformed conductor and motorman came tumbling out into Broadway. Frank began muttering — "Damn . . . Watch out, you fool! . . . Out of the way there! . . . Madam, would you remove your skirt from my spokes?" — as people hurried right out into the street to stop and point up, and beckon to still others. In the street around us men had begun taking off their caps and hats, holding them high and waving them in a little circle, and some of them yelled, "Hurrah! Hurrah!" pronouncing it just like that.

". . . all Manhattan went airship mad," my *New York Times* said next morning. "The news of the presence of this strange object in the sky quickly spread from Harlem to the Battery. From his lofty point of vantage a thousand feet above the sea level the navigator of the air was able to behold with equal ease the Statue of Liberty and Grant's Tomb, and everywhere within the territory lying between . . . He, in his turn, was visible to the little human ants that he saw crawling around in an excited way on the ground."

Just past the Astor Hotel a block up from the *Times* building, we had to stop, immediately becoming a little island like all the other cars, cabs, carriages, and streetcars standing motionless in what was now an almost solid pack, curb to curb

253

and up over the curbs, of people staring at the sky. Frank's motor off, we too watched — chins up, mouths open — as Roy Knabenshue sailed on down to the *Times* building. From here we couldn't judge distances too well, but the *Times* story the next morning said that "he reached a point on a line with the *Times* building and about fifty feet west of the tower," and that "he then turned his machine so that it pointed straight east. It remained stationary in that position long enough to allow him to wave his hand in acknowledgment of the greeting wafted up to him by members of the *Times* staff who were watching his flight from the tower." We could see them. Every visible window on the top floors of the *Times* building had been raised, and people — two, three, and sometimes four to a window — hung out, staring at Roy Knabenshue suspended there in space. We saw him wave, and then the women in the windows began waving handkerchiefs at him, and the men waved their shirtsleeved arms — and I felt wonderful; felt that damned, embarrassing lump in the throat you get sometimes at some very special human event. That man up there waving, those people in the tower, handkerchiefs fluttering back: I looked at the Jotta Girl and she looked at me, and we both nodded, smiling a little sheepishly, then looked up again at the sky.

Knabenshue must have moved his rudder, and for a moment or so we saw the strange shape of his balloon in silhouette. This is the photograph

— taken in those moments from the *Times* tower — that appeared in the *Times*, and is just about what we saw as he turned.

KNABENSHUE'S AIRSHIP.

A shower of something fell from the balloon. For an instant I thought it was water, but the shower widened into a shimmering cloud as it fell, too slowly for water, and I realized Knabenshue had dropped a shower of paper.

"Must be over Times Square," Frank murmured. "He's dropped the checks."

"Checks?" said the Jotta Girl.

Frank nodded, still watching Knabenshue. "Yeah, each good for a dollar." He glanced at her. "Find one, take it to the newspaper office, and they'll give you a dollar. It's advertising; they're paying him, that's why he's up there." Frank laughed. "He was sick all morning — I phoned him. Indigestion. Not used to New York food!" He laughed again. "But he needs the money, so he's up."

Sounding so let down I had to smile, the Jotta Girl said, "Oh. I thought he loved it."

"He does." Frank set his forearms on the big wheel to look across at her, puzzled. "He loves it. It's why he does it. But it takes money. And to get money, you'll go up long as you can get out of bed."

Knabenshue sailed on, that crazy cloth propeller catching the sun, shrinking, shrinking to a black speck under a thumbnail splotch of yellow, clear on down to about Madison Square. Then, quickly, helped by the western breeze, he turned to the east, occasional little flutters of paper appearing below him like tiny far-off insect swarms. He was far to the east now, above Second Avenue maybe, or even First; we couldn't tell. And over there, too, the streets filled. ". . . none but invalids and cradled babies," the *Times* reporter wrote, "could have remained indoors in the Borough of Manhattan. Every housetop as far as the eye could reach was filled with men and women and children, all of them gazing upward in rapt contemplation of the same object — the traveler in the sky . . . between the Park and Madison Square every sidewalk was crowded with people, some of whom seemed glued to the spot with faces turned heavenward and mouths agape. While others were running hither and thither in eager attempts to be Johnny-on-the-spot when the aeronaut should return to solid ground once more. Not less than three hundred thousand witnessed Mr. Knabenshue's cruise over Manhattan Island."

We too sat watching him slide down out of the sky in a long glide toward Central Park —

part of the time, we learned later, spilling gas to get himself down, because his engine had failed. And when he landed in the Park, fighting treetops a little to get down to the croquet field, he got into trouble with the cops, who ordered him out of the Park.

Broadway draining of people now, Frank started his engine, offering to drop us off wherever we were going, and we accepted — or at least the Jotta Girl did — a ride back to the Plaza. There we stood on the curb, smiling down at Frank in his roadster going *chunka-chunka-chunka,* the late sun polishing that lovely green hood, and I craved this car, I wanted to steal it. We asked him in for tea at the *thé dansant,* which I could hear going strong with "By the light! . . . of the silvery moon!" but he couldn't. There in his marvelous long-hooded open green beauty of a car, white shirt open at the collar, yellow hair mussed by the wind, he said his wife was expecting him, and I nearly smiled at the Jotta Girl's face. *Married?*

He said, "Come on down and see me, and I'll give you a ride in my hydro-aeroplane. Pier A, North River, near the Battery." We thanked him, both promising to show up soon for a flight, my mind simultaneously shouting that nothing could get me near his "hydro-aeroplane."

In the lobby we met Archie, to whom the Jotta Girl had spoken at Mrs. Israel's lecture. She introduced us casually, he invited us in for tea, and in we went. More dancing, at which I was exactly as good and as bad as before. But Archie was an easy, amiable guy, good company, we all had fun, and I stayed quite a while, before — all of a sudden — I was so tired I thought somebody, preferably the Jotta Girl, would have to carry me to my room. And I made my excuses, went up, and — shoes and half my clothes off — dropped down on the bed, and right to sleep: a big, big day.

18

DOWN IN the lobby before breakfast next morning, I bought a *Times*, then stood at the lobby theater-ticket window behind a man buying tickets for *Kismet*. And felt not even slightly surprised to hear just behind me, "Good morning, Simon. What are you going to see?" And I turned to face the Jotta Girl, glad of an excuse to smile — it was hard not to laugh. But I didn't mind being so obviously pursued: this was a good-looking girl. And while it was flattering, I knew my feelings for Julia couldn't be touched, so it was kind of funny, too. *"The Greyhound,"* I answered, and could have spoken her reply right along with her.

"Why, so am I," she said, her voice astonished at the coincidence. And, the man ahead of me turning away, studying his tickets, I stepped up and bought a pair on the aisle for today's matinee of *The Greyhound*. I didn't mind; I don't like sitting alone at a play or movie. And keeping the aisle seat for myself, I handed her the other.

But I like breakfast alone, and had it in the

259

hotel coffee shop, with only the *Times*. Read the advance review of *The Greyhound*, which said, among other not entirely flattering things, that "by checking your intelligence with your hat," you might like the play well enough.

And then I found this in the *Letters to the Editor* column.

A TAXI-AEROPLANE.

Frank Coffyn is Looking for Fares at Pier A, North River.

To the Editor of The New York Times:

I thank you for your comment on my trusting my aeroplane. You are like the boy in the well-known song in that you "guessed right the very first time." Aeroplanes, particularly hydro-aeroplanes, are very much safer than people think. In my opinion the machines are ahead of the men who pilot them, for probably 85 per cent of flying is in the machine one flies. That is immediately apparent when one sees that almost everybody who wants to learn how to fly does so very quickly. Aeroplaning is not for supermen, and they who fly are not supermen at all.

But aeroplaning, particularly in this country, has received several black eyes because of the carelessness, amounting almost to criminal recklessness, of some airmen and some aeroplane builders. Imperfect machines there are, of course, just as there are badly built automobiles. Chauffeurs who try to take sixty-mile-an-hour automobiles around street corners at that speed find imitators among the airmen. You will find such antics more or less common with every kind of vehicle, born, probably in the familiarity which breeds contempt for the factor of safety.

I agree with you that "it would be interesting to know how many people in this city would be willing to take a ride in an aeroplane." It costs money to operate a flying machine, particularly with the present types of motors. I cannot, therefore, much as I should like to do so, invite people to ride with me at no expense to themselves. But I will carry passengers, either male or female, from Pier A, North River, to and around the Statue of Liberty at a price that should not hamper those who really want to ride. Aviation has not yet reached the stage where it has become a poor man's pleasure, as the case is with the automobile.

My hydro-aeroplane is, in my opinion, a far safer machine than the average New York taxicab. Certainly I feel that I take far fewer chances in it than I do when I ride through New York's crowded streets in a taxicab, whose chauffeur is trying to take me to my destination as quickly as possible, regardless

of decent precautions for my own or pedestrians' safety, so that he may pick up
another fare at an early moment.

Again permit me to thank you for your
editorial. If the same class of people who
made the automobile industry, as it now exists, possible by their purchase of motor cars
were only to try aeroplaning, particularly
over the water, which is ten times safer than
flying over land, I am sure that aviation
would receive that stimulus which would
quickly put it on a sound and sane footing,
free from crazy exhibition features and dis-
gusting exploitation of circus stunts.

FRANK T. COFFYN

But Coffyn's "assurances" didn't even come close
to convincing me that "hydro-aeroplanes" were
"very much safer than people think." What did
sound persuasive to me was that "aeroplaning,
particularly in this country, has received several
black eyes because of the carelessness, amounting
almost to criminal recklessness, of some airmen
and some aeroplane builders." Even while reading
those bone-chilling words, the blood was with-
drawing from my skin with the sudden understanding that I actually had to go up in Frank
Coffyn's "hydro-aeroplane." *Had* to. *Had* to. Because how else — I sat looking across the restaurant tabletops — how else could I search the
length and breadth of Manhattan Island for something, it seemed to me, that I'd never seen or

even heard of? How else search for a building with a prow like the *Mauretania*'s? *Oh, Rube, Rube, what have you got me into?*

It was early, so I walked, taking my camera. This is Broadway and Twenty-third Street, south-

east corner of Broadway. And this is Broadway and Ninth Street, northeast corner of Ninth. Still

pretty nice and respectable down here. But as I moved further and further down into this 1912 New York, it got shabbier. I glanced into Max's Busy Bee Quick Lunch Room here, and thought

that if Max had ever eaten here himself, it must be his widow running it now.

But every sight and street sound, even these kids' voices (this is Ann Street) were a fascination to my hungry eyes and ears. Here on Fulton Street even this barber pole and tailor's shop — is this

understandable? — took my eye. And when I

reached the place those men are passing, I had to stop and — feeling foolish — take this.

Pier A was down where Frank said it was, sticking out into the Hudson on the west side of lower Manhattan not too far from the very tip of the Island. And today, strung out along the grassy riverbank for maybe a hundred yards on each side of Pier A, stood . . . I really don't know how many people; a lot. The crowd — men's dark suits and white stiff collars, women's long colorful dresses — stood silent, faces tilted up, absorbed and staring. I walked up to them, and stood looking between heads out at the gray Hudson. Out beyond Pier A a wooden raft lay swaying from the tiny waves, a rowboat tied to it. Then, far beyond this, I found what these silent people stood watching: a plane, not high, way off over the water toward the Jersey shore.

I wasn't sure at first that I actually heard it. Then, watching it, small and low but sharply clear and alone in the air, I did hear for sure the steady *stutter-stutter-stutter-stutter-stutter-stutter* sound. He was coming low, right at us; then he rose steeply and, over the trees of Battery Park, Frank Coffyn, his plane white on the blue, began swinging and swerving, entertaining us down here, gracefully tilting from side to side, the right wings dipping, then the left, and from the crowd came a long murmured *ohhhhh* of pleasure.

He flew away, dwindling, back toward the Jersey shore. We watched his slow, lazy turn, glittering for a heartbeat as the sun touched the taut cloth of the wings. Then, low over the water and straight at us he came, growing again but this time dropping, descending, the propeller a shimmering circle. Lower . . . lower still . . . then faster than a blink, a wind puff yanked up the left wings, dipping the other side to nearly touch the low waves. Instantly Coffyn did something to simultaneously level the plane and touch the river, a sudden jittering white scuff appearing at the front of the long boatlike hull, the plane sagging back into ungainliness. Then on she came, a clumsy boat now, bucking the wavelets, and I stood watching, badly scared. Scared for Frank and the passenger I could see now, and scared for myself, in the sharp understanding that this plane, that all these crude early planes, like Roy Knabenshue's strange balloon, could abruptly kill you.

On she bobbled and bounced, straight for the big anchored float, about to hit it; then Frank cut the motor, swinging the rudder, and — wings passing right over the raft — brought the body of his plane alongside the raft, and his passenger, a woman, I saw now, stepped expertly out onto the raft, a rope in hand. She tied it to a metal ring, Frank watching her, and in that moment I took this. Then he turned to toss out an anchor to hold the other end steady, and I stood staring, shocked at the flimsiness of this contraption. The thing sitting out there on the water wasn't much more than a kite! A pasteup of wood and stretched cloth. Only those flimsy wings to support that

great big heavy-looking circular motor mounted there right out in the open. This motorized kite looked like something you could put together in your garage. In about fifteen minutes. Go up in that? Sitting out there high in the air over New York City?

The passenger standing on the raft — Frank stepping over to join her now — was a woman in a long blue skirt and a middy blouse with a big square sailor's collar at the back. She looked nice standing there smiling at Frank, who stood grinning over at the crowd on shore.

Then they rowed in, Frank tied up the boat, and he and the lady stood on the pier in a little circle of reporters with notebooks; I recognized a couple of them from Roy Knabenshue's tent. "Did you enjoy your aerial sightseeing, Mrs. Coffyn?" one of them called out, and she turned, smiling. Oh yes, it was thrilling! Watching her face, I saw that she meant it: she may have done this before to drum up business, probably had, but she meant it. Everyone should fly over the city, she added, and Frank said, "Everyone with five dollars," and they all laughed. Frank turned for a moment to look out into the bay at an incoming ship. A reporter asked if this wasn't his second flight of the day. Yes, it was. Was he going up again? Yes, he thought so. Again he turned to look out at the distant ship, and I did too. Still far off, but now I could make out two threads of black smoke lining out behind its stacks. "Gentlemen," Frank said to the reporters, "on my first flight today, I saw that ship just entering the Narrows, and flew out to take a look. I flew over the vessel at a height of about four hundred feet, and saw the passengers at her prow gathering, as I supposed, for the first glimpse of the Statue of Liberty."

"Did they see you?"

"Oh yes indeed, greeting me with considerable enthusiasm." And waving their hats, I thought to myself. "The ship's horn hooted at me, and I then flew down alongside her just over the water to read her name, the *St. Louis*, as I learned. I then attempted to hover over her stern, but she traveled too slowly for me. Even flying at my minimum speed, I could not help but fly ahead of her. So I gave up the *St. Louis* as a poor competitor, left the vessel, returned to the Battery, and, as you are aware, have had time for even a second flight, and the *St. Louis* not yet here. I firmly believe that the traveler's future," and he pointed upward, "lies there." Then,

269

nodding toward the ship: "And no longer there."
Propagandizing for the cause, I thought. Still, I
felt a swift little thrill hearing him, he was so
spectacularly right. Did he really believe it?
Glancing over at the kite out there by the raft,
it was hard to think so.

Now he gave reporters and crowd a friendly
nod, a gesture with the chin, took his wife's arm
and walked on, and this 1912 crowd, including
the reporters, all respected their retreat to privacy.
No one followed with a last question, and it didn't
seem to occur to anyone to hold out something
to be autographed.

They walked on toward a smiling young woman
waiting for them a dozen yards from the pier;
then Frank glanced over and saw me. He grinned
immediately, beckoning, and the four of us came
together in a group, the young woman taking
both of Mrs. Coffyn's hands as they spoke and
brushed cheeks. I took off my hat as Frank introduced me to his wife, who looked at me with
lively, cheerful interest in a new person. Then
she introduced me to the very good-looking Harriet Quimby, "who is an aviatrix!"

"And will soon be the first woman to fly the
English Channel," Frank said.

"Soon will be *trying*," she said, then to me,
"Meanwhile I am occupied much more mundanely
as a dramatic critic. For *Leslie's Weekly*," and I
almost popped out that I worked for *Leslie's* too!
Instead, I managed to say, "Oh? Will you be
seeing *The Greyhound*?" and we talked about that

for a moment or so.

I liked her, this Harriet Quimby, was impressed, and long after, back again in a time at the other end of this new century, I sat in the reference room of the New York Public Library leafing through the pages of *Who Was Who*, not really expecting to find *Harriet Quimby*, because I had never otherwise heard of her. But her name is there. Harriet Quimby did fly the English Channel. Alone. The first woman to do it. On April 16, 1912. But the entry also included the date of her death a few months later. In a flying accident. But not now, not yet, not this day.

"You two off then?" Frank said, and Mrs. Coffyn said, "Yes, but if you're taking Mr. Morley up now, we'll stay a few minutes to watch." She smiled at me charmingly, and everyone turned and began walking toward the pier. And in the presence of a young and lovely "aviatrix" who planned to climb into one of these crazy kites and fly out alone over the English Channel . . . and in the presence of another woman, who'd just stepped out of the awful thing waiting out there beside the raft . . . I walked along too, the condemned man helpless to do anything but join the procession leaving from his open cell door. Over the grass to the pier and the rowboat, out there on the Styx. Then toward the raft and — oh Lord — that evil construction of cloth and sticks sitting there waiting for me.

On the float I stood on the rough wood planking beside the plane while Frank knelt down to tie up the boat. I said, "Frank, this is more than just sightseeing. I want to fly down the length of Manhattan to look for a building. A building, I guess, that's shaped like a boat. Has a prow anyway. Like the *Mauretania*."

He thought about it, then shook his head. "I don't remember anything like that. But if it's there we'll find it."

"And I want to pay you a lot more than five dollars."

"All right. We'll see how long it takes. Shouldn't be too costly." He stood up, the raft bobbling a little in a way I didn't like; should I grab my stomach and say I was seasick? The thing had two little bucket seats, one behind the other down in the flimsy fuselage. Frank walked around the front of the plane; I stood watching, then stepped as he did, onto the pontoon first, then swinging up and down into that terrible little seat, Frank behind me. There was a leather strap, the kind you'd find in an electric chair, and I cinched it tight around my waist. Frank leaned forward to pass me a pair of goggles, and I made my cheek muscles imitate what little they could remember of smiling, and put them on. Clear glass, not tinted.

Frank started his engine. Then drove out into the Hudson.

We waited, drifting sideways a little, for a tug to churn itself out of the way: it seemed to be heading upriver after the *St. Louis*. Frank taxied out in a wide downstream curve, made a swift

272

tight little turn into what wind there was, and — I wanted to squeeze my eyes shut but didn't — we began bouncing forward, *slap-slap*, over the miniature waves, a fan of spray from the pontoon hull wetting my face and goggles, which I wiped with my sleeve. Our motion abruptly went smooth, and just above the water we sailed right past the end of the pier, and I had a swift glimpse of Mrs. Coffyn and Harriet Quimby — she was actually beautiful — smiling, waving, and when I faced front again, being up here didn't seem so bad.

This was nothing of what I'd expected, sitting here putt-putting along above the water. This was no hundred tons of howling metal brutally thrusting through a thinned-out alien nothingness. This was another kind of thing, the sun on my face, the soft almost Indian-summer warmth of this strange 1912 early spring pressing my forehead: I could feel the air holding us up.

The engine putted along, the propeller revolved, and I heard it, but not loudly. We sat ahead of it, and possibly most of the sound poured away behind us. Sailing along here over the Hudson, gradually rising, I grinned and nodded at Frank.

And made a mistake. In moving my head, I glanced down over the side, then looked up fast, straight to the front, and it was all right again.

Frank began circling: slow, wide, easy circles leisurely lifting us higher, higher, and that seemed okay. Slowly corkscrewing up through the air,

273

Frank stayed over the water that would accept us engineless, if need be. I'd see the long heights of the Jersey shore stretching out, green and rural mostly. Then see the great harbor. Then, sliding away behind us, the endless brown-black fingers of the west-side Manhattan docks. Glimpsed the toy-size *St. Louis*, two even tinier toys shoving her sideways at the American Line docks. Saw a white scrap of sailboat . . . a greenish-black spot that was a tug . . . two little red ferries perched on the water . . . then Ellis Island far behind us . . . the little Statue of Liberty, turned green since last I'd seen it, its torch revolving slowly as it slid back behind us. "I flew around Liberty last week," Frank said, "with a motion picture cameraman right where you're sitting. He took motion pictures of the crown and the torch, while inside the crown *another* man took motion pictures of *us!*" I grinned and nodded, wishing I could see those films; had they survived into the other end of the century?

It felt good now, this lazy hawklike circling gradually expanding the entire harbor for me. Well behind us now lay the green spot of Battery Park flecked with the colors of dresses and drab suits — they were watching *us!*

"Took a motion picture cameraman up to photograph the office buildings at the tip of the island. Flew level with the top windows, full of rubbernecks watching us and waving while he cranked away at them. Then, right over the East River the bolts worked loose, the camera fell off the wing, and that's where it is now, bottom of the river somewhere."

Finally, moving north as we climbed — how high? Two thousand feet? Three? I didn't know — we turned in over the city, and I saw what I can still see in my mind: far down there, spread out for me in this faintly hazed morning, lay the city of this fresh new century, the city between the two other New Yorks I'd known, and it seemed beautiful.

I've never flown across the New York of the final years of the twentieth century, but I've looked at aerial photographs, and they're stunning, especially the glittering unworldly night views. But the tall, tall, and ever taller buildings, so thick and close in midcity, hide the city they occupy. Often the aerial photographer, searching with his camera, can't find streets or people, only layered walls, the city lost.

But not yet, not now. Now the long, slim, familiar map shape of Manhattan lay down there, its neat crisscrossed streets crawling with the specks and shapes of its life. And I began to search for — what? A kind of stone ship was all I could think of, an impossible stone ship with windows. Here and there the slim upward-pointing fingers of New York's "skyscrapers" stood mostly alone, easily found. As if reading a familiar page, my eyes moved down from the great green rectangle of Central Park, following the curves of Upper Broadway — I could see the specks of color that were its people and vehicles — and easily found the slim white tower of the *Times* building rising alone and unchallenged. To the west the nineteenth century lay almost untouched in long brown-fronted, black-roofed stripes across the city map. I picked out the shining white new-ness of the Public Library at Forty-second Street, simultaneously seeing in my mind the reservoir that belonged there too. Off to the east, a smudge of scattered lumber, cut stone, and dirt ramps: Grand Central Station a-building. I sat in comfort there on the taut fabric of my wing, floating on the air, looking down at the two not-quite-the-same grays of the enclosing rivers . . . followed the long sun glints of the tiny strips of El lines down each side of the city. Then, yes, that was Thirty-third Street, must be, because the great white rectangle just beyond it, sparkling in its newness, could only be Penn Station. And off to the east where one day the Empire State Build-ing would climb, lay the green peaks and domes and the fluttering flagpoles of the great Waldorf-Astoria Hotel.

But Frank Coffyn had seen all this again and again, and occasionally he leaned forward to talk, to ask questions. And while he listened to my replies, I realized something that possibly he didn't. That everything entering Frank's mind and attention came out into something about fly-ing.

So I'd come from Buffalo, eh? Well, before long I'd be able to travel from Buffalo to New York by aeroplane. How did I like the Plaza

Hotel? Just fine: my room overlooked Central Park. And Frank nodded, and said it must be almost like seeing it from a plane. "Frank, what would you have done," I said, "if you'd lived long before the aeroplane?" I'd turned to look at him, and his eyes actually went wide. "My God," he said softly, "what an awful idea. But it didn't happen, Si. And I'll tell you why. I was born to fly across the Atlantic Ocean. I'm going to, Si. I want to be the first."

I could only nod and say, "Well, Frank, it will be done."

"Oh, yes; if only I can raise the *money*. I need bigger engines. And a bigger aeroplane to hold them. And protection from the weather. Si, it's eighteen hundred and eighteen miles from New-foundland to the coast of Ireland." He was serious! He'd thought this out. "With a speed of forty-five miles an hour I could do it in forty hours. I've learned that from June to September" — his hands on the controls, his feet on the pedals moved frequently, carefully, but his mind was far away — "there is a prevailing wind blowing from the west which would give me from twenty to thirty miles an hour help." He knew all this, and it was right. "Once started, there could be no land-ing on the water, but I firmly believe that with two engines, one of which could be switched on in case of damage to the other, and with two hundred gallons of gasoline, the thing could be done. We're learning now, Si. We're all of us learning the hazards of aeroplaning. I've learned to be careful flying low over city streets; the currents of air that come up from a city are treacherous. We have to learn, and on the day a man flies the Atlantic, he'll need — well, what? Forethought. Careful preparation. Patience. All those virtues and more."

I sat nodding, silently saying, *Frank, there's a boy alive now . . .* where? Where was Charles Lindbergh at this moment? I didn't know, but silently I said, *You can't quite do it, Frank. Just barely not quite. But the boy who is going to probably knows your name.*

New buildings down there, moving evenly away under us — hotels, apartments, whatever. But still a low and comfortable city, still visible to itself. Ahead now — we seemed almost directly above Fifth Avenue — the one-corner-missing rectangle of Madison Square, and I would not move my head to look off to the east toward Gramercy Park. And then down there . . . why, yes. *Yes.* Oh my God, yes, yes, *yes!* There at the intersection of Broadway and Fifth Avenue, looking ready to sail up either one, I suddenly spotted what Z had seen, "her prow sharp and straight as that of the *Mauretania* herself." Yes, she *was* "a ship! Of stone and steel," steadily moving toward us as though in actual motion. And Z was right: it seemed all wrong to call this beauty (I took this later at ground level) by so ordinary a name as the Flatiron Building.

Nothing of this to Frank, of course. I sat silently elated; Z would be *down there tonight.* And I would

be too. I hadn't blown it after all; now again it began to be just faintly and distantly possible that I could join a course of events and alter them — so that a war might slip away into a new past as only a possibility that had never occurred.

On down Manhattan Island to the green slipper that was Union Square: I'd seen this last with Julia and Willy, watching a nighttime parade. Sliding toward us, and then underneath us, the maze of Manhattan's earliest streets: short, angling, curving, the planned orderliness above Fourteenth Street sliding behind us. I glanced at Frank, grinning, nodding, to say that I liked this. And he smiled the tolerant acknowledgment of a man who'd seen it all many times but is pleased to show it again.

The black sliver of Trinity's steeple still alone on the sky . . . Then Frank nodded to the east, and we began sliding downward toward the city — quite fast, the streets expanding up toward us, dots rapidly swelling into people. Frank out to scare me a bit, I think. Then I felt the pressure of my strap as we tilted to the left into a downward turn. A half-second glimpse of the basket masts of a gray battleship moored on the Brooklyn shore, and down we came, still turning, the flat gray of the East River widening to meet us.

We leveled, swaying, twenty feet — no more — above the water just under our wings. Frank, taking his eyes from the river for only an instant, sneaked a glance at me; I was supposed to be scared, and was, oh, I was. Because just ahead, and I understood Frank's glance and was terrified, hung the Brooklyn Bridge — we were going under it! We didn't know until we saw this photo in

the *Times* that in this moment a newspaper photographer, seeing what Frank was about to do, actually snapped this muddy photograph. An instant later, under we went, gloriously under the bridge, its shadow flashing across us. Then out, and directly over the stack of the tug there in the photograph. And the gush of hot, hot gas pouring up out of that stack seized our flimsy little kite, and shook it — heaved and tossed us helplessly, a dog mercilessly killing a rat.

Frank fought, forcing his controls, using his entire strength to hang on to control, only barely doing so. We nearly went in, we damn near hit the river. Frank's face like a carving in wood, he held on to that little plane, bucking, bucking, a steer out of the chute, fighting it, my strap dug into my waist.

Then abruptly we were out, not crashed, not quite striking the river, all suddenly serene, and we shot up into the sky, out of danger, in a fine and graceful curve.

I found my voice. I said, "Frank. Tell me again about flying the Atlantic. The careful preparation. The forethought. The caution. All those necessary virtues."

Frank said, "I'm sorry. I'm very sorry. Si. I was a damn fool." And, suddenly angry at himself: "That's not the way I fly!" On down toward Pier A now, an easy touchdown to the water, a nice slow taxi toward the raft. "But on the day a man flies the Atlantic, he'll need careful preparation, yes. He'll need rigorous forethought. Plenty of patience. All that, Si, all of those. But at the last, when he climbs into his aeroplane and sits facing the Atlantic Ocean, it's going to take a little wild and woolly recklessness too."

19

A LONG-HAIRED Gibson Girl handed me this program in exchange for two tickets to *The Grey-*

hound. She wore a gray uniform dress, big white Buster Brown collar with a huge bow tie, and a button that said *Usher.* She led us — the Jotta Girl and me — down to seats right on the aisle, and when a twelve-year-old boy in a red bellboy suit with brass buttons came along selling long thin boxes of chocolate mints, I bought one.

I glanced around: people coming down every aisle, edging into the rows. Z would be here, was maybe here right now; maybe I was looking at him. All over the the-ater splendid long-haired women in high-necked dresses sat re-moving their e n o r m o u s hats — care-fully, using both hands to lift them straight up, the Jotta Girl one of them. She wore a long pale dress and a pink hat not

quite ten feet in diameter. The men, all over the theater: stiff collars, short hair parted in the middle, mostly, some of them wearing pince-nez glasses. Would Z be wearing pince-nez? I didn't think so, but maybe.

Up ahead hung the tall and massive red curtain, the heavy gold fringe along the bottom at least a foot long, the velvet folds shadowed by the foot lights. Breathes there a man with soul so dead he doesn't find the moments before the mysterious curtain rise a thrill? Although I remembered that in years ahead theater curtains would vanish, leaving you to sit staring at the empty set until it turned stale, illusion gone.

Beside me, the Jotta Girl sat studying her program, and I looked at mine, then counted, and turned to say, "Hey, a cast of twenty-six!" but she didn't seem impressed. I counted scenes then: six! But didn't say anything. I was impressed, though, and pleased. I get tired of the same old set all through the play. And tired of only two actors.

I talked a little about Wilson Mizner then, one of the play's authors, and also something of a crook and confidence man. She seemed interested, which pleased me. It was nice having her along. I liked the Jotta Girl; liked people who like Wilson Mizner. He'd been up in the Yukon during the gold rush of the nineties, not out in the cold and snow but comfortably playing poker with the gold-bearing miners, and mostly winning. One day he sat playing cards in a Yukon saloon and bawdy house, when a man rushed in saying, "Someone just insulted Goldie!" And

Mizner, dealing the cards, said, "In God's name, how?"

The moment came: The houselights lowered . . . held . . . then flicked out, the theater suddenly black dark except for the gas flames standing behind the red exit signs. Then, always and ever a thrill, the swift rise of the curtain, this time, according to my program, on "A San Francisco Boarding House." And we saw a thinly furnished bedroom: a single window, a dresser, a cast-iron bedstead. At which Ying Lee stood making the bed.

Well, what can I say about Ying Lee? Except that I sat here in a 1912 theater, and that Ying Lee was therefore not a "Chinese" but a "Chinaman." We knew that, because his eyes were taped into a slant, his skin had been yellowed, he wore black cloth slippers, and his pigtail reached to his waist. And in the moment we saw him up there, carelessly making the bed, the audience reacted not with an actual laugh — he wasn't doing anything funny yet — but with a murmur hinting of anticipated laughter because . . . well, this was a Chinaman.

"Ying!" a woman's voice called from offstage, and Ying looked up, his face going stubborn, not replying. He accidentally dropped a pillow, clumsily stepping on it, and got a ripple of laughter. Then in came Mrs. Fagin, the landlady, my program told me. "Why don't you come when I call you?"

"Me make bed."

"You know less about making a bed than a mule."

"Me quit!" He folded his arms.

"Now?"

Ying thought about that. "By and by" — getting his laugh.

"Well, in the meantime go and straighten my room up." And Ying left — singing what either was or was meant to be a high-pitched Chinese song, and we laughed again.

"Claire" walked on — this was her room — and I took up my program because she was truly lovely: Alice Martin. She began telling her trouble to Mrs. Fagin, and we learned she was married to and deserted by "The Greyhound," a confidence man who'd treated her badly, though she still loved him. But I started to lose track of the plot because I'd begun listening less to their words than to the odd sound of their voices. And realized that, without microphones, their voices carried out to us oddly, absorbed instantly by our several hundred bodies. This curious deadened sound, flat and echoless, was strangely compelling, making the actual presence of the actors up there extraordinarily real.

I also sat waiting for witty Mizner lines, but wasn't hearing any. Claire and Mrs. Fagin exited, Ying and McSherry came on, and we learned that McSherry was a reformed card shark, now a detective, in love with Claire, and so forth. "Mrs. Fagin upstair," Ying said. "You wait."

"Well, maybe you can tell me something,"

McSherry said, and brought out a big sheet of red paper in such a way that we could see it was written in Chinese characters.

Ying glanced at it. "No sabby."

"That's too bad," said McSherry. Then, suddenly and loudly, "Sim yup tong!"

Instantly Ying reacted, because it turned out that this was a command from his tong, never to be disobeyed. Immediately servile, terrified, Ying shouted "Ni ha limya!" or something like that, snatching the paper, turning to face us as he read it silently, head moving up and down the vertical columns.

"You sabby now?"

"Mebbee."

McSherry pulled up his left sleeve to show a scar on his wrist. Ying Lee looked at it, consulted the red paper, looked back at the wrist, apparently checking the scar against a description of it. "This Chink's from Missouri," McSherry said, to the audience.

Wilson Mizner? The celebrated wit? I refused to think so. Looking at the red paper, McSherry said, "Looks like a bill for tearing up a shirt." When McSherry asked where Claire's husband was, Ying said, "He come by and by," and McSherry said, "To a Chink 'by and by' means two minutes or forty years. Which do you mean?"

"He come yesterday. One o'clock."

"What time the day before?"

"Seven weeks."

Well, the audience liked it. And I was part

of the audience, so I laughed with them. But . . . ?

Mrs. Fagin and McSherry advanced the plot: he was here to help Claire because he was in love with her himself. Then along came a line I'd read sarcastically referred to in the *Times* review. McSherry, speaking angrily to Claire's husband, The Greyhound, said, "Any man that can't go straight on his own, don't do it for a woman after he's got her!"

"Ain't it the truth!" Mrs. Fagin exclaimed up there on the stage, and I sneaked a glance at the Jotta Girl, and then at the audience immediately around me. They sat smiling, enjoying the play, but not taking lines like that any more seriously than I did.

A couple of times in the same scene, when McSherry was affected by the powerful emotion of his love for Claire, he did something that surprised me. He'd turn away, and stand with his back to the audience, shoulders bowed — something I'd never before seen an actor do. An acting convention of the time, I suppose, to show emotion so strong the face must be averted. I've heard that a ballet dancer, working hard and sweating, will seize an instant when her back is momentarily to the audience to wipe sweat from her face with a lovely wrist movement, then fling her arm gracefully out to flick the sweat away. Maybe McSherry, I thought now, was up there, back to the audience, making funny faces.

As he and Mrs. Fagin finished, Ying came in with a broom. "Me make sweep?"

Mrs. F. stepped back in astonishment. "First time in his life he ever asked to work!" When McSherry and Mrs. Fagin left, Ying's sweeping slowed till the broom was barely moving, no longer quite touching the floor, a Chinese Stepin Fetchit.

Act One pretty well laid out the plot: A group of con men and a woman were sailing to Europe in order to fleece a rich family aboard the ship. And I was wondering if maybe Wilson Mizner had personal knowledge of how that was done. I liked the gang's names: The Greyhound, Whispering Alex, Deep Sea Kitty, and The Pale Face Kid, so called, I understood when he first walked out onto the stage, because his face was so red. "You'll be in the way on this trip, Kid," said Deep Sea Kitty.

"Why?"

"On a first-class ship people wear garments, eat with their forks, and change their clothes to sleep!"

"I could learn all that in a week!" said the Kid, and I laughed, and nodded — I thought that had the raffish Mizner touch. But mostly this play seemed to me as if it might have been laid out of an afternoon. Over drinks.

I'd been careful not to read the scene description in my program. I wanted the little surprise I got when the curtain rose, this time on Act Two, the deck of a ship, and it was fine.

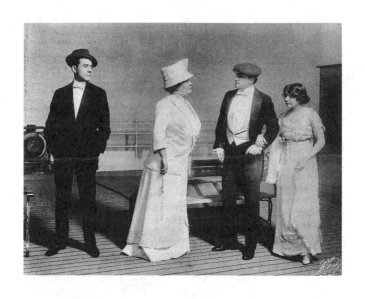

There it all was: people reading in deck chairs; others leaning on the rail to stare off at the sea and painted backdrop of sky and clouds; a very real-looking lifeboat; a radio shack; even a couple playing that shipboard game where you toss rings. And when I glanced down at my program I saw that this was "The Hurricane Deck of H.M.S. *Mauretania*." I'm one of those people who are fascinated by the great old ocean liners; who like to read about them, and stare at their pictures wondering what it had been like to sail on them. And of course the *Mauretania* was possibly the most loved of all the splendid old liners — was this really what the *Mauretania* looked like? I sat forward, studying the set, and — well, who could say? But this looked real, even the deck seemed like genuine ship's planking.

The *Times* later published a layout of scenes from the play; these are a couple of them. The people aren't overacting as much as their photographs may suggest; they're posing for a slow camera, I think, holding an expression not too easy even for actors. Wearing caps and hats was okay for this audience; all men wore one or the other outdoors. This flag-holding bunch — a Mizner comic touch? — are superpatriot hicks from Lima, Ohio: they're the rich family the crooks are about to meet with a forged letter of introduction.

Suddenly we all jumped: from the radio shack up there on the stage came a startling sound burst, a hissingly

electric *dit-dit. Dit-dit-dit! Dit-dit-dit-dit-dit!* And we sat up and paid attention. Wireless messages at sea were new in this world, and this was a new and thrilling sound. The rapid, sparking *dit-dit-dit* stopped, all the passengers staring at the radio shack. And a moment later a man in ship's uniform came out with a piece of paper. "Aerogram!" he called. "Aerogram for Foster Allen! Aerogram for Mr. Allen!" and off he went hunting for him.

It was a fine touch, I thought, and from time to time throughout the play, sometimes for reason of plot and sometimes not, that exciting *dit-dit . . . dit-dit-dit* would come sparking out to startle and please us.

I began to suspect that The Pale Face Kid was Wilson Mizner's creation and favorite, because he seemed in on most of what I took to be Mizner lines. On deck trying to make conversation with Etta, a good-looking young passenger, he had trouble finding something to say, and finally blurted out, "Did you notice the sea?"

And later, playing shuffleboard with Etta, he did pretty well even though it was his first time. Where had he learned? Etta wondered. "Used to play it all the time," said the Kid, "at home on the lawn."

"On the *lawn?* Can you slide them on the grass?"

"Of course not," said the Kid, thinking fast. "Ah . . . we used to roll them."

To Deep Sea Kitty, he said, "Can you get a lawyer to do that?"

"Sure! I could get a lawyer to scuttle this ship for the court costs." And: "When the time comes for perjury, we'll coach you like a first-class lawyer would." When a passenger asked the Kid, "Where do you stop in London?" the Kid said, "Westminster Abbey."

I thought I saw another aspect of the strange and contradictory Mizner in a deck scene between McSherry and a detective who was on board to help him with the crooks. The dinner gong had

293

rung, everyone else gone, and talking to Mc-Sherry, the detective noticed something in Mc-Sherry's inside coat pocket. He reached forward to tap it, saying, "Looks like a green baize shuffling board in your pocket." A *what?* I'd never heard of such a thing, and I don't think the audience had. But "a green baize shuffling board" could hardly be an invention, could it? McSherry said, "I shuffle sometimes when I'm thinking, but I don't play anymore." And when the detective left, McSherry sat down, brought out a marvelous little foldup board, and opened it to form a green-covered surface on his lap. Then, staring thoughtfully out to sea, his hands endlessly and fluently shuffled a deck of cards. Who would carry a foldup board just for shuffling? Nobody except a man practicing undetectable crooked shuffles. Did this come out of Wilson Mizner's own strange past? I'll bet it did. But watching McSherry up there, I wanted a green baize shuffling board too. *Dit-dit-dit-dit-dit!* said the radio shack, McSherry jumped up, and the play continued.

Curtain down on Act Two, houselights up, and out to the lobby for intermission, and some kind of pink stuff to drink. Then back for a fast curtain rise on what looked like and was a poker game in a smoky cabin, portholes on the back wall.

The *Times*'s advance review said, "That poker game was a delight," and it was. Because it seemed real, a poker game right out of Wilson Mizner's life, I was sure of it. The men up there in shirtsleeves, vests hanging open, puffing real smoke from real cigars, talked like real poker players. "Great draw, wasn't it?" said one grinning player, pulling in a pot, and a sour loser replied, "Never mind the ancient history." A player dropped out of a pot, throwing in his losing hand and saying disgustedly, "Fight it out between you." A man walked around his chair to change his luck. "Say, don't you ever ante?" one player said to another. "Sure," was the answer, "when forced." Looking up there at the players on the stage around a hexagonal poker table in "The Card Room: Evening, Same Day" was like watching an actual game. They said and did what poker players really say and do. "You couldn't open your mouth with these," said a player of his cards. A loser whose turn it was to deal started gathering up discarded cards, saying irritably, "Come on with the discards. Speed! Speed! Discards!" "I can't draw my breath," said another disgusted loser. A man laid down a winning hand of three kings, saying, as poker players probably always will, "Three monarchs of all they survey!" The steady obligatory insults never stopped. "You deal like you're dividing a box of soda crackers." This fine Wilson Mizner poker game ended with McSherry using his old skill as a former card shark, refined just before the game with practice on the green baize shuffling board, to outwit the con men by dealing from the middle of the deck.

The red velvet curtain came down on the climax of the scene, the crooks outwitted by McSherry,

the sucker raking in his huge pot. And then —
I counted — there were *seven* curtain calls just
for the scene, the play not over. Each call built
to growing applause, the sixth being the sucker,
who walked out for his bow with his hands full
of the money he'd just won — which brought
down the house. And finally McSherry, and we
really and truly gave him a great hand — he'd
just outwitted the crooks! Then, the applause
dying, we all sat grinning, the theater buzzing
with talk: we were loving this.

Fourth act, curtain rise on the thrilling *dit-
dit-dit-dit* from the radio shack — "Midnight on
the Hurricane Deck" — and the play pretty
quickly resolved itself. Finally — the gang out-
foxed by McSherry, the reformed cardsharp —
The Greyhound either jumped or fell to his death
over the side of the ship in the last and best
effect of the play. We saw him plunge over the
side . . . then silence through a long two seconds,
the others up there on the hurricane deck staring
down after him, horrified . . . Then *we heard
the splash!* Heard it, and an instant later saw the
top of an actual spout of water appear at the
ship's rail! *And* — a brilliant touch — this splash
appeared *a little further down along the rail* because
the ship, you see, was *moving.* "Man overboard!"
someone yelled, and with my lovely Claire in
McSherry's arms, the final curtain began descending to — don't ask me why — the wonderfully,
hissingly dramatic *dit-dit-dit* of the wireless. And
then, for the very first time in the play, a sudden

blast of sound filling the theater, shaking the walls, from the great ship's horn blasting over and over along with that urgent *dit-dit-dit* as the swaying gold tassels gradually lowered. You couldn't think for the sound, and we went wild, went crazy. For this we'd have pounded our palms if we hadn't even seen the play.

But I didn't forget why I was here. Got my hat from under my seat, swung my legs out to stand in the aisle, and, crouching low, hustled up the dark aisle; and the deep blast of the horn and the electric sparking *dit-dit-dit* of the wireless gave a wild urgency to what I was doing, a thrill of drama and excitement. Z would be out there. He really would, I knew it! Out on the walk in the next few minutes, and I'd be there waiting to see his face.

Across the tiled floor of the lobby, empty except for a pair of Gibson girls talking, and I was the very first of the audience to reach the sidewalk in front of the Knickerbocker. Somewhere, maybe a block or so away, the Dove Lady was walking toward me.

A man came out of the theater, glanced at me, carefully fitted on his derby, then walked off. Up the street the *Times* tower stood against the blue-white sky. Three women came out of the theater, all talking, laughing, none listening. A few more . . . Then suddenly the crowd came surging through every door, some immediately walking off, but a lot of them simply stopping dead on the walk to chatter. Now pedestrians

had to wind their way through this swelling crowd, and I stood watching, excited but worried. Because I didn't know what exactly I was looking for, and when the Dove Lady came walking by, as she would . . . with Z staring after her, as he would . . . just what would I *see?* What if "Dove Lady" was only a name, nothing I could actually recognize?

I moved away, toward a drugstore on the corner, to get a clear view of this fast-growing throng. An empty wooden box lay at the curb, half in the gutter, and I nudged it out with my foot and stepped on a little island. Because what if she were there right now this very instant and *I was missing her?* On impulse I brought out my camera, unfolded it, and snapped these views, of the beginning crowd, figuring that if I missed the Dove Lady, I might spot her and Z later somewhere in my photos.

The crowd kept rowing, and I wound back my film.

But no more than maybe a minute or so later, the crowd became a mob. A dozen Dove Ladies could be marching toward me now as I stood staring, looking for who knew what. Nervously now, I again wound my film forward, and got this mob scene.

Was the Dove Lady somewhere in *this?* Well, why not? Could

be a whole flock of them.

A pair of particularly fine-hatted women came walking toward me, glancing up at me on my box. And it seemed almost obligatory, only polite, to lift my camera and snap them here. But the viewfinder of my Kodak was about the size of an ordinary postage stamp, so I didn't notice the woman just behind them — see her there? — until I lowered my camera. Then, as she passed my box, I looked down and saw the stuffed-bird ornament on her hat, saw its round vacant little glass eye. And saw the eye close, then open again — the bird was alive!

And the bird was a dove — I'd snapped the Dove Lady! And somewhere back in that crowd, maybe still staring after her, was Z. As I leaned forward to search the crowd for him, a huge pink something moved before my face, filling my vision, blocking off the crowd. And in the middle of that great wheel of pinkness, the Jotta Girl's face looking up at me to say, "What in the world are you doing!"

I stood frantically waving her away, wanting to shove her to one side, and she did move aside, but the crowd had shifted like the revolving bits of a kaleidoscope, and Z and my moment, my one chance of spotting him, were gone, used up.

When I got back my roll of film, I had this

portion of the print enlarged, and here it is, this is the moment my camera's eye saw but I didn't. I'd stood squinting down at my gray little postage-stamp viewfinder as my camera took the Dove Lady — see the live dove on her hat? And I'd looked up from my viewfinder at nothing but the great pinkness of the Jotta Girl's *hat!* Hadn't seen the Dove Lady till she walked past me, my moment gone.

"Let's get a cab," I said brusquely, stepping to the curb, where I yanked open the passenger door of a big red cab. Then I ushered the Jotta Girl in, saying "Plaza Hotel" to the driver, and slammed the door, turning away as it pulled out into the Broadway traffic, before I said something I shouldn't.

Down the walk, as I turned, I could still see

the Dove Lady's hat, saw the startled faces of pedestrians as they glimpsed the living bird. I knew where she was going. I'd seen her photograph in the lobby of the Fifth Avenue Theatre, a bird perched on each shoulder. *This* was our Bird Lady, a vaudeville performer, now all mystery, all interest in her gone. And I turned away to walk back to the hotel, and cool off; it wasn't really the Jotta Girl's fault.

It's a twenty-block walk, and I was okay when I came into the lobby — and found the Jotta Girl waiting in a straight-backed chair right beside the elevator doors. No acknowledgment of my innocent smile of happy surprise. She simply stood up, and when the elevator doors opened, stepped in with me, saying, "Tenth, please." Then she just stood staring at the back of the elevator boy's pillbox hat, till he opened the doors on ten.

Then, doors sliding shut, she turned to face me and, voice icy, said, "Now. I *demand* an explanation of your astonishing rudeness." Down the corridor a man turned a corner to come walking toward us, room key dangling in his hand. "Wait." She walked by me, passing two closed doors, feeling in her handbag. Brought out her key, bent forward to unlock her door, then gestured me in with an irritated jerk of her chin. Door closed, she walked past me — a big room, larger than mine — then turned to face me. "Well?"

I was ready. "I'm very sorry. And I do apologize. But I can't really tell you much. I'm a . . .

kind of detective, you might say. I'm looking for someone. I was about to get in the cab when I thought I saw him, that's all. So I just closed the door —"

"Slammed it."

"I suppose. But I was in a hurry, couldn't take time to explain or I'd lose him."

"And — was it your quarry?"

"Nope. Wrong man."

She stepped closer to study my face. "Si, is this true?"

"Sort of. Fairly close."

She stood looking up at me, then did this fine thing women sometimes do: put a hand on each shoulder, her forearms on my chest. This does something to your arms; you can't let them just hang there. So it was not of my own volition, it really was not! She was so close, I could smell her perfume, and she was so good-*looking*, that my arms just rose up, went around her, and I was kissing her before I could take control, kissing her hard, pulling her tight against me. Then — the little man in my head running for the controls, hanging on to the levers, fighting them, I — and oh, I didn't want to, I was so aware that I *did not want to* — I dropped my arms and stepped back fast. "I didn't mean that. I didn't intend it."

She just smiled, nodding. "I know. But I did. It's my fault. You're a good loyal husband, aren't you. Well, sit down, Si; I won't chase you."

I couldn't run screaming out of the room, and

I walked over to a window chair. "Damn right it's your fault. You're too attractive. Much too."

"I don't suppose you'd like to slowly take off my clothes —"

"Hey! Shut up, okay? Just shut up."

"Of course I'd help! I'd unhook the —"

"Come on now."

"Okay. But it's too bad."

I didn't nod, but didn't shake my head either, because it was too bad. Why did it have to be like this? Why couldn't this be just a — just kind of separate from everything else. A sort of separate little island not connected . . . Enough, enough, and I stood up. "My goodness, just look at the time."

"Okay, I'll let you go." She walked to the door, then turned to me, hand on the knob. "But you know why I'm here, Si? In New York? I'm spending a small inheritance, that's all. Using it up, having a bit of fun. So why don't you let me help you? I have the time, and there must be something I could do to help."

"Sure," I said. "Fine, okay." She opened the door, and I made a little show of sidling past her looking scared, she made a fake little lunge, and we smiled. Then I headed for my room, only three doors down, still smiling; I liked the Jotta Girl just fine.

20

I HAD the evening to kill, but it didn't want to die and fought back. For a while I thought it might win, and nine o'clock never come. I had an armload of newspapers, and lay on my bed, shoes off, pillows stuffed behind me. But the *World*, the *Express*, the *Tribune*, the *Post*, all seemed like the strange newspapers you buy on vacation; funny-looking, the typefaces wrong, news headings about people and events that have nothing to do with you. Even the comics were strange: "Boob McNutt" . . . "Lady Bountiful" . . . "Foxy Grandpa" . . . "Buster Brown" . . . "Maud, the Mule." And they sure weren't funny.

I had the new *Variety*, still hunting for Tessie and Ted, but nope. I looked through *Artists' Forum*, the letters from readers section; also nope. One letter there said, *Cleveland, Ohio, Editor* Variety: *I ask that you investigate the truth of the report from Cleveland. While at the Grand this week, I wish it to be known that the true fact is I was the laughing hit of the bill. The undersigned acts*

305

on the same performance acknowledge this fact. Sam Morris.

Below this *Variety* said, *(Acts referred to, each signing above letter: Frank Rutledge, J. K. Bradshaw, Grace Bainbridge, The Four Bucks, Don Fabio, Miller and Mack, Onri Orthorpe and Co., and Wm. H. Rorkoph, stage manager.)*

Last week's *Variety* was over on the radiator, and I got it and, sitting on the edge of the bed, found the out-of-town review pages. These were dense with small-type reviews of vaudeville bills all over the United States, city after city, theater after theater, hundreds of terse, condensed, microscopic reviews — written, I thought, by locals in each town, attending with comps for whatever *Variety* paid them — not much, I imagined. Found *Cleveland, O*; then, far down in the middle of the long column, *Grand (J. H. Michel, mgr; agent, U. B. O.: Monday rehearsal 10)* — *Don Fabio, good contortionist; Miller and Mack, fair song and dance; Frank Rutledge and Co., featuring Grace Bainbridge, in "Our Wife," pleased; Onri Orthorpe and Co., spectacular dancers; Sam Morris, German monolog, did not please; Four Bucks, good cyclists.*

Then I sat back on my bed thinking about Sam Morris rushing down to buy this *Variety* as soon as copies reached his hotel newsstand. Taking it off to a corner of the lobby maybe, finding all the pages of small-type reviews, finding Cleveland, finding the Grand, bringing the paper closer, finding his own name . . . followed by

306

three sickening words, *did not please*. Not hard to picture a grimace then of — something: pain, anger, maybe fear. Then off at a lobby writing desk, keeping it brief and dignified, taking it to the Grand and carrying it around backstage to every other performer on the bill ("Sure, Sam, be happy to sign. Don't let that hick reviewer get to you!"). Finally, fighting to show that he was really the laughing hit of the bill, Sam Morris even gets the stage manager to sign his protest. A tough life. Oh, Tessie and Ted.

Still not ten o'clock, time frozen, Einstein right. It occurred to me that I might saunter down the hall, tap on the Jotta Girl's door, and say, "Hi! Just wondered what you were doing," but Julia didn't want me to. Neither did Willy. Rover thought it might be okay, but his moral standards were untested, so I just lay there and thought about England.

After a while, I walked to the windows and looked out. The sky was worth a look: clear and clean, a fine deepening blue out over the Park, and to the west, over the Hudson, a lingering touch of daylight that just hated to leave. And then, from around the corner on Fifth, the fish-horn squawk of a rubber-bulbed horn, and it was *l'heure bleu*, full of promise, and I opened the window to lean out into this new night, and was happy.

Ten o'clock did in fact come. Downstairs then, no hat, no outer coat. Little chilly for that, but couldn't be helped. And I came trit-trotting down the outside Plaza steps the way you do when you're momentarily nineteen again, and took a cab, a red one, down to Madison Square.

Broadway and Fifth Avenue cross each other just below Madison Square to make a giant X at Twenty-third Street. So that Broadway is suddenly east of Fifth. And on the little triangle this creates stands that peculiar structure, the Flatiron Building, shaped to fit its site. The neighborhood around it, relentlessly noisy all day, stood nearly silent now at ten twenty-five. I could hear my own footsteps, walking along Fifth Avenue directly beside the west wall of the building. Then as I walked around the narrow end — the prow — of the building, I looked north far up the night-time Broadway of hotels and theaters at the distant lights of the Great White Way. But rounding the prow to walk south along the Broadway wall of the building, I looked down an ordinary Broadway of dark storefronts and emptied office buildings.

A good meeting place, but I'd had enough of scouting it, nothing much to learn. So, around the broad back of the building; then again I walked north toward its narrow end, but this time, at the little street-level shop stuck onto the rounded prow, I kept on walking — across Broadway to the dark greenery of Madison Square. And there on a bench I sat down to stare over at the puzzle of the Flatiron Building.

No: there was simply no way to sneak up on a pair of men standing beside a wall of the building over there on an otherwise deserted sidewalk.

Maybe I could just stroll past them, a late passerby, and see their faces? Not if they didn't want me to, and simply turned away till I'd gone by. My mind strayed: Yes, it did look like a tall stone ship over there, ready to sail up Broadway or Fifth. I tugged out my watch, the face barely visible in the light of a park lamppost. Eleven minutes to eleven; I had to do something, and I stood up, walked across Broadway again, and stopped beside the building: What now? I'd passed the Flatiron countless times, but now directly beside it, really looking at it, I saw that its surface was cut stone in the shape of large blocks, mortised in the crevices. And I reached up, put my fingertips in a shoulder-height crevice, set the side of my right shoe in the first crevice above the sidewalk, straightened my knee, and stood, hung on the side of the building ten inches above the walk. And understood that I had to do it again, right now, before I could think, or I could never do it at all.

Hands raised one at a time to the next crevice, left toe to the next higher level, knee straightening. Did it again immediately, then again, the stone rough-cut, scraping my clothes, tugging at buttons, brushing my cheek, feeling cold.

Up, crablike, spraddled against the side of the Flatiron Building not daring to think, shoving thought aside, until I gently bumped my head on the underside of the stone ledge that runs clear around the building. There I hung, blocked: I could fall, some thirty feet, I thought, and no, not be killed — I didn't think so, but maybe. But certainly break bones, smash my shoulder easily if I hit wrong, or yes, crack my skull, that could happen. *But don't* think, *just* do *it,* and I very gently let go with my right hand, moved it up, knuckles brushing the underside of the projecting stone shelf, then out and back, my hand hooked over its outer edge. Then the other, very quickly, because now my feet couldn't hold, and I swung gently out, hanging over the sidewalk — and quickly, before my upper-arm strength drained away, I pulled myself up, steadily and fast, chin passing the shelf edge. Then, forearms going straight, I could bend forward and lie, legs still dangling, but happy with relief, safe.

Then, knees up too, I crept across, and sat down on this little stone ledging, the window washers' delight, running clear around the entire building.

A moment, a few seconds of self-congratulation, sitting there in the dark up on the side of the Flatiron Building, back comfortably against the stonework between a pair of dark office windows lettered with — I couldn't really read it, looking back over my shoulder. Just that moment or so, and then it flashed in my mind like a comic-strip light bulb: *On which side of the building were they going to meet?*

I sat facing Broadway, and now I stood up; quite dark here, no light from the street this high. The ledge was white; I could see it. And I began walking around the building, patrolling it. I felt

310

like an idiot, slowly strolling round and round the Flatiron Building up there in the dark, watching the empty walks below, careful not to trip, almost sliding my feet along the stone. It was getting cold, a small breeze. It must be eleven o'clock — where *were* they?

Around the prow then, slowly, not quite lifting my feet but sliding them along. Now a lone pedestrian across the street on Fifth Avenue. But not coming here, not even looking this way. I turned the corner at Twenty-second Street, and crept along the back. Nothing.

Around the corner, and now along the east, Broadway side, the busy white lights far ahead up there. On up to the prow again, and then it occurred to me: I stopped, and stood — a kind of figurehead against that prow, but facing the wrong way. And stood there watching Broadway and Fifth Avenue both.

And then here came someone, suddenly, out of Twenty-second Street, now crossing Broadway angling toward the building. And well, yes, I recognized him, as who would not, as he walked into a circle of weak orange light lying on the pavement under a streetlamp. I'd seen this figure often in black-and-white film — the decisive movement, the power in the tilt of the big head. And now, as the streetlight momentarily moved across them, the familiar small round glasses and mustache below them. Then as he stepped onto the sidewalk, the dark, wide-brimmed old Rough Rider hat.

311

He stopped beside the building wall, the hat turning as the invisible head under it turned to look north. I looked too, and now here came the other, from the north, crossing Broadway toward us, and I hurried along my ledge with no sound, or almost none, and arrived there over their heads as they met.

"Well, my boy. On time as always," said the surprisingly not deep but almost thin voice.

"I try to be, sir."

"And enjoying New York? But of course you are."

"Always, as you well know. Sir, I could have come to your —"

"No, too many reporters lurking about these days. Wouldn't do for them to see you arrive. I simply left by the back door, and down a — you know the passageway."

"Yes, sir."

Silence now, movement by the heavier figure; he was tall enough but not so tall as the other. *We were right about that, Rube: Z is tall.* And now a whiteness, something in hand. "I worked on these this afternoon, and I believe they are right, they will accomplish their object." The taller man's hand reaching out, taking the papers. "You have Howard's?"

"Yes, sir," tucking the papers away.

"Then good luck, my boy. Good luck, and be careful."

"Always.

"No, not quite always." And they both laughed

a little. Then, abruptly, suddenly embarrassed it seemed to me: "Good luck," once again, and a quick single handshake. Then they both turned away, and I stood there on my foolish little stone shelf staring down at first one, then the other of the two dark hats and wide brims which were all I'd ever seen, all I could possibly have seen from the only place I could possibly have hidden. There he went, the almost portly old Rough Rider, back the way he'd come, vanishing into Twenty-second Street. And there crossing Broadway toward Madison Square went the back of Z's hat, the back of his neck, the back of his coat, then was lost among the trees, and I stood up there on the side of the Flatiron Building trying to think what that meant. Z was gone forever now, no other clue to finding him left. The Great War? Well, the notion of a single man somehow preventing that enormous event had never quite seemed real; had seemed faintly absurd, in fact, and I just shrugged, and began to climb down to the sidewalk. But what about Willy? I didn't know; just have to think about that.

No cabs down here, and turning away from the great stone Flatiron, I began to walk. Z was gone, but Tessie and Ted were here, weren't they? *Yes*, here in 1912 New York. On Broadway, they'd always said. So why hadn't I found them? Crossing Twenty-eighth Street, glancing left, I saw the marquee lights of the Fifth Avenue Theatre a short block to the west. And in that moment they went out, but I stood motionless on the curb because just a little further down that short block a single light, a round white globe, still burned, and I realized that this was the stage door. I hesitated. I wanted to go *home,* I wanted my family, and I could go tonight, go to the Brooklyn Bridge, and within an hour . . . But I turned left, and walked the short block to that lighted globe.

Yes. Lettered on the green wood door beneath it: *Stage,* in washed-out white, and I stood on the walk looking at it, not knowing what to do now. The door opened abruptly, and a young woman walked swiftly out, on her way and knowing exactly where, enough makeup still on so I knew she'd been part of the show. I took a shallow little breath, pushed the door open with a forefinger, waited, then walked cautiously in.

21

ALONG A short dim cor-
ridor, up three wooden
steps, and — I sketched
this later from memory
— the stagedoor man
asleep. Sneak by him?
No. I didn't know where
to go or what I was
doing: I'd be caught, and
thrown out. I looked at
this sleeping man, then
got out my wallet, mov-
ing quietly, slipped out
a twenty-dollar bill, and
folded it twice. Holding
it in my closed fist, I
worked up my best timidly eager, I'm-harmless
smile, and tapped the man on the knee.

He didn't move, just opened his eyes slightly,
used to being caught asleep and pretending he
wasn't. He looked up at me steadily, and I said,
"Excuse me, but I wonder if I could possibly

see . . ." Who? I spoke the only name I knew here: "The Dove Lady."

He was going to shake his head, ask who I was, and all that, but, not looking at my hand, as though it were acting independently, I passed him my folded-up bill. He glanced at it, then up at me, eyes going hard, and I understood. I'd made a mistake; he'd seen the yellow back and the big *20*, and it was too much, ten times too much possibly, and it made him wary. But still . . . he glanced down at what lay in his palm, hesitated, then got to his feet. "Wait here."

The little wooden-floored area he left me in was maybe ten by ten. To my right I saw the dark stage and the edges of the many backdrops, mysterious ropes rising up into blackness. From down the corridor my doorman friend had walked into, I heard a woman casually singing. Heard a man's easy, skilled, good-natured laugh. Heard a man swear, not meaning it. The wall at my left was bare brick, a bulletin board fastened to it, and I walked over to see what the thumbtacked notices said.

One was a typed list of acts, with call times for afternoon and evening performances. A notice printed on cardboard — I had time to copy it — read, *Don't say "slob" or "son-of-a-bitch" or "golly gee" on this stage unless you want to be canceled peremptorily. Do not address anyone in the audience in any manner. If you have not the ability to entertain Mr. Keith's audiences without risk of offending them, do the best you can. Lack of talent will be less open to censure than would be an insult to a patron. If you are in doubt as to the character of your act consult the local manager before you go on the stage, for if you are guilty of uttering anything sacrilegious or even suggestive you will be immediately closed and will never again be allowed in a theater where Mr. Keith is an authority.* Wow.

Along the top of the bulletin board's wood frame someone had lettered pretty neatly in crayon, *Don't send your laundry out until after the first performance.* On the white-painted wooden surface of the board itself were more inscriptions, hand-printed in ink or pencil. *Don't blame the orchestra, they are too busy at the foundry to rehearse . . . Gee, what a small stage . . . Where's the mail? . . . We know the theater's rotten, but how's your show? . . . The dressing rooms are swept out every summer . . .* Tacked up in a corner, a printed calling card: *Zeno Brothers, acrobats, can be addressed care of Billboard.* A rubber-stamped inscription, *Luke Mason of "The Josh Wilkins Company" is America's Greatest Comedian.* In pencil on a little rectangle of paper carefully torn from an envelope: *Flo De Vere, of "The Belle of Boston" Company sending regards to the Wrangler Sisters of "The Merry Marauders Company."* A typed list of *Boarding Houses:* some twenty-odd addresses, mostly in the west Thirties and Forties. And added in pencil, half a dozen more. Penciled comments beside some of them: *Good . . . Good food but not enuf . . . A bum place — for acrobats only.* I heard my man walking toward me, and

317

when I looked up he poked a thumb over one shoulder, saying, "Go on back," and walked past me toward his chair; I felt like asking for my twenty back.

Down the same corridor, a right turn into another, wider corridor of dressing rooms, running parallel to the stage — I think; this was a little disorienting.

Corridors and dressing rooms were alive with people — tonight's performers, I supposed. I walked along, glancing into the dressing rooms, edging past and around the people in the corridor, fascinated. Mostly they ignored me, but nodded if our eyes met. Was it okay to glance into their dressing rooms? I didn't know how else to find the Dove Lady. Then — sitting at her dressing table, her back to the corridor but watching for me in her mirror — here she was, dressed for the street. Against a wall stood three large cube-shaped birdcages covered with a cloth. I stopped at her door, she said, "Come on in," and I thanked her for seeing me. "And what can I do for you?"

"There's a vaudeville act supposed to be in New York this month sometime. I have to see it, but I don't know where they'll be. Or when. Or how to find out."

She waited a moment to see if there was any more; then: "You know what the act's called, I trust."

"Tessie and Ted."

She thought about it, shook her head. "Don't know them. What's their act?"

"Well, she sings, I think. And he plays the piano, and dances."

"And how come you picked me?"

"Well, I had to choose from the cyclists, Joe Cook, Kraus and Raus, and the rest. Your photo looked the kindest."

"Oh, it does! And I am!" She smiled now. "Well, shouldn't be hard to find out." She picked up a copy of *Variety* from her table, opened it, turned pages, then folded it back to a page packed with small type, and handed it to me. "Take a look; you can see for yourself if they're on."

Bills Next Week in Vaudeville Theaters Playing 3 or Less Shows Daily. All houses open for the week with Monday matinees when not otherwise listed. Below this the page was dense with small type, and compact with symbols. *Theaters listed as Orpheum without any further distinguishing descriptions are on the Orpheum Circuit. Theaters listed with S-C following name and in brackets, usually Empress, are on the Sullivan-Considine Circuit . . . (P) Pantage Circuit . . . (Loew) Marcus Loew Circuit . . .* An entire world I knew nothing about.

New York was the first heading, naturally. And the first theater listed was this one, the Fifth Avenue. Beginning this last Monday: *The Doyle Family . . . Kraus and Raus . . . Smith, Smith, Smith and the Smithies . . . Vernon and Vera . . . The Back Fence Banshees . . . Madam Zelda . . . The Dove Lady . . . Joe Cook . . . Merlin the Great.*

At the American (Loew), another long list of acts . . . another at the Colonial (U.B.O.) . . . and on and on, dozens and dozens of vaudeville acts on this week in New York, Brooklyn, the Bronx. But no Tessie and Ted. Following New York, the listing became alphabetical, acts opening this last Monday in Atlanta, Georgia . . . Atlantic City (Young's Pier), and in Oakland, Plattsburg, Portland, Pueblo . . .

The listing continued onto the next page . . . and onto still a third: hundreds and hundreds — thousands, for all I could tell — of vaudeville acts playing this week all over the United States, more than anyone could read.

"Find them?"

"Not in New York." I offered her paper back.

"Keep it if you want, I've read it."

"I never imagined there were so many vaudeville acts. And I'd like to see every one of them."

"Oh no you wouldn't. Those are the big-time listings, the two-a-day or three-a-day. There are even more small-time acts — six, seven shows a day. Which is murder, believe you me. And there's medium small-time" — she was leaning toward her mirror, turning her face, lifting her jaw, inspecting — "that's four, five shows a day. And big small-time, little big-time, medium big-time, big big-time." She laughed, glancing at me in her mirror. "I'm kidding, but there's something like two thousand vaudeville houses in the U.S. of A. and that means all kinds of vaudeville, and a lot you don't ever want to see. New York gets the best, naturally. If you like vaudeville, you're in the right place. You sure your act got to New York?"

I nodded.

"Well." A final glance at her mirror; then she turned off its lights and stood up, leaning forward to brush off the front of her dress. "I'm going home now. Meaning my New York boarding house. If you want to come along, somebody there may know about Tessie and Ted."

"I'd like to," I said. She lifted a corner of the cloth covering the cages, I heard a kind of rustling, and she said, "Good night, chickees," and we left. Outside, she walked straight across the sidewalk to a waiting hansom cab. "Evenin', Miz Boothe."

"Good evening, Charley. It's home sweet home tonight." And she climbed in while I trotted around to the other side. The driver clucked his horse awake, flicked the reins, and we pulled out into Twenty-eighth Street, heading west. "I don't like the automobiles," the Dove Lady said. "They stink."

"Yes. But so do the horses."

"They stink nice, though."

"Yeah." I thought so too. "I like the hansoms. Nice and slow so you can really see things."

"And they give you time to think. What's your name?"

"Simon Morley. Si."

"Okay, Si. And I'm Maude. Maude Boothe." We clattered over the bricklike stone paving blocks under the Sixth Avenue El and its overhead station, then over to Seventh Avenue, and as we turned into it, I think my face must have shown something, because there up ahead stood Penn Station in all its majesty. I sat forward to take it in, great tall windows shining on the night. "Lovely, isn't it," Maude Boothe said, and I nodded yes, oh yes. "I came in there last time," she said, "and it's beautiful inside. It makes you feel good, proud to live in New York." I nodded again: we were passing it now, my head turning to watch its white newness slide by.

Somewhere in the Thirties we turned west into a long block of four-story brownstones all more or less identical. We stopped in front of one, beside a streetlamp, and I sat forward making motions of paying. She waved me away, and I got out under the light, waiting to help her down. Two men in button sweaters and caps sat on the stoop watching us: one elderly or old, the other maybe forty. The cab clopping away, Maude Boothe turned to them. "Either of you ever hear of an act, Tessie and Ted?"

They thought, then shook their heads. "Knew Tessie Burns once," the old man said. "Burns and Burns, the House-Afire Act. No Tessie and Ted. What's their act?"

"Song and dance. This is Si; he wants to get in touch with them. Si, that's John, the talkative one. And this is Ben. He's an acrobat, they can't talk." They grinned, reaching out to shake my hand. "I'm going up to change," Maude said.

"Stick around if you want. There'll be others out here: somebody must know Tessie and Ted. I'm beginning to feel I do." She went up the stairs, and John, the old one, said, "Take a load off your feet, Si," and I sat down halfway up the steps.

"That *Variety*, — he nodded at my coat pocket. "Mind if I borrow it?"

I gave it to him, and to Ben he said, "You seen this yet?" Ben shook his head. "Well, you know LaMont, LaMont's Cockatoos?"

"Yeah, I played with LaMont. In Des Moines. Bird act. Noisy, squawking damn things. Not like Maude's."

"Well, he's got a squawk himself here in *Variety*." John took a pair of old-style specs with narrow oval lenses from his shirt pocket, flicked out the thin wire sidepieces, and put them on with one hand. A young good-looking woman in slippers and a long patterned kimono with wide Japanese sleeves came out of the house, sat down on an upper balustrade, pulling out a square of knitting from her kimono pocket, and began to knit. John said, "Dolores, this here's Si," and she smiled beautifully at me, and I nodded back, trying to equal her smile. John raised paper and chin high, turning his back to the streetlamp to bring its light fully on the page. " 'New York, New York,' " he read aloud. " 'In last week's *Variety* George M. Young wrote a review of Keith's bill, Philadelphia, wherein he made mention of an act playing the Victoria there that was

323

either a copy of LaMont's Cockatoos, or there was difficulty in understanding how the routine of both bird acts could be so much alike. I think Mr. Young has made a big mistake in comparing any other act with LaMont's Cockatoos. LaMont's Cockatoos do back somersaults, giant swings, and so forth, which other bird acts are not on record as exhibiting. LaMont's birds, fifty in number, are all trained, where the other act has but three birds, and features one trick like LaMont's; i.e., the bell trick. But LaMont does not make the bell trick constitute the entire act as the other act does. In fact, the act spoken of is nothing like LaMont's. It is like all other acts that are in the same line. They try the bluff of putting it over, but fail to accomplish the results of LaMont's Cockatoos. Signed, LaMont.' " As he folded the paper to hand it back to me, I smiled and nodded to show I appreciated the humor of the letter he'd read. But none of the others smiled; they glanced at me quickly, then looked away, and I felt my face go hot. Dolores reached down to touch my shoulder reassuringly. "Don't blame you, Si. LaMont's letter does sound funny. All that fuss. But his act is all he's got, you see. It's everything, it's his livelihood, it's *him,* he's nothing without it. None of us are. And he has to protect that. Bookers read the goddamn reviews, you can bet on that, *bookers.* So LaMont can't let his fifty-bird act get confused with anything less." She smiled at me. *"Verstehen?"*

I nodded, and so did the old man, who said,

"You got to fight for your act. Hell, they'll even steal it from the thief who stole it from you. Listen to this one." He took the paper from my lap, opened it to the same page of letters, and read aloud. " 'Chicago. January 8. Editor *Variety*. Re: the letter accusing James Neary of stealing Mike Scott's act, that of wearing dress coat, green tights, with medals on. I wish to state that I and Tom Ward produced it originally at the Odeon Theatre, Baltimore, Maryland, February 13, 1876. I can refer you to Steve Finn and Jack Sheean. Signed, W. J. Malcolm.' " John grinned at me, letting me know he agreed this was kind of funny. "Knew a guy once," he said, "claimed he thought up the line 'Beautiful but dumb.' Got mad every time he heard anyone else use it." He lifted *Variety* to his glasses again, and read, " 'London, December 19. Editor *Variety*. I desire to call your attention to an injustice which artists often have to suffer in the use by other artists of an expression or form of advertisement. For instance, with my daughter, Alice Pierce, who presents a series of "impressions" of stars, I find that the word "impression" is now being used for the first time by several artists. Signed, M. Pierce.' "

I nodded, not smiling now, at this little glimpse of an old man fighting for his daughter. "Steal your act," Dolores said as a young man in shirtsleeves, no attached collar, appeared in the doorway behind her. "Worst thing they can do."

"Oh, there's worse than that," the new man

said; then Dolores interrupted to introduce us. His name was Al, and he'd never heard of Tessie and Ted. He sat down beside Dolores, and continued his story. "You know Noble and Henson? Songs and crossfire?" They all nodded, murmuring yes. "Well, I saw Pat last week at the Hoffman House. He's not working now, but he says they're booked. Well, Pat says last summer he was offered the Orpheum Circuit for the team at a salary of two hundred per week. He was to sign the contract next day. Well, he told people about it, and that night he runs into a fellow name of Burt Bender; you know him?" Nobody seemed to. Maude Boothe came out in a dark blue bathrobe and slippers; she sat down opposite Dolores and Al. "Well," said Al, "Burt was the male member of another team not quite as good as Noble and Henson."

"I remember them," Maude said. "Played with them once in San Francisco."

"Well, Burt meets Pat Henson, and came in like a million dollars. Says, 'What do you think of Beck: wants me to sign for the Orpheum at two hundred and fifty. I been fighting him for the other fifty for six months.'" Two very tiny women, not quite dwarfs, came out, and sat down next to Maude. I'd become aware that, two houses to the west, a similar gathering had formed; and several more across the street. "Well, Pat said that after this gink left, he thought about that for the rest of the evening. Here's The Benders, not as good as they were and everyone knew it. But the Orph Circuit offers them fifty bucks more!" The street before us stood empty, motionless; not a car had passed since I'd come here, and none were parked in the entire block. "So Pat talks the whole thing over with his partner, and next day they turn down the Orpheum Circuit at two hundred. Well, they laid off all winter, and he spent his savings. This last spring Pat finds out what happened. Somebody told Burt Bender about Pat's offer, and Burt hotfoots it over to the Orpheum booking office. He tells the Orpheum he and his partner will work for one fifty. So they took him and his partner 'stead of Noble and Henson. Burt says he's been layin' for that guy ever since."

Maude Boothe said, "Anybody ever hear of an act Tessie and Ted? Si down there is looking for them." The two tiny women thought, then shook their heads. "Well, stick around," Maude said to me. "Eventually somebody'll know." Later Maude told me who everyone out here was. Al and Dolores were married, and had an act together: they were magnificent dancers, the tango especially. They were on at the Victoria. Upstairs they had a year-old baby, and Dolores always sat where she could hear it if it cried. The two tiny women were twins, though not identical, born in Toledo to a pair of English music hall performers in the States on a tour, who never went home. Their twins became teenagers, and their parents taught and rehearsed them in the act they still used — the act was their inheritance. In it, one of them, heavily rouged and powdered, acted as a ventriloquist's dummy for the other. Presently the dummy would rebel, and they'd trade places: audiences loved that, it was the high point of their act. They'd sing a little then, dance a little, not badly but not especially well. Didn't matter because audiences always took them to their hearts, and the pair was always booked, and always in big time. They were shy, never went out, at ease only with vaudevillians. Old John was long retired. Like many vaudevillians, though by no means all, Maude told me later, he'd saved money, owned property, had several bank accounts: for safety. And a diamond ring he could hock if he had to. He lived in theatrical boarding houses like this one, moving occasionally for a change or because he got mad at somebody. Everything tangible he owned was in his old dome-topped trunk, professionally lettered with his name and his agent's address. Ben was a fairly new arrival and Maude didn't know much about him. "Yet," she added, smiling. She thought he had or once had had a family somewhere. There were other boarders, either up in their rooms or not at home. Nothing about herself.

Ben spoke up, surprising everyone a little, I thought. "Something worse than stealing a booking. Or even an act," he said. "Anyone ever hear of Sauer and Kraut?"

"I think maybe I did," said old John. From other front stoops up and down the quiet street — no cars yet, not a one — quiet laughter and

328

voices. From somewhere across the street, piano music from an open window. "Sauer and Kraut were strictly small-time," Ben said. "German comedians: the little derbies, the padded stomachs, the awful accents, the pratfalls. *Small* small-time."

Across the street a woman's voice joined the piano notes, and she sang, as we all paused to listen, "When the town is fast asleep . . . And it's midnight in the sky . . . That's the time the festive Chink . . . starts to wink his other eye . . . Starts to wink his dreamy eye. Lazily you'll hear him sigh, Chinatown, my Chinatown, when the lights are low . . ."

Down the street under the nearest streetlamp, a pair of men in street clothes stood practicing a balancing act, one on the other's shoulders. "But Sauer and Kraut wanted to move up," Ben said, "so they bought a new act. A lot better stuff than anything they had. They rehearsed it, tried it out, and got booked." A boy came noisily down the center of the street on a contraption made from a two-by-four, roller-skate wheels nailed to each end, a box nailed upright to the front, a tin can "headlight" nailed to that. One foot on the two-by-four, he pushed himself along with the other. He stopped to watch the balancing act. ". . . almond eyes of brown. Hearts seem light and life seems bright, in dreamy Chinatown . . ."

"I was on the same bill they were," Ben went on. "At the Adelphi? In Guthrie?"

Al said, "Guthrie next week, and I don't drink."

"I never played Guthrie, but I played Norman," said Dolores. "Before we were married, I was booked in Cleburne, Texas, by Swor Brothers of Dallas. I took the week for less money than I'd been receiving on account of it was a short jump. I was led to believe it was a week stand, and I got there to be informed by the manager that he only played acts three days, and that he had an agreement with the agent not to pay transportation on split weeks. And three days was a split week." Dolores never stopped knitting. "So I paid my transportation, and after the three days I worked the rest of the week in Gainesville. For the next week I accepted booking by phone for Norman, Oklahoma, and was told that the contract would be mailed to me there. On arrival I found the house was booked by Jack Dickey, and no contracts. I went to my hotel, and immediately phoned Swor Brothers, but they refused to talk to me." A barefooted boy of ten or eleven walked by, looking inquiringly at our stoop, and John beckoned him over. He gave the boy some money, so did Ben, and Al got up and walked into the house. "Went to the Western Union office," Dolores said, "and wired them, requesting an answer. It was ignored." Al came out with a large, shiny metal bucket, came down the steps, and handed it to the boy, gave some money, change, to John, and the boy left. "So I think artists working Texas and Oklahoma better watch out with these agents. They don't look out after

330

your interests, and the truth ain't in them. You have trouble in Guthrie?"

"No, it was okay," Ben said. "The Adelphi's okay."

I waited; no one said anything. Down the street, the acrobats finished their practicing, walking back to their stoop, the kid on the skate-wheel contraption scooting on, wheels grinding. I worked up my nerve, and said, "What happened with Sauer and Kraut?"

"Well, they were on maybe number four spot, and I saw them come out early, in costume, all ready, and they stood waiting in the wings watching. Opening act was a juggling team, I think, and then for some reason, some booking mixup maybe — nothing to do about it, you have to fill the bill — on comes another comedy team." From one of the stoops across the street, a young man of maybe twenty came angling across the street toward us. "Hey there, Dippy." He stopped before us, smiling at the general murmur of greeting. "Evening, folks." This was Van Hoven, I learned, The Dippy, Mad Musician.

"You seen the beer boy, eh?" said John.

"Sure." Dippy grinned, and sat down beside Ben. "Don't let me interrupt."

"Well, this other comedy team walks on, right past Sauer and Kraut, and they're dressed the same! Looks like two pairs of twins! They go on, and do the *same act!* Word for word, joke for joke, same knockabouts, everything! The guy sold the same act to the both of them."

The others nodded, saying, "Yeah," or, "Wouldn't you know," and the like. After a little time I said, "Well . . . what happened? To Sauer and Kraut?"

"Oh," said Ben, voice surprised at the question, "they were canned. On the spot. They were no use now. Had to borrow money to get out of town. We all gave them what we could."

Across the street, "Chinatown" ended. A pause, then piano and the same young voice began: "Honey, honey, can't you hear? Funny, funny music, dear . . . Ain't the funny strain goin' to your brain? Like a bottle of wine, fine. Hon', hon', hon', take a chance! One, one, one! One little dance! Can't you see them all swaying up the hall? Let's be gettin' in line!" Then the familiar chorus: "Everybody's doin' it, doin' it! Doin' what? Turkey Trot!" And Maude groaned, and said, "Everybody's *over*doin' it."

A middle-aged woman came out of the house and sat down on the step just below Maude, and Maude leaned forward, murmuring something to her. Then she called to me. "Si, this is Madam Zelda, Mind Reader. That's Simon Morley. She never heard of Tessie and Ted either."

"I'll let Maude know if I do," Madam Zelda said, and I nodded and smiled, thanking her.

The beer boy came walking toward our house, tilted to one side, his arm pulled straight down by the weight of his filled bucket. Dolores went into the house, Ben was digging into his pants pocket, and I stood up quickly, saying, "Let me," and got out a pair of quarters. Ben took the filled bucket; I gave the quarters to the boy, who looked down at them astonished. "Gee! Thanks, mister!"

Dolores came out carrying a Coca-Cola tray full of assorted glasses, Maude just behind her with cups and a pot of tea on another tray. Then we all sat comfortably leaned back against the stone, sipping. Across the street I saw a boy coming slowly from Eighth Avenue carrying two tin buckets. And over at Eighth saw the corner saloon I thought he'd come from. It was a good moment sitting here sipping beer with these people. The night was turning a little cool, but no one left, and in the easy silence it occurred to me that my morning newspaper had had columns filled with Taft and Roosevelt struggling for the Republican presidential nomination; and other stories on the growing troubles in Europe. But these people sitting out here lived in another world, the only one that mattered. Did they ever vote? I suspected not, and I'd have bet that in the entire house behind us, up in the rooms they lived in, there wasn't a newspaper not called *Variety* or *Billboard*.

The easy, lazy, mildly gossipy talk resumed. I heard about a vaudevillian called Sparrow; they all seemed to know or had heard of him. His act was unique. He stood up on the stage and tossed oranges, tomatoes, and other soft fruit out to the audience. Then he'd put a fork in his mouth, and the audience threw all that garbage back at him while he tried to catch it on his fork. He'd miss, and in no time his suit and face were dripping. And always, some of the audience knew his act, and brought along hard stuff like potatoes and turnips and threw them. Threw good, a lot of them, fast, hard, and right at his face. So he had to catch it. On his fork. If he missed, as he sometimes did, too bad; black eye, bloody nose. He carried his own floor cloth, and wore a dress suit made of black and white oilcloth. And when he came off, walking along backstage toward his dressing room, he got a clear path.

Another act was Sherman and Morissey, who did a comic trapeze act in funny costume. What they did was fall. Off a six-foot-high wire onto the stage. Singly and together. Then they'd get mad, and knock each other around, and fall some more. And the falls were real, no way to fake them. They hurt so much that they couldn't take it for more than eight minutes; the shortest act in vaudeville, Ben said. Back in their dressing room, it was liniment, bandages, and pulling splinters out of each other, getting into shape for the next show.

I must have looked astonished, and Dolores smiled and said, "It's vaudeville, Si. And it's better to be in it than out." That led the talk into failures, people who could no longer get bookings, the worst thing that could happen. A man most of them knew had gradually slipped from medium- to small-time, and then into no bookings at all. Friends had coached him then into being a storewindow dummy. He'd stand in store windows, face whitened and rouged, motionless as a real dummy. Then he'd rap on the window at a likely passerby, who would stop to stare, and he'd make a stiff mechanical bow, with a jerky mechanical smile. Then absolutely still and motionless again. People would gather, rapping on the window at him, boys making faces trying to force him to smile, and he'd point to a sign in the window advertising something inside. "It wasn't show business," Al said, "but it was close as he could get," and everyone nodded.

Something strange happened then. Young Van Hoven began to talk, and he went on and on and on, no one interrupting. As well as I can remember, this is what he said. I wouldn't have blamed anyone who got up and left, though no one did, but I listened and could have gone on listening all night long.

"It's hard," he murmured, voice genuinely sympathetic to the ex-vaudevillian store-window dummy. "I was in the show business and I wasn't putting it over either. Misery loves company, so I joined a partner who also didn't have any money. I was broke all winter, and it was one of Chicago's hardest. We roomed in South Clark Street near the alley of the stage door of the old Olympic, and talk about Ding Bat not knowing the family above — it's a joke!" (I have no idea what that meant.) "The landlady never saw us, and we never saw her: when you look like we looked, you didn't want to see anyone.

"We rehearsed a burlesque magic act, and put

it together in a couple of days in our room by the aid of gaslight. That was the only way you could even find yourself in our room night or day, and we slept all day to try to forget we ought to eat." Dippy smiled. "Now sometimes when I'm eating big meals I wonder if I'm awake.

"My partner, Jules, poor old Jules! He was sick and he was getting bald-headed. He wanted to give up, but one day I landed a job for three days for twelve dollars for the team, and our supper Sunday night. It was a German joint, and Jules was German, so we put it over. And on Sunday I ate like I eat now.

"The next week we played a joint on the far north side, got our money, paid a few debts, ate a couple of times, and were broke again. Couldn't even get our laundry. Got a job then, supposed to pay us twenty dollars a week, and we had to walk to it; no carfare, nearly five miles. When we stepped into the place the bartender said, 'Harding sends me two men? I don't want men, I won't play men, I want women, my audience wants women!' Well, I don't want to say I'm so stuck on show business that tears came to my eyes, but they did — for another reason! I begged this big dub to please play us, as I was sick and Jules was sick, and I showed him Jules's hair. I did everything until finally he did play us. We flopped and the two old soubrettes he had on the bill with us were a knockout. So I knew the fellow was right, and I hurried out to a place on North Halsted Street and I actually begged for a job. He gave in, and I rushed back to get Jules.

"Well, we went to work for eighteen dollars for the team, and supper on Sunday night again. Booked direct, no commission. The place had a small German stock company. Our double-up magic act was a riot, but my own single was a fliv. I felt pretty blue because the manager wanted to keep Jules, and join up with the stock company. But I almost knew Jules would stick with me, and he did. But the next week was the finish: we both got canned. It was the first time since we were together. I'd often gone it alone, and when I saw the stage manager talking to my partner with some money in his hand, I knew it was finished with the two of us as a team. I stepped outside, on that cold rainy April night, and it just seemed I never could make good, and my good suit and cuff buttons and everything were in soak. I was desperate, and went back into the front of the house where Mr. Murphy, one of the owners, was sitting with two ladies. I pleaded with him to please keep both of us boys, and I showed him my clothes. He could easily see I didn't have on all a human being should have. So he let me finish the week out alone, at twelve dollars.

"I did it, and did it hard. I drew fifty cents every night, and Jules would meet me after his turn, and we'd eat, and just go to sleep back at the boarding house. The next day I'd walk back to save carfare. Well, the next week Jules and I split up; he thought he could do better with a soubrette. So I was flat in Chicago once more. Jules went with a turkey burlesque. He took my muffler and a shirt, and all I had left was a summer suit of old clothes, and my trunk.

"Well, Williams of Williams and Healy put me next to a wagon-show job, and another friend bought my ticket. I jumped to Boswell, Indiana, to Adam Fetzer's one-ring wagon show, and believe me, it was some bum circus. The room where we slept was upstairs, and the big top, or the big tent, was laid out on the floor, and it was full of ropes. Well, you can see what a chance you had to sleep lying on a lot of ropes, so I decided to move out. Now, Fetzer's had a lion in a big cage with two partitions in it, and only one lion. So I slept in the empty partition. I got some horse blankets and all was fine. The other fellows thought I was swellheaded because I was sleeping outside with a lion instead of them.

"Fetzer was afraid I was a lemon, though, and I thought I was, too. So he made me do extra work like shining harness, painting wagons, and doing everything he could think of. And he was a good thinker. So I did as he thought best, because I was up against it. Nine dollars was the limit with that show, and all I got was seven. But I did my best. I fed the lion, and he wasn't like a regular lion that got up early. He was old and nearly ready to die. Still, he was the best thing in the circus, so you can see what kind of circus it was. I used to have to wake him up to eat, and grind his meat, too, and when we gave a special show in the sideshow, I used to have to poke him with a hot iron to make him growl a little. A couple of times we nearly got run out of town for doing that. I felt sorry for poor old Jake, but I was in no position to pity a lion.

"I got to feeling pretty blue at times, but you can't let yourself stay blue around a circus for very long. Those circus fellows are made of iron. There was one who had been with Fetzer for years, and to hold his job he did a dozen acts. One was a revolving ladder act, and he got me into it. I had to hang on because it would revolve and bring me clear to the top, and then he wanted me to clown up there to make him a bigger hit, but believe me, all I did was hold on, and I held on tight. Every time I saw that ladder, I thought I saw my finish.

"Now, come April the roads dried, and April twenty-fifth our first show on the road opened. Well, I'd practiced on my own in the winter, and now I pulled aside the canvas and waited; the band played, and I ran out into the ring and did a comedy juggling act, and as true as I'm alive, I was one big hit. I also did a magic act that was not so good but good enough.

"Well, that night I slept in a regular hotel room, and Adam, the manager, was all salve. I was called Frankie, and all that soft stuff. The next day they used me in the sideshow, too, and honest, folks, I was needed bad. It consisted of a dwarfed bearded woman and her giant husband, a couple of old alligators, two cages of monkeys, the lion, and myself. I lectured on them, and did the best I could to make the thing look like a real sideshow, but the more I see of Broadway today, the wiser I think those rubes are. Old P. T. Barnum might have fooled them, but I couldn't. The best thing in our show was always our move to the next town.

"I got canned before my notice was up — I won't go into that — and with ten dollars in my pocket I jumped to Dayton. No job there, so I went to work in a restaurant. Finally landed a job with Gus Sun, and I jumped to Elkins, West Virginia; had to sit up all night. And when I got there, all in, was told I wasn't booked. Oh boy. But they couldn't lick me, and I borrowed enough from the manager to get to my next booking in Fairmont, West Virginia, where I opened. Well, the manager was a real fellow. I was on that circuit for eighteen weeks — eleven weeks in theaters, and seven weeks in hotels and restaurants. I hate to admit that, but what's the difference: I was as good as some of the theaters I played in. If I'd been a full-grown man instead of just a kid, some of those managers wouldn't have done me the way they did. But it's all over now, and I did my crying in my room in those days. I used to wonder if I was really bad, but it's all in the game; only I sure held a bad hand pretty often.

"Got thrown off the Sun Circuit, and joined

a rep show. The manager kept me on because he knew I had the nerve to do anything. And I did; did everything with that show, and I stuck with it till spring. It was the longest job I ever had, and to this day I write the manager letters; he was a regular fellow.

"The season closed, and I jumped back to Chicago, and all that summer I did eight shows a day on State Street. All day long from nine-thirty A.M. till eleven P.M. I couldn't stand it, so I jumped to Des Moines, and when I got there was told business was bad, so I didn't go to work, but landed a job in Oskaloosa at twenty-five dollars. From there I jumped to Manhattan, Kansas, and a couple of other small towns.

"Then my true friend, Frank Doyle, saved my life by giving me some time in Chicago, where I stayed all winter. Finally, the next summer on July fifth, came my chance. I opened at the Majestic — and to tell how I got that would be another whole story. Anyhow, I was a hit. Still, I'd sit in my dressing room and wonder if I was going to stay all week or get canned again. But I stayed all week, and up to now I have played in every first-class vaudeville theater in America and Canada, and I can only say it's a hard game. Even to this day the thing I can't bear is the manager who cans acts. That and the poor weak-minded simpleton who steals another man's act when maybe the poor fellow he stole it from battled even a harder battle than the one I have just related.

"Well, let's cheer up. I'm twenty-three years old in February, and I was born in Sioux City, on the Orpheum Circuit. And it's great to have a room like I've got this week, and a dinner like I had tonight. And fine dressing rooms, big stages, and to sleep in sleepers and belong to clubs where you meet George M. Cohan and Andrew Mack and all those fellows, even have them ask you to join their show. Oh, it's no use talking, this thing is great when you get it right. If it's a dream, don't ever wake me up. And if it's true, oh, please don't let the Commercial Trust Company fail, because that's where I have all my money. So I say, good luck to all, and success comes if you deserve it. Do your own act, and let your brother live. Good night, folks, 'nuff said now."

They replied, "Night, Daffy. Come again," and John dug out a watch, snapped open its case, looked and groaned. Everyone was standing, stretching a little, and I stood up to shake hands, thanking these fine people for having me here. I think my voice told them that I truly liked being here this evening, because when they invited me back, smiling, I could see and hear that they meant it.

The others going on inside, I stood a moment or so longer with Maude Boothe. She asked me where I was staying, brows rising in mock awe when I told her. And said she'd phone if she heard anything about Tessie and Ted.

I walked clear back to the Plaza, a long way and it was late, late, late. But this evening had been exciting for me, and I walked for time to think about it. And think about just *being* here in this strange New York, everything almost but never quite entirely familiar. Walking here along the Lower Broadway I knew so well, passing buildings Julia and I had walked by, I heard — strange on Broadway — no sound but the scuff of my own shoe leather, not a headlight or car ahead or — I turned to look — behind me as far as I could see. From blank dark store and office fronts, only the occasional dimness of a light far back inside.

Then a change, momentarily puzzling till I recognized that a fragrance had come sifting through the air, only a hint then gone. Then back, stronger and now persistent. And a pleasure. What? New-baked bread, the air filling with it, and I inhaled, pulling it in. And saw up ahead an almost dream-like sight: a silent, motionless crowd. There they stood as I walked closer: hardly moving, a crowd of silent men standing out here in the night. Suspended over the street corner — this was Broadway and Eleventh — a painted wooden sign reading, *Fleischmann's Bakery*. Walking by, I looked over at this line of forlorn and silent men in pocket-sprung suitcoats, safety-pinned overcoats, some only in shirtsleeves.

A cop stood at the curb watching them — tall helmet of heavy tan felt, belted blue coat to just above the knees. He glanced at me, approaching, saw I was a gent, I suppose, and said, "Good evening, sir."

"Good evening, officer." I stopped. "What's going on?"

"Fleischmann's gives away day-old bread at midnight." We both glanced away to the north at a pair of headlights, huge, round, dim, moving toward us, jouncing a little. Then stood watching the car slow and stop here at the curb; a limousine, long, polished, expensive. "Officer!" called a woman as she climbed out under a streetlamp — young, good-looking, long pale dress, big big hat. An older woman getting out of the car now, wearing the vague kind of dress that wasn't a uniform but was. She had a satchel in her hand.

"We are giving a party!" the young one cried gaily to the cop, her tone inviting him to join the fun. "You see," she said, confident of his interest, "I had thought at first of giving a dinner party to my friends. Then I thought how much better to give a dinner party to the poor." She turned her head to smile beautifully at the line of watching men, sweeping out an arm to include them all. "I want to feed every man here! So, you see," she explained kindly to the cop, "I want your help. For I am afraid some of the more anxious men will not be willing to wait their turn."

I recognized this lady; I'd seen her before in a Sunday comic section along with "Bringing Up Father," "Petey Dink," "Doc Yak," and "Der

344

Captain und Der Kids." This was a genuine "Lady Bountiful," an actual type of this time, I felt sure. Lady Bountifuls really and truly existed here, superbly certain of themselves and their goodness, and the cop knew it. "Yes, ma'am," he answered her quickly. "If you will stand here beside the curb, I'll call them out two at a time. And very kind of you, ma'am; what is your name?"

"I had rather not give it; names won't count at this party! Send over the first two." The cop gestured, and two dirty-faced young men at the head of the line came over, pulling their caps off. "My friends," said Lady Bountiful, her tone compassionate, "I want you to have dinner with me!" She reached into the satchel held open by the older woman, brought out two half-dollars, and gave one to each of them, who took them, ducking their heads, muttering their thanks. "This is a birthday party!" cried Lady B, "and I wish you well."

At the cop's signal, the waiting men came over two at a time for their half-dollars; actually a fairly large gift, I had to remind myself. When the satchel was empty, the older lady brought out another full one.

Standing there watching, I made a rough count: there were maybe four hundred men waiting here in the night at Fleischmann's, and each got his half-dollar. And each thanked Lady Bountiful politely, a lot of them in a foreign language. She turned graciously to the cop then. "It's been quite a birthday party," she said, "and I thank you very much for assisting us. I don't know what we would have done without you!" The cop touched his cap, and she glanced at me; for a moment I thought I was going to get a half-dollar. Then both women got back into the car, and as it pulled away I saw that a uniformed chauffeur was driving.

Fleischmann's had opened up a door at the head of the line, light edging out onto the walk, and the line began inching forward. "What do they get?" I asked the cop, and he said, "Coffee and bread." I said good night then, and walked on to the Plaza thinking of what I'd just seen. And of the vaudeville people out on their front stoops in their own tight, cozy, dangerous world.

At the hotel a pink-slip message lay in my box: Phone Madam Zelda. I knew she'd be up, still out on the front stoop, most of them, still talking vaudeville, vaudeville, vaudeville, so I phoned from my room.

Her call time for tomorrow's performance had been changed; someone had just phoned her. Vera of Vernon and Vera had been taken to the hospital from their boarding house, apparently with appendicitis. And Madam Z had phoned me immediately because the replacement act coming in tomorrow from Albany was called Tessie and Teddy. If I was going to see it, Madam Zelda's act was scheduled to follow; would I stay and see her? And I said that I certainly would.

22

I WAITED out the morning in Central Park, walking around, sitting on a bench, getting up, following the sun: *Tessie and Ted, Tessie and Ted.* And arrived at the matinee far too early, no more than eight or ten other early birds, down here on the big main floor; all men, some of them reading newspapers. And because the houselights were on full, I saw that the fancy plasterwork, elaborately painted, was — not quite shabby, not yet, but getting there. And my red plush seat and those around me were worn, not quite to the nub yet, but getting there too.

Now a few women coming down the aisle, young, mostly alone, careful to pick seats with plenty of room on each side, then busy with their hats. Finally the orchestra coming in fast, up out of a black cave under the stage, heads ducked for the tiny doorway, carrying instruments. Settling to just below our eye level behind their little green curtain. Little music-stand lights coming on, tootlings and tuning and violin scraping beginning. And then lots of people, a rush of

347

them, moving down the aisles, mostly single men, and now the women in pairs. Houselights lowering, then abruptly out, footlights sliding up the green curtain folds. On each side of the proscenium, a glass panel lighted up: *A*, it read, and I looked at my program: *Orchestral Selections*. The program began with a fast march tune; plenty of fife and snare drum. On the next page *Vernon and Vera* were listed as *E*. But *Vernon and Vera* now meant *Tessie and Ted*, didn't it?

A went out, and *B* lighted up for *The Hurleys*. A baton tap, then the orchestra, soft and with a definite beat, footlights winking out, curtain rising fast on . . . this was a garden, wasn't it? Yes. A formal garden. Two shallow marble steps at stage front led up onto a balustered terrace the full depth of the stage back to a painted drop of gardens extending in perspective to a far-off horizon. Beside the steps, standing on two short newel posts, a pair of life-sized bronze statues of men with folded arms as though on guard, bronze bodies shining under spotlighting from far overhead.

What was coming? Music soft, beat strong, the stage stood empty through a well-timed moment. Suddenly a human figure flew across the stage in a descending arc: a man in tights standing on a flying trapeze that nearly brushed the floor of the verandah. He rose to the top of his arc, stepped gracefully off onto a pedestal, and turned to face the direction he'd come from. And in that instant a girl in tights flew past him to rise to her pedestal across the stage, and the pair, facing each other, stood smiling.

Then, to the music, they began a kind of aerial ballet: not dangerous but wonderfully graceful. He'd catch her wrists as she released her trapeze to turn toward him in the air . . . they'd swing out on one trapeze, two other trapezes swinging in toward them from the wings, each stepping onto one . . .

It was fun to watch, charming really — except that people were still coming in, walking down the aisles, sidling into the rows, banging seats down. In the semidark one girl called to another, "Edna, here's two!" If this was customary, and it seemed to be, bothering no one as far as I could tell, I could understand why this first act was entirely silent.

Onstage the two aerialists finished, dropping to the stage, bowing to applause, smiling, gesturing one to the other with open palms, wrists turning upward. And when they skipped off hand in hand I thought — was supposed to think — the act was over.

Then my mouth actually popped open in real

astonishment because — orchestra swinging into a fast tempo — the two motionless statues stepped forward down onto the stage and into a marvelous clog. Not tap but wooden-soled sandals clacking away in effortless rhythm, arms swinging, bronze faces grinning out at us. It was great, just great, and when they'd finished and the aerialists came out again, the four of them took their bows to a huge wash of applause, my hands smacking away with the rest. It was a fine finish, the green curtain up and down three times before the footlights again slid up onto the folds and gilt of the swaying curtain.

Now the audience was alive, pleased, eager for whatever came next. *B* had gone dark, and now *C* lighted up, but I didn't bother checking my program, just waited to see.

Curtain rising on — what *was* this? Before a backdrop of mountain scenery stood a long something extending across the stage. Cages. It was a long row of foot-high cages with wire-mesh fronts, standing up there side by side on spindly wooden legs. Movement in the cages . . . animals . . . They were *cats*. Ordinary cats, each in its own small cage, so narrow they had to face front, though they didn't seem unhappy; one sat washing its face with tongue and paw. But the tail of every single cat hung straight down behind the cage — well, of course: now I saw it; the tails were artificial. A row of artificial tails hanging straight down behind the cages. And walking on fast, here came a small thin man in evening clothes: thin pale face, thin trimmed black line of mustache. Coat with a swallowtail to his ankles. A single low bow, arms swinging up, then sweeping down to almost brush the stage. Then he walked quickly backward — skipped, really — to stand behind the first cage at the right.

A pause; then a very soft orchestral accompaniment creeping in, he yanked the first tail hard and simultaneously howled like an angry cat, his mouth hidden by the cage. It was getting harder to startle me, but that terrible cat howl made me blink. Then — sitting below stage level, we could see the black top of his bowed head sliding above the roofs of the cages. And underneath them, see his running legs and the rapid yanking of fake tails. Yanked in some sort of order, an awful yowl each time. Some he yanked twice, then raced past three or four tails to yank one down the line, and with each yank, yowling, howling, spitting, sobbing, lips closed but it had to be him, the cats seeming undisturbed. But his cries sounded real, and he was playing — or singing, or yowling, or whatever — "The Bells of Saint Mary's"! *Oh, the yowls of . . . screech-howl-howl!* Each note true but the snarling death moan or scream of a back-fence cat, and it was hilarious, the audience going crazy, laughing to almost drown out those terrible musical howls.

He finished with a tail yank that shook the cages, and stepped forward past the cages to make a low bow, an arm again swinging down through a great half-circle to sweep the stage. Then he leaped back, and resumed his crazy race behind the cages, yanking tails as he sobbed and yowled out the notes of — what else? — "Turkey Trot." He finished with "Just a Song at Twilight" — *Just a yowl at cat moan . . . when the sob is screech . . .*

The audience wanted more, and our applause said so, but he was smarter than that. Because one more, I think, and suddenly the act would have turned boring. But he left us with a marvelous finish. Again and again he bowed to our applause, then walked forward and in some way — brows lifting, some subtle change in manner — conveyed to us that he wanted our attention. Our applause tapered off fast, we sat watching in expectant silence, he took one last step to the very footlights, leaned out over them, and — the house eagerly still — he *purred*. A growling catlike purr that could be heard in the second balcony, I'm sure, and it killed us: he skipped off, the curtain descending in a rain of applause, a few of the audience imitating his cat yips.

Curtain down, audience still buzzing, some still laughing quietly, I sat wondering: Who *were* these vaudevillians? To what strange kind of person would it ever occur to turn a talent, if that's the word, for meowing and yowling like a cat into a lifetime career?

The Bird Lady: Curtain up, and there she stood, in a sequined dress, arms straight out at her sides, a dove perched on each wrist, elbow, and shoulder. Smiling, chin up, and looking regal. Looking younger, better-looking somehow. On four perches mounted on stands at each side of the stage, a dozen or so more birds, facing us. Then a snap of her fingers, and up they all flew, spiraling, climbing high over the stage. Now Maude Boothe — the Bird Lady — had a little whistle in her mouth. One silvery chirp, and every bird turned in the air and — they didn't fly but glided down over the suddenly murmuring audience, then up to the balcony railing, where all perched, turning on awkward bird feet to face the stage.

Orchestra came in, very much in the background, and, with small whistled signals, the Bird Lady put the doves through their maneuvers. They flew, they perched on aisle-seat arms, patrons leaning away, smiling uncertainly. They lined up on the stage perfectly, I thought, and stood motionless till the whistle released them. They passed some object, I don't know what, from beak to beak down the line. They clustered, every one of them, on her arms, shoulders, head, while she walked about. Again, this time in a straight line, they flew out above us, then divided, every other bird, into two curves arcing back to the stage in a kind of heart shape over our heads, and . . . I didn't want to feel this way, it seemed disloyal, but for me it just wasn't very interesting. Surprising that birds could be taught these things, but . . . so what? And although I applauded as loud and hard as I could, out of loyalty, I was relieved when it was over.

But frightened. Because *E* was next, Vera and

Vernon . . . Tessie and Ted. I very nearly — feeling the actual muscle impulse — stood up to walk away. *I did not belong here.*

But I stayed. The Bird Lady took her last bow, the curtain down then, proscenium cards changing from *D* to *E*, and I abruptly cowered far down in my seat, arms crossing over my stomach, trying to become invisible, trying not to be here. But my head came up. A backdrop onstage now: vaguely painted trees, a stream — nothing. A baby grand piano and a stool. And oh, *oh,* here they *were* walking on. Tessie, my great-aunt, maybe thirty years old now? I'd never seen her, never known her. And walking beside her, smiling, almost grinning, the twelve-year-old boy who would grow up, be married three times, and in early middle age father a child in his final marriage, and still only in his forties die before his son was two.

I had two photographs of him. In one he is a grinning college boy in a porkpie hat sitting with a friend in the front seat of an open Ford touring car on the hood of which you can read in white paint, *Peaches, here's your can!* The other is a formal professional photograph: head and shoulders; necktie, stiff collar, stiff smile, mustache. Thirty-five maybe.

I knew those photographs, knew that face. And here was another version of it, right *there* up on the stage now, smiling, nodding at us as he twirled the piano stool to proper height. I knew he had already begun to drink, had probably just had a stiff one. A twelve-year-old boy with a knack for the piano, there with his ambitious aunt, she smiling out at us, placing herself by the piano, he — my *father* up there — turning a page of sheet music, positioning his fingers, looking at Tess — their moment, the very pinnacle of their lives — and as she began to sing, accompanying her on the piano. "Some . . . where a voice . . . is caw-ling," she sang, "Over land and sea . . . Some . . . where a voice . . ." The fingers on the piano keys doing well, playing well, in this their greatest moment. "Caw-ling to me-e-e . . ." She sang all right, I guess, I didn't know, couldn't tell. I just looked, sitting frozen, staring up at this forbidden sight. My own father: Was I going to cry? No. But I stopped looking at the stage, and just sat waiting, eyes downcast.

Applause, and she sang again, something — I don't know. Applause, and she sang once more, and I looked up and he was there, still there, hunched over the keys, smiling, glancing sideways, sending the smile out to us, up there playing, the smooth young cheek moving, weaving, in time to his music, the failed man, of failed marriages, the alcoholic-to-be already begun, here in the very peak of their lives, the famous days — not even a full week — when they "played Broadway." I shouldn't have come here, Danziger was right, always so right; this was a forbidden thing.

It was over then, the applause dying pretty fast, and they were gone. I hadn't applauded,

I'd separated myself from this, had no right to participate, this seat vacant. I sat wanting to go home to Willy and Julia, and stay there, and I was going to, I was finished here now.

But *F* lighted up, Madam Zelda, and I'd said I'd stay for her act. So I sat there in the momentary darkness waiting for whatever I was feeling to slow down, to begin diluting and become able to be thought about.

Madam Z's act began in what I supposed was a traditional way, but still effective. Curtain up slow on a nearly dark stage, a small compact glow of light at the center. This intensifying as we became silent — a tiny spotlight focused on a large glass globe which sat on a kind of pillar. Now the light expanded to include Madam Z's face from below, then gradually her entire upper body. Absurd but effective. She sat there cross-legged in a sort of harem costume, I guess, a turban on her head, motionless, staring down at the glowing globe. And we sat silent and waiting.

Abruptly — spoken down here on the dark auditorium floor — a man's voice, impressively deep. "Mad-am *Zell*-da!" As he spoke, a spotlight picked him out, standing in an aisle: tall, broad, tan suit, white shirt and dark tie. "Are you ready?"

A pause just long enough so that maybe she wasn't going to reply. Then, "Yessss," holding the hiss, "Madam Zelda . . . is ready!"

The spotlight broadened to include the member of the audience seated beside the big man standing

356

in the aisle. The seated man looking up at the other, smiling, waiting. "I have here, a letter belonging to a gentleman, and addressed to him. What . . . is his name?"

"His name . . . is Robert . . . Lederer."

"And what is the address below it?"

"The address is . . . One-eleven West Eighth Street, City!"

"Is that correct, sir?" — handing the envelope back, the man nodding, smiling, looking sheepish. "Quite correct!" The big man moved quickly up the aisle, ignoring several letters or cards or whatever held out to him, and stopped to lean into an aisle and pick up the hand of a young woman. "This young lady, Madam Zelda! Is wearing a ring! Tell us, Madam Zelda, what is the ring like?"

"The ring . . . the ring . . ."

"Yes! Describe it please!"

"It holds a diamond, a beautiful diamond, and on each side of this magnificent stone is . . . a lustrous pearl!" How was she doing this? Code, I supposed, an elaborate code buried in whatever the tall man called to her.

"Correct!" he shouted, the girl looking pleased and abashed, the tall man stalking swiftly up the aisle, moving on behind me so that I couldn't see him without twisting around, but I listened. "A gentleman here, Madam Z! Tell me, tell me now, the name . . . the name . . . of this man's sister!" Code or not, how could he know that?

"Her name is . . . Clara!"

"Is that correct, sir? *Yes!* The gentleman says you are entirely correct! And now, Madam, I am holding this man's watch! Tell me, concentrate, think, think! What is the number . . . of this man's watch?"

"The number of his watch is two . . . one-eight-seven . . . six-nine — no, seven-nine . . ." She paused, hesitating, the man in the aisle insistent: "Yes!? Yes!?" and I sat bewildered because I — not quite, but almost — recognized the numbers as he spoke them. I — almost — knew them too. Triumphantly Madam Zelda finished. "Seven! The number of this man's watch is two-one-eight-seven-seven-nine-seven-one!"

"*Is* that correct, sir?" I was twisting around in my seat to see. "*Is* that the number of your watch?" and I sat staring as Archie nodded, smiling at the Jotta Girl beside him. "Yes," Archie said, slipping his watch back into a vest pocket, "that is quite correct."

"Archie is Z," I said to myself stupidly. His watch number was the number I'd seen in Alice Longworth's letter. The tall man in the aisle turning away toward someone else, the Jotta Girl looked up to see me staring back at them. She spoke to Archie, who looked up, then gestured, indicating a vacant seat beside them. And I stood, edged out into the aisle, walked back a half-dozen rows, and . . . *Rube, Rube, look: I'm sitting down next to Z. Now what? What do I do now?*

What I did was . . . sit there. Talking a bit to Archie, to the Jotta Girl. And all I could think of to do was . . . stick with Archie now, as best I could. Become his buddy. It sounded empty, vague, but . . . what else?

We sat applauding Madam Zelda as the curtain went down, Archie delighted with her. *G* lighted up on the proscenium, and a moment later the heavy green curtain was bumped from behind, wavering its long velvet folds, drawing our attention. Then a movement at the very bottom of the curtain, lifting it slightly into an inverted V. A face appeared there, just over the stage floor, tipped sideways, peeking out, the eyes widening at sight of us, mouth opening in comic dismay, to a rustle of laughter. "Joe Cook," Archie said happily, and the audience sat waiting, murmuring expectantly.

I *think* Joe Cook was funny. The audience thought so. He came out, moving fast, in funny hat and costume, heading for a cottage at center stage. Rapped loudly on the door, the landlord demanding rent. Did it again, then simply picked up the whole cottage — of canvas and light wood frame — and walked offstage with it. He had whatever it takes to make that hilarious, generally explained by talk about "timing." And the audience howled. And I sat, not actually howling — but yes, I *did* know . . . that Tessie and Ted were standing in the wings watching Joe Cook too. Watching, laughing genuinely, and — oh yes — grinning and nodding at him as he came off, maybe actually speaking to him, one vaudevillian to another.

Almost immediately Joe Cook was onstage again, staggering across it with three men on his back, each with his feet on the shoulders of the man beneath him. It looked genuine, their clothes real and fluttering, and he staggered so realistically under their weight, but — the "timing" again — now he somehow let us see they were papier-mâché just exactly as he entered the opposite wings. And as we exploded in laughter I knew — *knew* — who stood grinning backstage, looking at each other to nod in the joy of actually knowing Joe Cook, a vaudeville "headliner."

We sat watching Joe Cook's act. Watched as this vaudeville aristocrat came out, sat down in a chair facing us, and waited, looking benignly out at us till the house became quiet. Then entirely silent as he waited some more. Finally, not a cough or stir; I could hear the faint sound of Archie's breathing. How did Joe Cook *do* that? If I'd been up there facing the audience like that, waiting, smiling, my nerve would have broken, and I'd have had to run off the stage.

Then, speaking into our utter silence, he said in a quiet conversational way as though to a friend, "I will now give you an imitation of four Hawaiians," and began what may be vaudeville's most famous monologue. I sat smiling. Not at Joe Cook but at the pair I knew must be standing just out of sight, listening, happy with each other in their "week," the famous three-day "week on

Broadway" in the most illustrious company of their world. *I hope the great man speaks to you, I said silently. I hope he has troubled to know your names and uses them at least once in this famous time which will have to last you for the downhill rest of your lives.*

Z. Well, he would get to Europe; Rube and I knew that. He was okay here in New York. So — find out where he was going, because . . . I'd have to go along, it looked like. Who was Z? Z was Archie, but who was Archie? In the cab back to the hotel I said, "Would you two join me this evening? For . . . cocktails? Dinner. A night out. I'm in a celebratory mood; maybe you'd guide us around, Arch."

"Very kind of you, Simon. I'll be happy to."

The Jotta Girl, seated between us, said, "Me too." Then turned to murmur in my ear, "Found your man, haven't you," and I nodded.

In the lobby I bought an *Evening Mail*, and we rode up, Archie getting off at four. On up to ten; then I walked on right past the Jotta Girl's room, but as I stood unlocking my door she was beside me. "Oh, I should have bought a paper too; there's a sale at Wanamaker's. Do you mind if I tear out a little teeny bit of their ad?"

Yes, I minded: I minded her coming in with me. But in my room I just stood waiting as she found the Wanamaker ad, carefully tore out a little section on a shoe sale, which I didn't believe for a moment she would ever attend. Then I walked to the door, opened it, saying, "See you at six, then. Downstairs."

"Oh, yes; downstairs, of course. Where else?" And she left, moving past me in the doorway, facing me and grinning, and I just rolled my eyes upward, shaking my head.

23

THE GIRL WITH THE WINKING EYE

THIS IS the enormous 1912 face which will always mean the Great White Way for me. Archie, an out-of-town New Yorker, had planned this; sent our cab west on Thirty-second Street so that as it turned up Broadway, there it was. And as I hung out the cab window staring up at the immense face, the Jotta Girl's head beside mine staring too, that great big electric left eye *winked* at us. I clipped this photo from a *New York Times* story on Broadway's spectacular new light-bulb signs that seemed to move; the chariot race with revolving wheels, flying hoofs, and cracking whips up ahead on the roof of the Normandie was another. "New York is crazy about them," Archie said, and I nodded and grinned. "So am I."

Nighttime Broadway lay ahead, so different from the almost quiet daytime street I'd walked down. Now sidewalks and street were jammed and glittering whitely: this was the Great White Way because it *was* white, no neon, every automobile and streetcar headlight, every street-level shop window and theater marquee blazingly lighted by clear, spike-ended white bulbs. And Archie sat grinning: this was *his* town; he'd personally screwed in every shining bulb around us.

Then he disappointed me. The driver swung left, across the street to park heading the wrong way in front of — the Astor Hotel? I didn't want to go here, into a place still existing in my own time, in which I'd often been, and the Jotta Girl, glancing at me, didn't either. But in we went, to the elevators, where Archie — Mr. Manhattan — simply nodded at the elevator boy, forefinger pointing straight up. And then we stepped out into this, the Astor Roof Garden; I didn't know it existed. Roof gardens all over town, Arch said as we were led to a table overlooking Broadway; on hotels and even theater roofs, the plays moving

364

ON THE ROOF OF THE HOTEL ASTOR

out and up under the sky when the weather was right. Now as we sat down, we could feel the great gas heaters, all around the perimeter. And then, under the glitter of the night sky, we had — what else? — champagne. And talked. Or Archie did; I mostly questioned. This tall, pleasant, red-haired, red-mustached, freckled man was a major in the U.S. Army *and* — I wasn't surprised — chief aide to President Taft, as he had been to the preceding President, Theodore Roosevelt. And I nodded, impressed, thinking of their nighttime meeting beside the Flatiron Building. But now Arch had a six-week leave; he needed a rest, though he didn't look tired to me. First, some time in New York, which he loved. "Then a few weeks in Europe."

"Oh? When are you going?"

And it was this easy: "Wednesday, this coming Wednesday; on the *Campania*. She's small and a bit slow, but I like that, and she's a Cunarder, so I expect I'll enjoy the sea voyage; I am never seasick. I have a friend, Francis Millet, the well-known painter" — a little pride in his voice — "who is off on the midnight sailing of the *Mauretania* tonight. Wouldn't wait for me; doesn't like New York, if you can imagine that."

"Midnight sailing?" The Jotta Girl sounded interested.

"Oh yes. They're enormous fun, you know. Come along, why don't you. Both of you. You'll enjoy it, they're like an enormous party."

Rube . . . are you sure this is Z?

Champagne up there in the sky; then we walked catercorner across Broadway, Archie not saying where we were going. But — not running across the street, hardly even looking, just walking between the few slow-moving cars trundling along — when I saw the huge stone griffin over the entrance, I knew; this was Rector's.

Inside, it was big, lavish, crystal-chandeliered, luxurious, and crowded. We had to wait, but they knew Archie, and we didn't wait long.

At our table — more champagne on the way — the Jotta Girl and I looked at our napkins, embroidered with the griffin; at the tablecloth marked with the same, at our glasses and silverware engraved with the Rector griffin. And part-time New Yorker Archie watched us, delighted.

Then he entertained us with Rector stories: the

former jockey, now rich, who occasionally had his giant servant carry a small cannon to the roof, where he shot it off to celebrate various occasions, such as his wedding; the rich miner from the West who showed up annually, always with a vest pocket full of pearls

which he'd finger and play with on the tabletop. The giant apples imported from France in season, all grown with a paper griffin pasted to their skin so they ripened with the Rector trademark.

Elegant people all

around us, including one beauty who caught me staring. A fine orchestra, and it occurred to me, half listening as Archie talked, how many songs of this time have been remembered ever since: they played "By the Light of the Silvery Moon" . . . "I Wonder Who's Kissing Her Now" . . . "Meet Me Tonight in Dreamland" . . . "Oh, You Beautiful Doll" . . . Then, right in the middle of "Let Me Call You Sweetheart," Archie just finishing about the apples from France, the orchestra cut off in midnote and swung abruptly into "I'm Falling in Love with Someone," and Arch leaned discreetly across the table to whisper excitedly, "There he is! By the door!"

I looked, saw a man in evening clothes, in his early fifties, I'd say, who stood nodding, smiling, bowing slightly, acknowledging a spatter of applause. Then he turned to walk to the orchestra. "He's going to thank them now," Archie said. "He always does."

"Who is he?"

That startled Archie. "Why, Victor Herbert! The moment they see him enter, they invariably stop and play one of his compositions. And invariably he walks over to thank them — see him? Very gracious man."

We ordered dinner, the Jotta Girl nudged me to pour more champagne, and after we'd tasted, I asked Archie if he knew Alice Longworth.

Of course! Everyone knew Alice, she was leader of a set, of which he was pleased to be a minor member.

368

Oh? What was she like?

"A madcap. Quite insane. Her husband, Nick, is a member of the House, but she finds that no barrier to her impulses. If one is awakened at three in the morning by pebbles dashed against one's window, it will be Alice down below forcing you up and dressed to join some sort of impromptu party. We've played golf with Alice driving a ball through the empty streets of Washington at some unlikely hour. I am in hope that she and Nicky will come up to New York for at least a day before I must sail."

I think dinner — rack of lamb for me — was maybe the best I've ever had. Then — this was my evening — I ordered brandy, and when I asked Archie about his two Presidents, he got serious. Had enormous regard and respect for President Taft, liked him immensely, an honor to serve as his aide. But his real love, I could tell from his voice, was President Roosevelt.

What about Roosevelt, what did he admire so? Well, T.R. was himself always. Took a walk once with the French ambassador, reached the Potomac, and sent his two Secret Service guards home. Then — a fine summer day — the two men stripped down, swam the Potomac, swam back, sat on a rock in the sun, drying, got dressed, and walked back to the White House. Independent. And a spirit of fun.

But tough. "He believes in physical fitness, and had ordered the officer corps of the Navy to make a ninety-mile horseback ride each week. And he said to me, 'If you could see the protests against my order prescribing the riding test for the Navy, you would understand that a great coterie of both the Army and the Navy are only waiting for me to leave the White House to deluge the next President with applications to modify the order. But I know the order is not too severe; and if it is, I also want to know it. But if two naval officers, and you and I can take this ride of ninety miles in one day, we will never hear a word again in protest of the order. It will silence all critics, and the Army and the Navy itself will see to its perpetuation as a matter of esprit de corps.' "

Across the dining room from us, a large, portly man, dining alone, stood up at his table and began to sing in a fine loud baritone. The song was something about "I *want* what I *want* when I *want* it!" from a musical, Archie said, in which this man starred. And as he sang, most of the Rector's patrons picked up glasses, knives, or whatever, and began banging the tabletops in unison with each "want." "I WANT what I WANT when I WANT it!" sang the man, each "WANT" almost lost in the united pounding.

He finished and bowed, everyone applauding including waiters and members of the orchestra which had softly accompanied him. Then he sat down, resumed eating, the restaurant's conversational buzz resumed, and Archie said, "And so on the day of the ride — or not the day, I should say, but in the middle of the night — the President came pounding at my door, we had breakfast, and it was just twenty minutes to four when the President, Admiral Rixey, Dr. Gregson, and I mounted our horses. The President rode Roswell and I had my faithful Larry. The two naval officers had their own mounts also. We started at a dogtrot down Pennsylvania Avenue and made the bridge in ten minutes. But oh, the wind was cold, Si! And everything frozen hard.

"The greater part of the roads we traveled over had been deeply furrowed and cut up since the last thaw and snow, and had frozen in this way. But we managed to reach Fairfax Courthouse by six-twenty. I had ordered two cavalry orderlies to leave replacement horses at Fairfax, Cub Run, and Buckland, but gave no explanation of whom they were for. Consequently the horses were the most ordinary cavalry mounts.

"At Fairfax we found the first detachment of new horses waiting for us in charge of a trooper from Fort Myer. It took only fifteen minutes to change horses, and without waiting a minute we started at a brisk trot toward Centerville. At Cub Run we found our second change of horses, and for the President and myself it was for the worse. The new horses were rough, slow, and mine was vicious.

"But the President was in the best of spirits, and joked Admiral Rixey about the Virginia roads, and wondered what the old veterans would say if their spirits could see him riding over Bull Run with these rebels, as he called us."

"Is that Jack London?" said the Jotta Girl, gesturing with her chin at a table across the room, and we looked.

"I believe it is," said Archie, and I thought so too. He had that look, that early-years-of-the-century face that you see in photos of the Yale football team of the times before they wore helmets; the longish hair, the turtleneck jerseys, a look that eventually vanished from the earth. It was Jack London all right. "And I believe the men with him are Richard Harding Davis and Gerald Montizambert."

I didn't say anything; I didn't know who Richard Harding Davis was, though of course I knew, as who didn't, who the sinister and notorious Gerald Montizambert was.

Arch said, "By the time we reached Gainesville we all felt that the trip would be a success. Each had measured his strength, and knew about what we could do, and when we reached Buckland at nine thirty-five we were in a fine humor.

"We changed our horses there, and started on our last lap to Warrenton. We had planned to reach the town by eleven, but it looked hopeless for a time, as part of the road was so furrowed and cut up that we could only make any time by keeping off the roads and riding up on the embankments. We took advantage of every good stretch, however, to gallop, and just as the town clock struck eleven we entered the main thoroughfare of the town. Several people recognized the President, and soon the news spread. They would not believe we had ridden from Washington. He made a short address to them, but the result was that he had to eat his lunch in ten minutes.

"We left Warrenton at twelve-fifteen and did not reach Buckland on our way back until one thirty-five. I had a horse which fought the bit the entire way. And once when I got off to look after the girth of the President's saddle, I was fifteen minutes getting back on again. He would plunge and rear, and once he struck at Dr. Gregson and came near putting him out of business. Finally I made a flying leap for the saddle and made it. I was mighty glad to turn him over to the orderly at Buckand, I can tell you.

"Between Buckland and Cub Run our vitality was at its lowest. Admiral Rixey was on a fine animal of his own, and he had set the pace at a jog trot which was all right for him but it was hell on the President and myself, who were riding the roughest troop horses which Fort Myer could turn out. Finally as we reached Cub Run and started afresh, the President ordered Rixey to the rear and told me to set the pace. I set it by walking slowly when the roads were bad and galloping like mad when they were good. We made better time this way, although one is not supposed to; but the pace had the effect of resting us up when very tired, and when galloping to warm our blood and exhilarate our spirits.

"Just before we reached Centerville we met a blizzard, which came from the north in the shape of a blinding sleet storm, and this storm was continuous from this point to Washington. The wind was blowing a gale and the ice cut our faces so that I thought mine must certainly be bleeding. We kept up a fast gait to Fairfax, however, as every mile covered now was that much made certain, for it was beginning to look doubtful whether we would be able to make Washington on account of the heavy fall of sleet. When we reached Fairfax we got the horses on which we had begun the ride, and I never felt more relieved in my life than when the orderly told us that both Roswell and Larry were in good condition and not lame from the ride in the early morning. On any other horses I don't think we would have made Washington without an accident, if indeed we had made it at all.

"We left Fairfax in the inky blackness of night, and walked practically the entire way to Falls Church. From Centerville the President had been going it blindly, for the ice would cake on his glasses so that he could see nothing ahead of him. He simply trusted to Roswell now. I took the lead and he came immediately behind me, followed by Gregson and Admiral Rixey.

"I dared not gallop, for we were too near our goal to run the risks of an accident. Once, when I began to trot, the President's horse went into a ditch, but luckily recovered himself without injury to himself or his rider. At Falls Church we began to trot, for the roads were better, and strange to say, by the reflected lights of Washington nine miles away, we could keep fairly well in the roads. Enough snow had fallen with the sleet to make them fairly safe, so we trotted the entire way in to the Aqueduct Bridge. As we turned into the lighted approach, we saw the carriage from the White House which I had ordered to meet us before we left Fairfax. But when the question came up as to whether the asphalt streets were safe for the horses, the President settled it by saying, 'By George, we will make the White House with our horses if we have to lead them,' and we started across the bridge.

"Mrs. Roosevelt was watching for us from the window of Miss Ethel's room, and by the time we alighted she was standing in the doorway to welcome us. We were all covered with ice, but the President in his black riding jacket with fur collar and pockets, and broad-brim black hat, looked for all the world like the pictures of Santa Claus. Mrs. Roosevelt made us come in and gave us a julep, which was the first drop of liquor any of us had during the entire ride.

"I was stiff the following day, and did not feel like getting up. But I was out of the house at the usual time, and reported to the President at ten. I could not refrain from stopping at my club and showing myself in passing, for I knew that everyone there would be expecting us to be laid up for days. It was a ride of a hundred and four miles."

We sat there then, in the crowded, fashionable restaurant, and I didn't say anything for a minute or so. I was thinking about American Presidents.

Nothing original, but only that they come in many varieties. And that possibly the earlier vintages had something the newer ones don't seem to know about. Anyway, if it was true that here in 1912 the causes of the Great War were still small, still manageable, could still be altered and the war actually prevented . . . maybe this tall, pleasant, competent, and honorable man, and the two Presidents he served, might just possibly be able to manage it.

Archie said, "It's nearly ten-thirty. We must leave now if we are to join the party on the *Mauretania*."

24

DOWN SEVENTH Avenue then, in our cab, chain-driven at maybe twenty miles an hour. West on Fourteenth Street toward the Hudson River; then the three of us sat frozen in midsentence, mid-laugh, by the most thrilling, evocative, literally hair-raising sound — felt on the arms and back of the neck — that I know, the oh, so deep growl of a ship's horn. It went on, jumbling the very molecules of the air, and on, and on, and was never ever going to stop, so low, so deep, pervading your bones. Then it did stop but not in my brain and nerves, and we turned onto West Street, moving along directly beside the smooth flat river and its docks. And in that moment, very suddenly, up there ahead just a few docks further on we saw them rising above everything else, lighted by searchlights below — the four tremendous stacks of the *Mauretania*, painted Cunard Line red, black-banded around their tops, the glorious shining white superstructure below them. Now the deep ship's horn again, then finally stopping, to leave nothing in mind or emotion but its own mental echo and the thrilling actuality of those four astonishing stacks against the night. The great growling horn sounded again almost immediately, and I wanted nothing more of the world than to sail out on this waiting ship.

We rolled to a slow coasting stop at the curb, behind a dozen other unloading cabs and cars, and stepped out into an oasis of light, noise, chatter, laughter, and shouts; an oasis surrounded by an apparently dark and deserted lower Manhattan. All but the prow of the ship — astoundingly almost touching the sidewalk, and lettered with the magic name *Mauretania* — all but that and the four great stacks rising above everything else was hidden now by the huge, ugly, shedlike wooden dock, its shingled roof a story above our heads. Beyond it, at the other empty side, lay the Hudson, the moon tipping the ripples with yellow glints. A magic moment for me, and maybe for the Jotta Girl, because as we stood waiting, Archie leaning into the cab to pay the driver, she slipped her arm under mine.

From the curbside cabs and cars, people were stepping out: some confidently, others cautiously, looking around worriedly, afraid the ship might suddenly leave. But most were almost boisterous, one party, six of them in a single cab, all in evening dress, shouting drunk.

Some had luggage strapped to racks unfolded behind their cars or cabs, or roped onto the flat railed roofs. Others had none, visitors or experienced travelers who'd sent theirs aboard during the day.

A cop at the curb stood gesturing cabs away as soon as they'd unloaded, and as ours turned out into West Street again, a large gray limousine, one inch shorter than a freight car, came rolling silently in behind it. The cop's hand went respectfully to his cap visor, and a pair of derby-hatted reporters — I was sure they were reporters — came running, and a third trotted along beside the car.

Archie, Jotta Girl, and I stood watching as the limousine stopped glitteringly under a curbside streetlamp. In the open front seat, a chauffeur in a peaked cap and a footman in silk topper, both in dark green uniform. The footman was down, out on the walk before the car had fully stopped, walking along beside the rear door, reaching for its big nickeled handle. He opened the door as the chauffeur set his brake, a long ratcheting sound, then jumped down and walked back past the limousine to an open-bodied snub-nosed truck labeled *Ludlock's Express Company*, which had pulled in behind. Now the footman had the car door open, one of the reporters leaning down to smile and nod at the people inside.

They got out daintily, two women helped at the elbows by the footman, the younger one first, silk ankle reaching for the wide running board, hardly needing to duck, the car roof was so high. An older woman stepping carefully out behind, given token help by the chauffeur. The younger woman stood glancing around, looking marvelous, and the Jotta Girl very softly said, "Wow."

Her coat was long and dark — blue or black, I couldn't tell — with an ermine collar. She held an ermine muff, and wore a dark hat, a kind of turban, on each side of which lay a scarlet wing, an actual bird's wing; spectacular. The reporter beside her said something, she half turned to reply, and the light of the curbside streetlamp moved across a winking, diamond-studded strand around her neck and touched a big oval lavaliere suspended from it, which burst into light like a tiny fireworks display. "Real," said the Jotta Girl beside me. "Really real . . ." The woman's profile had come into the light and I saw she was — well, while you wouldn't say beautiful, you certainly wouldn't say merely pretty. Distinctive, maybe; like absolutely no one else. You saw that she knew exactly who she was, and that it was someone important who always had been. The older woman, dressed plainly but not in uniform, though you saw she was a servant, had walked back to the express truck, up on the bed of which the driver stood dragging trunks to the open tailgate, chauffeur and footman heaving them down to the walk by their strap handles.

The cop had sauntered over, an iron filing to a magnet, and the lady gave him a pleasant but not-too-large smile. "They won't be too long," she said, and the cop quickly touched the peak of his cap again, and lay down on the walk to lick her shoes — well, he didn't but he wanted to.

I'd drifted closer to the curb, very curious, the Jotta Girl right along with me, Archie hanging back, unwilling to eavesdrop. Pretending to look out into the street, watching for someone who hadn't yet arrived, we heard the reporter — he had pad and pencil out now — say, "And may I tell our readers that you enjoyed your stay here?"

"Of course! As always. I do love America." She turned to check the unloading; the trunks, eight of them so far, were stacking up on the walk.

"And do you still feel the suffragettes will win the vote?"

"Of course they will win. Here and in England. As of course they should."

"And you are . . . a socialist still?"

"Yes, certainly I am a socialist. And expect to remain one."

"And you stayed at — was it the Ritz-Carlton Hotel?"

"Yes indeed, as why should I not?" She looked back to the truck. "John? Rudy? Alice? They are all here? You'll see them safely aboard."

"Yes, ma'am," said the maid, and the lady walked on toward the steps leading down to the *Mauretania*'s side. To the reporter who stood staring after her, I said, "Who is it?"

"The Countess of Warwick."

"And a socialist?"

"So she always says. So I guess she is."

The trunks were all down on the walk now, the footman beckoning to a band of blue-smocked porters, and I counted. There were eighteen great big black trunks, brass-cornered, brass locks, heavy black straps, and around the center of each had been painted a broad yellow stripe, for quick easy identification, I suppose. Painted in black on each stripe, a number. Painted on the lid of each trunk a coronet, the letters *F.E.W.* underneath it. On the end of each trunk, a single new label reading, *Cunard Steamship Line*. But at the side of the stacked trunks sat a large suitcase, and it was nearly covered by labels for Cunard, White Star Line, Hamburg-American, and for hotels in every important city of Europe, and I knew that this was the maid's.

More cabs, cars, and luggage-loaded trucks, filling curb space as fast as emptied, the countess's car pulling away. Archie, Jotta Girl, and I looking at each other to nod and grin, then turning to the stairway down to the dock. I felt wondrously happy; just to *be* here, to have seen the countess, and to be walking down these wooden stairs. And was willing right now — eager — to sell my soul without asking for change, to be sailing out on this great lighted thing.

She lay there miles long, three never-ending rows of shining portholes, hundreds and hundreds and hundreds of them, dwindling off to dots. I've read that an ocean liner is the largest thing that moves, and this — walking down the wooden stairs, I stared — was hard to understand. How could it be so long, so large, how could it have been made, how could this monster float?

Down, then, across the scruffy wood floor of the dock, then up the gangplank, and it was exactly that, a wide plank, railed and slatted. And crowded, busy with laughing excited people. I glanced off, now strangely a little higher than the city down at my right, and then I stepped out of the world I'd known.

Into a world I'd never seen the likes of, its looks, warmth, its strangeness and even its smell told me so. Welcoming us stood a row of smiling men and boys in uniform, the bellboys or whatever they were called in brass-buttoned blue suits. All happy to see us, skillfully moving us on. On into a great room jostling with passengers, visitors, and sweating stewards. Booby-trapped with golf bags leaning against the walls, with tall flaring wicker flower baskets to be delivered to cabins. With brown paper packages on the floor against the walls, and, on little tables, enormous boxes of candy and stacks of telegrams, cablegrams. And with two-wheeled handcarts for luggage and baskets of fruit. And potted palms, and people, people, and the sound of people, and always more people stepping curiously in.

We moved on, the three of us, had to move with the flow, down a narrow passageway, then out into a great and beautiful room. Arching above us, a magnificent canopy of patterned colored glass, the walls of — what? I don't know — glowing dark wood. And a long, long, white-cloth table, behind it smiling men in starched chef's hats and knotted kerchiefs waiting behind food, food, food. Including pâté de foie gras. Including black caviar. Including roasts. Cold cuts. Tiny steaks. Stews. Fruit, cakes, ice cream, anything, *anything*. Sliced salmon. And we ate, plates in hand, and grinned at each other, walking around the big room looking at wall paintings. People moved in and moved out, and we lost the Jotta Girl, she vanished. And I set down my plate and wandered, curious. Out into the corridors again, squirming with people, most of them laughing and happy, not all. Not the uniformed stewards battling along with buckets of ice.

On past staterooms crammed with fun-lovers yelling at me to come on in and have a drink. Past a room, door slightly ajar, a woman sitting alone on the edge of a bed, crying. Past worried people talking about luggage. Past others urging wild, insane children to bed and sleep.

In and out of the great public rooms, I hardly knew where. What to say about them? I don't know, except that every one was different and all were the same. Each had a tremendous glass canopy almost covering the ceiling — to admit daylight from the open deck above. Each canopy different, yet all the same. One was cream and gold, the dining room with magnificent deep red carpets, upholstery a deep pink. Swivel chairs around the tables bolted to the floors; which said something to me about the ocean crossing ahead. Crystal chandeliers, carpets matching the drapes.

Carpets in rose, carpets in green. Out of one crowded jabbering room into another, sometimes almost deserted. The lounge. The smoking room, which had an enormous working fireplace. The music room. The library. Dark polished wood everywhere. Paintings, luxury, a *luxury* liner; it was that all right. And everywhere, more potted plants.

I peeked into empty cabins, and one that wasn't, yanking my head out before they saw me. In the bedrooms, dresser tops with rails to keep things from sliding off; glasses set in wells; a ship ready for rough water.

In the library, nearly empty, I stood looking around: another glass canopy, more dark paneling, shelves of books, a lot of upholstered chairs, all looking new. I'd heard a voice in a corridor say the *Mauretania* was just out of dry dock, refurbished. I sneaked a look around: nobody. And took a twenty-five-cent piece from my pocket, stood on tiptoe, and dropped it behind a row of books: even though I could not, something of mine was going to sail tonight. The Jotta Girl came in, glass in hand, and we went out and up to the promenade deck. Funnels, looking like enormous white saxophones, stood everywhere, the deck crowded with them. They scooped up air from the ship's forward motion, no air-conditioning. We strolled past lifeboats, reaching a hand up to touch the bottoms. Found Archie leaning on a rail talking to his friend, to whom he introduced us: the painter Francis Millet.

From somewhere a boy's voice: "All ashore that's going ashore!" and I must have looked excited, because Arch smiled. "No hurry," he said. "They'll say that half a dozen times yet, and no one will pay a bit of attention. But when you hear the ship's horn, they mean it. Let's meet up on the sidewalk near the top of the stairs; the dock will be pretty crowded. And first one up hold a cab; they'll be scarce for a while."

But after that — the Jotta Girl and I wandering, getting a little bored, finally — the all-ashore calls came more frequently. Then they came with chimes, boys moving through the ship tapping out chime notes, calling their warning. And finally the panic-inducing repeated blasts of the ship's terrible horn, and for an instant I was back hurrying up the aisle of *The Greyhound* matinee. *Blast! Blast! Blast! Blast!* — hurry off *now* or be carried out to sea!

At one of the open hatchways in the side of the ship, the Jotta Girl and I edged into the crowd moving toward a gangplank. Then, holding hands not to get separated, we walked down the steep slant to the solid safety of the dock, back into reality. But didn't yet climb the stairs to the street; we stood watching, gaping up at the great ship. Passengers gathered along her railings now, calling down to friends, while stewards walked among them handing out something or other. Handing out thin rolls of colored paper, which the passengers tossed out now, holding on to one end, to unroll down toward friends here on the dock

386

who caught the other end. So that suddenly hundreds of these many-colored paper ribbons hung between ship and shore, gangplanks down and being wheeled away fast, black hatchway openings slamming shut and dogged down to become parts of the long sides of the ship. Behind the great *Mauretania* the slow, sluggish beat of the tug engines, black smoke popping from their stacks. Gulls crying now, lifting, gliding; a strip of gray water appearing along the side of the ship. Then her huge growl, the great lonely departing cry again. And again, and again.

The *Mauretania* came sliding past us, backing out into the Hudson, the hundreds of paper ribbons going taut, breaking, the voyage begun. And we stood staring up at her mesmerized. The backward-sliding prow came toward us, then slipped on past, and we stood gazing up at her lighted decks, and the waving passengers, and Archie — *Archie up there at the rail* — his palm facing us, giving us a final small embarrassed and, I think, apologetic farewell.

25

---

*AND SO I lost him, Rube. Well, what did you think!
What did you expect? I could have done this, should
have done that, you bet. But I'm not supersleuth.
Did the best I could, which wasn't very good, I
know, I know.* These defensive thoughts moving
uselessly through my mind as I stood in my tenth-
floor room looking down onto the darkness of
Central Park. I was very tired, shucking off my
coat, wondering what I ought to feel about my
failure. Well, I said to myself, whatever Rube
had argued me into, it had never seemed real
or possible to me that anything I could do could
really and truly prevent an enormous war involving nearly all the world. And I felt no sureness
at all that Dr. D wasn't absolutely right: Don't
ever, ever alter the past . . . or you'll alter the
future in a way or ways you cannot know.

But I did feel stupid, looking down onto the
paving and the shining tracks of motionless Fifty-
ninth Street. Then, as sometimes happens, another
thought came winging along out of nowhere and
inserted itself. And I swung around, walked out

of my room in my shirtsleeves, and actually trotted down the staircase to the lobby, where the night clerk glanced up at me walking fast across the lobby. The newsstand had closed, but the papers were left out; you dropped your money into an empty cigar box on the counter. There were two copies of the *Evening Mail* still left.

Back in my room with one of them spread open on the bed, I turned pages, found the Jotta Girl's Wanamaker ad, and — as well as I could approximate what she had done — carefully tore out a section of the ad, for a woman's shoe. Glanced at it, then turned it to look at the other side. Out into the hall fast then, and tapped on her door.

She opened it cautiously, saw me, closed the door to remove the chain, then let me in, looking at me as I walked in past her, waiting for me to explain. She'd removed her bedspread, the bed still unopened, so I sat down on the edge of the bed, nodding at the chair near it, expecting her to take it. Instead, she sat down beside me, a little too close, so I lay back, on my side, head propped on elbow. She was having fun tonight, and did the same, and we lay there, faces about three inches apart, while she blinked at me slowly, smiling. It flustered me, as she knew it would, and for something to say, I murmured, "The Jotta Girl."

"What?"

"It's what I've called you. In my mind. The Jotta Girl. From the song." I began quietly singing the foolish nonwords that had once so appealed to my five-year-old mind. "Jotta . . . jotta! Jotta, jotta, jink-jink-jing!" She smiled, nodding, and when I continued, "Yes, jotta," she joined in, and we both sang, "Everywhere you go you hear 'em sing." Grinning at this two-in-the-morning foolishness, we sang, "Jotta! Oh, jotta! Jotta, jotta, jink-jink-jing" and ran out of words. Still smiling, I said, "How come you know that?"

"I don't know: always have. From an old song, isn't it?"

I nodded, quite slowly. "Yes. A song from the 1920s." I waited for her reaction, her confusion at knowing a song that wouldn't be written for years to come. But she didn't get it, didn't realize, just lay watching me, waiting.

So I said, "Did you get your shoes?"

"What shoes?"

From my shirt pocket I took the little rectangle of newsprint I'd torn from the *Evening Mail*, unfolded it, and held it up to show her the ad she'd torn from my first copy of the paper — for a woman's shoe. "This is the shoe you said you were interested in." Then I turned my little clipping to show her the other side. "Or was it really this you wanted torn out of my paper so I wouldn't see it?" Printed on the side now facing her was a column of type headed: *Departures.* Below that, in small type: *Sailing tonight on the* Mauretania *for Le Havre and Southampton: Colonel and Mrs. William T. Allen, Kenneth Braden and Susan Ferguson and daughter, Mr. and Mrs. Oliver*

Ausible, Marguerite Theodosia, Tom Buchanan, Ruth Buchanan, Miss Edna Butler, Major Archibald Butt, aide to the President . . . I said, "You didn't have to tear this out of my paper; I'd never have noticed it."

She shrugged. "I had to be sure." She didn't move; just kept lying there, head propped on an elbow, waiting, so I said it.

"Dr. D sent you, didn't he?"

She nodded. "We were afraid you'd remember me: because I was at the Project when you were. But he didn't have anyone else to send. I remember *you* at the Project!"

"Yeah, well, sorry. Your hair is different or something."

"Sure, but still."

"Well, I'm teddibly, teddibly sorry. I do apologize. He sent you here to sabotage me, didn't he?"

"I suppose you could say so. Simon, Dr. D knew who Z was the moment you first mentioned him! On the phone that night."

I nodded.

"*Everyone* knows who Archibald Butt was! Everyone in the world but you and Rube."

I nodded again.

"So yes, sure. I was here to keep you apart if I could. Till he sailed. I think Archie was suspicious of you anyway; you came on pretty strong and fast."

"Yeah, well, I didn't have a lot of time."

She moved her face slightly closer. "So I'm

guilty. What are you going to do about it?"

"Oh, I'm not mad. Or even sorry about it. I even think Dr. D may be right."

"Oh? Then how come — really, Simon, how come you were willing to try such a stupendous thing?"

"As preventing World War One? Oh, just as a favor to a friend."

We lay looking at each other, lying very close on a bed behind a closed door at two in the morning. Separated by the length of a lifetime from everyone who might care. We lay there looking at each other, and didn't move. Looked some more, and didn't move. Then smiled a little, the moment, if there'd ever been one, gone. "You're going home," she said. "I can tell. Back to dear old Julia." And I nodded, and we sat up.

"As soon and as fast as I can. I told Rube I'd report back, and I'll do it. Then it's home forever. You?"

"I guess so. Sure."

"Wisconsin, isn't it?"

" 'Fraid so."

"How do you go?"

"There's a place beside the East River. Sit there at night when you can't really see the other shore . . ." I was nodding, and she said, "You?"

"Brooklyn Bridge, if I were going home. But tomorrow — Central Park."

"So strange. This thing we can do. To be able to *do* it. I've never really gotten used to it." She leaned close, and I thought she was going to kiss me, just lightly kiss me goodbye, but she only touched my arm for an instant, and I nodded, and we smiled, and I left.

An hour or maybe a little less before sunset next day, I checked out of the hotel, spare clothes left behind for whoever found them, and walked into the Park. From Fifty-ninth Street behind me, as the Plaza's doors opened and closed, I heard the music of the *thé dansant,* and the occasional merry-melancholy fish-horn honk of a cab. It wasn't *l'heure bleu,* not today; there was a sharpness, a hint of rain in the air. But my bench when I found it was sheltered, and I sat down, and began the relaxation of mind and body, began the strange, actually indescribable mental search and simultaneous renunciation the Project had taught me.

And when presently — dark now, Fifth Avenue streetlamps on — I came around the last turn of the path, the Plaza had a spotlighted fountain twinkling before it, and cars pulling up to and leaving from, and people walking in through and out of, the Fifth Avenue entrance. And all around, and behind it — a great backdrop for it — the hard-glittering towers of Manhattan in the time I'd been born into.

26

AT RUBE'S apartment I had the easy chair, sitting by the windows in a parallelogram of late-afternoon sun, coffee mug in hand. But Rube — well, he didn't pace, wasn't nervous. He just walked, in his army pants, leather slippers, and white shirt. Wandered around his little living room listening, smiling, nodding, *interested*. I'd actually found Z but Rube didn't seem to care about that. What had I *done* in New York? What had I *seen?* What was it *like?*

He laughed genuinely when I quoted from *The Greyhound*, then wanted to know what the usherettes wore. And what the audience wore, and what they said in the lobby during intermission. And Mrs. Israel, and Professor Duryea, the dance teacher — and *Jolson*, my God! *Tell* me about them. And what the streets looked like. And Broadway.

He couldn't get enough, walking the room listening, smiling, nodding. Didn't give a damn about Z, far as I could tell. Finally I asked him about it, and he said, "Oh, we've been working too, Si, since you left. And now we know all about Major Archibald Butt. Your Jotta Girl was dead right. 'Jotta Girl,' " he repeated mockingly. "How'd you come up with that?" I shrugged, a little annoyed, and he said, "I remember her all right. From the Project. Hot little number."

" 'Hot little number.' Rube, if you ever develop the ability, head for the 1920s; you'll be right at home."

"I only wish I could. Anyway, your Jotta Girl was right: Everybody in the world but us knew who Major Archibald Butt was. The checkout girl at Safeway knows. Your paper-delivery boy knows. And Dr. D sure did, once you'd blabbed to him. But now I know too. I've read all about him. Your pal Major Archibald Butt sailed for Europe. As we learned too late to brief you. We also know that he got his papers; the letters of intent or whatever. And that he sailed for home. We know the date now, and we even know the ship. But he never got home." Rube stood at my chair grinning down at me like a little kid.

"Well, if you should ever happen to feel like it, you might let me know too."

"He sailed . . ." Rube began to laugh, shoulders jiggling. "*Huh, huh, huh, huh,* oh my God. He sailed — ah, *hah, hah, hah, hah!* Si, he sailed for home on the goddamn *Titanic!*"

After a moment I said, "Maybe you won't mind if I don't laugh. I *knew* him, God damn it!"

"You disappoint me. Always have. Because you don't really have any imagination. This absolutely astounding ability is wasted on you, *wasted*. All it has ever really meant to you is going back to 1880-whatever, and *Julia*. Willy. And your goddamn *dog*. Add fireplace and slippers, and that's enough for you."

"Well . . . yeah."

"What I could do with your ability!"

I pretended to cross myself at the thought.

"Simon, old fellow, even though you know that it isn't so, I believe you still actually think of the past as immutable. The *Titanic* sank. Major Butt drowned. World War One happened. Nothing to be done about it. You've never really and truly got hold of the idea that if you can go back before these things hap—"

"Rube, its you who's never understood. I've had time — and reason — to think, and the notion that Dr. D is right keeps sneaking into my mind. Whatever has happened *is* our past. What *reason* to go back and interfere with it? We're formed by our past; we'd change our own fate — blindly."

"Dr. D and his timid convert." Then, briskly, as though the nonsense were over now, he said, "Si, I want you to go back. And keep the *Titanic* from sinking." I smiled but he ignored it. "We have a 1911 passport made up for you, a real one, a good one, only a name change. It's just a big printed sheet, no photos then, thank God. You've got to go back, Si, because — we've researched this — the sinking of the *Titanic* seems to have been an event that changed the course of the world it belonged to. Even more than the loss of the people who went down with her was an *attitude* lost with it. A way people thought about the world and the century. After the *Titanic* things were never the same. It was a kind of Big Bang that changed everything. And the world veered off in another and wrong direction, the century that could have been, derailed. But . . . could you get yourself back to May 1911?"

I sat grinning, openly laughing at him. "Sure, but I won't. I just goddamn well *won't*. Why? What lunacy do you have in mind?"

He told me, and I just grinned some more. "Home, Rube. I'm going *home*."

He stood blinking at me, his face regretful, and said, "Si, I hope you will forgive me for what I have to do," and turned to walk to a little desk he had across the room. There he pushed aside a flat glass paperweight and picked up what I could see was a folded sheet of computer printout, holes down the sides. He brought it over, handed it to me, and I took and unfolded it, a long double sheet.

I couldn't tell what it was, no heading, just a long list, several dozen lines down the page in slightly faded computer print. Every line began with my name: *Morley, Morley, Morley,* clear down the left side. Following the first *Morley,* a comma, then *Aaron D.*, a string of numerals, and *HD, July 1, 1919.* Then *Morley, Adam A.,* a string of numerals, and *HD, Dec. 17, 1918.* Six or eight more *Morleys* followed by *HD*, meaning *Honorable Discharge*, it occurred to me. Then *Morley, Calvin C.*, his serial number, and *MIA, June 11, 1918*, and I knew what this sheet was, and my hand began to tremble minutely, the paper vibrating, and my eyes wouldn't quite work right, and didn't want to, but I couldn't possibly help it, and looked down at the last name on the list just above the torn-off edge, and it was there: *Morley, William S. — S* for Simon — his army serial number, and *KIA, Dec. 2, 1917. Just in time for Christmas!* my mind screamed. And I looked up at Rube, waiting, his face a little desperate. Before I could speak he said, pleading, "You had to *know* about Willy, Si! And you *want* to know, don't you? Don't you? Because I didn't fake that; don't ever think that. It's real. It's true."

I knew it was, and that in a single instant everything had changed and that I was going — had to try! — into the New York of May 1911, to attempt the craziness that could only occur in the mind of Ruben Prien.

"No, I don't blame you," I said. "It's not your fault. Not your fault at all. You son of a bitch."

27

NO TROUBLE in May 1911 booking a first-class passage on the *Mauretania* at the Cunard Line office on Lower Broadway. Next month maybe, but plenty of space now. Just time after that to buy clothes, right there on Lower Broadway: shirts, linen, shoes, pants, Norfolk jacket, cap, for walking on deck. Even dinner clothes. Along with two leather bags. Then a cab to Pier 52.

Unpacking in my cabin as we moved down the Hudson — the ship rock-steady, our motion smooth as a billiard ball rolling on felt — I'd glimpsed the city, so close, sliding swiftly past my cabin window. And by the time I reached the promenade deck in my spiffy new walking duds, we'd passed the tip of Manhattan, passed the Ambrose Lightship, and the great open sea lay ahead.

The *Mauretania*, the most loved of them all. Franklin Roosevelt said, "She always fascinated me with her graceful, yachtlike lines, her four enormous black-banded red funnels, and her appearance of power and good breeding . . . if there ever was a ship which possessed the thing called 'soul,' the *Mauretania* did. . . . Every ship has a soul. But the *Mauretania* had one you could talk to. . . . As Captain Rostron once said to me, she had the manners and deportment of a great lady and behaved herself as such." In the Smithsonian, if you hunt for it and ask enough questions, you'll find it: F.D.R.'s own model of the loved *Mauretania*.

There is nothing to do aboard an ocean liner, nothing you need to do. You're a child again, everything taken care of by Mommy and Daddy. So you change clothes, several times a day. Go out and walk the promenade deck, around and around, counting the laps, breathing the utterly clean air, feeling new health move through your veins. Then you sit in a deck chair, and a steward brings you hot bouillon, which you never drink anywhere else, but here you like it. You're a prince but a prisoner, too: you can't change your mind now. You are here on this ship and will stay here, nothing to be done about that. But this new absence of ability or need to decide is liberating. And you give in to the deliciousness of being taken care of. Spend hours in a deck chair, blanket tucked around you by a deck steward, your smile of thanks almost that of an invalid. The immense book you brought along, or got from the library, may lie unread as you doze or stare at the sea or chat with your neighbor.

Nothing to do, and it keeps you busy. I moved through and lounged in the great rooms I'd seen the night Archie sailed, the splendid arched ceilings of patterned glass now bright with the daylight of the open sea. These majestic rooms belonged to us now, the chosen few, never crowded, ours alone.

You eat; astonishing meals, delicious, and anything you want, anything, the *Mauretania* boasted, and lived up to it. And on the deck of this lovely ship, the ocean as you've never experienced it before. You're afloat in it, you're of it now, it's the element you live in. I loved it; here I saw that the horizon is a circle, with us always precisely at its center. I watched the distant glints of far-off waves, saw them rolling away beside us, saw a far-off school of porpoises curving in and out of the ocean.

Nothing to do, and all the time in the world to do it. For an hour at a time or longer, I'd stand at the stern of the *Mauretania* leaning on the rail, watching the wake endlessly line out behind us. Watching it had the hypnotic fascination of staring at the flames in a fireplace, seeing the broad light green road we'd just traveled, lying in sharp contrast to the gray-black of the sea beside it. Those deep, deep propellers, taller than a small building, endlessly thrusting up that green water so powerfully that I never saw the wake behind us subside. Always it lay stretched out further back than I could see, the long road along which we had moved. Now and then as it lined out behind us, a little squiggle would appear at right or left, a little bend in our path over the ocean, reflecting the small turns of the helmsman's wheel twitching the great rudder into endless tiny corrections of our course.

I talked to people leaning on the rail beside me. Or sitting in the next deck chair. Or barstool. And of course to the people beside and across from me in the great dining room. And I fell very easily in love with the *Mauretania*.

But for me and everyone else, beginning after breakfast on our last full day at sea, it all changed, life's demands again reaching out for us. And we talked about arrival times, destinations, and plans, and when the sea turned rough, and we reduced speed, and were told we'd be late, arriving in Liverpool well after dark, we grumbled.

Finally, at anchor in the Mersey just off the Liverpool dock — not deep enough for the draft of this ship, or the tide too low, I never learned which — the passengers for Ireland stood at the railing watching the others go off in ship's boats.

And at ten-fifteen, our luggage already transferred, we stepped from an open hatchway at just above sea level — lighted by a *Mauretania* searchlight — onto the deck of T.S.S. (twin-screw steamer) *Heroic*, a slim handsome little one-stack ferry. At my steward's advice I'd booked a cabin; the Irish Sea would be rough, and nothing to see in the dark anyway.

It *was* rough. I slept pretty well, but awakened a lot; we rolled from side to side, and we pitched stem to stern, moving at eighteen knots. And I heard the sea, loud and close. During the night someone passing my cabin said, "Allaman," as it sounded, and I understood that we must be passing the Isle of Man, but I didn't care.

Around five-thirty or six, daylight, I went out on deck; our motion much quieter now because we were steaming up the land-sheltered Belfast Lough, the mouth of the River Lagan, an Irish passenger told me. We reached the Dunbar's Dock a little past six, but berthing took a while, and I stood looking out at what I could see of Belfast: sheds . . . a mountain dominating the skyline . . . chimneys, already smoking . . . a clock tower . . . a city. A real city; four hundred thousand people lived here.

Cabs waiting on the broad dock — I guess you'd say cabs. These were pony-drawn traps, some open, some closed, not an automobile to be seen. And for the Grand Central Hotel, there stood an omnibus — it looked to me like a stretch stagecoach, four windows long — two horses, and a uniformed porter waiting. He loaded my luggage up on top, along with that of two other passengers, one a woman in full mourning including black veil. Ten minutes to the hotel on Royal Street, the best hotel in town, the *Mauretania* steward had told me. I liked it; lots of polished wood, glass, tile floor, and potted palms in the lobby. A stack of newspapers on the desk as I registered, and I bought one, the *Northern Whig*. A nice large room then, with a big brass bedstead, long lace curtains, heavy down comforter, washbowl and pitcher on the dresser.

No bathroom; that was down the hall.

Back in the lobby, I said to the clerk, "I have business with Harland and Wolff; is it a walking distance?" Yes, if I enjoyed walking, and he brought out a map and showed me the route, easy enough, it looked, always heading toward the River Lagan.

Outside then, but not to Harland and Wolff, not yet; now I just wandered in Belfast, and what I saw was a crowded, noisy, cluttered, purely Victorian city, nothing I saw newly built. This was a city of stone, at least downtown here, mostly low two- and three-story commercial buildings. Streets clanging with traffic, all horsedrawn except for some of the great double-decked red buses, upper decks unroofed. These were trolley buses on electrified streets, but horse-drawn on other streets. On the front of every bus, a sign reading, *Marsh's Biscuits*. Besides the buses, every kind of horsedrawn vehicle, and I saw a two-wheeled cart pulled by three boys. Not a single automobile — I saw none. Pedestrians crossed the streets wherever and whenever they chose, and there were advertising signs everywhere: *Cerebos*, whatever that meant, and *Co-Op Bread*, and plenty of music hall ads.

I wandered through a block or two of music halls and a theater, the Opera House, with an Arthur Pinero play. And looked over the hoardings of two-a-day music halls: *Cherburn's Young Stars* at the Empire, plus *Elton Edwin, classical banjoist. Kitts and Windrow, The Fair Imposters and their Mélange.* At the Royal Hippodrome, *Alfred Cruikshank, a droll clown, in song and story. Horton and Latriska,* and so on and so on. None of my vaudeville friends, though I knew they sometimes had bookings in England and Ireland.

Back to the hotel in the late afternoon, where I tried to read the *Northern Whig.* And finally, a little after ten o'clock, a flashlight in my pocket, I walked through the lobby, deserted now, then outside, where I followed the clerk's directions, in which the key word seemed to be "Queen." I crossed Queen's Bridge . . . passed Queen's Quay Station . . . walked along Queen's Road. . . .

The closer to my destination, the quieter, meaner, and uglier the streets became. And presently, the street slanting down toward the Lagan ahead, the houses were ugly little two-story stone dwellings, built wall to wall, and directly beside the stone sidewalk. These were workers' houses, dockyard and shipyard laborers. No lights now, no sound except from one where I could hear a baby crying. The roadway beside me cobbled with field or river stones. Dark through each silent block, streetlamps only at the corners, ragged-edged, smoky, orange-flame lights; I could smell the kerosene as I passed under each, my shadow bunching under my feet, then lengthening and fading off into the darkness ahead.

Now a road T-crossed this, the intersection dimly lighted. I walked across it; brick-paved, deserted, silent. On the other side, a narrow walk beside a brick wall a couple feet taller than I, easily climbed. On the other side of this wall, a scattering of buildings, some with a dim light inside, some dark. I could read the painted names of some: *Foundry . . . Fettling Shop . . . Storage . . . Timber Drying Shed . . . Electric Generating Station . . . Brass Fitting Shop . . . Galvanizing . . . Pattern Stores . . . Fitting and Bolt Shop . . . Upholstery Shop . . . Paint Shop . . .* and many more as I walked. Mostly dark, no movement, no sound but the soft scuff of my shoes, here on this night of 1911.

Now a break in the wall, the road branching into the walled area, a wide wooden gate across the opening, a black-and-white painted sign: *Harland & Wolff, Ltd., Shipbuilders.* Then the wall resumed, and more shops: *Coppersmith's Shop . . . Brass Foundry . . . Boiler Shop. . . .*

On through a long dark block, then both wall and I made a right turn, down toward the Lagan. A final turn, into Queen's Road, and now I walked between brick-walled areas on each side. *Time Office . . .* then *Main Office*, a dim night-light inside this one. And between it and *Mast Shop*, a narrow passageway.

Through a long minute I stood listening . . . then reached up to press my hooked hands onto the wall top. Then I heaved myself up to hang supported on my stiffened arms, listening. No whistle blast, no running feet or snarling dogs. Nothing, and I lay across the wall on my belly, squirmed my legs around and over, dropped, turned around and stood staring at what I'd known I would see from here, but hugely larger, impossibly larger than I'd ever imagined.

28

THIS—NOT my photograph, and taken in daylight — but this is what I saw now, only in black silhouette, a giant cutout sharp against the moonlit sky over the river waiting to receive her in two more days. Just under the knife of its prow, the shadowy reviewing stand waiting for the lady with the christening champagne, I supposed. Who would smash her bottle against that black steel, and — I had read — "the hydraulic launching trigger" would be pulled. Then the almost imperceptible slow widening between prow and dripping bottle: a foot . . . a yard . . . then with abrupt speed, down the incline she'd slide, this enormous black mass, her stern smashing into the Lagan, waterspout soaring, then this great black hull bobbing a little, afloat at last. To be towed to the dock where cranes would lower her superstructure, the ship would be fitted out, and in a remarkably short time the *Titanic* would sail out on her black, murderous, only journey.

But no; now it would not. Standing in the dark between my two buildings, I looked at and — abruptly, surprisingly — hated the new ship rising to the sky there across the yard. We personify ships, they seem to have human qualities; there are good ships, stubborn resistant ships, and now I saw this giant silhouetted shape as evil, blackly malevolent: she knew — this monstrous bulk *knew* she would betray the hundreds who, trusting her, would sail out on her only voyage. At this moment somewhere across hundreds of ocean miles the great berg lay drifting toward their rendezvous, this black prow waiting now to slide along the mass of blue ice it might just as well have missed by the feet or even inches that would have made the difference.

Well, I was here to prevent that rendezvous, and I walked out — moving from shadow to shadow, pausing to listen — toward the *Titanic*, her cargo ports open. This was Rube's simple idea: launch her *now,* down the ways into and under the Lagan.

At the prow just past the ceremonial stand, I used my flashlight to hunt for "the launching trigger." It would have to be somewhere forward here easily in sight of lady and bottle to synchronize trigger pull with, "I christen you *Titanic*!"

I couldn't find it; nothing that to my mind even resembled a trigger, and I walked back and around to the starboard side. Not here, nothing like a launching trigger, and I walked on and into this tunnel directly under the *Titanic*'s hull

— again, not my photo but it's what I saw now in the wavering oval of my flash: this forest of stumps supporting the unimaginable bulk just above me. And here in the almost dark, as alone as I've ever been, I felt my face flush. How, *how* could we have been so stupid? No ship could be left to be easily or accidentally launched! More, much more had to be done here before the final ceremony. Something, some sort of rolling support riding on the track — I could see this easily here — had to replace this forest. And all these stumps had to be knocked out by swinging sledges in the moment just before the launch. How had we ever supposed that somehow I could send this monster prematurely sliding down the ways? I felt like a child, and shut my eyes, ashamed.

Hopelessly crouched under this great black evil, I moved my light across the peeled roundness of these endless supports, then lifted it to slide the little patch of light along the riveted rows forming the *Titanic* just over my head. The thing had beaten me, no contest, this monster untouchable. In frustration and weak anger, I lifted my fist and brought it up hard to strike the riveted steel but even in anger I turned my fist, defeated, to strike with the soft edge of my hand, not the knuckles that this thick cold steel would have crushed. And the ship didn't care, the steel cold and wet with dew, my little blow no more making a sound than striking granite.

There under the *Titanic* I switched off my light, crouching helplessly for a moment longer, then

411

crept out. Out and back the way I'd come, back along the streets to my hotel. Nothing, nothing, nothing could be done to prevent what I alone in this world knew was going to happen.

And yet, walking back, I began to feel that I wasn't finished. Something *had* to be done. And what I did next was to walk the length of Ireland.

I'd always wanted to, had occasionally thought about it, and now here near the century's beginning, the country unspoiled, this was my chance. And in the morning I bought what I needed: hiking shoes, canteen, knapsack, map. I talked to store clerks, to hotel people, and got plenty of advice. Shipped my luggage ahead by train, and set out the following morning.

This isn't the story of that long almost happy journey, but I saw what visitors to Ireland always see, that the fields truly are a shade of green seen nowhere else. I walked dirt roads, standing aside for great flocks of sheep, shepherd and I nodding, touching caps. Stopped at a farm for water, was welcomed by a shy, truly charming couple with faces and hands permanently dirty, seldom — ever? — washed. Who gave me water, and food I hadn't asked for in a kitchen through which live chickens wandered. Back on the road, miles ahead, I looked for a place to throw away the sandwiches, empty my canteen, felt ashamed, and ate them and drank.

I stood staring across fields at the strange castlelike fortresses of centuries past, still standing, their entrances high above the ground, against siege from — Vikings? I wasn't sure. Sometimes I stayed overnight, a couple days, a week if I felt like it, in a village or town that took my interest. At the local inn or hotel, getting clothes washed, walking around, talking to people, usually friendly though not always. Twice I camped near a cliff overlooking the sea, once for almost a week. And spent days mostly sitting on the edge watching the waves far below flood up onto the stony beach, then wash back down; not actually thinking, not quite, but letting the problem waiting for me move through my mind. Spent a month in Dublin, walking it, visiting Joycean pubs. Was he here in Dublin now? I couldn't remember, if I ever knew. If he was I never saw him, or if I did, didn't know it.

And then finally, on a late afternoon of the following spring, the necessary time pleasantly killed, I walked into the little port called Queenstown, almost only a village, its houses scattered over a series of terraces rising above the enormous bay of Cork harbor. At the edge of a wide dirt street I stood looking down at the great enclosed sheet of water flashing under the late-in-the-day sun, two small ships at anchor, a lightship far out at the harbor entrance. An almost empty harbor now, but not tomorrow, and I felt abruptly tired, depressed, the problem with no answer back. I found Queenstown Inn then, and a hot bath, a drink, another, then dinner, and bed.

At just past eight next morning I stood in a short line in the downtown office of James Scott

& Co., agents for Cunard, Hamburg-American, White Star, and apparently every other steamship line calling in Queenstown. I wore a white shirt now, a tie and suit, weightless after tweeds and heavy boots, which I'd left behind in the Queenstown Inn closet along with my knapsack. My luggage had been waiting for me a long time now, and I had it sent to James Scott & Co. In the line ahead of me stood two men, both wearing caps and worn suitcoats with unmatching pants; and at the head of the little line, talking to the twenty-year-old clerk at the wooden counter, a young woman and an eight-year-old-girl, wearing shawls over their shoulders and black straw hats.

I felt sick, looking at the child, wanting to *tell* them, knowing I could not, and stood watching and listening as the young woman bought a second-class ticket. Leaning to one side, I saw it, a surprisingly big sheet of buff paper imprinted with the White Star legend, and a cut of a four-funnel steamer. Thirteen pounds it cost her, which she had ready in her hand.

The clerk glanced at the two men in caps then, and without asking brought out two identical-looking tickets, but on white paper. "Steerage," he said, not even a question, wrote on each ticket, and said, "Ten pounds, ten shillings," and again, each had exactly that ready in his hand. I'd edged forward, curious about the ticket lying on the counter, and saw that it was actually a contract, everything spelled out including *Bill of Fare: Breakfast at eight o'clock: Oatmeal Porridge and milk, tea, coffee, sugar, milk, fresh bread, butter . . .*

My turn, then, three more men in caps now behind me. "Sor?" said the clerk. Sounded like *sor,* anyway.

"One first-class."

"First-class? *First?*" He smiled, happy about it. "Never before have I sold one of them." He had to hunt through two drawers to find a first-class ticket, looking about like the others but on tan paper — and with no bill of fare. Then — no hurry, everyone behind me could wait — he brought up and unrolled on the counter, turning it to face me, a deck plan. He weighted it at two corners with an inkwell and a paper-spike. "And where would you like to be, sor? We have vacancies on every deck, many a cancellation; Southampton telephoned me only last night."

"The boat deck. Which is the boat deck?"

"That would be Deck A, sor, the top deck." He touched the deck plan, but I saw that all the cabins were well forward: they'd rise and fall with the sea, and I'd had enough of that. But Deck B just below, also a Promenade deck, had cabins along its entire length except for restaurants near the stern. "Maybe Deck B would be better; something near the middle and as close to the staircase here as you've got." I touched the little printed stairs on the plan which led up to the boat deck and boat number five. Closest to the stairs was a three-room suite with its own private Promenade, but next to it, a single. "This one?"

"B-fifty-seven." He looked at a typed list, then

at a penciled list of cancellations. "Taken, sor, but B-fifty-nine beside it is available."

"I'll take it." I brought out my wallet, looking at him questioningly, and he had his big moment: watching me slyly, not sure I understood what I'd gotten into, he said, "Yes, sor. That will be five hundred and fifty American dollars."

"How about a hundred and ten English fivers?"

"That will do very nicely indeed."

I had ready, in an inside coat pocket, an inch-thick sheaf of the strange English five-pound notes printed on one side only of a sheet of white paper big as a dog's blanket. The little room was absolutely silent, every eye watching as I counted out a hundred and ten of these. The clerk picked them up, tapped them into alignment, and — I admired this — put them into his cash drawer without recounting. He pushed over my ticket. "Safe voyage, sor." And I thanked him, and left, every eye following me out to the street.

Around noon I walked onto Scott's Quay with my suitcase, set it at my feet, then stood with several dozen Irish immigrants staring out toward the distant harbor mouth. I had my camera again and, not really wanting to, I took this. There

she lay waiting for us, lazy wisps lifting from her funnels; arrogantly waiting, my enemy and the enemy of us all, the great evil blackness under whose riveted hull I had stood helpless. She *knew*, and she knew that I knew, I alone. And I looked out at that black smoking silhouette and did not know what to do with my knowledge of what — far over the horizon ahead — lay waiting for us.

We left Scott's Quay here, standing crowded together on the deck of the tender *America*, following this tender crammed with mail for the States. Plenty of excited chatter and laughter,

though one young girl stood silent and white-faced. As we chugged across the bay, the waiting ship ahead began to grow, and the murmur of talk lowered. Our steady passage across the calm took maybe half an hour, details slowly emerging on the great silhouetted ship: a thin gold sheer line at the hull's upper edge . . . a roughening of the black surface of her side becoming rows of rivets. I'd seen one of our passengers, as he boarded the tender, wearing kilts, but hadn't noticed his bagpipe. But now as we drew near the waiting ship he began to play, a mournful squealing, and a young woman in a shawl murmured respectfully, " 'Erin's Lament.' " Fortunately he wasn't too close to me — when you've heard one bagpipe tune you've heard them both — but the crowd listened quietly. When he finished, the enormous ship filled our view, and the vibration of our steam engine suddenly slowed under our feet, and now I looked far up at the great white letters that spelled *Titanic*.

29

WE LAY beside her, rocking on the water, men
in a portside cargo opening fending us with boat
hooks, and I snapped this, Captain Smith himself

way up there at the top watching us board. They'd run out a gangplank, and now we moved on up it and into the black cargo opening.

Inside we separated forever, everyone else gestured off to the left by uniformed crew members. I alone, tan ticket in hand, politely gestured toward a staircase. But, my foot on the steel tread, I stood for a moment watching the others walk off, chattering, most of them soon to drown, unless . . . unless what?

Up through the ship I climbed then — didn't yet know where the elevators were or whether they came down this far — up and up toward my deck. The stairs turned from bare steel to carpeted treads, the staircases widening, stair landings becoming more ornate with each flight up, banisters becoming heavy with carving. A new deck, and now the newel posts of the next flight up bore a pair of bronze figures supporting lamps, and I saw stained glass, framed paintings, and above the staircase a great curved ceiling of stained-glass washing stairs and carved banisters in multicolored light. Each of the great public rooms, lounges, and lobbies through which I ascended seemed more lavish than the last, and I'd begun passing glorious women in fashionable hobble skirts, and their cigar-smoking men in suits, vests, watch chains, stiff white collars, some wearing shipboard caps, a few still actually wearing derbies. Nearly everyone smiling, pleased and excited at new sights and sounds. Moving up through this mighty ship on newly carpeted stairs,

I'd become aware of the special smell of the *Titanic*, different from the *Mauretania*, both saying that we were at sea, but pervading the air of the *Titanic* the unique smell of — I recognized it now — newness. Of newly dried paint, newly woven and still untrod carpeting, new wood newly glued, new cloth, new everything, this magnificent luxury liner still unused: we were the first.

To the pleased, excited passengers moving up and down through the ship with me, I think everything said pleasure ahead. I saw it in their faces, smiles, and heard it in their voices, and it affected me. For a forgetful few moments moving up through this ship, I shared the anticipation of a beginning voyage. Then I stepped off the stairs onto the floor of the first-class salon, and saw the shining, possibly never-yet-played grand piano. And remembered the story of an Irish immigrant girl saved in one of the lifeboats — had I glimpsed her on the ferry? The ship slowly sinking, she'd climbed up from steerage into this magnificent salon, along with a group of fellow steerage passengers. She continued on up, heading for the boat deck, but glancing back she saw one of her fellow immigrants stop at the piano in awe. He touched the keys, then began to play, sliding onto the piano bench. Others of the group gathered around him, and they began to sing along, staring around them at the unimaginable luxury of the room they'd found themselves in. And that was the last the girl ascending the stairs ever saw or heard of her friends.

421

True or not, the memory of that story abruptly separated me from the other passengers on the stairs; these splendid women and the cigar-smoking, pince-nezed men. Who of these would be saved? Most of the women, few of the men. I had to shut off these incapacitating thoughts; I was here on this ship for a powerful reason, and I forced my mind to focus on that.

My cabin was where the White Star deck plan had said it would be, very near the staircase I stepped from onto B deck. This is it, B59 on the *Titanic*, door ajar, key in lock, steady as a hotel room as I stood in the door taking this picture. Just behind me a steward said, "Boarded

at Queenstown, did you, sir?" and I understood that he wanted to see a ticket and turned: he wore a brass-buttoned green jacket, white shirt, black bow tie. *Will you be saved?* my mind asked as I handed him my ticket. He gave it back, nodding: I was the only first-class boarder at

Queenstown, so my luggage should soon be here. I nodded and walked out to explore.

Up one last flight to the boat deck, but just before reaching it, I stopped. Beside each stair, one at each side, a little glassed-in light was set, all unlighted now. Wasn't this the staircase, I stood wondering, and weren't these the lights that Second Officer Lightoller saw as he stood loading women and children into the portside lifeboats? Glancing down from time to time to see the green ocean water slowly creeping up the stairs toward him, these lights shining eerily under the ascending water? I thought so; thought I remembered from so much I had read that this was Lightoller's staircase, waiting now for the midnight just ahead when the ocean would enter to slowly climb higher and higher, stair by stair.

I shut down on the thought, and stepped out onto the new teak of the boat deck, the very topmost deck out under the pale sky and weak sun. Through the leather of my soles, suddenly, I felt the vibration from many decks below of the ship's great turbines, and we began to move out to sea. Here hung the lifeboats, here was the deck soon to be crowded with men, women, and children in life jackets. Some of them stone-faced calm, some crying, some terribly frightened, some laughing at what they supposed was a false alarm. Up here the confused, botched lowering of half-empty boats — *Cut it out!* I turned to walk over to the starboard side of B deck, and the shining white paint of boat number five. There it hung secure in its davits, glittery white, tautly covered with canvas, and I reached out to touch the new paint of its wooden side. Under my fingertip, the painted wood felt smooth, faintly warm from the sun. But above all it felt solid and real. *Titanic Boat Five*, said the fresh black lettering at its prow, and I touched the *T*. Then touched the cool solidity of the varnished ship's rail below Boat Five, and then I was really here. On the new *Titanic*, its speed steadily increasing, a doomed ship, carrying me and every other soul aboard toward the immense icy mass waiting ahead. And once again I stood bleakly alone, eyes closing against this useless knowledge.

I walked on; beside me, large as a ten-story building, a great beige and black stack marched in line with three more identical monsters back toward the stern. They rose immensely up through the roofs of the various superstructures, their thin wash of black smoke streaming out to merge and dissipate behind us. Huge air scoops sprouted from the deck like giant ear trumpets. I turned to look forward, and just ahead, the enclosed bridge of the ship stretched across the entire forward end of the deck. A door at its side stood ajar, swinging slightly to and fro with our movement, and I walked up to peek in. There they were, four officers, three in blue, the fourth, Captain Smith himself, still in his whites. Not quite shoulder to shoulder, they stood in a line facing forward, staring out through the long square windows. Captain Smith's arms hung behind him, one hand clasping the other wrist. Behind them, in his own little glassed-in enclosure, was the helmsman, hands on his great wooden wheel, eyes on the compass in the brass binnacle before him. He stood directly opposite me, only a dozen feet or so off, and before he could glance over and see me, I turned away.

For a moment or so longer I stood alone out here, glancing up at the aerial strung between our two masts; it would be the first ever to signal an SOS. Through the web of black guy wires bracing the enormous stacks, the wind of our passage moaned steadily, mournful and lonely, as though it knew and was telling me what was going to happen, and I walked back to my stairs.

Down here on B deck, the sides sheltered from the sea in places by long glass windows, it was warmer, and I walked along on the sun side toward the stern. A boy spinning a top on the steady

deck had a little audience, and I joined them long enough to snap this. *Will this boy survive?* I was sick of the question, unable to prevent it, and walked on toward the stern. At every entrance passengers were turning in to the warmth of the interior, but I kept on toward the stern and the entrance to the Verandah and Palm Court. Near the stern, second-class passengers stood up on their limited deck space watching the privileged

first class, and me with my red leather camera as I stood taking them. As I saw this in my tiny little viewfinder, my mind said, *Most of you are going to drown Sunday night.* I left to walk back along the port side, then wished I hadn't. Very little sun, no one out, and the rows of empty deck chairs made it seem like a deserted ship. My own solitary steps sounded along the deck as though I were the only passenger, and up there ahead I rounded the turn near the prow. I wound my film, and saw the last of it appear in the little red window. Over the rail I used it for this bleak sight: the *Titanic,* racing now, on to-

ward the night over this strange deathly calm sea.

I'd had enough, and spent the rest of the day in my cabin; had the steward bring dinner in. I didn't want to see any more people who might be living their last day or so; or to encounter Archie prematurely, to stutter and stumble and say it all wrong. If there was a way to convince Arch of the unbelievable, I had to find it, and I tried to work it out in my mind, lying on my bed feeling the easy motion, hearing the quiet, regular, almost reassuring creakings of a ship moving through a quiet sea.

I could have learned from the purser in the morning which was Archie's cabin, but instead I simply wandered in and out of the great public rooms till I found him in the lounge in a big leather chair: gray suit, plain blue tie; smoking a morning cigar.

Suspicious, he sat watching me approach, making my way around and between tables and big lounge chairs. And didn't smile: whoever I was or whatever I might be up to, he knew from my very presence aboard that I must be more than the casual New York acquaintance he'd supposed. I thought he wasn't even going to stand, and possibly he thought so too. But at the last moment instinct brought him to his feet, and when I said, "Hello, Archie," and put out a hand, he took it and replied politely, watching me with sharp, inquisitive eyes.

He said, "Sit down," nodding at a chair facing him.

I sat down, leaned toward him, and said it the

way I'd worked it out. "Archie, I know about your mission. I'm not your enemy: I want it to succeed. But let me tell you something you can't possibly believe. Just hear me out. And then, Arch . . . wait. And when you actually see the proof . . . you will know then that I've spoken the truth." I saw the flick of impatience and got down to it.

"I know something that is impossible to know, and yet I know it. This is Friday. On Sunday night, around eleven-thirty, this ship will strike an iceberg. Two hours later it will sink." He sat watching me, waiting. "A good many people will be saved in lifeboats in those two hours. But many of the boats will be lowered only partly filled. And fifteen hundred people will drown. Do I really know this? Sunday night will tell, won't it. It will happen, and when it does, I want to take you to boat number five, which will be lowered with only a few people. Some women in first, then with no others around, the men standing by will be allowed in. You and I can be there —"

"Si. I've seen a few inexplicable things; I know they happen. And possibly somehow you know what you say you do. Maybe so. Maybe somehow you really know. But you don't seem to know me. If you did, you could not possibly think that with women and children left behind to drown, Archibald Butt would be standing beside a lifeboat scheming to climb into it!" He sat there looking at me, then smiled a little. "I would be

429

where every other gentleman aboard would be: waiting quietly somewhere out of the way for whatever fate intends. Very likely here in this lounge, accepting God's will. Along with a glass of brandy. Not cowering beside a lifeboat while women drown. I believe it's where you'd be too, Si. When you'd thought about it. I'm sure you would."

"But what about your *papers*, Arch? Shouldn't they be saved at least?"

He looked contemptuously at the crackpot. "I don't know what you're talking about." Leaning forward in his chair, he looked past me at a quietly ticking grandfather clock across the room. "And now if you'll excuse me." And he stood, smiled but only just barely, walked out, and I understood as though he had said it that I was not to trouble him again.

And so, finally, I'd failed. Archie would drown, the Great War would happen. But I'd never quite been able to make myself believe that something I could do, *anything* I could do, would actually prevent that enormous war. Yet watching Archie walk away and out of the lounge, my eyes stung.

Willy, what about Willy! Well . . . decades lay between him and the December 2, 1917, date followed by *KIA* that Rube Prien had shown me. Someday I'd have to tell son Willy who I was, and where I'd come from. Well, I'd simply warn him about that date too. Forewarned is forearmed, and he could protect himself: report sick that morning, turn left instead of right, do *something*,

430

anything, that would slightly alter the events of the next few hours. I could give Willy the means of saving himself.

Strange, sitting here in this quiet, nearly empty lounge, thinking my thoughts, knowing what I knew — that this was the *Titanic*'s maiden voyage and her last. That Sunday night she would sink into an ocean so astonishingly calm survivors would remember forever the light of the stars shining on the face of the nearly motionless sea. And strange that this great disaster would be a matter of almost inches: if she'd passed the huge berg only slightly more to one side, I sat remembering, she'd have sailed right on by the deadly spur of underwater ice that opened her plates to the sea. And steamed triumphantly into New York harbor, pennants flying, tugs spouting.

But now? I took myself to my cabin, and — meals brought in by the steward — spent the day there, confused, baffled. I knew what was coming, *knew;* but what to do? Just wait till time to step into a lifeboat I already knew would be lowered nearly empty, leaving half the ship to drown?

In the morning, sick of the question and of my cabin and view — through a curtained window, not a porthole — of the endless flat monotonous gray sea and unbroken horizon, I showered, dressed, and began roaming. Heard the ship's bugler blow breakfast call, hesitated, then skipped it, too agitated to eat. Walking the boat deck, enclosed but unheated, I'd get chilled, then inside again through the revolving doors. A pair of electric heaters glowing orange stood just inside, and I liked that. The days' runs were posted on the smoking room bulletin board, and I went in and read yesterday's: Thursday noon to Friday, the *Titanic* had steamed 386 miles. Another passenger there turned to ask a passing steward if we'd do better today, and he replied that he thought we'd post over 500 miles. I said, "Excuse me, steward, but — how can I speak to Captain Smith? It's quite important."

"Well, sir, at half after ten, and it's nearly that now, he should be coming along the deck just outside with his morning inspection party. I should think that might be a good time, sir."

So out on the deck again, I sat in a wooden deck chair watching the almost imperceptible roll of the ship, the horizontal top deck rail dropping slowly, slowly below the distant horizon encircling us, then holding there, holding . . . before it began to slowly rise again. Soothing to watch, it calmed me, and when I heard and saw the inspection party down the deck moving toward me, I knew I could stand and say what I had to.

Here they came, five ship's officers led by the captain himself, all in full-dress blues with medals, all wearing wing collars. One of the party making notes, the captain's big white-bearded head turned steadily side to side, looking, watching, commenting, nodding and smiling at passengers but moving briskly along, conversation not encouraged now, and I made myself stand, stepped out before the little group, and made my mouth speak.

"May I have a word with you, Captain? It is truly important."

He stood looking at me carefully. "Yes?"

"Sir. Captain Smith." How could I make sense? "I happen to have some . . . special knowledge." Didn't sound right! How to *say* this? Oh hell, just say it! "On Sunday night, if you maintain this course and speed, sir, we are going to strike an iceberg. We will! I —" I stopped, amazed; he was grinning at me.

"Oh, don't worry, don't you worry, sir!" He clapped a reassuring hand lightly on my shoulder. "We know all about the icebergs; this is the iceberg season, and we've had plenty of warnings, isn't that so, Jack," glancing at one of his officers.

"Yes, sir, from *Empress of Britain* and *Touraine* so far. They report field ice, some growlers, some bergs between forty-one fifty north latitude and forty-nine fifty west. Bound to hear more reports as we approach, sir."

And this impressive, neatly bearded, likable captain smiled at me pleasantly. "So we're well warned, sir," Captain Smith said, "but I do thank you" — he touched me lightly on the shoulder again. "Not to worry." And they moved on.

So . . . yes. What else could he have thought or said? And now? Now there was simply nothing else I could do. Except wait. And because I knew what I knew, I was no longer able to talk to or even look at other passengers. At my assigned dining room table I'd been seated with a not-quite-elderly man and his wife, he newly retired; and another, forty-year-old man, all English. And I was not able to continue making light conversation with them, all of us laughing a lot, with me wondering all the time: *What will happen to you tomorrow night?*

I had to find a refuge from the sight and sound of living people whose shoes — I'd compulsively glance at them — were going to lie alone on the ocean floor through decades to come, their clothes and entire bodies dissolving to nothing. And Sunday afternoon, restlessly wandering, I found my refuge at the very stern, overhanging the sea, protruding further back than even the great rudder. This was a separate little poop deck reached by a short flight of stairs from the main Deck B. And in this desolate, deserted little place crowded with ship's machinery — winches, cranes, capstans — I stood, here at the very stern, forearms on the rail, trying to isolate my helpless self from the horror of what was going to happen. And I resumed my old game of watching the greeny-white wake peel endlessly out behind us.

It empties the mind to stare down at the ever-changing sameness of a ship's wake. There behind us it lay on the quiet gray sea, handsomely green, squirming with bubbles, a wide watery road over which we'd just come. Arms on the stern rail, hands clasped over the sea, I stood watching the great propeller bubbles blossom up from the deep; watching the helmsman's occasional small corrections appear as a squiggle in the wake, slightly bending the long green road to left or right. Watched a bird appear here far out in the ocean. A tern, was that what they were called? He'd follow us, wings spread motionless, getting a free ride on the invisible tunnel of warmed air lining out behind us. Then he'd move, he'd tilt; it looked like fun. Presently he lowered to the surface and, wings tucking, bobbed away behind us on our flat green wake. They slept on the sea, I thought I knew.

And out here, bent over the roadlike wake, I escaped. The deck under my feet, the rail under my forearms were solid, the people inside the warmth of this ship truly alive. But for me, only for me but nevertheless, all this finally became the distant past. My own reality lay far away, and what was going to happen tonight out here in the Atlantic was an old, old story from a long-ago time about which I could do nothing at all.

But I couldn't hang on to that truth. From behind me on the deck of the ship whose fate and people I'd tried to turn from, I heard approaching footsteps, then the mumble-grumble of a man's voice, a woman's reply, everything turning again to real and now, and I stood frantic with helplessness.

Someone materialized beside me, sleeved forearms sliding into vision on the railing beside mine, hands clasping, and I knew whose they were, and could not possibly have prevented the wild rush of happiness. And, no way to stop this, none,

I turned, my arms reaching, and grabbed the Jotta Girl to me, kissing her hard, kissing her long, and just did not want to stop. But did; *Julia, I did.* And now out here on the gray Atlantic, we stood grinning at each other. I said, "Dr. D just never quits, does he."

"He had to be certain. So I sat in the lounge watching you and Archie from an armchair behind a pillar till I knew. It's over now, Si; Archie won't change his mind."

"I know. Jot, what will you do when it happens?"

"Dr. D says go to Boat Eighteen. It was lowered with plenty of room left. You?"

"Boat Five. There were only a few women in it, no others around, just a few men. So the men were ordered in too."

Side by side then, forearms again on the stern rail, we stood watching the long green wake endlessly come into being, straight as a road for a while, then the little squiggle to one side or the other of the helmsman's small correction. Occasionally people walked by on the deck behind us; we'd hear their wooden footsteps approach, hear the murmur of their talk. We heard a man, a woman, and a small girl; then the child spotted us, and scampered up our stairs just enough so that, turning at the sound, we saw her little face and red knitted cap appear. She stared at us for a moment, her eyes bright with mischief, then called, "Hello!" delighted with her own daring. The Jotta Girl smiled, calling an answer, but when she looked back to me her eyes glittered wet. "Oh *Christ,* Si, *what can we do?*"

I shook my head. "There's no warning them," and I told her what had happened when I spoke to Captain Smith. And we turned back to stare down at our wake again.

But not for long. She turned from our rail to the little flight of stairs down to the main deck, and I followed. A few steps across the deck below, then up the outside stairs to the boat deck, I almost trotting along behind her, wondering. Forward along the deck, glancing at her as I caught up. But her face was set, purposeful, not a glance at me, and no explanation.

On past the lifeboats in their davits — big, *big,* seeing them this close. And now the Jot pulled the scarf from her neck, a thin gauzy thing patterned in lavender, and carried it hanging loosely between her hands. We walked fast, the length of the port side, the steady wind of the ship's passage mournful in the guy wires spidered out from the huge beige stacks rimmed in black.

At the very end of this deck, as far forward as we could go, she stopped beside the ship's bridge, a long narrow enclosed space lying across the entire width of the ship. A door here stood open, and inside the bridge, as always day and night, stood a line of four ship's officers, among them the captain, hands behind his back, one hand clasping the other wrist. The front of the bridge was a line of tall glassed windows, giving them a clear view of the sea ahead. They stood silent, staring. They couldn't see us, here beside the door at the rear, but the helmsman could. He stood several feet behind the officers, his outspread arms gripping the great wooden wheel, eyes on the face of the big lighted compass floating in the waist-high binnacle before him. He glanced at us standing there in the open doorway, but only for a moment, used to the occasional curious passenger. But he'd seen the Jotta Girl's smile, her very best smile, which was very, very good; and, watching his compass again, he was slightly smiling, couldn't help it.

Now the Jotta Girl smiled even more, a dazzling supersmile, and walked in toward the helmsman, lifting her hands as though to show him the scarf hanging loose between them. She stopped beside him, raised her hands, and gently laid her scarf across the helmsman's face, pulling it taut, then tossing the ends up onto the flat top of his British seaman's white cap. The scarf clung to his face, a hand rising to pluck it off, but he couldn't quite pinch up the thin material, and had to lift both hands to get hold of and drag it off. I'd seen his wheel make a quarter-turn, and — scarf off — he grabbed it, glancing quickly down at his binnacle, and corrected his course. Then — we stood back outside the door again — he turned to us, glaring, but the Jot stood beautifully smiling at her little prank, blew him a kiss, and he had to grin, shaking his head.

We walked a step or two away, then ran — racing back along the port side, past the lifeboats again, clattering down the little staircase, across the bit of open deck, then up to our little poop deck perch at the stern. And there it lay, written on the water, already well behind us but clear and plain — the graphlike squiggle on the long greeny wake which told us that the Jotta Girl had just slightly altered the course of the *Titanic*.

Not much but very little was needed, just the tiny bit — a few *inches* enough — to make the enormous difference between riding over the underwater ice spur that would buckle her plates and kill her . . . or sailing unknowingly just past it. The Jotta Girl had made that difference, and — I couldn't help it, didn't want to help it — I grabbed and kissed her in a little ecstasy of joy and relief.

We celebrated — had drinks in the Cafe Parisian, sitting beside each other, grinning nonstop, clicking our glasses in toast or salute or whatever; to each other, the helmsman, Dr. D, Rube Prien, Captain Smith, this splendid new ship. People at nearby tables were smiling at us, and we raised our glasses to them, feeling just fine. To tease the Jot I said, "Never interfere with the past. Never, never, never, never! Ever!"

"Oh, shut up."

"Broke the sacred rule, didn't you? What would Dr. D say?"

"That I did exactly right."

"Oh no he wouldn't. But I will. You did just right, you did great."

We were careful not to drink too much, and

at dinner not even wine. And at 11:15 we sat waiting in the lounge at a table for two beside a starboard window: the great iceberg would pass close, and we wanted to see it. We talked, I don't know about what, glancing often at a big round wall clock across the room. It worked by air pressure, a steward had told me, the big hand advancing a full minute at a time. And when it jumped from 11:19 to 11:20, we stopped trying to talk, and sat waiting.

Outside, I knew, up in a crow's nest on the forward mast, a seaman bulky with heavy clothes sat staring out at the black sea and starlit sky. At any moment now, he should lean forward, eyes narrowing, making sure . . . then reach swiftly for the lanyard of his warning bell. A dozen seconds . . . several more, the clock hands across the room still at 11:20. Then we heard what we alone had known we'd hear, the fast triple sound, *clang, clang, clang,* of the warning bell, faint and distant through the window glass. A long pause, the lookout on his phone to the bridge, we knew. Then, grinning at each other, we felt it, the slow-motion swing of the great vessel as the rudder swung hard. And then, abruptly, astoundingly, here it was sliding past just outside our window, a great ice-white cliff filling the window glass bottom to top, side to side — we could have touched it except for the glass. And then, on her new course . . . *on her new course* . . . on the very slightly altered course the Jotta Girl had sent us into . . . the *Titanic*

440

just barely touched the enormous mass she would otherwise just barely have missed.

And we heard — not at all loudly, feeling it through our shoe soles as much as hearing it — the long slow tearing sound, the prolonged ripping, as the ice spur deep under the sea in precisely the right place raked along the ship's riveted bottom to let in the first rush of the unstoppable sea that in two hours would sink her. The Jot's eyes widening, widening, as she listened, the color emptying from her face, she whispered, "Never. . . ." Her eyes glittered with sudden tears. "Never alter . . ." She stood up swiftly, and as I pushed back my chair she said, "No!" Then, almost ferociously, "*No,* don't come after me! *Don't!*" And swung around to walk away very fast.

Outside my window a ship's officer walked by, in no hurry that I could see. The berg was gone now, far off in the dark behind us. I looked around the room for, and found, Archibald Butt, sitting with several other men at the table where, I knew, he would remain. And I sat back — there were two long, long hours to get through, no rush — and picked up my drink.

30

I'M HOME now. For good. And sitting out here in the not-quite-darkness of our front stoop — there's a streetlamp down at the curb — I'm okay, I'm all right. Pretty much, anyway. But I don't want to leave here again, don't ever want to be anywhere else. And don't want to ever again even think of Rube Prien. Or Dr. D and how right he was. Rover's out there across the street somewhere. He glances over here a lot; I see his eyes glint green from the streetlamp on that side. Wants to be sure I'm here while he checks out that the neighborhood is still unchanged.

Which it almost is, though not quite. Last night I walked down the block a way, checking out the neighborhood myself, and saw the funeral wreath on old Mr. Bostick's front door: the stiff dark wreath with small lavender flowers that we hang on our front doors to say that someone in this house has died. Old Bostick was born in 1799, the year George Washington died; for a few months, weeks, or maybe only days they might have been alive together. Imagine it. Now he's gone, a thread to the past broken. But they break every day, don't they, the past ever receding, growing stiller and stiller in our minds.

Gloomy obvious thoughts, sitting out here. But I'll stop pretty soon. Stop thinking so much of what happened. And stop thinking of the Jot; I hope she got off, I'm sure she did. She wouldn't let me come with her; she was crying and actually ran away.

Yes, Rove, I'm still here: haven't slammed the door and left you to go seek your fortune. I'm here, and Julia is upstairs putting Willy to bed. I'm sure he'll be okay in years to come; forewarned is forearmed. Julia will be getting ready for bed herself soon, and I'll go up to join her, and that's a very nice thought. But sneaking in under the tent — damn it, I don't know how to stop this! — is the Jotta Girl. The knowledge that we could have, might have, and almost did. Even worse is the tiny twinge of regret I feel about that. No denying it, and I wonder — oh hell, I wonder how that would have been. Cut it out, cut it out, cut it *out*.

Old Rove crossing through the little puddle of streetlamp light, coming up the steps now, tongue out, to join me companionably, sitting down here with expectant certainty of a splendid, nonskimpy ear rub. In a couple of minutes, then, I'll go in and upstairs to Julia. And tomorrow I'll make a start on planning; making notes and lists. Have to seal all the ground-floor windows, I think, in our house and Aunt Ada's. Maybe have her move in with us for a week, that would be best. Figure how much food to get in, and coal and wood; at least a cord. All the things I'll have to do — *okay, Rove, in we go* — to get us ready for the Blizzard of '88.

PICTURE CREDITS

PAGE 38: *Frank Leslie's Illustrated Newspaper*, November 11, 1876

PAGE 92: New York Bound Archives, New York City

PAGE 97: *Frank Leslie's Illustrated Newspaper*, September 14, 1889

PAGES 104, 209 (top and bottom), 212 (top), 215, 241, 242, 243, 255, 268, 365: Collection of the author

PAGES 197, 198, 315, 366, 367 (top and bottom): From *Welcome to Our City* by Julian Street (P. F. Collier & Son, Inc., copyright 1912)

PAGE 205: United States History, Local History and Genealogy Division, The New York Public Library, Astor, Lenox and Tilden Foundations

PAGE 206: The Plaza Hotel — Statue of William Tecumseh Sherman, Museum of the City of New York

PAGE 207 (top): East Side of Fifth Avenue from 59th to 58th Streets, The Byron Collection, Museum of the City of New York

PAGES 208 (bottom), 210, 211 (top), 212, 214 (top and bottom), 217, 218, 235 (bottom), 236